SOLID AS STEELE

STEELE GUARDIANS SERIES - BOOK 5

SUSAN SLEEMAN

Published by Edge of Your Seat Books, Inc.

Contact the publisher at contact@edgeofyourseatbooks.com

Cover design by Kelly A. Martin of KAM Design

1

The body lying on the front porch wasn't included in Mackenzie Steele's vacation home rental.

But there he was. Out front of her rustic cabin in the Oregon High Desert as she peeked out the front door.

A large, broad-shouldered man. His back to her. His legs curled up. Wearing dirty and torn athletic pants and a navy blue sweatshirt stretched tightly over his muscular back. Blood caked in his deep brown hair, and he looked like he'd traveled a distance on foot, reached her porch, and dropped.

Unmoving.

Was he dead?

Now what? Her coffee was only starting to brew. How could a girl think after only four hours of sleep and no java?

So what should she do? *Yeah, what?*

She was alone in this desert cabin sitting on one-hundred-fifty private acres and bordering government land for miles and miles. Her only company included deer, coyotes, and other small animals.

If this guy was alive, she couldn't risk talking to him. Not yet. Not while unprotected.

She closed and locked the door without a sound then

backed up to the bedroom she'd chosen for her stay. Her gun safe sat on the floor where she'd dropped it last night after she arrived in the dark. With shaky fingers she tapped in the combo. The door popped open, the click like a trumpet siren to warn the man of her actions.

Stop. Just your imagination. The safe opening had actually been quiet. The most important thing—she had a weapon and could protect herself while checking to see how severely the guy was hurt.

She shed her pj's, put on jeans and a T-shirt, then clipped the holster on her belt and shrugged into a zip-front sweatshirt to hide the gun. She might be in a desert, but overnight low temperatures hovered around freezing, and she also needed it for warmth.

Heart thumping in her chest, she strode over the wood floors to the rough wood door and cracked it open to poke her head out.

The sun, a magnificent red ball of fire, rose over mountains in the distance, and the breathtaking red and orange striations of the Painted Hills in the foreground took her attention. For only a moment. Gorgeous, but if she stopped to enjoy God's colors radiating across the sky and barren land this morning instead of paying attention to the man, she could lose her life.

He hadn't moved. Not one bit.

She took a breath.

"Hello," she called out.

No movement. Nothing.

"Hey you," she said louder.

No response.

Fine. She had to get closer. Check his vitals.

She inched forward. Caught sight of his chest moving. *Okay, good. He's alive.* But obviously injured.

"Sir," she said. "Are you okay?"

No answer.

She moved even closer, standing over him now. One more attempt to get him to move via a voice command.

Failed.

She squatted, put a hand on his shoulder to shake him.

Flash.

He came awake. His hand clamping onto her wrist. He flipped her over his body and pinned her on the rough worn floorboards with a forearm to her throat.

"You're hurting me," she eked out as his arm pressed the breath from her body.

His eyes flew open, and he lurched back, releasing his hold. "Sorry. Oh, man. Sorry."

She scrambled away from him and rubbed her throat. "You should be. You're on my porch, and I just wanted to be sure you're okay."

"Yeah, right. I know." He looked around, dark eyes piercing yet confused. "Where? Who?"

She should be afraid of him after that move, but his confusion turned to panic, and she felt sorry for him.

"What's your name?" she asked.

"I'm..." His words fell off. "I don't...I mean, I can't remember." His gaze swept the area, panic lodged in every shift of his eyes. "What in the world is going on here? Who are you? Where are we?"

Was he for real or faking? She would go along with him for now and watch for anything that said she couldn't trust him. "I'm Mackenzie Steele, and this is my vacation rental in John Day, Oregon."

"Vacation? Oh, man, I ruined your vacation by landing here and tossing you around, didn't I? Sorry. I would never hurt a woman. Guess I overreacted. All I know is I woke up with a hand on my shoulder. I felt threatened for some reason."

He ran a hand through his hair and winced. "Hair's sticky."

"Blood. You're injured."

"I..."—he blinked long lashes and looked down—"I can't remember hardly anything. Just flashes really. Waking up at the base of a small butte surrounded by miles of nothing. I didn't have a phone or anything in my pockets. No watch. Nothing. So I started hiking. Took me most of the night, but I saw your lights. Got this far and must've collapsed." He frowned. "Sorry I scared you."

"It's okay," she said, but it really wasn't. She'd never been manhandled like that, and it would take some time to get over it and trust him.

What was she saying? She would ask him to move on and there would be no need to trust him.

But wait. Was that fair? He needed medical attention, and she couldn't send him packing. At least not without some food. Water. A look at his injuries.

"Let me get you some water." She jumped to her feet and took a wide berth around him to enter the small two bedroom cabin. The rustic interior and rugged stone fireplace that she'd found incredibly charming last night held no appeal right now.

The view now only reminded her of her vulnerability, and she had to be careful if she wanted to stay alive. Very careful.

∾

She was running from him, this Mackenzie Steele. Of course she was. A gorgeous woman with glossy blond hair, big eyes, and a toned body. She had to be careful around strangers. Especially strange men. Dangerous men.

Men like him.

His gut cramped. He wasn't the guy she must be thinking he was. Or was he? *No.* That he knew for certain. Sure, he didn't know his name or any details of his life. Not even the reason for his injury, but he *did* know he would never hurt a woman on purpose. Never. Knew that deep in his core.

And yet, he had. Grabbed her like a sack of potatoes and flung her to the floor. Slamming his arm into her neck. Would his rough handling leave a bruise? Leave evidence of his behavior?

God, please, no.

Well, there you go. He'd prayed. That was something else to go on. He must believe in God for a prayer to pop into his head. A comforting thought for sure. The first one since she touched him. Or maybe the second one. She comforted him too, even while those big eyes were filled with panic.

Another thing he knew?

This woman—this curvaceous beauty—was carrying. He'd caught the bulge of her holster through her sweatshirt. Didn't fit with her very feminine appearance. Not at all.

Listen to him. Profiling her like that. Stereotyping. What did he know? Nothing right now.

Dread inched up his throat in rancid bile. He swallowed it down. He had to ignore these thoughts. Make a plan. Take action.

What was his next step?

The door opened. She stepped out carrying a bottle of water and a plate holding a large bagel slathered in cream cheese. "I figured you would be hungry too."

"Thank you."

She stepped halfway to him. "No offense. I won't hand this to you, but I'll set it down on the floorboards and go back for some coffee."

"I understand. You have to be careful," he said with as much conviction as possible.

"You want coffee?" She placed the plate and bottle near her feet.

"Please. Black as can be." Okay, great he knew how he took his coffee. Something else to go on. Not really of value but something.

She backed into the cabin.

He didn't want to scare her, so he waited for the door to close then grabbed the plate and propped his back against the rough cedar siding. He cracked the water bottle and nearly drained the cool liquid before she returned with two large stoneware mugs of coffee. Without a word, she set one on the floor then backed up to a rocking chair and sat.

She wasn't overly tall. Five-eight, he guessed, but her height was in her legs, which she elegantly crossed. She sipped on the mug, staring ahead.

"I don't want to scare you," he said. "But I can't resist the smell of the coffee, and I'm going to grab the mug now."

She peered at him. "I've been scared since I spotted you."

"I get that, and I'm sorry for it." He smiled at her as he leaned over to grab the rich dark coffee with steam rising into the frosty morning. "Thank you for being so generous and giving me something to eat and drink."

"I considered sending you packing." She sounded very earnest and straightforward and he liked that too. "But my faith wouldn't let me do it."

He took a long sip of the strong coffee and stifled a groan over the deep, nutty flavor. She liked her coffee the way he did. Strong and potent. Though it looked like she dosed hers liberally with cream. "I might not know much about myself, but I prayed a minute ago. Guess that means I believe in God too."

"Could be." She rested the mug on her knee. "But some

people who aren't practicing Christians call out to God in times of extreme duress."

"I hope you're wrong, and I'm a man who lives his life by faith." Another sip of coffee and he traded the mug for the bagel.

"Me too." She met his gaze and locked on. "So what now? Should I call the county sheriff's office? See if anyone reported you missing?"

"No!" His outburst startled her, and she jostled her coffee, the caramel-colored liquid sloshing over the top.

"Sorry," he said. "I don't know why I reacted like that."

"Maybe because you were breaking the law when you got hurt, and you don't want to get law enforcement involved."

He took a breath to cool down. "That's possible. Doesn't feel right though."

Her eyes narrowed. "What other explanation could there be for such a response?"

"I don't know." Thoughts raced through his head, and he chomped off a bite of what turned out to be a cinnamon and raisin bagel. He chewed the sweet dough and swallowed. "Maybe I don't trust law enforcement."

"Then you don't trust me."

"You're an officer?"

"Not now, but I was a detective in the Oregon State Police investigations division. Worked for OSP for over five years."

Explained her reason for carrying. "And now?"

"Now I work at my family's business. Steele Guardians. We provide security guards for companies and events. We're based in the Portland metro area but have clients all over the Northwest."

"Sounds impressive." He took another big bite of the chewy bagel with crisp edges.

"My dad and uncle started the business after they retired from law enforcement. Now they're wanting to retire, and my sisters and cousins have left law enforcement to take over."

"A family of cops." He polished off the first half of the bagel.

She nodded. "My dad and uncle have a rule. If we want to run the company, we had to serve in law enforcement for five years first. They said it would teach us to think like a criminal."

"And did it?"

"More than you can know."

"Which is why you're suspicious of me."

"That and you could snap my neck without breaking a sweat."

"Yeah, there is that." He took a long pull on the earthy coffee. "But I wouldn't. At least I don't think I would."

"Any memories come back yet? Like your name?"

He shook his head.

She lifted a delicate eyebrow. "Can I make some observations?"

He reached for the other half of the bagel. "Sure."

"No wedding ring or telltale ring from wearing one. Probably single. Your clothing and shoes are top-of-the-line. Your haircut isn't a cheap one. You reacted to my touch like someone with martial arts training or military background. Maybe even law enforcement training."

He swallowed. "Which could mean I'm a good guy."

"Or a successful criminal." She wrinkled her cute nose and smiled.

He laughed. Man, what a good feeling to lighten up here. With this beautiful woman.

"I've been thinking about it since I first saw you," she said. "You could be from anywhere. Even out of state. We need to look close first then expand our search if needed. I want to call OSP. I have plenty of contacts there and can get what I need without many questions."

He might agree to let her do that. Actually, if she wanted to make the calls, he wouldn't stop her. That would take physical restraint, which he would never do. "What will you tell them?"

"Nothing much. Just ask if there are any missing person's reports for men fitting your description."

"Okay. I guess." He took another bite of the bagel that now tasted like the dust swirling in the dry desert landscape.

She set down her mug and used her cell phone to make the call. "Jeffers, hi. Mackenzie Steele."

"Steele!" The responding voice boomed over the phone.

Mackenzie held her cell away from her ear. "I have a favor to ask."

Jeffers muttered something.

She explained her need. "I'll hang on while you run the search, if you don't mind."

She looked at him. "He's running a check in the Oregon database. If he strikes out then he'll move on to NaMus. National Missing and Unidentified Persons System. A database of missing people searchable by law enforcement. With all the records, the search could take some time."

"There are that many missing people?"

She nodded. "Estimates say nearly eight million people around the world go missing every year. Ninety percent or more are found, but still, that's a huge number."

She turned her attention back to the phone. "No. No facial scars or visible tattoos."

She cupped her hand over the phone. "Can you check for tats elsewhere?"

He ripped off his sweatshirt and found a shoulder tattoo.

A black cross. He ran a finger over it. Scar tissue. He covered up a wound or surgical scar. Maybe the cross meant that his faith had a part in that. But what?

He leaned closer to display it for Mackenzie. Her eyebrows lifted but she didn't say anything other than to relay the information to this Jeffers guy.

Okay, she wondered about the tat too. Maybe this tattoo held the answer to his memory loss and injury and knowing about it would help him recover his identity. Maybe.

2

Mackenzie held on the phone while Jeffers added the black cross tattoo to his search. She looked at the man. He might really be a believer. Or not. A rough, almost violent-looking cross didn't necessarily mean it symbolized Christianity. And why did he keep running his finger over it?

If the cross did relate to being a Christian, it gave her a bit more confidence in his trustworthiness. But she'd spent years as a trooper and knew cross tattoos didn't always symbolize Christianity. In fact, they often didn't. For now, she would take this new bit of information at face value.

"Owen," he blurted out.

"What?"

"Owen seems familiar." He sat forward, his eyelashes beating rapidly. "I mean, I don't know if it's my name, but it feels right."

"Then that's what we'll call you."

"Okay." The insecurity in that big tough body that she imagined would portray a demeanor of confident and in charge behavior had to leave him hurting something fierce.

At least she'd be hurting. She liked to control things. Way too much. One of her downfalls.

She turned her attention back to her call. "Hey, Jeffers. Add the first name Owen to the search too."

She picked up her coffee and took a long draw. Cold. Yuck. She hadn't had her fill this morning and would get another hot cup when she got off the call.

Then what? What if Jeffers didn't locate any matches? Could she send Owen packing?

She could hear her dad and grandad lecturing her on safety. Her cousin Thomas had been violently murdered, and everyone had a heightened sense of the bad things that could happen. Not only had they personally experienced the terror of violent crime, but they'd also witnessed it on the job for years.

But when everything became too much to bear, her mom and gran would remind her to have compassion and live her faith. Which she did.

But which should win out here? Safety or faith?

"No matches on the tattoo," Jeffers said. "And really nothing remotely resembling the description you gave me. But I can dig deeper and keep at it if you want."

"That would be great."

"You want to tell me what's going on?"

"No."

"You know I don't like that, but I have to respect your decision." He let out a noisy breath through the phone. "Be careful, Steele. You might not be one of us anymore, but we don't want anything bad to happen to you."

"Thanks." She ended the call and looked at Owen. "Would you agree to be fingerprinted?"

"Fingerprinted?" He gaped at her as if she'd asked for his firstborn child. "Man, I don't know. I just don't know."

"It shouldn't be a problem if you don't have anything to hide, right?"

He tilted his head, and that razor-sharp gaze locked on

her again. "What if law enforcement is involved in whatever incapacitated me?"

Interesting take on things. "The odds of that are very slim."

"But not impossible."

"No, not impossible." She resisted sighing over his stubbornness. "Ever think it's as simple as you fell and hit your head?"

"My gut says it's more than that, but I could be exaggerating things."

"What if I take your picture and do an internet image search?"

"Hey, yeah." His expression brightened. "That sounds good."

She stood and moved closer to him. "We might get a better match if you smile."

He smiled, but the lines were tight and forced. She wished she could make him smile for real.

Why on earth was she trusting this stranger? Sure, he claimed to be a Christian, but people could claim anything.

Just get the work done. The sooner you know something about him, the better.

She snapped a few pics and stepped back.

"After I do the search, we should get you into town for medical attention."

He lifted his hand to his head. "I'm fine."

"You might feel fine, but you blacked out, right?"

"Yes."

"Often a sign of concussion and a head injury's not something to mess with."

"I suppose not."

"After that, we can stop at the OSP outpost in town to get your fingerprints taken."

"Right." He frowned. "I'm still not sure that's a good idea."

"You want to know who you are, right?"

"I do. But if they search my prints, won't my ID only show up if I'm a criminal? I don't think I want to hear that I'm a bad guy."

He sounded sincere again, but she had to hold off on deciding how to deal with him. "The database also includes law enforcement officers. Federal applicants. Employees and military too."

He let out a breath. "Okay, I'll do it on one condition. Before we go to the police, I want to try to retrace my steps. See if I can figure out where I've been and what happened."

She didn't ever like conditions placed on her actions and wasn't keen on this one. "Are you up to doing that? Physically, I mean."

"Not sure."

"Maybe we should wait until tomorrow. Let you get a good night's sleep first."

"And where do I sleep? No money. No credit cards. Means a hotel is out. No car." He tilted his head. "I don't suppose you'd let me sleep out here again."

"With as cold as it gets at night that's not a good idea."

"Yeah, I didn't think so. Maybe the hospital staff can help me find a shelter."

"There's a guest house out back," she said before thinking it through. "You can stay there."

His eyes flashed wide. "You sure? I mean, I don't plan to hurt you, but..."

"But you don't know who you are or what you're capable of."

"Exactly."

She knew that to be true. Just like she knew she probably shouldn't let him stay on the property or even go out into the wilderness alone with him. But he shouldn't be

14

hiking alone for who knows how many miles in his condition.

She needed help. *But who?*

She thought about the trek through the desert. About how they might follow his trail. They needed help. "We should have a guide for the morning. Someone who knows how to follow your trail."

"I don't suppose you know someone like that."

"I do. A whole team of guys actually. They own a company called Shadow Lake Survival where they teach off-grid survival techniques. I'll call to ask one of them to come out tonight to stay with me. Then escort us tomorrow."

"Sounds good." He actually sounded relieved. "But it's something else I can't pay for."

"I'm friends with the owners—the Maddox brothers. I grew up going to their resort every summer with my family, and we became friends. They'll do it for me without charge."

He sat forward and planted his hands on his knees. "Then I would be thankful for their help, but once I remember who I am and can access my finances, I *will* pay them."

If you remember and have the money, she didn't say aloud. No point in kicking the guy when he was down.

The small but modern hospital had newer navy-blue chairs and a beige tile floor in the waiting area that smelled like strong antiseptic. The registration staff were kind, but Owen had a hard time getting registered. Apparently, if you didn't know your name, their kindness evaporated, and they looked at you funny.

So yeah. No ID. No insurance. No service?

Maybe not.

"Take my ID and credit card to guarantee payment." Mackenzie showed her ID and slapped her credit card on the counter.

The clerks held a discussion among themselves then agreed to let him in and generated a mound of paperwork.

Owen watched her, her tongue peeking out the corner of her mouth as she read down each page and ticked boxes with solid checkmarks.

No questions asked. No hesitation. Just compassion and kindness in action.

What kind of stranger did that for another human being?

A Christian, that's who.

Did she believe him to be a good guy? He hoped he was, but with the suspicious circumstances of his injury and not having any ID meant the odds were probably fifty/fifty that he was a bad guy too.

Still, she was one of the good ones. And sharp too. She'd called a rideshare for the drive from the cabin instead of getting into a vehicle with a stranger who could overpower her. Had already overpowered her. He rode in the backseat. She rode in the front. If the driver thought it odd that she requested to be separated from him, he didn't comment.

"Done." She pushed the clipboard across the counter to the clerk.

The older woman gave a wavering smile. "Have a seat in the lobby, and we'll call you as soon as possible."

Turned out as soon as possible meant an hour later, but once Owen reached the exam room, he quickly undressed and discovered ugly purple bruises on his abdomen and chest. He'd not only fallen and hit his head, but he'd also hit something hard with his body.

Or he'd been attacked with fists. Ambushed, maybe.

The young doctor who looked like he was just out of med school and sleep deprived, entered the space before Owen could get his gown lifted over his shoulders. "I'm Dr. Patterson."

He moved closer to Owen. "Those are some impressive contusions. Leave the gown where it is so I can examine you." He gloved up and palpitated Owen's bruises while running through a list of questions. He moved to Owen's back. "Multiple contusions here too."

He listened to Owen's heart and lungs. "And you don't remember what happened?"

"All I know is I came to at the base of a butte and a large boulder next to me had blood on it. Figured I might've fallen off the butte."

Patterson tightened his mouth into a hard slash. "How high was the butte?"

"Not sure, but it wasn't high. Maybe ten feet max."

"In that case, the many contusions seem unlikely. I more suspect you've been beaten."

Yeah, Owen did too, but he didn't want to admit it as that might indicate criminal activity.

"Let's get a look at that head wound." The doctor pulled Owen's head forward and probed the open wound. He stepped back and performed what Owen knew to be a neurological exam, and Owen thought he passed the tests.

Patterson ripped off the gloves and disposed of them. "You're not exhibiting any of the classic symptoms of a serious head injury other than loss of consciousness."

Seriously? "What about the memory loss?"

"We can discuss that after we do a CT scan, but I don't think we'll find your injury caused the amnesia."

Owen took a second to try to digest that information. "Then what in the world would've caused it?"

Patterson looked Owen straight in the face. "I suspect

we're looking at an emotional shock that caused psychogenic or dissociative amnesia."

"Maybe I saw something before I was injured?" Owen clarified.

"Could be." Patterson continued to peer at Owen. "Or like I mentioned, You could've suffered an intense beating. But let's get that CT for your head and take a good look at your internal organs, too. I want to see if they suffered any damage. Then we can go from there."

He spun and marched out of the room.

Owen pulled up his gown and tied it at his neck. Thoughts pinged through his head like the steel ball in a pinball machine. But like the machine, the levers failed and the balls of thought fell away without revealing anything.

What could he have seen that would be so shocking that he didn't want to remember it or anything else? He couldn't even begin to figure it out without knowing his identity and why he'd been in the desert all alone without ID. Or had the person who hurt him stolen it?

The technician arrived to take him down for the CT, and Owen settled into the wheelchair for the ride. He wanted to pound his hand against his head to jar something loose in there, but held off. The doc didn't think Owen had a serious head injury, but he wouldn't risk hitting himself just in case. Not to mention it would hurt and do no good other than to alleviate some frustration.

The staff efficiently performed the scan, and Owen quickly returned to his exam room again, the young doctor standing in front of him.

"The good news is you don't have any internal injuries or bleeding," Patterson said. "And just as I suspected, no brain hematomas or skull fractures. However, since you did lose consciousness, you fit the diagnosis for a concussion. A mild one, I suspect."

"So I can go home?" Owen asked though he had no idea where home was.

"Yes, but I need you to be cautious and watch for certain symptoms." He went on to describe a list of symptoms and things that might or might not happen. "Do you have someone who can stay with you tonight to wake you every few hours to be sure you can awaken normally?"

If his memory came back, would he have anyone in his life who would do that for him? Somehow he believed he might be a loner.

"Sir?" Patterson asked.

"Yeah, sure. The person who brought me in," he answered quickly so the doctor would discharge him, but he couldn't possibly ask Mackenzie to let him stay in her cabin. That she was allowing him to spend the night in the guest house was beyond generous. And maybe a little foolish, but then she did have a gun for protection and she was calling the guide to stay with her.

Owen would simply have to monitor himself. Or the outdoor guide could stay in the guest house too. But Mackenzie's friend would already be doing Owen a favor just by coming to lead them through the desert. Having to get up every few hours when they had a big day ahead wasn't a fair ask.

Owen was on his own.

Why did that bother him almost as much as losing his memory?

Mackenzie paced the sidewalk outside the ER, a brisk wind whipping her hair in her face as she held her phone to her ear. "C'mon, Ryan, answer."

"Mac, is that you?" His breathless voice came over the phone, sounding like he'd run to answer.

"Yeah. Am I interrupting something?"

"Just finishing a run. What's up?"

She told him about her situation. "Could you or someone on your team make it out here ASAP then guide us tomorrow? Tonight would be best."

She explained her reasoning, held her breath, and waited for his response.

"We've got a big gig tomorrow, but let me check with my brothers to see if they can handle things without me."

"I don't want to cause any problems."

"No worries. You've always been a problem in my life, so what's new?" He chuckled.

She laughed with him, but deep down, there was some truth to his statement. In their early teens, he'd taken a liking to her. Boyfriend/girlfriend kind of liking. She never thought of him that way. It had caused an issue for two summers, but then she started dating in high school, and about the same time, he fell for a girl named Mia Blackburn whose uncle owned the resort next door, and that was the end of his interest in Mackenzie.

"If the guys give me a pass," Ryan continued. "I could be there by six."

"Sounds perfect. Owen will bunk in the guest house and you can stay in the cabin with me or with him. Your choice."

"Hmm, a potential criminal or a beautiful woman? No contest." He laughed again. "I'll take the crook."

She hadn't seen or talked to Ryan in about a year and had forgotten what a joker he could be. His good nature would help lighten the mood with the very serious Owen.

"How long of a trek are we talking about?" Ryan asked.

"We're not really sure. Owen said he believes he walked most of the night."

"Then I'll bring provisions for an overnight campout."

"That sounds great." She took a moment to consider other items she might need to mention to Ryan. "Since this guy doesn't know who he is or if he has any money, he can't pay you, but I can."

"You still make that earthquake cake?"

Odd question. "I haven't for years, but I sure can."

"That will be payment enough if you can rustle one up by the time I get there."

"That I can do." She laughed. "Text me when you know if you're sure you can come."

"Will do."

She ended the call and went back through the sliding doors of the ER's main entrance, the whoosh as they slid drawing attention from the patients inside. She spotted Owen striding across the lobby, his gaze seeking the area around him. He had the look of a cop. A person who was always assessing his surroundings for potential danger. Or maybe a desperate criminal who feared he was being hunted.

She'd never realized how similar the look could be between the two types of people. But there were differences too. The officer's expression usually held confidence. The criminal mostly held fear. And Owen was marching like a man with purpose. Shoulders back. Long, fast strides. Chest thrust out.

A man who was used to being in charge. That was her take on it, anyway.

He approached her, but kept on walking, moving past her, striding through the door and outside. She followed him. He took deep breaths as if being inside smothered him, and he needed fresh air. Maybe he'd gotten bad news. She opened her mouth to ask.

"I'm ready to go," he said. "Can you arrange another ride?"

"Sure." She thumbed through her phone to the rideshare program and requested to be picked up. "Good news. Only five minutes out."

She stowed her phone and looked at him. "What did the doctor say?"

"No serious head injury. Not bad enough to cause the amnesia."

Curious. "Then what?"

"He thinks I suffered some sort of traumatic shock." Owen shoved his hands into his sweatshirt pockets.

What in the world had he witnessed out in the desert that was bad enough to make a strong guy like this lose his memory? She desperately wanted to know, but even more—feared the answer.

Maybe he did too as he fell silent, and they stared ahead until the four-door sedan arrived. He opened the front door and asked if she could ride in front. The female driver agreed. Probably because he smiled at her. And man, what a smile. Mackenzie caught it only from the side, but all those rugged good looks turned into charming and playful.

He moved out of her way, and that smile traveled with him, broadening as he locked onto her face. Mackenzie had a pure shot to the heart. Then it changed to fear.

A sociopath killer could turn on the charm like this too.

She climbed into the silver Honda that held a strong scent from a pine tree air freshener dangling from the mirror. Owen settled in the back, the car shifting with his weight.

Which guy was she going home with? The charming man he seemed to be or a man who might be planning to kill her?

She'd always been good at reading people and didn't like

him for the sociopath vibe, but she wasn't always right. She had her gun, and hopefully, Ryan would be there tonight for added protection.

She faced the driver. "I need to stop at the nearest grocery store. I only need a few things, and I'll pay extra for you to wait."

"Sure thing." The young woman fixed her attention on merging into traffic and soon pulled into a small mom-and-pop grocery store.

The older store was clean, and the mouthwatering scent of freshly baked bread drifted down the aisles. The smell urged Mackenzie to grab a loaf for dinner, but she'd brought a nice whole wheat loaf that her gran had baked for the trip so resisted the urge. The loaf was supposed to last Mackenzie the whole week but probably wouldn't make it through a day with Owen and Ryan eating with her.

She jerked a small cart free from a stack, the metal grinding and clanging as the back dropped down. She started for the baking aisle and felt Owen's attention on her for the trip through the store.

"I might not know much," he said. "But my Spidey sense tells me you're going to be baking something."

She grabbed a bag of coconut and squeezed it to confirm freshness. "A cake for Ryan Maddox, the guy who'll be guiding us tomorrow. That's his payment."

An eyebrow went up. "Not much of a payment."

"You haven't tasted my cake." She laughed.

Owen cracked a smile.

"I'm also going to grab food for a meal tonight and breakfast for the three of us, and Ryan will bring supplies for on the trail. Anything else you want while we're here?"

"I'm good with whatever you have."

"You don't have to do that."

"Do what?"

"Think you're putting me out so much. You're not. Really. I like to help. And if I were in your shoes I would hope someone would do this for me. Jesus would, you know."

"Yeah. Guess I'm not good at accepting help."

"Hey, this is a good thing." She smiled at him. "You've learned something about yourself."

He frowned. "Might be better if it was a positive thing, but yeah. Guess I know myself better now."

Please let this guy figure out who he is. And please, please, let him be one of the good guys.

3

Mackenzie swirled a knife through the cream cheese, butter, and powdered sugar mixture she'd dropped by spoonfuls into the chocolate fudge cake batter. Satisfied it was incorporated, she sprinkled a layer of chocolate chips on the top then inserted the sweet-smelling cake into the oven and set a timer.

Her phone chimed from the counter, and she looked at the text from Ryan. *We're a go. See you at six.*

Thank you! Cake's in the oven, she replied.

The timer set, she had to go to the guest house to tell Owen when to arrive for dinner. He would've had plenty of time to shower and change by now. They'd made a final stop at a clothing store, and she'd bought him clean clothes so he could bag the ones he was wearing in case they needed them for evidence collection. He'd argued the whole time about her paying, but she promised to keep receipts for him to repay her if he could.

His natural behavior seemed to be that of an honest man who didn't want to take advantage of her, but she couldn't be sure she wasn't letting her physical attraction to him get in the way of her judgment. She'd never had such an intense reaction to a guy before, and it was hard to separate that from anything else she felt about him.

Forget that. Try to act like the detective you once were and keep an open mind. And your eyes open.

She stepped outside into the brisk wind and tugged her fleece closed as she crossed the dusty soil littered with tufts of dried grass to the one-bedroom log cabin. The rental listing said this was the original building on the property and was constructed in 1920. The current owner had restored it and built the main cabin and other outbuildings.

She knocked on the rustic door and stood back. She'd been renting this property every year since leaving college. All but last year when she'd started working at the company and couldn't take the time off.

It was her place to be alone with her thoughts and with God. To recharge. When she'd been a state trooper, she hadn't been able to recharge on a daily basis. By the end of her duty, she'd lost her joy in so many things and was heading toward burn out. But then, for some reason, when she'd left the force, she'd started a podcast on faith in her daily life, and it had restored her faith and joy. She was just now starting to fully live and embrace life again.

The door opened, and Owen appeared as he pulled together the front of a button-down shirt. He got it closed, but not before she spotted massive bruises on a firm torso. He fastened a button.

"Stop," she said. "Let me see those bruises."

"It's nothing. Really. Doc says no internal injuries. Only surface bruises."

She took hold of the fabric and separated it, working hard not to gasp. "And your back?"

She asked as she turned him and tugged the shirt down over his broad shoulders to see the answer. "These bruises

26

are fresh. Someone beat you up before hitting you over the head."

"Looks like it." He shrugged the shirt over his broad shoulders.

"You didn't just fall, then," she muttered as she considered the situation. Maybe he hadn't been alone out there. He'd been brutally beaten. But that could've happened before he arrived in the desert too.

The big question right now was how in the world was he moving and not in terrible pain?

"You need some pain relievers," she said.

"They gave me Tylenol at the hospital." A tight smile crossed his face as he continued to button his shirt. "Have you heard from Ryan?"

"He's officially coming at six. Which is when I would like to have dinner. Does that work for you?"

"Sure. I can get a good nap in before if that's okay with you."

"Of course. There's an alarm clock by the bed." She started to leave but turned back. "Is there anything you need before then?"

"You've been more than generous." He tugged on the shirttails. "I'll repay every cent on your tally."

"We'll figure it all out."

He frowned. "Your generosity floors me."

"Faith in action," she said and departed.

His gaze was on her as she made the trip back to her cabin. She was sure of it, and she had to force one foot in front of the other to keep moving. She really wanted to stay at the guest house with him to make sure he didn't require any help and got the rest he needed. But he'd made no secret of his independent nature and wanting to be alone. She was fine with that. She really was. She'd come to the desert to be alone too.

Then why did she keep wanting to look back. Worse yet, turn around to stay with this man? He could be the worst kind of criminal who was very skilled in masquerading as a decent guy.

Her very life could be in danger and she'd best not forget that.

~

The smell of roasting beef wafted out of an open window, accompanied with laughter, and drew Owen toward the cabin. A newer model Ford Bronco in a cactus gray color sat in the drive. Ryan, Owen assumed.

The guy had arrived in style as newer Broncos could be pricey. Funny how Owen could recognize the make and model of a vehicle but not his own name. Some things seemed natural. Others appeared like a black wall in front of his face. The doctor had told him that was normal and not to let it freak him out, but it still did.

He knocked on the door, and the laughter died. Boots pounded on the floor from the other side of the door, and it was soon snatched open.

An intense guy with dishwater blond hair and a weightlifter's build stood there, hiking boots planted wide. He had on green tactical pants with a T-shirt and wore a gun at his hip. "Guess you're Owen. I'm Ryan Maddox."

"Hey, thanks for coming, man," Owen said. "I really appreciate it."

"Yeah, well, Mac's a longtime friend. My brothers and I will help whenever she needs us."

Okay. Staking his territory? Certainly making sure that Owen knew that leading them into the wilderness was a favor for Mackenzie—not Owen.

Barefooted, Mackenzie crossed the room to join them.

She was wearing a flowing skirt and clinging knit black top that contrasted with her light hair color.

Ryan turned to smile at her, and she tucked her arm in his to pull him away from the door. "Back off, Ryan, and let the guy in."

Ryan frowned, but let her lead him back to the kitchen island where she pushed him onto a stool. He kept his gaze pinned to Owen.

Was every minute with this guy going to be a battle?

Owen closed the door and crossed the room toward them.

Mackenzie lifted a glass pitcher with honey-colored liquid and clinking ice cubes. "Can I get you some iced tea?"

"That would be nice." He smiled. "Dinner smells great."

"I made a beef roast with carrots and potatoes. I know Ryan likes it, and it's an old favorite with my dad and grandad."

Ryan's stomach growled.

Mackenzie looked at him and rolled her eyes.

"What? I haven't had a home-cooked meal in a long time." He laughed. "I don't get over to my mom and dad's place often enough for my stomach's liking."

"You need to find a woman who can cook then." Mackenzie poured the tea and set the glass on the island in front of Owen.

Ryan frowned.

She peered at the guy. "Right. Still pining over the one who got away."

"Would that be you?" Owen asked and instantly hated that he needed to know the answer.

Her gaze flashed to him. "Me? Hah. No. Mia. Ryan's high school sweetheart."

"Enough." Ryan turned his attention to a backpack sitting on the stool next to him. He took out a laminated map and slid items out of the way to lay it on the island. "A map of this property. Can you show me the direction you arrived from?"

Owen moved closer and looked at the terrain and lay of the buildings on the land. He ran his finger from the front porch that faced west in a straight line through barren land. "I started out at dusk and walked most of the night, but my injuries made me rest often. Not sure about the distance. Once I spotted the cabin's lights, I aimed toward it."

Ryan pressed his lips into a thin line. "And that's it? That's all you can give me to go on?"

"Yeah, except for there being a ten-foot butte and rock with blood on it where I started." Owen held Ryan's challenging gaze.

"No idea how you got there?" Ryan didn't back down.

"None."

"That's freaky."

"Tell me about it."

Ryan folded the map. "I'd hoped we could drive at least part of the way, but with not knowing your direction, I'll need to be on foot to track your movements. And hope what I locate are *your* movements and not someone else's."

"I haven't seen anyone else on the property." Mackenzie set the pitcher on the island. "But someone could be out on the far reaches of the land, and I wouldn't know it. Owen showing up proved that."

Ryan looked at her. "You get the police involved yet?"

"No," she said.

"My fault." Owen picked up his tea. "I'm hoping when I go back out, something will jog my memory, and we won't need the police."

"Not notifying the police at all is not an option," Mackenzie said. "Someone hurt you. The massive bruises you sustained prove that, and we need to make them pay."

30

"Yeah," he said, but depending on the situation, Owen might not involve law enforcement.

A timer sounded from the stove.

Mackenzie turned to silence it. "Dinner's ready. Head to the table, and I'll serve."

Owen stood. "Can I do anything to help?"

She slid a Tylenol and Ibuprofen bottle toward him. "Take some of these and take the bottles to your cabin for later tonight."

"Thanks." He picked up the bottles. "But I was more thinking about carrying food or something like that."

"Don't bother asking." Ryan grabbed his iced tea glass. "Her gran taught her to serve her guests while they recline in comfort, and she continues to be old school."

"I wouldn't go that far, but yeah. When you come to dinner at my place, I do the work. You reap the rewards." She made shooing motions with her hands. "Now off you go."

Owen followed Ryan, taking his tea to the table set with basic white plates and bright blue plaid napkins. Ryan sat on the far side, and Owen took a seat across the table.

"I'd like to head out at dawn, if that works for you." Ryan pulled his chair closer to the table, and the legs scraped on the wide wood floor planks.

"Sure thing."

Mackenzie brought in a platter with a browned roast and vegetables laced with slices of onions. Owen's mouth watered at the sight, and he couldn't wait to dig in. She spun and went back to the kitchen.

"Way I figure it." Ryan eyed the platter. "A night in the wild is likely, and you should bring a change of clothes."

Thankfully, Mackenzie had bought him two sets of clothing and toiletries. "No backpack to transport things, but I have a bag from the store for my things."

"I'm counting on you to carry a pack with provisions. We should be able to fit your things in there. If you're up to carrying the pack, that is."

Owen didn't like seeming weaker than this macho outdoorsman, and he especially didn't want to seem like a wimp in front of Mackenzie. "I'll do whatever it takes."

"His back won't let him do that." Mackenzie brought in a plate of thickly sliced wheat bread. "He has severe bruises. I'll carry the pack."

Ryan nodded. "You should be fine hauling it. After all, you always hauled a pack around at camp filled with everything but the kitchen sink."

They laughed together, and Owen felt like a third wheel.

Mackenzie passed the meat and veggie platter to Ryan and the bread to Owen. Ryan filled his plate with hefty slices of beef and browned carrots, potatoes, and onions, and Owen didn't hold back either. If he planned to hike tomorrow, he needed to gain some strength.

He would carry that pack. No matter the pain. No matter how much Mackenzie argued with him.

She sat and held out her hands. "Let's pray."

If Ryan wasn't a Christian, he didn't balk at the request but readily took her hand. Owen took the other one. It was warm and comforting as was her prayer for their meal. But she also added a plea for God to be with Owen and help him recover his memory. Despite his lapse in knowing much about himself, the prayer brought him a sense of peace. For a moment anyway.

The perfectly roasted meal melted in Owen's mouth and filled his gut. He slathered the bread with butter, the soft but hearty wheat tasted simply amazing. He didn't want to waste time talking between bites, but Ryan discussed his tracking methods and how far he hoped to travel on the first morning.

"We'll stop for lunch." He put down his fork on the nearly empty plate to grab his glass. "I'll evaluate then if we need to spend the night under the stars. I have everything we need except personal items." He looked at Mackenzie. "I suggest you don't plan to bring makeup and all those girlie things you carried at camp as the pack is full."

She wrinkled her nose. "What makeup? This is all natural beauty."

He chuckled then turned serious as he looked at Owen. "I don't suppose you remember if you know how to fire a gun."

Owen chewed his bread and tried to remember. "I don't know."

Ryan set down the tea and stabbed his remaining beef, but held it midair. "We could do a little target practice at the crack of dawn. If I think you're good to go after that, I've got a handgun you can use."

Owen drained his tea and pondered his stance on guns. He had no idea what he thought about them. He knew he didn't have a problem with Ryan and Mackenzie carrying. Maybe that meant he was fine with guns. The morning would tell.

Ryan faced Mackenzie. "Time for that cake?"

She set her fork down. "I don't know what it is about that recipe you like so much."

"Coconut. Cream cheese. Cake. Sweetness overload. What's not to like?" Ryan grinned.

She pushed back her chair. "I'll take your plates and get it."

Owen stood to help.

She raised a hand. "Sit. You're still my guest."

He dropped back down but moved his place setting to the end of the table and stacked it on top of hers. Ryan got out his phone and focused on the screen, but Owen watched

Mackenzie's fluid movements as she moved into the kitchen. She had delicate feet, and she glided as if she'd been a dancer at some point. He had a hard time placing her in a state trooper uniform and stopping a car on the roadside. But she'd done the job for five years and been promoted to detective, so she had to be good at it.

What about tomorrow? What might they find at the end of his trail? Something illegal and she would then turn around and arrest him? She couldn't make a legal arrest, but she could arrange to have law enforcement waiting for him when he returned. In that case, would he go along peacefully or would he try to evade the arrest?

It seemed wrong to leave her hanging when she'd been kind to him—beyond kind—but he had to think of himself first. Right?

Not if you went by the Mackenzie Steele philosophy of life. If you did that, then you not only didn't think of yourself first, but at times, you didn't think of yourself at all. That drew him to her even more than her good looks and likable personality.

4

The shrill alarm clock reverberated through Owen's bedroom, and he could barely roll over to turn it off. His arm and leg muscles, everywhere actually, screamed at him to remain still. The bruises felt like fire and laying on a bed of nails at the same time.

He dug deep for strength and rolled the final distance. A sharp bruising pain made him gasp as he slapped the alarm button. He'd set his alarm for two hours before their scheduled departure time, allowing him to take a hot shower and additional acetaminophen. He tossed back a few Ibuprofen tablets too and eased his feet to the floor. Each step toward the bathroom was like climbing a mountain of pain.

But he made it to the large shower and let nearly scalding water sluice over his battered body. He stayed in the stream of water until it turned cold.

Better. He felt a bit better. Good enough to be able to dress and gather his belongings for the trip.

Then he poured a cup of strong black coffee from the pot he'd set the timer on to brew at the same time as his alarm and sat before the television to catch the local morning news. He sipped and waited for a story showing his face connected to some crime. Thirty minutes later, the broadcast ended, and his face hadn't been splashed across the screen. Nor his name even mentioned.

Did no one notice he was missing? Care? Or was there no one in his life? Was he truly the loner he seemed to think he was?

At least he didn't learn anything bad about himself. "Now you better hope we don't find anything bad on the other end of today's journey."

Hope *and* pray. Which he did. With uncertainty as he didn't remember what being a believer entailed. It just felt natural. The doctor said Owen could remember things like making coffee or how to set an alarm, but not remember other things. Muscle memory, he'd called it.

"Speaking of muscles." He stretched his arms overhead to test the level of pain. "Good. Drugs are working."

He got up and went through a stretching routine. Seemed like he knew what to do to ease the pain and had done it before. Maybe every day. Who knows. Not him. And he wanted to—desperately. For himself sure, but also so he could interact with Mackenzie on a legitimate level. Would he be romantically interested in her if he had his memory? Did he have a wife? Girlfriend?

He held out his left hand. As Mackenzie had said, no indication of wearing a ring for any length of time, but not all people wore wedding rings. And guys didn't wear engagement rings.

A knock sounded on his door, and he whirled to face it.

"Jumpy much?" He shook his head and went to open it.

Hoping for Mackenzie, he stifled a frown when he found Ryan standing there. He carried a handgun and a box of ammo. "Mac's making breakfast, and we have enough time and light to do a little shooting. You ready."

"Let me grab my bag." Owen turned off the coffee pot

and picked up the store bag sitting on the counter. "Lead the way."

"I've set up an improvised firing range at the base of a butte. Hopefully, you at least won't miss the butte." Ryan chuckled.

Owen didn't laugh. Nothing funny here for him. He felt totally incompetent around this man. Owen had no idea what he was capable of or what he did for a living and couldn't counteract the power that Ryan exuded. They, whoever *they* are, often said that a guy gained his worth and identity from his occupation. Owen could surely believe that now.

The sun was barely peeking above the horizon, the sky filled with soft layers of reds and oranges, and a burning ball of fire sat in the middle. The colorful hills he'd seen yesterday, a black silhouette in the foreground.

Ryan glanced over his shoulder. "Nice view, huh?"

"Fantastic."

"I never get tired of it. Especially when the Painted Hills come to life under the sun. They change colors as the sun moves through the day."

"How long have you been a professional guide?" Owen asked.

"Been doing it unofficially since high school when my dad would take me along on his tours."

"Your dad got you involved in it, then?"

"My whole family really. We own a resort on Shadow Lake. Not a fancy billionaire's place. We've kept it rustic and primitive to give our guests a more natural experience. For as far back as I can remember, my dad taught my brothers and me how to track, hunt, fish, and camp. That sort of thing. Then, like I said, in high school I started taking out overnight camping groups under his supervision."

"That when you met Mackenzie?"

"Her family started coming to the resort every summer when we were in grade school. Dad had me and my brothers doing chores on the resort that early in life. Meant I interacted with the guests on a regular basis. Mac was a real tomboy back then, and her sisters more girly girls. She preferred to hang out with me."

"You ever fall for her?"

Ryan's shoulders tensed. "I did actually. But then I met my high school girlfriend and knew it was only a stupid crush with Mac. Glad we never ruined our friendship over it."

"And now? You're not attached?"

"Nope." Ryan passed the handgun to Owen.

The weight felt familiar in his hand, and he automatically checked the safety then released the ammo magazine. "Glock 17. 9mm. Full mag."

"Nice," Ryan said. "Looks like you know your guns."

Owen pushed the magazine back into place and turned to face a large piece of paper with big red circles. Owen lifted the gun and fired twice, hitting dead center.

"A double tap," Ryan said.

Owen glanced at the guy. "What?"

"Double-tap. A tactical shooting technique to fire not one shot but two. Used to be a technique taught to law enforcement officers. Nowadays, they more commonly teach shoot to stop the threat. Still, a lot of officers do the double-tap first."

"Sounds like you think I might be or have been a cop."

Ryan shrugged and took the gun back. "Could be. Or could be coincidence. Either way, you can handle a gun, and it'll be good for all three of us to be armed out there if needed. I'll keep this weapon in my backpack and give it to you if we encounter danger."

Translated—I don't trust you enough to carry all the time. "Are you expecting trouble?"

"I don't usually expect it, but I'm always prepared for it." Ryan engaged the gun's safety and placed it in his backpack. "That's what wilderness survival training is all about. Expect the best, but plan for the worst."

Owen was starting to let his need to compare himself to Ryan go and was becoming impressed with this guy. "I might need to take a class from you."

"You'd be welcome." Ryan locked gazes. "That is, if you don't hurt Mac in any way. She's one special woman, and she deserves only the best in life. You hurt her, and you deal with me. Got it?"

"Got it." Owen knew the man would follow through on his warning.

"Breakfast is ready," Mackenzie shouted from the cabin's open doorway. "Come get it before the food gets cold."

"And she makes a mean cake too, which can always be added to the breakfast menu." Ryan laughed and jogged toward the cabin, leaving Owen behind.

Owen started off behind Ryan. Owen wanted to take confidence in what the double-tap shooting might say about him. He could be a cop. Didn't mean he was a good one. Or he could've left the force and joined the criminal element. It happened.

Mackenzie left the door open, and the savory aroma of frying bacon drifted into the dry desert air. His mouth watered, and he would run to the cabin if he could.

He found her and Ryan sitting at the island. Their plates held fluffy scrambled eggs dotted with green peppers and shredded cheddar cheese. They'd also added thick slices of bacon and the same wheat bread from the night before, toasted golden brown with butter melted in pools on the top.

She looked at him. "Morning. Help yourself."

"Say what?" Ryan blinked at her.

"Yeah. I'm letting a guest fend for himself. Shocking." She laughed.

Her early morning humor brightened Owen's mood. Today was starting off to be a pretty good day.

He didn't have to be told twice to grab some food. He loaded his plate, the gooey cheese in the eggs fighting against the spoon. He poured a steaming black cup of coffee and a glass of orange juice and turned. "Thanks for cooking. Can I get you anything while I'm over here?"

"We're good." She stabbed her mound of eggs. "Ryan says you're a natural with the gun, and you did a double-tap. Hope that means you're one of the white knights of law enforcement and will get back up on your trusty steed soon."

"White knights?" He sat on the far side of her. "That's a lot to live up to."

"Not for me. Just being a law enforcement officer, especially these days, qualifies a person for that honor."

Ryan held his slice of bacon midair and eyed her. "Hey, what about a former one?"

"Yeah, you count."

Owen swallowed a crispy bite of bacon and swung on the stool to face Ryan. "You were an officer once?"

"Right after I got my master's in public administration and found out I don't like being inside all day. I did a four-year stint as a deputy, but I was still craving the outdoors. Then the executive director for Wilderness Ways resigned, and I stepped in."

"Wilderness Ways?" Owen sipped his coffee, made as strong as the day before.

"A wilderness counseling program for troubled teens. We lease the resort next to my family's place."

"You do both? Work as the director and at the family business?"

"Yep." He poked his fork into a clump of eggs. "Now that my parents retired and moved to town, my oldest brother Reid runs the survival business. My brother Russ and I help out when we can, but business is booming so Russ and I will have to step up more."

"You're a busy guy."

"A guy who works extremely hard so he doesn't have to think about Mia." Mackenzie arched a brow at Ryan.

"About today," Ryan said.

"Ah yes." Mackenzie kept her attention pinned to Ryan. "Avoid the topic as usual."

Ryan cast her a sharp look. "That's water under the bridge and not worth talking about."

She sighed. "Not sure you're right, but I give up."

"So, today." Owen brought them back as he wanted to get going as soon as they finished their meal.

"Right." Ryan grabbed his orange juice. "I'll do the tracking for the most part, but we all need situational awareness. Which basically means observing and correctly interpreting your observations."

"I can do that," Mackenzie said.

Ryan looked at Owen. "Might be harder for you since your memory's impaired. In tracking, we rely on mental models. Basically, it's the way we look at and understand the world. These models create expectations of how the world works for us. We grasp what occurred before, what's happening at the moment, and that gives a sense of what will likely happen next."

"And I don't have the past."

"Exactly," Ryan said. "Today we'll be concentrating on the environment and don't need to deal with the human behavior and psychology. We know where you've been and that you were fleeing. Gives us some of your mental mind-set. Unless I'm wrong."

"You got it right."

"I won't discount the psychology totally, but it'll take a back seat." Ryan took a long drink of the juice, draining the last half of the glass. "We'll use two procedures. Scan and search. Scanning the area to get a big-picture overview while keeping an open focus. Then I'll do an in-depth analysis of an area or of an object."

"Sounds like you know what you're doing," Owen said, once again impressed.

"I'll explain more as we move, but time's wasting." Ryan pushed to his feet. "Let's take a bathroom break and get on the trail."

"You guys go first while I load the dishwasher."

Ryan took off for the bathroom.

Owen helped carry dishes to the sink. "I wasn't trying to butter the guy up. He really does seem to know what he's doing."

"Has for years." She settled a plate in the dishwasher. "One time when I was in junior high and we were staying at his family resort, I got into a fight with my cousin Londyn and stormed off. Of course, I got lost in the woods. Panicked. Scared my parents to death, but Ryan found me within an hour."

She looked at Owen, a sheepish expression on her face. "If we hadn't been friends I would've been mortified. But he was cool about things, and it was much better that he found me before they had to call in the official search and rescue team."

Owen put the orange juice in the refrigerator. "Well, I'm thankful for his help for sure."

She locked gazes. "Are you sure you're ready for what we might find?"

42

"Ready?" He closed the refrigerator door. "Probably not, but I want to know who I am, and I'll risk learning anything to figure that out. Even what we might uncover today."

∼

As they started their trek over the dusty soil in the warmth of the morning sun, Mackenzie didn't like the grimace on Owen's face. He'd insisted on carrying the backpack and was holding his hands under it to keep the pack suspended above his back. He had to be in a lot of pain. Senseless pain, if anyone asked her. He didn't have to suffer when she could be doing her part. But he'd insisted, and she didn't want to further tax what she suspected was an assault on his perceived male worthiness.

Guys associated way too much with their occupations. Women too, but usually not to the same extent. Still, she knew if she suddenly had no idea of who she was, she would be stressed to the max. Imagine not knowing if you were a good person or a criminal? If you were compassionate or a sociopath? If you were Christian or someone who lived without a guiding faith?

She'd probably lose it, but he continued to hold things together. Stoic most of the time, but he did occasionally crack a smile and even laugh. Then she saw a man who would be fun to get to know.

Ryan squatted next to a large footprint and looked at Owen. "Are the shoes you're wearing now the ones you were wearing when you arrived?"

"Yes."

"Let me see the bottom."

Owen lifted his foot.

"See the waffle print and rounded toe and the way the heel is worn down on the outside? Matches your shoe and

43

the size is right. These are your footprints for sure, and this shoe print is the same as all of the ones I've seen."

Mackenzie eyed the footprints. "Owen was alone as he said."

"At least at this point." Ryan stood. "Let's follow the trail."

She and Owen traipsed after Ryan and walked all morning over dry dirt, scrub, and tufts of brown grass. Huge boulders were scattered around and a few buttes rose up from the gritty soil like desert skyscrapers. Otherwise, the only interesting sight for her besides the Painted Hills was Owen. He had determination, she'd give him that. At their water breaks, she'd tried to grab the pack but he'd been adamant about carrying it and gingerly lifted it onto his battered body.

She'd made sure to compliment him on his resolve. She should've mentioned the stubbornness instead, but Ryan interrupted as he scanned the surroundings.

"Hang on." He charged across the area running parallel to their trail. "Yeah, tire tracks." Bending down, he got out his camera and snapped pictures. He took out a small red flag on a metal stake and pushed it into the ground then returned. "Heavy vehicle. Large tires. Good tread. I'd say a full-sized pickup carrying a heavy payload of some sort."

"A person can tell all that from the tracks?" Owen asked.

"Not all guides, but I've been a tracker long enough that I've seen all kinds of tire tracks and am sure of my assessment." He looked at Mackenzie. "Can we split up and you follow the tire tracks while I keep on Owen's shoe prints? You'll be in eyesight the whole time. If either path veers off we'll get back together and follow one trail at a time."

"Sure," she said.

"Just let me know if anything seems to change."

"Like what?"

"Like if the tracks deepen or lighten. That would tell us if they offloaded or added to the truck cargo. And if you see footprints. That kind of thing."

"Roger that." She gave him a quick salute and headed for the red flag.

They moved on. Stopping. Scanning. Searching. Walking some more. And more.

"Hold up." Ryan squatted.

Mackenzie crossed the area to join them.

"Footprints are changing," Ryan said.

Owen crouched next to Ryan. "How so?"

"So far the footprint impressions have been shallow and close together. That indicates you were walking. These are starting to appear farther apart from each other and deeper in the toe. Indicates you were running."

Owen's forehead knotted. "Something or someone could've been chasing me."

"Sure. Or until this point, you had some strength and wanted to move fast, but your strength started to wane, and you had to resort to walking."

"Or decided to conserve energy, right?" Mackenzie asked.

"Right." Ryan stood. "This might be a good time to stop for lunch."

"That's my cue then." She'd insisted on them having real food for their first meal, and they could eat the ready meals Ryan brought along for dinner that night if it was needed. "We're only having PB&J, but at least it's on my gran's home-made bread."

"Which might I say is some fine bread." Ryan off-loaded his pack and sat on a boulder. "You'll have to thank her for us."

"She's very adventurous and will be happy to hear she

45

had a part in the search." Mackenzie handed a thick sandwich to Ryan and one to Owen.

"I remember that night at the campfire when she told the story about her riding on the wing of your grandfather's crop dusting plane." Ryan took his sandwich from the bag and chomped a huge bite.

Owen shot Mackenzie a questioning look. "She really did that?"

"All the time." Mackenzie got out her own sandwich. "My cousin Peyton looks like her, but I have her adventurous spirit."

Ryan swallowed. "I can see that. How many times have I had to rescue you from doing something, um...well...ill-advised?"

"Thanks for not saying stupid." She opened her zipper bag. "You rescued me way too many times, but I'd like to think I'm a little more responsible now."

"No offense, but you took me in," Owen said, his tone very serious. "Probably not the wisest decision."

She didn't take offense at his statement. He was right, but... "Sometimes you have to trust your gut. I didn't let you stay in the cabin with me, and I called Ryan."

"Yeah. You took precautions." Owen polished off a quarter of his sandwich in one bite.

"Have you remembered anything as we've walked today?" she asked him, wanting to change the topic.

He shrugged and swallowed. "I have a vague memory of this area, but then I might've expected to see this after seeing the landscape around your cabin."

"He has a point." Ryan stuffed his plastic bag into a trash container he'd brought along. "The terrain has all been very similar."

She nodded. "Another sandwich?"

"Do you even need to ask?" He grinned.

She handed him a second one and handed one to Owen too, who gave her a thankful smile and resumed chewing.

Ryan looked at his watch. "Sunset is at a little after five today. Means we have a few more hours of solid daylight left. At four, I'll call the search for the day to give us time to make camp for the night."

"We'll be out overnight no matter what, then?" she asked.

He nodded. "Even if we reach our destination, we'll want to have time in the light of day to carefully evaluate the area. I want to follow those tire tracks too."

Owen looked at her. "Is it okay if we're stuck out here overnight or do you want to head back?"

"We've come this far," she said. "And I won't quit due to a night in the cold."

She made sure to sound unstoppable, but before she'd agreed, she probably should have asked about the sleeping arrangements.

5

"There!" Owen shouted. "That's the area I remember. And the rock."

He dropped his pack and ran toward the butte, but pain forced him to slow to a fast walk. He skirted clumps of desert vegetation and rushed toward a large boulder that was burned in his memory. Dried blood caked the rock. Exactly like he'd remembered.

Flashes of memories peppered his brain as he walked. Pictures of him trudging through the wilderness. Alone. No one chasing him. Tiring. Wanting to quit. But something kept pulling him forward. Step after step until he reached Mackenzie's porch and collapsed.

What had made him keep going? And what had stolen his memory? Nothing terrible here other than the bloody rock, and that surely wasn't traumatic enough to make him forget.

"Blood." Mackenzie's voice came from behind him.

He jumped. He'd forgotten she and Ryan were with him.

He looked at her. "Guessing it's mine."

Ryan joined them. "I brought containers to take forensic samples of any evidence we locate."

48

"If I decide not to notify the police, what good will that do?" Owen asked.

"We could have a private lab analyze them," Mackenzie said.

Owen nodded, his mind racing. "Law enforcement will want to take their own samples for chain of custody anyway. Wow. Oh wow. That's weird. For some reason, I knew that. Couple that with the double-tap and maybe I really am a cop."

Ryan's eyes narrowed. "A cop or guy skilled at breaking the law?"

Poof. Owen's positive spin he so desperately wanted vanished. *Thanks, for that.*

"We need to get camp set up," Ryan jerked his head in the direction of his backpack resting where he'd placed it on a large boulder. "If there's still daylight when we're done, we can check this out again. If not, it'll have to wait until morning."

Owen didn't want to leave the spot, but the safety and comfort of Mackenzie was more important to him than anything. Even recovering his memory. Video flashes of this woman in danger popped into his brain. His gut hurt. Was his stress for her alone or did he want to protect all women? Another thing he didn't know.

He followed Ryan, who stopped near a twisted juniper tree. "We'll camp in the flat clearing near this tree. We should catch a breeze yet today, and the tents will receive full sunshine first thing in the morning."

"Sounds good," Mackenzie said. "We're yours to command."

"Wow, I think that's the first time I've ever heard that from you." Ryan laughed. "I packed three individual tents. Since I know how to set them up and how to choose a good site, I'll take care of that. But we'll need firewood."

"I noticed a dead tree back on the trail a bit." Owen jerked a thumb over his shoulder. "Will that work?"

Ryan nodded. "I'll get my saw and the two of you can cut the branches into manageable pieces and bring them back."

In Owen's wounded state, he wasn't terribly eager to saw wood and tote it back here. His body was about ready to collapse. He'd only gotten this far spurred on by the hope of finding the area he needed to see. And he'd foolishly believed that when he arrived, his memory would come flooding back and part of his trauma would be over.

Not so much.

Why God? Just why?

He waited for an answer.

Nothing came.

He knew in his gut that he'd asked the question many times in his life and hadn't received answers. Maybe he was a believer but not a very strong Christian, so he didn't know how to listen for answers. Or the right way to listen. Was there a secret to unlock God's communication? A secret he didn't know but would discover once his memory came back?

Ryan gave him a folding saw. "It's small but mighty."

"Like a mustard seed of faith," Mackenzie said, as if she were able to read the doubt in Owen's mind.

"Can move a mountain." She paused and locked gazes with him. "Give our search for your memory time. We'll figure it out."

He didn't know how to reply, so he set off for the tree, pondering her comment as he walked.

She caught up to him.

He looked at her. "You really do believe that, don't you?"

"I do," she replied with certainty.

"I just asked God why He's allowing me to go through this."

"And?" She stepped to the dead tree and rested a hand on one of the twisted branches.

"And no answer."

She looked up at him. "Can I make a suggestion?"

"Of course," he said and really meant it. He'd already come to see she lived her faith, and whatever she had to say actually might help him.

"When I'm troubled about something, I try to remind myself the problem isn't forever. That things will change. Evolve. Maybe not get better but change. So say I'm having a bad day. I say to myself that I'm upset *for now*. Adding the *for now* to whatever problem I'm dealing with helps me remember that it's temporary."

"I can try that." He unfolded the saw blade and locked it in place. "But I might never get my memory back. Then what? Your *for now* doesn't work."

"But each day that you don't have it you'll get better at dealing with the change. Soon you'll find yourself stronger and more able to cope."

"And if I want to wallow in my misery instead?" He hated hearing that come out of his mouth, but that was the state of his emotions right now.

"That's your choice. I mean, I do that too. Let myself mourn the loss of something, but then I know I have to get over it and move on. With God's help, I manage it."

He looked for the best branch to start sawing. "You make it sound so easy."

"Easy? Hah!" She laughed. "Not at all. It's simply a choice you make. But don't think you can make it on your own. Maybe instead of asking God why, ask Him to help you accept and deal with the problem."

"Good advice," he said, but wasn't at all sure he could carry it out. That involved trusting God to do whatever *He* wanted. Not what Owen wanted. And he was so very desperate to get his memory back when that might not be God's plan at all.

Still, if he wanted to look at the positives, he could appreciate the fact that God put this woman in his life. She was so full of surprises. Surprises that Owen liked. Liked a lot. And he liked her. The depth of her being was even more impressive than her looks or the fact that she put others first.

And what about him? Was he deep enough to hold his own with her? To earn her respect?

He was beginning to doubt it. But he would embrace her advice and try to take this recent event in stride and stop being frustrated. *For now.* Maybe those two little words could help him do it for short periods of time, and they would morph into longer periods of time as she said.

He sawed off a dead branch then cut it up, his muscles and body screaming to stop. She stacked the branches, then carried an armful back to the campsite. He waited until she was out of sight and let out a long breath, then took in a few more and let his arms fall limp at his side. Time to admit that he couldn't keep sawing long enough to produce the quantity of wood they needed.

Could he stand to watch her do the work while he stood back? Or would he completely tire his muscles and not be able to move tomorrow?

That would be foolish. Tomorrow was too important. He needed all of his reserves for scouring the area.

He rested against the trunk and waited for her to return. "My arms have given out."

"Let me." She gently took the saw from his hand, a soft look in her eyes. Not pity. Not weakness. But compassion and what he suspected was Christian love.

"Thank you," he said sincerely.

"Hey, just cause I'm a girl doesn't mean I can't do the

same work. I'm an equal partner in this trip with you and Ryan."

"You're right. I was being sexist." He moved out of her way.

"You were being a guy." She wrinkled her cute nose and sawed away.

Grace. She was extending God's grace to him when he was acting like one of those he-man guys who believed women didn't have equal footing. But he believed this woman could do anything she set her mind to. Especially with her faith, which was clearly far bigger than a tiny mustard seed.

Her actions were precise and effective. Not a wasted movement.

He took a long limb from her. "You've done this before."

"We have a wood-burning fireplace in the farmhouse I was raised in. And of course, I chopped wood with Ryan in the summers. At least until his dad invested in a chainsaw."

Man, she *was* full of surprises. "You grew up on a farm?"

She paused to look at him. "I did. My parents' house is on one side of my grandparents' farm and then my aunt and uncle's property borders the other side."

"And here I had you pegged for a city girl."

"What gave you that impression?"

"I think the skirt you wore. It was soft and feminine. Very stylish."

She propped a hand on a hip. "So you think all country girls wear bib overalls and flannel shirts."

"Yeah, maybe I did." He laughed.

"There's a lot of that, of course. Doing barn chores in heels and a skirt isn't very practical, but we did all the other things our city counterparts did." She cut the limb into smaller pieces. "Well, maybe everything but drugs, alcohol, and sex, but that probably has more to do with the way we were raised than the availability."

"I wish I knew how I was raised."

"You look pretty clean-cut. Fit, like you work out. So maybe you were an athlete."

"Maybe." He let her comment ruminate in his brain as he gathered an armload of wood and took it back to the campsite.

Under the setting sun, Ryan had erected three lime green and gray nylon tents that were long and skinny and held a sleeping bag. Just the right size for one person each. And part of the reason his and Ryan's packs were heavy. They were carrying gear for three people.

Owen didn't mind, but wanted to know why Ryan didn't have Mackenzie carry her own gear. So he asked.

"You want the honest answer?" Ryan asked.

Owen nodded.

"I figured with your injuries you'd give out and not be able to carry the pack. Mackenzie could take it, and I wouldn't have to repack things on the fly."

Owen didn't like the answer, but it was a fair assessment. "I've already had to let her saw the tree. And she might have to carry the pack tomorrow. We'll see."

"No shame in that." Ryan cocked an eyebrow. "She told me you're a bruised mess. We both understand."

"Yeah, well, I don't." Wishing he could accept it as readily as the two of them, Owen started back for the tree.

Mackenzie had sawed the rest of the last branch into smaller pieces and had started on the next one.

"Stay back." She swiped the back of her hand over her forehead and laughed. "This is sweaty work."

"I can take over again," he offered.

"No worries. I don't get to the gym as often as I'd like these days and it's good for toning my arms."

"Nothing wrong with your arms. Or the rest of you for that matter," he said, then clamped his mouth closed.

Why had he said that? And in such a flirtatious tone. The last thing she needed was to be stuck in the wilderness with a guy who had no idea of his identity and was hitting on her. The very last thing.

She didn't say a word but resumed sawing. He carried, and she sawed until darkness descended on them like a heavy black cloak littered with stars, and Ryan declared they had enough wood to make it through the night.

Ryan had created a fire ring with rocks and stacked the wood next to it. "We'll take shifts tonight keeping the fire stoked to ward off any coyotes and badgers."

"Any worries about them attacking?" Mackenzie knelt by the fire pit.

"Worry? Not really. But I like to be cautious."

Owen lowered his aching body to the ground. "Then I'd like a gun for my shift."

Ryan shared a look with Mackenzie. She nodded.

"Fine. You'll get the gun." Ryan squatted next to the fire ring. "Let me get some water boiling so we can fix the MREs. On the menu tonight is beef stroganoff."

"Is it any good?" Mackenzie tucked her legs under her.

"I've tried most all the brands out there and this one seems to be the best. As a bonus, it requires less water and time to cook." Ryan struck a match and the kindling and dried brush he'd put under the wood teepee caught and flamed into life.

"The last thing I need right now is heat from the fire." Mackenzie laughed and fanned her face.

Suddenly hyper-alert, Ryan cocked his head. Owen soon heard the sound taking Ryan's attention. A sound coming from the west. A rumble. Like an off-road vehicle.

Owen met Ryan's gaze. "We have company."

Ryan drew his weapon.

"I want to arm myself too." Owen's calm voice surprised him when his heart was racing.

"Gun's in my backpack in the tent." Ryan didn't shift his gaze but got to his feet.

Owen jumped up, his whole body groaning in pain, to follow Ryan. Owen wanted to not only be protected but do the protecting of Mackenzie if needed.

Ryan shoved the Glock into Owen's hands then dug back into his pack.

Owen checked the ammo clip.

Nearly full.

He clipped the empty holster on his belt and looked up in time to see headlights coming their way.

Ryan drew out a pair of binoculars. "Night vision."

"Perfect." Owen turned to check on Mackenzie.

She'd taken cover on the far side of the thick trunk of the juniper tree. Ryan dropped behind a boulder, and Owen joined Mackenzie. The headlights cut through the inky night. Two sharp beams. Aiming their way.

"Why would someone be out here on private property at this time of night?" Owen asked.

"You think someone tracked us here?" Her tone was breathless, but he couldn't see her expression.

"I don't think so. Not when they're coming from the north, but who knows." He stepped behind Mackenzie and leaned close. For his own safety, yeah, but mostly to protect her from an attack from behind. Her body trembled, and he wanted to wrap his arms around her and hold her until she let go of the fear and stopped shaking.

The vehicle came into view. Too dark to make out many details, but it looked like it carried one helmeted rider. No way to ID the driver, but the size said male.

Owen's brain flashed with a memory. The sun setting. A

56

red Polaris Utility Terrain Vehicle racing toward him. One man in the UTV wearing a sleek black half-helmet that left his face uncovered. Leaping out. Calmly swaggering toward Owen, helmet still in place. Not saying a word. Owen trying to introduce himself and ask what the guy was doing there.

The rider tossed a fist to Owen's face, catching him off guard and spinning him. The guy got behind Owen and pummeled his back. When Owen turned, the rider landed a fist to Owen's gut. Another. And another, before Owen got a punch in of his own to the man's gut.

Owen didn't get another chance. The rider shoved Owen. He plummeted backward. Head striking the rock. Then nothing but blackness until he woke up in the dark. Alone. Left for dead. His vehicle gone.

The roar of the engine rocketing toward them snapped Owen back to the present. Back to the potential threat. Back to protecting Mackenzie.

The driver suddenly slammed on the brakes, the vehicle fishtailing to a stop. He stood. Surveyed the area. Sat and turned the vehicle, racing back in the direction he'd come from.

Owen wasn't ready to back off on protecting Mackenzie yet. Not until he couldn't hear the sound of the vehicle as rifles had good range out here in the flatlands. Not that he believed that they were dealing with a shooter. There had been zero evidence of that, but caution was the word.

"You make out anything on the vehicle?" Owen made sure to talk loud enough to be heard over the departing engine.

"No, did you?" she asked.

"Just that it was a two-seater UTV with a single male wearing a helmet."

The engine's rumble disappeared into the night, and Owen finally stepped back. "Let's join Ryan but be alert."

They strode to Ryan who was backing toward the firepit.

"What did you see?" Owen asked.

"Polaris UTV. Red and black. Male driver. Helmet. Big guy. Put him at six feet, maybe two thirty. Wore a leather jacket and jeans."

"Sounds like the guy who attacked me yesterday, and the same UTV he was driving. I think he took my vehicle or had someone else do it. Assuming I drove out here, but I'm not sure of that."

Mackenzie flashed her gaze to him. "You remembered?"

He nodded and described the attack. "The guy wore one of those half helmets so I could see him, but it was too dark to make out any features other than he wore glasses. That's all for now. Not sure why the guy attacked me though."

Mackenzie sat by the fire and drew her legs in again. "It's good news that something came back, and the glasses could help us locate this guy."

"Yeah, and the doc said if I start to remember bits and pieces, I have a better chance of gaining all my memory back."

"Keep watch." Ryan gave them both a pointed look. "And I'll get this water boiling so we can eat."

Mackenzie gaped at him. "How can you eat after that?"

Owen agreed. His stomach was churning. Not from seeing the vehicle, but from remembering the vicious assault.

"We have to." Ryan stoked the fire and put the collapsible kettle on a rack above. "With all the hiking today, we have to keep up our calorie intake if we're going to function tomorrow."

"I'll take the first watch starting after we eat." Owen challenged Ryan with a just-try-me look. "And I'll need those binoculars to do the job right."

Ryan lifted the cord from around his neck and handed

them over without a single question. "It's a little early for shuteye, but I can always try."

"Not too early for me," Mackenzie said. "I'll probably crash once my adrenaline wears off."

Owen hoped so. And he wouldn't wake her for a shift either. There was no way he was sleeping tonight. No way at all. Not when there was a chance this man who beat him to a pulp would return and Owen could nab him and unravel this mystery.

6

As the sun woke from a good night's sleep, Owen sat across from Ryan at the firepit and stared at the lime green tents, knowing his gaze held longing for the sleeping bag in his tent. But he'd taken every shift last night. Not that Ryan had shirked his duty. He'd taken a stint while Owen dozed a bit by the fire. Maybe Owen's decision to stay up all night would come back to bite him today. His body screamed from the hike yesterday. From the beating. From the lack of sleep.

But at least the night awake taught him that he was made of some pretty stern stuff. Made him unreasonably proud. Maybe that would make up for the pain and fatigue.

Mackenzie crawled out of her tent. Her hair was messy, and she had that sleepy just-came-awake look. A little bewildered. A little sultry. Her breaths coming in little puffs in the near-freezing temperatures.

Did she look this way every morning?

Man, he'd like to find out.

"You guys let me sleep all night." She stretched her arms overhead, her top lifting and showing a creamy sliver of skin above her jeans.

Ryan looked at Mackenzie. "Were you warm enough last night?"

"Perfect." She looked at him and then at Owen. "And before either of you say anything when we leave today, you schlepped all of these things for my creature comfort, and I'm carrying the pack out."

"Fine by me," Ryan said.

"Me too." Owen was struggling this morning, but still wished he didn't have to let her do the work.

She offered them both a victorious smile that shot an arrow right to Owen's heart. This woman got to him in a big way, but Ryan didn't seem affected by the smile at all, confirming his platonic interest in her.

"Did either of you get any sleep?" she asked.

"I did." Ryan glanced at Owen. "But overachiever here took watch all night. Guess he didn't trust us to stand watch."

I guess I don't. "Can never be too careful."

Ryan held up a scrambled egg MRE. "It's gonna take a bit for the coffee and water to be ready for breakfast if you want to make a quick sweep around the area. I know it's barely light, but you might see something."

"Better than sitting here shivering and my muscles getting stiffer." Owen unfolded his legs to test the strength.

Mackenzie looked at him. "I'll come with you."

He marched across the open space to where the UTV had stopped last night. He bent to study the tracks, his back appreciating the stretch. "Are these tracks like the ones you trailed?"

"No. Closer together. Much smaller tires. Not as deep."

"Not the vehicle that drove toward your rental, then."

She shook her head. "You said they took your vehicle. I wonder if those tracks belonged to your vehicle."

"Could be, though I don't know what I was driving, if

anything. Ryan said those tracks were from a truck." He ran a frustrated hand through his hair.

"You seem like you might be a truck kind of guy."

"I do, do I?" He grinned as he didn't mind her thinking that way. He felt a kinship with pickups for some reason. Maybe he was exactly what she'd pegged him to be. "Why's that?"

"You seem like Ryan. Kind of rugged. At home in the outdoors."

"And what do you think about that?"

"Think about it?"

"Do you like guys who are rugged?"

"I like guys who like adventure. Often that can mean rugged, but I've had guy friends who like adventure and aren't overly rugged," She locked gazes with him. "I like you, if that's what you're really asking."

He was unreasonably happy by her answer. "You're very direct."

"Not most of the time. I'm more the peacemaker in a group and can often be found lost in my thoughts and philosophizing."

"But this called for a direct answer?"

"I just wanted you to know I like you."

"And what if I'm a criminal?"

"You're not," she said with conviction. "You went out of your way last night to be sure I was safe behind that tree. Then let me sleep all night. Those actions show me you're very much a gentleman, even if you are a man of few words. So there." She laughed.

He laughed with her, the moment more refreshing than a night of sleep might've been. He wanted to slide his fingers into that thick mane and pull her close for a kiss. But he wouldn't. Not before he knew who he was. She was a special woman and deserved a good man. He only hoped she was right and he was that man.

"Can you take pictures of the tracks?" he asked, getting them back to the business at hand.

"Sure." She took her phone out and snapped several photos in succession, the clicks echoing into the quiet.

He turned toward the base of the outcropping and studied every inch of the area, trying to remember the things Ryan looked for in tracking.

He squatted, and his thighs screamed in pain. "Another set of footprints. Looks like boots. Big size. Male."

"Agreed." Mackenzie bent and took pictures. "And a unique pattern."

He looked at her. "You're thinking we might be able to match it to someone's boots."

She stowed her phone. "If we can find a solid suspect, yes, but otherwise, no. Most of the guys around here wear boots of some kind, and it would be like playing Cinderella to find the person who made these prints."

The sight of Mackenzie sitting in a chair and all the men of the area coming forward to show her their boots came to mind. He chuckled silently as he stood and continued along the base of the outcropping.

A blackbird swooped into a rock crevice, drawing his attention to the dusty bottom of a small winding creek. The curving indentation was several feet deep and dotted with rocks worn smooth from years of the creek flowing over them. It looked like someone had taken bags of rocks and tossed them in a random pattern when coursing water had laid them there.

"Looks like a dried-up creek bed," she said from behind him.

He looked back at her. "I wonder how long it's been dry."

She joined him. "I don't know the area well, but we've

had some pretty dry years lately and maybe it's been this way for a while."

He started up the creek and wound around the outcropping of jagged rocks.

He came to a stop. Flashed a hand in the air. Tried not to gag and empty his stomach. "Stop. Don't come around here."

His heart thumped. Raced. But he stood strong to block Mackenzie from seeing the horrific sight.

Had this been what he'd seen to cause his memory loss? The sight before him was shocking enough to take his memory and more.

Mackenzie appreciated Owen trying to protect her. She really did. Found it endearing even. But she was a strong woman and could handle seeing whatever he'd discovered. Even if it did make his face go white.

She pushed past him. Wished she hadn't. Came to a stop.

"Oh. Oh my." She turned away.

"That's why I told you not to come back here."

"But I'm too stubborn." Her stomach roiled. She was glad for two things. They hadn't eaten breakfast yet, and the sun only inched above the horizon, so the horrific sight in front of her wasn't completely visible. But in moments, the sun would beat down on the creek bed.

Still, what she'd seen was burned in her brain for all eternity.

She looked at Owen. "It's a woman, right?"

"The clothing would suggest that."

"Seems like the body was submerged in the creek until the water dried up to reveal her skeleton." Mackenzie held his gaze. "I'd heard with all the drought in the west lately that's happened with some lakes. Water receding and revealing bodies, I mean."

"Sounds plausible."

"And do you think this is what you were trying to forget?"

"Seems possible." He swallowed hard, his Adam's apple bobbing in his tan throat. "Wish I could forget it now."

"We need to call the authorities."

He nodded and frowned. Dark panic consumed his expression.

"Means you'll be fingerprinted." No point in dodging his worries. Better to confront it head on. "Maybe even be asked for a DNA sample."

"Yeah."

"And you're okay with that?"

"A woman's likely been murdered. I have to be."

Mackenzie got out her phone, but wasn't surprised when the screen displayed zero bars. She'd checked her phone as they'd hiked and hadn't gotten any bars since early yesterday morning. "No signal."

"Maybe Ryan carries a SAT phone."

"Yeah, I bet he does." She scrambled back around the rock and tried to let go of the image of the skeletal remains held in some sort of large bag that had been ripped open at the top to reveal the remains. The woman was wearing a dusty pink sweatshirt and matching pants that looked like they were designed for hiking. Her ankles were tied with thick rope, and she wore hiking boots. She'd been murdered. Had to be with the rope around her ankles and the bag holding her body.

Mackenzie took a long breath and let it out. "Looks like the bag kept the skeleton intact."

"Yeah."

"Which would maybe help confirm that she'd skeletonized in water where predators didn't carry bones away."

"Makes sense."

She didn't like his short answers, but he was likely trying to process too. "Do you remember seeing her before?"

He tilted his head. "I keep trying, but nothing is coming back."

"I'll continue to pray that it does." And she would pray for much more. Like he hadn't killed this woman and come back to move the body and been discovered by the UTV driver.

They needed answers even more now. And she had to consider that Owen actually remembered and was lying to her. She didn't think so, but the former law enforcement officer in her told her not to lose sight of that.

She started for the campsite. "If Ryan can get a call through, I want to get ahold of Dr. Kelsey Dunbar too. She's a forensic anthropologist at the Veritas Center in Portland."

"The name seems familiar."

"The Center is a private lab devoted to forensic testing for law enforcement agencies, and they're world renowned for their facility and skills." Mackenzie looked at Owen. "If you're an officer, you might've worked with them."

"Maybe."

"Anyway, due to the status of the remains, the sheriff will likely turn this investigation over to OSP, and they'd have to call in a state anthropologist. I might as well see if they'll agree to let Kelsey recover the remains instead."

Mackenzie paused to make strong eye contact and rest her hand on his arm, hopefully telling him that she was on his side. "You want answers, and she's the best. On the cutting edge of research and data. If a lead can be found in those remains, she'll find it. And I'll ask her to bring Sierra Rice with her too. She's their trace evidence expert."

66

He frowned. "It's going to take them time to get here."

"Not to worry. They're driven to help. If they agree to take the investigation, they'll drive through the night to be here at first light."

He offered her a tight smile. "Then let's get back to Ryan and hope he has that phone."

Owen paced the campsite. He was at once uncomfortable and comfortable with the sheriff department's presence. Two young deputies—one thin and wiry, the other tall and stocky—raced onto the scene, their lights and sirens blaring when there was no one in need of warning.

Ryan had given them coordinates and asked them to approach the campsite from the south to not disturb the tire tracks. They complied. Both deputies stomped around the end of the butte and came back looking pale. They shared their story with Sheriff Wheeler when he arrived on scene.

The guy looked to be in his mid-fifties, short. Squat, but powerful. His men wore black uniforms, but he was dressed in a long-sleeved green shirt, dark jeans, and had a holster and badge clipped to his belt that sported a large gold buckle under a burgeoning belly. He marched with purpose behind the deputy he called Dahl toward the creek and disappeared behind the rocks.

Owen looked at Ryan and Mackenzie. "Either one of you know anything about the sheriff?"

"Not me," Ryan said.

"All I remember is that he unseated a long-term sheriff by a landslide when he was elected," Mackenzie said.

Owen nodded. "Popular guy."

"I think it was more that there was a question about the prior sheriff's business dealings."

Wheeler came back around the corner and stomped toward them. His ruddy complexion remained intact. No loss of blood in his face at the sight he'd witnessed but his jaw was clamped closed as he took long steps, kicking up dust with each one.

He came to a stop in front of them. "Sheriff Sterling Wheeler. Who called this in?"

Ryan stepped forward. "I did."

Wheeler fixed his steely blue eyes on Ryan. "And you are?"

"Ryan Maddox, guide for Mackenzie Steele and Owen, whose last name is unknown." Ryan shared the story of why they were there and Owen's memory loss.

That earned Owen a long look and raised eyebrow from the sheriff. "Now isn't that something." He jerked his thumb over his shoulder. "You all touch anything back there?"

"No. We know better than that." Mackenzie took a few steps closer. "I'm a former OSP detective in the investigations division, and Ryan served as a deputy in Emerson County."

"Well, I'll be." Wheeler sounded like a slow-going good old boy, but his sharp gaze told Owen something else. "Good you didn't disturb anything. After Deputy Dahl here gets the scene cordoned off, he'll take your statements and you can be on your way."

Translated—sit back and wait until we say you can go and don't interfere.

"We don't mean to step on your toes." Mackenzie smiled. "But I wanted to make one suggestion."

Wheeler looked put out. "One's all I have time for."

"With the state of the victim, I know you'll have to call in a forensic anthropologist to recover the body."

"And?"

"Might I recommend Dr. Dunbar at the Veritas Center in Portland?"

His forehead creased. "That frou-frou place where they charge my entire year's budget to step into the lobby?"

Mackenzie stiffened at the comment but quickly recovered. "They often do work pro bono, and I have a connection to the partners. I'm sure they'd agree to do it for free, and they could get here far faster than the state expert."

"Far's I know, sixty-five miles an hour on I-84 is sixty-five miles an hour for anyone. Even a specialist who charges premium fees." He gave a snide grin. "Unless you want to tell me they'll be breaking the law, and in that case, I'll be waiting for them."

"They have access to a helicopter."

"Right. Of course they do."

"Dr. Dunbar can also bring a trace evidence expert with her to process the scene."

He arched an eyebrow. "What's in this for you? Or are you hoping to cut me out of the loop?"

She shook her head. "You'll sign a contract with them. Unless you authorize someone other than yourself to receive reports, you'll be the only one who will receive the info."

"You don't say? A contract." He tapped his chin with his wide index finger. "The state folks are notoriously behind. I don't have the budget to station someone out here round the clock until those remains are recovered."

"We have a SAT phone, and I can call Dr. Dunbar right now. Maybe have her here in a few hours."

He nodded. "Go ahead then."

Mackenzie didn't waste time. She raced to Ryan's pack by the fire. She glanced at her cell phone first, then tapped a number into the SAT phone.

Wheeler turned his attention to Owen. "So no memory at all, huh?"

"The name Owen seems familiar and right. I also remembered the attack yesterday." He described the assault and the vehicle that had come upon them last night. "I'd like to file an official report so you can investigate that too."

"I'll have my deputy take your information, but don't hold out much hope. Got a Polaris dealership nearby. Means lots of Polaris UTVs in the area, so that's not likely going to be a big help."

Owen figured as much, but he still needed to report what had happened.

He heard Mackenzie say goodbye, and she hurried back to them. "Kelsey—Dr. Dunbar—agreed. She'll arrange the helicopter and be here as soon as possible."

"Good." Wheeler gave a tight smile.

"Might you authorize the forensic person to process the area where the attacker hit me too?" Owen asked.

"If it's free, why not? Tell my deputy where, and I'll have him cordon off that area too." Wheeler clapped his hands. "Then Dahl will get your statements, and you can be on your way."

Mackenzie's shoulders rose, and Owen was starting to recognize that look in her eyes. She was going to try to find a way to be here when the chopper landed and maybe longer. And Owen had no doubt that whatever she put her mind to, she would achieve.

7

Just over three hours later, Mackenzie closed her eyes and held her breath as the thumping helicopter rotors stirred the dust and sent it swirling into the air. The machine was landing a good football field away, but dust carried on the flat terrain, grittiness irritating her eyes and face. She waited for the chopper to land, and the blades to slowly wind down before approaching.

The deputy had taken their statements and cordoned off both areas. Sheriff Wheeler had gone back to his office to coordinate his resources, warning her and Owen to stay clear of the crime scene, but he didn't come right out and say she had to leave the area after that.

Ryan didn't hang around but caught a ride to the rental cabin with the sheriff to retrieve his Bronco and bring it to the crime scene so she and Owen didn't have to hike back to her rental.

The chopper's front door swung open, and Cooper Ashcroft jumped down. Coop was one of the pilots for the Blackwell Tactical team out of Cold Harbor. He was an intense guy with black hair and was often mistaken for an unapproachable tough guy, but once people got to know him, they soon learned he was a marshmallow inside.

He slid open the back door and held out his hand to assist first Sierra and then a very pregnant Kelsey. According to Mackenzie's calculations from the last time she'd seen Kelsey, the woman was around seven months pregnant, and her large baby bump confirmed that.

Mackenzie stepped over to greet them and introduce Owen. "Thank you for coming so quickly."

"Of course." Kelsey shook hands with Owen. "And what's your connection to all of this?"

Owen explained his situation concisely and robotically.

Coop glared at him. "Mighty convenient to forget things when a body's been discovered."

"She's skeletonized, so I doubt Owen had anything to do with her death." Mackenzie felt compelled to come to Owen's defense.

"You think it's a she?" Kelsey asked.

"Female clothing," Owen answered.

"The remains are completely exposed?" Kelsey asked. "Nothing buried?"

"That's right," Mackenzie said.

Sierra looked at Owen. "Must really be tough not to remember."

"It is. But things are starting to come back. I hope I'll soon know what I was doing out here other than discovering these remains."

Coop made a noise that was half a harrumph and half a grumble clearing of his throat as he eyed Owen.

Okay, what do you really think, Coop? Sheesh.

"What can we do to help?" Mackenzie asked.

"We'll need to unload the helicopter and set up our canopy and supplies," Kelsey said. "But first we'll want to

72

suit up and get a look at the remains to know what we're facing."

Coop smiled at Kelsey, his softer side coming out. "Let me know when you select a location, and I'll get the cargo unloaded."

Kelsey pointed at the helicopter door. "We need the red bin now."

"On it." Coop disappeared into the chopper.

Kelsey wound her near-black curly hair into a ponytail and looked at Mackenzie. "I want to be clear right up front that even though you called us, our contract is between the county and the Veritas Center. Means we can't share any information with you without the sheriff's consent."

"That's what I thought." Mackenzie smiled to ease the doctor's concern. "We appreciate the position you're in and will do our best not to ask anything of you."

"Thanks. I figured you knew that, but needed to make it clear."

Sierra followed Kelsey's lead in putting her hair into a ponytail, but she had dishwater blond hair, straight and falling below her shoulders. Coop brought the bin, and she dug out white Tyvek suits, handing one to Kelsey.

Kelsey quickly tugged the garment over her tan dress slacks and a floral print blouse with sheer sleeves, but struggled with getting the zipper closed. "I'll have to get a bigger size soon. I'm only seven months."

"I remember those days." Sierra raised her suit over black tactical pants and a black Veritas embroidered polo.

"And hope to experience it again someday?" Kelsey asked.

"Absolutely. But not before Asher turns two." Sierra pulled up her zipper, the rasping sound echoing in the quiet desert.

Kelsey got her zipper sorted out and glanced at Sierra. "Ready?"

"As I can be." Sierra looped a camera strap around her neck and the pair set off for Deputy Dahl.

Mackenzie and Owen trailed behind the couple. Mackenzie stifled a chuckle when Kelsey's pregnant waddle, black hair, and white suit brought a penguin to mind.

"They seem like an interesting pair," Owen said as they walked side-by-side.

"They are. Kelsey especially. She's super feminine and doesn't at all look like the kind of person I expect to unearth bones."

"Yeah, I can see that."

Sierra and Kelsey held out their IDs to the deputy.

"Deputy Dahl." He lifted the crime scene tape for them. "The sheriff requested that you look for any ID as soon as possible."

Kelsey nodded. "I will if it doesn't compromise the scene."

Mackenzie stepped forward. Dahl rolled his eyes and dropped the tape before she could follow, then picked up a clipboard and scribbled something on it. Probably recording Kelsey and Sierra's names as having accessed the scene.

Mackenzie followed along the tape toward the body, but Dahl had cordoned off a wide area for the scene's outer perimeter, and she couldn't make out everything the Veritas team were saying. On the bright side, she was impressed with the way Dahl had handled the scene. Not every small-town deputy did a by-the-book job.

"How long do you think it will take them?" Owen asked her.

She looked at him, his eyebrows drawn together. "No idea, but that's one thing they should be able to share with us."

Deputy Dahl pinned his focus on Mackenzie and Owen. Did he think she planned to jump the crime scene tape? She must look eager to get a better view of the skeleton now that she'd come to grips with finding it, but she wouldn't cause any problems with the crime scene. Besides, she suspected the good deputy and sheriff wouldn't mind arresting her to prove a point.

So she ignored Dahl, and lifted a hand over her eyes to block the sun. Kelsey had put on disposable gloves and was searching the victim's pockets. Hopefully, looking for that ID.

She stood, something silver dangling from her hand. She marched over to Dahl and held out her hand. "No ID but this might be unique enough to identify her."

He put on a glove and took the item from Kelsey. He let what appeared to be a necklace dangle from his fingers. "Seems pretty unusual. Let me get on my computer and run it through NaMUS."

He took off for his patrol vehicle and got behind the wheel. Kelsey went back to the remains. Mackenzie and Owen both kept their eyes on Dahl. Didn't take long before he got out and came back to Kelsey. "Necklace matches a woman named Cassie Collins."

Owen startled and took a step back.

Mackenzie looked at him, his face as white as the fluffy clouds overhead.

"From Vancouver." Dahl mentioned the Washington city right across the Columbia River from Portland. "What in the world was she doing out here?"

"That's what we hope to help you figure out." Kelsey held out her hand. "Now I'll need that necklace to log into official evidence."

"Let me take a quick picture for the sheriff." Dahl snapped a photo and handed the jewelry back to Kelsey.

"I'll let you know the minute we have additional information that might be helpful." Kelsey stood with the necklace dangling from her fingers.

Mackenzie snapped a picture of the heart-shaped pendant with an infinity sign in silver mounted over it.

Mackenzie turned her gaze back to Owen who was pale and looked like the name or the sight of the necklace sent him reeling even more. She leaned closer and whispered, "Do you know her?"

"I think I might." He worked his jaw muscles. "At least the name sounds familiar and puts a lump in my throat."

Had he come here to find this girl? Or worse, had he been involved in her murder? Questions Mackenzie would get to the bottom of as soon as possible.

Owen couldn't think straight. He'd been thrown for a loop by the name.

Cassie Collins.

That necklace... This woman's relationship to him sat at the fingertips of his brain. If only he could jar the information loose from the lost file where he'd housed it.

"Let's go over to the firepit and sit down." Mackenzie took his arm and steered him across the opening to a rock big enough for the two of them to perch on.

She watched him carefully, and unknowingly transmitted her expectation for him to remember too. But he didn't.

"We'll figure this out." She squeezed his arm and let go to sit.

"I hope so." He sat next to her. "It's so unsettling. It's like I'm looking at a black TV screen when I should see my life."

She shifted to face him. "I can't even imagine how hard that must be."

"I'd like to say it's the hardest thing I've ever faced, but I have no way of knowing."

"If it helps, I'm praying for you."

"It does help. I have the feeling you have a direct line to God and mine seems more circuitous." The blood started to return to his head and strength to his legs.

"We all have a direct line to God, but maybe we all don't take the time to be still and hear Him answer our call."

"Yeah, that could be it." Owen had suspected as much. He took a long breath and let it out. "So what happens next?"

"We go help Sierra and Kelsey unload their supplies." Mackenzie glanced at her watch. "By that time, Ryan should be back, and we can return to the cabin. But before we go, I want to invite Sierra and Kelsey to come take a break and have a light dinner with us."

"That would be good."

"If they accept, I'll have to go to the grocery store for more supplies. But after that, we can search the internet for information on Cassie Collins. I can also call Nick Thorn, the IT expert at Veritas, to run a deep background check."

"Sounds like a plan."

She made the call on the SAT phone Ryan left for them in case they needed it, and it was short and to the point, but he could tell that this Nick guy agreed to do the background check on Cassie.

Mackenzie ended her call. "He'll do it as soon as he can, but might not be until the morning."

"Thanks for arranging that." Owen stood and made sure not to show his disappointment in the check taking longer than he'd hoped. "We should help carry supplies."

He wanted to be of help, but more than that he wanted

to do something to stop wondering about this Cassie woman, and ignore the fringes of his memory that were tempting him to remember but keeping the memories out of reach.

He headed for the helicopter where the pilot had taken the supply bins out and set them on the ground.

Kelsey sauntered over to them and swiped a hand over her forehead. "It might not be hot this time of year, but I have my own little heater and need to get that canopy erected or I'll melt in the sun."

Owen grabbed the canopy. "I'm glad to carry it over there for you, but I doubt Dahl will let me set it up."

"Sierra and I can do it." Kelsey smiled and grabbed a tote. "If you all could also help bring the table to the perimeter and the rest of the bins, that would be incredible. It'll help us get going much faster."

"You got it." Mackenzie picked up the nearest bin and followed.

Owen carried the canopy to the edge of the fluttering yellow tape. While Sierra and Kelsey erected the canopy over the remains, he and Mackenzie marched back and forth, getting the bins in place. Then Sierra and Kelsey unfolded a long table and filled it with tools and equipment, most of which Owen couldn't name. Mackenzie stood next to Owen and waited for Kelsey to return.

"How long do you think the recovery will take?" Mackenzie asked.

Kelsey leaned against the chopper. "Shouldn't be more than five hours or so. But all depends on what we find under the remains."

"Will you want to spend the night?" Mackenzie asked.

She shook her head. "Coop is going to take off. Sierra's and my assistants are on the way in the van, so there will be four of us to take turns driving straight through."

Like Mackenzie had told Owen, this team really was dedicated to their work.

"If something changes," Mackenzie said. "You're welcome to stay with me."

"Appreciate that."

"We'll be leaving in a bit, but I wanted to offer dinner and a break with your feet up at my cabin if you'd like."

"That would be amazing." Kelsey rested her hand on her belly. "This little one will be thankful for the meal and the rest."

"Either you or Sierra have any food allergies?"

"None."

Mackenzie looked at her watch. "I'll come out to get you at about five for dinner."

"Sounds perfect." Kelsey unzipped her suit and took a pen and business card from her pocket. "I have one of the Center's SAT phones, and you can call me on this number if you need to get ahold of me."

Owen wasn't at all surprised that Kelsey and Sierra had a SAT phone.

Mackenzie took the card.

Kelsey grabbed a blue tarp and turned back to the crime scene as Ryan's Bronco rolled in.

Owen was jonesing to get away from the reminder that he likely knew the woman lying in the dry creek bed. "Let's go meet Ryan."

They strolled to the end of the flapping yellow tape, but instead of continuing on, Mackenzie stopped next to Deputy Dahl. Owen wanted to move her along, but the urge to know what she wanted with Dahl stopped him.

"I'll be getting dinner for the Veritas team," she said to Dahl. "Would you like me to bring something back for you?"

"Oh, man, that would be great."

"Food allergies?"

"Nope."

"I'll be back around five."

He nodded. "And hey, I slipped up before. Letting that name out when you could have overheard me. The sheriff told me to be careful."

"Yeah. We heard."

Dahl frowned. "Wheeler will have my hide for that. Don't suppose you could see your way clear to not report me to the sheriff?"

"You got it."

He swiped an exaggerated hand over his forehead. "Thanks. He's kind of a stickler, and I really need this job. Got a baby on the way."

"Congratulations." Mackenzie smiled and resumed walking.

"That was very kind of you," Owen said. "Not only offering dinner, but not calling him out on his error."

"It was an honest mistake."

"Mostly, you're just a very nice person."

"You think so, huh?"

"I know so." *And I can only hope I'm the kind of man you won't run from when we find out who I am.*

She headed toward Ryan who was squatting by the backpack he'd left behind. Owen could swear it looked like the guy was stocking his pack, but why, when they were heading back to the cabin?

"You going for a hike?" Mackenzie asked.

He glanced at her. "Figured I'd let you drop me off where I first spotted the tire tracks yesterday, and I'll see where they lead."

"You want us to come along?" she asked.

Ryan shook his head. "No offense, but I'll move faster and have less distractions if I go alone."

"You sure?" she asked, looking like she felt guilty over

riding in a comfy car instead of toughing out the terrain. At least that was how Owen was feeling.

"Positive." Ryan shoved a water bottle in the outside pocket of his pack then zipped it closed. "I'll drive to the marker then you can take over."

He led the way to his vehicle and climbed behind the wheel. Owen opened the front door for Mackenzie, then he slipped into the backseat. Owen sat back, and Ryan got them moving over the flat terrain, swerving to avoid clumps of tall vegetation that randomly grew.

Mackenzie looked at Ryan. "Can we use the Bronco to come back to get Kelsey and Sierra for dinner? It handles much better than my car."

"You sure you won't get lost?" He cocked a smile.

"I can follow your tracks."

"Then sure. And I have my SAT phone in case you do get lost and need to call me." He chuckled.

She swatted a hand at him. Playful. Like Owen would like to interact with her. But he had no right to engage with her in anything other than the business of figuring out Cassie Collins's death—and if he had a connection to it.

He wanted to hold out hope that he'd just stumbled upon her body when he'd been out hiking, but that wouldn't explain why her name put this deep ache in his gut. Plus he really hadn't been dressed to be out in the desert hiking alone, and he wouldn't have gone hiking on private property.

They soon arrived at the marker, and Ryan left the Bronco running while he jumped out.

"Want me to drive?" Owen asked.

"No license."

"Right."

She slid down and gave Ryan a high five as they passed each other. Owen joined her in the front seat.

She had to move the seat forward, but soon got them going. "When we run into town for some groceries for dinner, we should stop at the OSP office and get your prints taken."

"Dahl said we should go to the jail to have them taken."

"Those prints are for him, and he may or may not share. These will be for us."

"Right. Good idea." Not having enough energy to engage in small talk, Owen watched out the window and let the past two days play in his head, looking for any lead that might bring him closer to figuring out what, if any, relationship he had with Cassie Collins.

Please tell me how I know this woman. If I do. And don't let me be a criminal. Worse yet, a killer.

He desperately wanted answers, but his gut, already in a tight ball, told him he wasn't going to like what he learned.

8

Mackenzie led the way into the small OSP outpost, Owen's footsteps trailing behind her. She didn't waste a moment but marched over to the reception desk to introduce herself to the female wearing a trooper's uniform. Mackenzie added that she was a former investigator. That earned her a raised eyebrow but nothing else.

"Is there someone we can talk to about a missing person case and getting some fingerprints done?" Mackenzie made sure to sound polite.

The trooper reacted with a testy flick of her head. "I can help you. Do you want to file a missing person's report?"

"Not exactly." Mackenzie shared Owen's story but didn't mention the remains found today. "We hoped if you ran his prints, we could find out who he is."

The trooper's dark eyebrow went higher. "You'll need me to open a report for that, which I can do and take your prints, but the only AFIS terminal in the area is at the county jail."

Mackenzie had expected something like this. A terminal to run prints through the feds' Automated Fingerprint Identification System was costly, and such a small office and

83

small rural county wouldn't spend the funds on a terminal if they could go to the jail to use theirs.

"Then let's get that report going and prints made so you can get them to the jail for processing," Mackenzie said.

"Have a seat." The trooper pointed at the chairs by her desk and turned her attention to her computer screen.

Owen pulled the hard wooden chair out for Mackenzie. She gave him a sincere smile. Kind gestures like this and opening her car door earlier were things that gave her hope that they weren't going to get bad news when it came to his identity.

The trooper began rattling off questions, and they answered the very few that they could.

She shook her head. "The report is so empty it looks like it's riddled with bullet holes."

Owen frowned. "We'd give you more information if we had it, but we don't."

"Then let's get these prints done." She shoved her chair back and went across the room to return with an old-fashioned ink pad and fingerprint cards. "This probably looks archaic to you, after your time as an investigator, but money doesn't stretch out here to doing electronic prints."

She slipped the white ten-print card into a holder and came around the desk. "Go ahead and stand next to me and give me your right thumb."

Owen stood, and she rolled his thumb across the ink pad then pressed and rolled it over the appropriate square on the card. She followed the procedure until all ten digits had been completed, then inked his fingers further down and pressed each hand on the bottom of the card.

"All done." She slid individually wrapped alcohol wipes across the desk to him. "This should take care of most of the ink, but you'll also want to wash up in the restroom."

He scrubbed at his fingers.

"Any idea how long these will take to run?" Mackenzie asked.

"I can't deliver them to the jail until my supervisor returns. And then they'll have to run them, but the terminal was down recently. I'm not sure if it's operational now."

"Will you call us as soon as you have results?" Owen asked.

"I will if you're clear, i.e., no outstanding warrants." She eyed Owen. "Otherwise, one of us will be out to arrest you."

He frowned. "Where's the restroom?"

She jerked a thumb over her shoulder. "All the way to the back."

When he was out of earshot, the trooper sat on the corner of the desk. "You aren't staying alone with this man, are you? Because I wouldn't advise it."

"I'm not," Mackenzie said, though she no longer had qualms about doing so. She briefly considered asking the woman to look up Cassie Collins in the database, but Mackenzie didn't want to raise suspicions, and she also didn't want to get Deputy Dahl in trouble with the sheriff. Better to wait and call her own sources for the info.

Drying his hands on paper towels, Owen returned. "Thanks for your time. You have my contact info."

She pinned a pointed gaze on him, likely because they'd had to add Mackenzie's contact information on the report as Owen didn't have any. "I do."

Mackenzie got up to leave and end this trooper's suspicious looks.

Outside, Owen glanced at her as they walked to her car. "She didn't like me."

Mackenzie unlocked the car doors. "She was only being a good law enforcement officer and keeping an open mind."

"Not sure how open it was."

They got into her car, and Mackenzie made the drive to

the same grocery store they'd previously stopped at. They gathered the items they would need for dinner, and Mackenzie also grabbed supplies for breakfast.

Back at the rental, Owen fell quiet again, but helped unload the groceries.

"You should go rest while I prep dinner," she told him. "I slept all night and can do this on my own."

"You're sure?" he asked.

"Positive. It's only sandwiches and sides." She shooed him out of the house and put on an apron to start plating the meats and cheeses she'd bought for the build-your-own-sandwich night.

After everything was ready, Mackenzie got Owen, and they returned to the crime scene to pick up their guests and deliver the deputy's dinner. She wanted to let him rest, but she feared she might get lost in the waning light as the sun sank toward the horizon and wanted to have him along.

It took thirty minutes round trip, and Sierra and Kelsey were soon seated at her table, where she served the platter of deli meats and cheeses and store bakery buns. She added a bowl of fresh fruit and another one with the last of the thick gooey chocolate chip cookies from her gran. She saved the cake for Ryan.

"It's ready, Owen," she called to him where he'd been staring out the window. He'd grown pensive on the drive, and the mood seemed to have settled in for the duration. She couldn't even imagine his emotions right now.

Sierra grabbed a bun and slathered it with mayo. "Thank you for doing this for us."

"It's nothing special, but I hope it helps give you energy." Mackenzie filled glasses with iced tea. "Besides, it's the least I can do after you all came so quickly."

Kelsey put her hand over her glass. "No caffeine for me. The water is great."

Mackenzie sat next to Kelsey who had her feet up on another chair. "Still think you'll be done in five hours or less?"

"Looks like it." Kelsey piled smoked turkey slices on her bun and added Swiss cheese. "Sierra already finished all the scene photos so I can get started on the recovery, and our assistants should arrive by the time we're done here. They always make things go faster."

"Anything unusual yet?" Owen asked.

Kelsey raised her eyebrows. "I can't give you the details, but yes there was an oddity that I didn't expect to find."

"Will it help find the killer?" Mackenzie asked.

"Not sure." Kelsey looked at Sierra. "What do you think?"

"Could be. All depends."

"You two are very good at evasion." Mackenzie laughed.

"We have to be. Sorry." Kelsey added lettuce to her sandwich.

"No problem." She smiled to reassure Kelsey and Sierra.

"Would you pray with me so we can get started," Mackenzie said as she knew all the partners at Veritas were Christians.

They took hands and bowed their heads. Owen sat at the end of the table. She didn't connect physically with him, but she hoped her prayer connected emotionally.

"Can you at least tell us how long the body has been there?" Owen asked after she finished praying.

Kelsey took a long drink of her water. "Even if I could, I don't yet know."

Mackenzie looked at Kelsey. "Since we can't talk about the investigation, tell us what's new at Veritas."

"Ainslie and Grady had their baby about a month ago. A girl named Emma." She looked at Owen. "Grady is our weapons expert and Ainslie our crime scene photographer.

Normally she would've come along today, but she's on leave."

He nodded. "Do you know if you're having a boy or a girl?"

She shook her head. "We decided to be surprised, which isn't easy these days with the ultrasounds."

"After losing my memory, I think I would want to know. It would at least be information I could control."

Kelsey frowned. "I can't imagine how hard this is on you. Sierra and I are praying, and if you don't mind, I'd like to ask the rest of our team to pray too."

"That would be great." He smiled but it was forced. This was clearly still very disturbing for him.

Mackenzie wouldn't dwell on it. "Please give them my congratulations. Any other news?"

"We've hired a number of new techs to keep up with demands from law enforcement," Sierra said. "It's keeping me hopping to get them trained. And we've interviewed a few new staff members. That's all I can say for now, but it will be great to add additional disciplines to our team."

"Sounds exciting," Mackenzie said.

"It is. Always great to be on the cutting edge. I'm partici- pating in a new research study regarding burnt bones." Kelsey's face brightened. "It involves scanning the bones and then printing a 3D model. Might be very timely for today's discovery."

Was she saying the skeleton was burned without saying it? A hint. Sounded like it. Mackenzie hadn't noticed any charred bones, but then she'd only taken a quick look. "What does the study involve?"

"Now you've done it." Sierra grinned. "Kelsey will talk your ear off."

Mackenzie laughed. "That's probably good since we keep asking things we shouldn't."

"Since you insist." Kelsey set her sandwich on her plate. "Burnt human bones can be very fragile to hold. When there are fragments, we often have to do what is called a physical fit analysis. Basically we match bone fragments and put them together. That relies on the manual handling of the fragments. These fragments are often fragile, sharp, or embedded in other materials and it's difficult to do. So we're piloting a program that makes 3D models of the fragments which keep us from manually handling the delicate bones."

Owen leaned forward. "Sounds fascinating."

"It is, but like any new development in forensic science, we have to set precedents in the courtroom to be accepted." Kelsey sipped her water. "Getting a jury to buy into the technique is the easy part. Getting judges and defense attorneys to buy in is a whole different story."

Owen picked up his sandwich. "Mackenzie said you all were the best at what you do, but I'm most impressed."

"We're most blessed." Sierra set her glass on the table and reached for a cookie. "We're offered many opportunities to pilot projects and that allows us to stay on the cutting edge."

Owen fixed his gaze on Kelsey. "You mentioned that it might be timely for today's discovery."

"Did I?" She blinked her long lashes. "Hmm."

"In other words, that's all you are going to share."

She smiled and then chomped on her sandwich, obviously ending the conversation.

"Do you all have snacks at the crime scene or should I pack some things for you?" Mackenzie asked.

"We're good." Sierra held out her cookie. "But maybe a few of these cookies would be a nice add. We often reach that point in a recovery when things seem particularly dismal. A cookie would be nice right about then, and these are extra good."

Mackenzie couldn't imagine what they must go through but the horrified look on Owen's face said he could. That left many questions in Mackenzie's mind, but as she was clearly coming to care for him, she didn't know if she wanted any answers at all.

～

After delivering Sierra and Kelsey to the crime scene, Mackenzie led Owen to the slipcovered couch with down cushions that felt like sitting on a pillow. She'd appreciated his effort to try to join in the lighthearted conversation at the end of dinner, but he failed and put his focus on the food. Was he just not a social guy or did he fail because he didn't know much about himself, and it was hard to participate? And how could he when he knew nothing much about himself? He couldn't possibly know his opinion on anything.

Mackenzie settled her laptop on her knees and entered Cassie Collins into a search engine. She turned the computer allowing him to see several articles that appeared in *The Oregonian* a little less than two years ago, declaring the woman missing.

Mackenzie opened the first story. It included a picture of an apartment building in Vancouver where Cassie had lived with her husband, a Vancouver police officer. Her parents were the last people to see her the morning she'd disappeared. She was dressed in hiking clothing and said she was going hiking, but not where.

Owen stared at the picture of the upscale building like he was hoping it would jar a memory.

"Anything?" she asked.

He clutched his hands into fists on his knees. "Nothing but that same familiarity and feeling of dread."

Mackenzie resisted resting her hand on his and read the article.

"Sounds like she disappeared, car and all," Mackenzie said, even though he was reading the same thing.

Mackenzie scrolled down, and Cassie's photo opened in front of them. She was young and beautiful with long blond hair and high cheekbones. Big eyes were coated liberally with mascara.

Owen drew in a sharp breath.

Mackenzie glanced at him. "So you *do* know her?"

"She looks very familiar and seeing her is like a knife to the gut."

Mackenzie continued down the story, which didn't really give many more details other than Cassie's parents reported her missing when they couldn't get ahold of her, and the outfit she was wearing matched the one the woman in the creek had on.

"I think it's time I call a contact at Clark County to see what we can learn." Mackenzie reached for her phone on the end table and scrolled through her contacts until she located Bobby Harmon. She glanced at Owen. "Full disclosure. Detective Bobby Harmon and I dated for a while. Didn't end badly but I broke things off with Bobby, so we'll see how cooperative he'll be."

"Might he be the detective on the investigation?"

She shook her head. "He's only been a detective for the past two years. One of the reasons we broke up. He couldn't handle the fact that I made it to detective before he did."

She tapped his icon, and the phone rang.

"Bobby." She hit the speaker button. "Mackenzie Steele."

"Mac? For real?" He paused. "Long time no hear from you."

"Yeah, it's been a minute," she said, waiting for him to take over the conversation as he always did in the past.

"I heard you left the force."

"I went to work with the family after my cousin Thomas was murdered."

"Oh, yeah, right. Saw that on the news. I was really sorry to hear about him."

"Thanks."

"So what can I do you for?" He sounded wary and a little bit testy but that could just be because of their past.

"I'm on vacation in the John Day area and one of Clark County's missing investigations came to my attention. Cassie Collins is the missing woman."

"Now that's odd. You're the second person who's called in today to ask for information on her."

"Who else called?"

"You know I can't tell you that."

She wouldn't just give up. "Was it Sheriff Wheeler?"

Bobby blew out a short breath over the phone. "Again. Can't say."

He was either holding a grudge or had suddenly become a stickler for the rules. She didn't think he'd changed so likely the grudge.

"What can you tell me about the investigation?" Mackenzie asked, ignoring Bobby's stonewalling.

"Now, come on, Mac. You know I can't share that either. I can't tell you a single thing."

She gripped the edges of her laptop. "Can you at least point me to the detective who worked or is working the investigation?"

"Not really." He didn't respond for a long moment. "But I can tell you what I told the other person who asked. It doesn't look like anyone's working it. Says here the investigation went cold, and we closed it some time ago."

An answer but not one she wanted.

"Wait a second." Bobby's voice ticked higher. "I missed

this before. The original detective retired, but the file's been flagged. It's come up in conjunction with a current homicide investigation."

Interesting. "Can you put me through to the detective working the connected homicide?"

"No can do," he said, but didn't sound the least bit sorry about it. "The guy took a leave of absence a week ago. Not sure why. My lieutenant just said it was something personal."

Mackenzie wanted to reach through the phone and strangle Bobby. He had the information they needed right at his fingertips but wouldn't share out of spite. "But you'll ask your lieutenant if you can give me contact information for someone who can help me?"

"Will do."

Sure, but on what time frame? Bobby wasn't known for his timeliness, and Mackenzie didn't want to wait for him to stonewall them even more.

"Please go talk to him right away," Mackenzie said, doing her very best not to sound as irritable as he was. "This is very important."

"No need to lecture me, Mac. I'll go see him when we get off the phone."

"Will you call me no matter what he says?"

"Yeah, now let me go so I can get this done and you off my back." Bobby ended the call.

Mackenzie shook her head. "Thanks for nothing, Bobby."

"You think he'll actually ask?"

"Fifty/fifty chance I'd say, leaning a little more toward a big fat no." Mackenzie opened her laptop. "Let's see if we can find a recent homicide investigation in Vancouver and learn the detective's information that way."

"We might find a detective's name, but how can we link the investigation to Cassie?"

"Yeah, that'll be tough. But we need to do something while we wait for Bobby to get back to us—if he even does."

She searched until the return call came precisely fifteen minutes later. But it wasn't Bobby.

"Mackenzie Steele." She put the call on speaker.

"This is Lieutenant Sage. I hear you want to learn more about the Cassie Collins investigation."

Mackenzie told Sage about her interest, still leaving out finding the body and Owen's involvement. "I would appreciate any information you can provide."

"Do you know Ms. Collins?"

"No."

"Were you a witness to her disappearance or somehow have a connection to the investigation?" Confusion lingered in the man's tone.

"No, but like I said, her name came up while I was vacationing here, and I wanted to see if there was anything I could help with on the investigation."

"Not a typical response."

"Did I mention that I'm a former OSP detective? Left the force to work with my family's business after my cousin was murdered. Company is Steele Guardians. Perhaps you've heard of us."

"Right. Sure. I heard about your cousin too." His tone had softened. "I'm sorry for your loss."

"Thank you. So do you think I could get some information on Cassie or speak to the detective in charge?"

"No one's actively working that investigation right now." Exactly like Bobby had said. "But we do have a detective working a connected case and is fully versed on the Collins investigation. He's on leave for a few weeks, but I can text a picture of his business card to this number and you can contact him when he gets back."

"Is there anyone else who can help me?"

"Sorry. No. It's up to him."

"Okay, please send the card and thank you." She disconnected and sat back.

"Sage seemed helpful yet reserved," Owen said.

"Typical cop speak. Can't tell you how good I once was at it and that says a lot because I'm normally an oversharing kind of girl."

"I noticed you don't like to hold back." Owen chuckled.

"I don't and I don't plan to wait for this detective to get back from leave either. I'll text him as soon as I get the card. Hopefully he's a typical detective and has his phone on even if he's on leave."

Her phone dinged, and she looked at the image. Her heart dropped into her stomach, and her dinner churned. "Oh. Oh my. You're not going to believe this."

She held out the phone to Owen. "The name. It can't be a coincidence."

"No." Owen's face paled. "No, it can't."

9

Owen jumped up and paced the floor, his legs like rubber.

He felt Mackenzie's gaze pinned to him. "It's you, isn't it? The detective. His name is Owen. Owen Greer. You must be the detective and were investigating the case when you were attacked, right?"

"Yeah," he said as pictures flickered through his brain.

Years and years of special times spent with Cassie. Not only did it look like he was the detective, but she was his sister. No wonder he'd blocked the memory of finding her. He didn't want to remember. His grief came back in waves. Fresh now, but the deep ache of knowing she'd been missing and likely dead for years also returned. Pain to the bone. A jarring ache.

His parents. Their pain. He had to tell them she'd died. *No. No, no, no.* He couldn't do it. Just couldn't.

Mackenzie joined him and rested a hand on his arm. "Are you okay?"

"I'm starting to remember. Flashes of Cassie. Of my parents. She's my sister. She disappeared during my first year as a detective. Of course, they wouldn't let me officially work the investigation, but I kept up with it. At least as much as they would share with me."

She released his arm and looked at him, her eyes wet with tears. "I'm glad you're remembering, but I'm so sorry to hear Cassie was your sister."

"Thanks." He shoved his fingers into his hair. "After time passed, it was hard not to believe she'd died, but we tried to hold out hope. Until the day I found her. Guess the shock was too great."

"I don't mean to be insensitive, but how did you know it was her?"

"Her clothing. She stopped at my parents' place that morning. My mom took a selfie of them. It's what she was wearing at that visit. And now I know for sure because of the necklace. She was a foster child that my parents wanted to adopt, but her mother wouldn't allow it. So my parents gave her the infinity heart on her eighteenth birthday to signify that she was their daughter even without an adoption certificate."

"Finding her had to be hard."

"I guess I couldn't face it. Now I have to, and we need to find her killer." He fisted his hands and willed his emotions away to think like a detective. "It had to be whoever hit me over the head. The driver of the UTV."

"Sounds like it."

"The good news, as a detective, I might be able to get the sheriff to share his information or let the Veritas staff share it."

"You think he'll do that?"

Did he? "Rural guys can be pretty territorial. Still, you would think he would want to solve the murder and let me help."

Mackenzie's forehead narrowed. "What if we ask him if Veritas can share info with you after they give it to him?

That way he's getting the information firsthand and can act on any of it while you're second in line."

"Sounds like a good way to approach him." Owen couldn't wait to get started. "And no time like the present."

"You'll need ID."

"My shield. Sidearm. I don't remember if I had it with me or left it at home. Like Sage said, I'm on leave and not officially investigating Cassie's disappearance."

"You think you took leave to look into this? At least that's what I would do."

"Sounds like a good possibility." He looked at her. "Can I use your phone to call my LT back?"

"Sure." She unlocked the phone and handed it to him.

He hit redial for the last call and resumed pacing. He got voicemail.

"It's Owen. Need to talk to you about Cassie. I found her body. You can reach me at this number." He ended the call and hoped his supervisor got back to him, but he had a lot on his plate and might not return the call on a timely basis. "We should head into town. Talk to the sheriff."

"Yes, of course. Let me leave a note for Ryan on the door." She wrote the note and then grabbed her jacket and purse. She poked the note onto a nail on the front door and marched to her vehicle. He quickly followed, but she got there before he could open her door for her.

In the car, she placed her phone in the holder before inserting the key into the ignition. "For when your LT calls back."

He slid in. "I guess this means I'm not a criminal." He tried to smile at her but couldn't manage it.

She cranked the engine. "I really didn't think you were, but I have to admit that I had my doubts at times."

"I'm surprised with your law enforcement experience

98

that you didn't think I was. Especially after we spotted Cassie together."

"I got the sense that you're a good guy, and I'm usually a pretty good judge of character."

"I might not have been acting like myself, though." Owen clicked on his seatbelt.

"True enough." She glanced at him before getting the car on the narrow road. "But it's over now. We know you're one of the knights in shining armor."

"Unless I'm a crooked cop."

"Oh, please. Do not go there." Her attention changed to her driving, and she fell silent.

So did he. Looking out the window as the flat, barren land passed by. Thinking about Cassie and their life. His dad was an attorney, commuting to downtown Portland, and his mom stayed at home. But his dad was very involved in their lives. Coming to every football game Owen played. They were great parents and didn't deserve to lose a child.

"You're deep in thought," she said.

"I'm thinking about telling my mom and dad about Cassie. I'll have to get home somehow to do it. No way I'll give that information over the phone." He considered his next move. "No ID means I can't rent a car and a rideshare or taxi would be expensive. Maybe there's a bus."

"Don't be silly. I'll drive you. And bring you back here if you want to come."

"This is where she was murdered, and I'll have to continue investigating here. If you don't mind, I'll pick up the case files while I'm home."

"Don't mind at all."

She turned onto the road leading into town, and her phone rang. The caller ID identified Clark County Sheriff's Office. She swiped and answered on the car's Infotainment system. "Mackenzie Steele."

"It's Lieutenant Sage again. Detective Greer gave me this number to call."

"He's right here."

"Hey, LT," Owen said.

"Man, that's rough about Cassie. I'm sorry for your loss. You have everyone on the team's sympathy."

That put a lump in Owen's throat, and he had to swallow hard to keep from letting his emotions get out of control.

"I knew you weren't going to leave this alone," Sage continued, his baritone voice sounding loud over the car's speaker. "You stood right in my office and lied to my face."

Owen had figured this was coming, and he had no real response to the accusation. "Yeah, and?"

"And I'd have done the same thing. Maybe minus quitting."

Not the response Owen had expected, "I quit? I don't remember quitting." He shared about his memory issues since he first found Cassie, and how he'd spent time not having a clue as to his identity. "Did you accept my resignation?"

"Nah. But you gave me your shield and sidearm. Sounds like a good thing you did, or the person who assaulted you might be running around out there with them."

Thankfully, no one stole his service weapon and used it to commit a murder or other crime. "I'll be heading back to town to get my files, and I can pick them up from you then. That is if you'll let me work Cassie's investigation in conjunction with the Bussey case. If not, I'll be going rogue."

Sage didn't answer right away, and Owen could easily visualize the frustration on his supervisor's face. "Rogue doesn't get you Cassie's or the Bussey files."

"I suppose not," Owen said, but hoped for once that he'd violated department policy and had copied all of the files to bring them home.

"Let me think on it," Sage said. "I'll have an answer for you by the time I see you."

Owen glanced at the clock. "First thing in the morning work for you?"

"See you then."

The call ended, and Owen glanced at Mackenzie who was focusing on navigating the streets of John Day.

Owen sat back, thoughts swirling through his brain. "Let me take some time to think about how to approach Wheeler to get the most mileage."

She glanced at him. "Gee, if only I knew a thing about investigations and how to get an uncooperative sheriff to comply and could help with that." She finished with a snarky smile.

"Point taken." He grinned at her. "What do you suggest?"

She pointed her focus on the road ahead as they turned off of the main street of John Day. "Not sure yet, but maybe you should tell him right up front that you're not authorized to investigate Cassie's death, and then play on his sympathies."

He swiveled to face her. "You think he'll go for it?"

She shrugged. "I don't know a single law enforcement officer out there who wouldn't want to investigate the murder of a sibling. Including Wheeler. If we can prove to him that you're a detective, I think we can get the information we need."

"We?"

"You don't think I'm walking away now, do you? Because if you do, you don't know a thing about me."

He really didn't know her as well as he wanted, but he'd definitely seen her determination. "Wheeler will call my LT."

"Who is going to say you're a detective because he won't

air his department drama with another law enforcement officer."

"You're right. And that's really all I need." Owen was starting to like her plan. "Maybe we can find a picture online of me in uniform to show Wheeler."

"Go for it." She swiped her phone awake and unlocked it.

He took it and entered his information into the search engine. Several photos came up. One just last month, where he'd received an award for distinguished service in community policing when he'd gone the extra mile to solve a triple homicide.

"Got one that should help." He left it on her screen and put her phone back into the holder just as she pulled into the sheriff's office parking lot.

Inside, they found an older woman with helmet-shaped gray hair sitting behind the reception desk. She had a stern look, but gave them a sincere smile. "Can I help you?"

"Clark County Detective Owen Greer to see Sheriff Wheeler," Owen said, the words feeling familiar and strange at the same time.

She cocked her head and peered up at him. "Mind telling me what this is about?"

"The discovery this morning." He left it at that in case she didn't know about the body.

"Oh, that. Poor, poor thing." She lifted her handset and put it against her ear. "Sheriff, a Detective Owen Greer with Clark County Sheriff's Office is here to see you about that woman you found this morning."

A loud voice came through the phone, and she frowned.

"Yes, sir, I'll tell him." She set the handset down. "He's waiting on another call, but said he'd be out as soon as he can."

Owen suspected he didn't say it quite so nicely as this

comment wouldn't likely be enough to make the woman who worked in a sheriff's office frown.

"Have a seat." She pointed at the stiff wooden chairs in the small lobby that were worn from years of use. "And help yourself to coffee or water."

"Thank you." Owen made sure to smile at her. People in these front-end positions were invaluable when it came to getting needed information. If the sheriff blew them off, maybe he could count on her.

"You want coffee?" he asked Mackenzie as she settled into a chair and scooted around as if trying to get comfortable.

"I'm good."

He sat next to her, and his leg automatically started bobbing. Now that he knew his identity, the last thing he wanted to do was sit around and cool his heels.

Mackenzie pressed her hand on his knee. "If you don't relax a bit, you'll burn yourself out."

He would. He knew that. But there was no better cause to burn out on than finding his sister's killer.

Mackenzie couldn't miss the skepticism on Wheeler's face as he propped his shoulder against the open secure door but didn't come all the way into the waiting area. "So you remember who you are."

"I do," Owen said confidently.

Sheriff Wheeler eyed Owen. "Called your LT. Told me you've worked for him for three years and are an exemplary detective." Wheeler's words came out as more of an insult than a compliment.

Mackenzie clamped her lips together to keep from offering a smart reply. He was going to be a tough nut to crack, but they would crack him. "Is there somewhere we can talk in private?"

"Follow me." He spun and marched through the secure door.

Owen lurched forward and caught the door before it closed. He held it for Mackenzie. She followed the older officer down a narrow and dingy hallway to a small office with walls covered in orangey-brown color sixties wood paneling. Two green vinyl chairs sat in front of the desk, one with a wide crack running the width of the seat.

"Sit," Wheeler commanded as he moved around the neat but old metal desk.

She took the cracked chair. Owen looked like he wanted to remain standing but gave in. He probably figured if he wanted Wheeler's cooperation he would need to pick his battles and this wasn't a hill to die on.

"Now that you know I'm law enforcement and my investigation is connected to Cassie Collins's murder, I hope you will read me in and keep me in the loop on your investigation."

"What? You don't want to take over?"

"Well, sure." Owen grinned. "But you won't allow that to happen."

"See, you know me already." Wheeler placed his hands flat on the desk. "And you should also know I'm not real good at sharing. Started with my toys when I was a toddler and hasn't changed." He let out a booming laugh.

Owen didn't respond at first. "Cassie Collins was my sister."

Wheeler's eyebrow shot up. "My deputy didn't leak the victim's name to you after I told him not to, did he? He's known to do that no matter how hard I try to break him of the habit."

Mackenzie didn't know how to answer, so she let Owen take care of it.

"The return of my memory..." Owen shrugged off the end of the sentence, effectively not answering Wheeler's question.

Mackenzie held her breath, waiting to see if Wheeler would push it further.

The sheriff lifted his hands behind his head and leaned back. "Real sorry your sister lost her life and in such a terrible way."

Surprising. The sheriff sounded sincere. She was equally surprised he accepted Owen's answer. Maybe he would circle back and ask again. She didn't want to get Deputy Dahl into trouble and would do her best to make sure Wheeler didn't find out what had actually happened.

Owen leaned closer. "I need to figure out who killed her."

"I get that, but—"

"But nothing." Owen eyed Wheeler. "Put yourself in my shoes. If you lost a family member this way, I know you wouldn't sit on the sidelines."

"You got that right."

"And I don't want to have to go behind your back or investigate on my own. Figure if we pool resources, we can work this faster and more efficiently."

Wheeler dropped his hands to the arm of the chair and tilted his head. "I'll consider it."

Owen frowned. "What do you want in return?"

"What makes you think I want something?"

Um, gee. Because you're kind of difficult to get along with.

"I just do," Owen answered, his tone diplomatic.

Mackenzie was impressed with how calm and rational Owen was while the sheriff was pushing Owen's buttons.

"If I let you in on this investigation, you'll owe me a favor, and I'll call it in someday. You can be sure of that."

Owen blinked a few times. "Fine. I owe you."

The sheriff snapped his chair forward. "What do you want to know?"

"First, I want to be read in on the forensics. I won't push for getting the information before you, but I'd like to be read in after you've received the details. And I'd prefer to hear them straight from the Veritas staff."

Wheeler pursed his lips. "Think I'll keep things from you?"

"Not at all. I'm not as experienced as you. This is probably all old hat to you, but I like to get details and ask questions of forensic experts. That's the way I learn."

Wheeler nodded as if buying Owen's answer and liking the compliment. "Makes sense."

Owen's eye twitched. An indicator that he was playing Wheeler? Could be.

Wheeler grabbed his cell phone, tapped the screen and set the phone on the desk. It rang over the speaker.

"Dr. Dunbar," Kelsey answered.

"Sheriff Wheeler here. What do I have to do to have another agency detective read in on the forensics after you notify me?"

"Easy," Kelsey said. "We'll simply modify your contract. Give me the name and agency, and I'll have a new contract to you in an hour or so."

"Detective Owen Greer. Clark County Sheriff's Office."

"Owen Greer?" Kelsey asked. "The Owen I met at the crime scene?"

"Yeah," Wheeler said. "Turns out he's Cassie Collins's brother."

Kelsey remained silent for a long moment. "And he's approved to investigate her death?"

"He has my approval to be read in on the forensics, and that's all that should matter to you."

"You're right. It is." Kelsey let out a breath.

"Now, I'm a busy guy," Wheeler said. "So if you don't need anything else..."

"I'll get the revised contract to you." Kelsey's words were clipped. She was doing the work out of the goodness of her heart and didn't deserve Wheeler's attitude.

"I'll watch for it." Wheeler tapped his phone and looked at Owen. "What's your number two request?"

Owen sat forward, and rested his hands on the desk. "Tell Deputy Dahl I have access to the crime scene."

Wheeler picked up his phone again and instructed Dahl to give Owen access. He didn't say anything about Mackenzie, but they could fudge that with the deputy when they arrived on scene. Assuming that Owen allowed her to continue working with him. They wouldn't be able to fudge with Kelsey and Sierra though. Still, Owen would get the info and share with Mackenzie, right?

"Done." Wheeler dropped his phone on the desk with a clunk.

"Now you can update us on what you know about the murder," Owen said, his tone unyielding.

"I don't know anything more than you already know." Wheeler frowned. "I requested your sister's file while I was talking to your LT and am waiting on the first forensic reports to come in."

"Hopefully." Owen kept his gaze on Wheeler. "I can bring you a print copy of the file tomorrow."

"Works for me." Wheeler tilted his head. "Now it's time for you to answer my questions. What brought you to John Day in search of Cassie?"

"It has to do with a current investigation. Mind if I take a pass saying more for now. Just until I get to Vancouver to review my files and refresh my memory on how everything went down."

"You better not plan on stiffing me on this." Wheeler eyed Owen with an intensity that spoke to his position in law enforcement. "I can refuse to sign the updated Veritas contract."

"I'm not. I want to give you accurate facts, and my memory hasn't fully returned."

"You have a report to me by lunchtime tomorrow, you hear?"

"That shouldn't be a problem. After stopping by the crime scene, we'll head straight to Vancouver."

"See that it doesn't *become* a problem." The sheriff stood. "I'll see you out."

"One more thing," Owen said, stopping Wheeler. "I would ask that you don't contact my parents or Cassie's husband until after I tell them about her. I think it would be better coming from me."

"Of course. Let me know when you're ready for me to interview them."

Never, Mackenzie suspected as she followed Wheeler down the hallway and stepped outside, Owen right behind her. She shielded her eyes against the warm sun after being in the dark, dank office.

She took a breath of the nippy fresh air and looked up at Owen, whose blank expression she couldn't read. "That went as well as can be expected."

Owen nodded. "As long as Wheeler follows through, we should be on our way to finding Cassie's killer."

10

———

Owen almost wished the deputy had forbidden Mackenzie from entering the crime scene. Owen didn't want her to have to see Cassie again. But thankfully, Kelsey had recovered the remains, and she and her skinny male assistant were sitting under the tarp while Sierra worked with her assistant at the creek bed.

Kelsey stood and locked her gaze on Owen. Sympathy flowed from her expressive face. He recognized that look. He'd seen it for years, but especially from fellow church members who meant well but didn't know what to say or do. They tried to comfort him, but how could they when he'd honestly lost his faith for some time? Not his parents. Their faith had grown stronger, setting a solid example for him. After about a year, he'd finally moved on to acceptance and returned to his relationship with God, though it remained weak.

"I'm sorry for your loss, Owen," Kelsey said. "And to have found her like this. That must have been hard."

He nodded.

"It certainly would be traumatic enough to forget."

He nodded again, but needed to move them on before

he lost his cool and let today's shocking discovery take over his control. "Did you receive the new contract from Wheeler?"

"I did."

He pressed on. "Have you had a chance to update him? Is there anything to share?"

"I did, but all I can really tell you at this point is that the skeleton is a female of your sister's stature and age, matching the statistics listed in her missing person's report."

"So you believe it's her?" he asked, still holding a bit of hope that they had been wrong on the ID.

Kelsey frowned. "I'd really like to give you a concrete answer, but I never speculate. I won't go on record stating a positive ID until we have DNA or dental records to confirm. Did your parents turn in a DNA sample and dental records when she went missing?"

"DNA, yes. Not sure on dental."

"Then we'll get a sample from today to our DNA expert. I'll ask Emory to rush it, and request the results from Cassie's file for comparison. I'll request dental records and review them as soon as possible. The DNA should return something within twenty-four hours after preparing it."

"Evening tomorrow or early morning the next day, then," Owen said. "I don't suppose your people will be working then and can provide the results."

"We have techs who run DNA around the clock, but Emory might not be working, and you'll want to wait for her to review the results. Not that the techs aren't capable, but she's the ultimate expert. It's possible you'll have to wait until the following morning."

Owen couldn't ask for more. "I can't thank you all enough."

"We're glad to help you find closure."

Closure. Yeah. He needed that and even knowing Cassie

had died didn't provide it. Not until he had an answer to the question of how she died and who ended her life. "You mentioned something about burned bones at dinner."

"I did." Kelsey grimaced. "The right side upper body is severely burned."

His gut churned. "While she was alive? Maybe tortured?"

Kelsey shook her head, and a strand of hair fell free from her ponytail. "My preliminary findings tell me the burns occurred post-mortem."

"In your experience have you found anything like this where just a portion of the body is burned?" Mackenzie asked.

"No." Kelsey picked up a disposable wipe to clean her dirty hands or maybe wipe off her frustration from recovering the remains of another young woman cut down in her prime. "It's almost as if the killer decided to dispose of her body by burning it and then changed his mind before more of it could be consumed by the flames."

Owen sucked in a breath. "So you do believe this is murder?"

She nodded and discarded the wipe in a trash bag. "I discovered an obvious bullet wound to the skull, and Sierra recovered a slug from the outcropping nearby. We'll give it to our weapons expert to analyze. Grady's the best, and you can be assured he'll be able to tell us everything that's possible to know about it."

Owen nodded, though his gut twisted as visions assaulted his mind of Cassie falling victim to a bullet. At least her death would've been quick.

"Sierra also found a piece of optical glass near the area where you'd been knocked unconscious," Kelsey said.

"How will that help us?" Mackenzie asked.

"Sierra will consult a forensic optometrist and—"

"A what?" Owen had never heard of such a job.

"Forensic optometrist," Kelsey said. "The same kind of doctor who examines your eyes, but has forensics training too. He or she can study even the smallest shard of a broken lens to reveal someone's prescription. If you discover a suspect who wears glasses, then we can compare these findings to their prescription."

Owen shook his head. "I know I clocked my attacker, and he wore glasses so maybe I broke them. Or maybe he stumbled and fell on the rock. Either way. It's both interesting information and a good lead."

"Exactly." Kelsey smiled. "One other thing. Cassie's pockets were filled with heavy rocks."

"To keep the body submerged," Mackenzie said.

Owen took another breath and shoved his hands into his pockets.

"I'm sorry." Kelsey's sympathetic gaze landed on Owen. "This must be hard for you to hear."

"It is, but I can at least spare my parents from finding out these details unless it's critical to convicting her killer."

"That's one advantage to you being involved, I guess." Kelsey blinked a few times then a look of resolve replaced her concern. "We'll also process the recovered slug for any prints and DNA."

"With killers watching CSI shows and learning how not to get caught these days," Mackenzie said. "What are the odds of finding prints or DNA?"

"The odds are good. Many of our investigations are for crimes of passion and these forensics still provide a lot of answers because the murders are rarely premeditated."

She sounded so confident, but Owen had been disappointed in forensics many times over his detective career and remained skeptical. "Do you think you'll get good results even after the bullet's been in the rocks for so long?"

"Even then. Especially since we located the slug in a protected area. If prints or DNA were left on the slug, that is." Kelsey's mouth curved up in a slight smile. "Remember, you're not dealing with mere mortal techs here, but the best of the best scientists."

Owen forced a laugh. Not easy when he wasn't finding anything funny right now. "I don't have my phone right now, but can you update Mackenzie the minute you can?"

"Of course."

"Is it okay if I step over to the creek bed?" he asked. "I just need a minute there."

"Not at all. I know Sierra and Chad would like a break, and you can be alone if you want."

At her continued kindness, Owen nearly let his grief free but swallowed hard to contain it. "I would appreciate that."

She turned to her assistant. "Shawn, would you run over to tell them to take a break?"

"You got it." He charged away, his baggy suit flapping as he moved.

Mackenzie looked at Owen. "You want me to wait here?"

Did he? No. He'd already come to appreciate her support and wanted it now. "Mind coming with me?"

"Of course not."

They strode over to the area without speaking, passing Sierra and Chad on the way.

He stopped by the dry bed and stared at the soil and rocks. "No visual evidence of Cassie ever having been here now."

Mackenzie came to a stop by his side. She was close enough to touch him, but she didn't. Still, the heat radiated from her body, and he knew she was there.

"The good news is Sierra could find additional forensics," he said.

"Let's hope so." She finally took his hand. "Do you want me to pray or be quiet?"

He reveled in her touch for a few moments before answering. He didn't know if his faith had wavered again—he just didn't know much of anything yet—but her offer of prayer couldn't hurt. "Pray. Please pray."

She bowed her head and gave such an eloquent prayer that his eyes swam with tears. His little sister. Cassie. The baby of the family who couldn't be more of a sister if she had been officially adopted, had been lying here less than an hour ago. A mere skeleton. Her life brutally cut short. Now in a container ready to be clinically examined in a sterile lab.

His throat threatened to close, and he could barely breathe. He lost track of Mackenzie's words that floated into the dry desert air, empty to him now.

Why God? Why? Please. Are You there? Can You help me through this? Help me to understand? To trust? To believe?

"Amen." Mackenzie ended her prayer but didn't let go of his hand.

He came back to the present. To the reality of his loss. He took a few deep breaths. "When Cassie first went missing, I lost my faith. Totally."

"But from what you've said, you're still struggling, but you got it back?"

He stared ahead. "Thanks to my parents. Their faith actually deepened when she went missing. They said they had no choice. They could work hard to find Cassie, but they knew they had no control over whether she came back or not. It was ultimately up to God. And they helped me remember that He sees things we don't and allows things we can't possibly comprehend the reason for. I get that, but I still keep asking why things happen. I just asked it in the middle of your prayer. And after this? I don't know. How do you find hope again after something like this?"

"Doesn't most everyone at some point in their lives lose hope? Sure there are those who become bitter for life, but most people find it again because God wants us to have hope. He's built a longing for it into our fabric."

He shouldn't be questioning God right now, just thanking Him for putting such a godly woman in his life to set an example and help him navigate Cassie's loss. "You're right. I guess I see so many families of homicide victims suffering...I never thought it would happen to me. Not only losing my sister but my hope. I was raised in the church. Lived my faith. Wasn't even one of those kids who rebelled when they went off to college. But Cassie going missing has shaken me like nothing else."

"You need time to process. To come to grips with finding her and go through the stages of grief we all face when we lose someone we love."

"Yeah," he said, but wasn't all that convinced he had the depth of faith to work through this.

"I know it doesn't seem like it right now, but it will get better." She squeezed his hand. "And that's not a platitude. It really will. I promise."

She couldn't really promise that any more than he could promise to renew his faith and trust God through this loss. He wanted to, but he couldn't promise that he would manage it.

"We should get back to the team." He pointed at the canopy.

Thankfully, she didn't look disappointed in him, but released his hand and set off across the desert to where all four Veritas workers stood in the shade of the canopy.

"How long before you finish here?" Mackenzie asked.

"I've got maybe thirty minutes left," Sierra replied.

"Then we have to pack up. So say an hour. The good news for me and Kelsey is that Coop is coming back for us."

"We were supposed to drive back with Chad and Shawn, but someone..." Kelsey cast a pointed look at Sierra. "... called Coop and told him my pregnancy had me exhausted, and I needed a good night's sleep."

Sierra responded with an innocent grin. "Coop's wife is pregnant again, so he totally understood my request and is on his way."

"I don't suppose there's room in the helicopter for one more person," Owen asked.

"You wanting to go back to Portland?" Kelsey asked.

Owen nodded. "I need to notify my parents. It would be great if I didn't have a six-hour drive, and I could do it tonight. I would hate for them to hear about Cassie's death some other way."

"There's plenty of room." Sierra stared at her empty hands as if she wished she could do more. But why? She was already doing so much.

"I'm coming with you." Mackenzie didn't wait for him to respond but glanced at Sierra. "Assuming there's room for me too."

"There is," Sierra said.

Owen studied Mackenzie. "You don't have to cut your vacation short."

"Let's not waste time arguing. I intend to win." She cracked a cute smile. "We should find Ryan to drive us back here in time for the ride."

She was right—no point in arguing when she was one determined woman. So he nodded.

She glanced at the other women. "Thanks. We'll be back in plenty of time."

She marched back to the Bronco and got the vehicle going. She made a wide arc that would take them along the path where Ryan had been hiking. He'd almost reached the cabin and was moving at a good clip. She honked, and he turned and stopped.

She pulled up next to him and lowered her window to explain. "Can you put a marker here and then take us back to the crime scene?"

"Sure." He opened the door. "But I'm driving."

Mackenzie scrambled out, and Ryan went to place a marker. Owen had so many people on his side that it was like God had sent an army to help—and here Owen wasn't trusting God. How could he be questioning God and miss seeing and be thankful for this incredible support? Owen would do a better job of thanking people. Starting with Ryan.

Ryan climbed in the driver's seat and set his SAT phone into the console.

Owen faced him. "Hey man, thanks for all the help."

"Glad to do it."

Mackenzie leaned between the front seats. "Did you find anything?"

Ryan shifted into gear. "Two sets of tires."

"Two vehicles, then." Owen let the news sink in. "Could be my vehicle if we figure out it's missing."

"Seems likely," Ryan said. "I'm still pretty sure one set is a truck carrying a heavy payload, and the other looks like an SUV. What do you drive?"

"I'm guessing since I quit my job to pursue Cassie's investigation, it wasn't my work car. So I have a F-150 pickup and a Jeep Wrangler." Owen explained the return of his memory to Ryan and that Cassie was his sister.

"Oh, man, I'm sorry for your loss." Ryan glanced in the mirror.

Owen gave a sharp nod and hoped that moved Ryan along.

"The tracks could be from a Jeep," Ryan said. "I took pictures of both sets and will forward them to you. Maybe your forensic geniuses can find a match."

Owen figured if anyone could do this it would be the Veritas team. "Mind if I use your SAT phone to call my parents?"

"Help yourself."

Owen picked up the phone and made the call. His mom answered in her usual cheerful greeting, and he got a lump in his throat. He cleared it. "I'm getting back late tonight. Might not be until eleven. Mind if I stop by for a few minutes?"

"Always glad to see you no matter the time." She truly meant it, and that was never in doubt. "Of course, your dad will be sound asleep in his recliner. Just resting his eyes as he'll say when we wake him." She chuckled.

Owen felt like a traitor, knowing about Cassie but not telling his mother. "I'll see you then."

He quickly ended the call before she questioned him. A heaviness settled into the vehicle, feeling like an oppressive, muggy day.

"Guess with you two gone," Ryan said, "it means I'm free to eat the rest of the cake."

Mackenzie laughed, and Owen appreciated Ryan lightening the mood before Owen moved into a dark place and brought everyone down with him.

Mackenzie leaned forward again. "You can spend the night, Ryan. Raid my food supply or even go home. But we'll be coming back tomorrow, so be sure to tell me where you leave the key."

He glanced at her. "You want me to stay on?"

"I think our tracking's done," she said.

Ryan lifted his gaze to the mirror. "I'm not talking about tracking."

"Then what?" She batted long lashes. "Oh that. My safety and all. Nah. Owen's a detective and I don't have to worry about him."

"I figured him more for a bad guy." Ryan chuckled.

Mackenzie laughed with him. Owen surprised himself by laughing along with the pair, but he knew with the mission ahead it was likely his last laugh for the day.

11

Mackenzie scanned through the clear night to the Portland lights coming into view outside the helicopter window. She and Owen sat on one side of the chopper facing Sierra and Kelsey. So far the flight had been smooth, and Kelsey had gone to sleep right after takeoff, her head resting on Sierra's shoulder.

Before they'd departed, Mackenzie had arranged for her youngest sister Ryleigh to pick her and Owen up at the heliport where Coop would put down. Sierra and Kelsey had left their vehicle at the heliport and had offered a ride, but Mackenzie didn't want to keep them out later when the point of Coop flying them back to Portland was to get home earlier.

"Told you she was tired," Sierra whispered through the headsets they all wore, including Coop. The sets allowed them to communicate with each other over the loud beating of the rotors.

"ETA five minutes," Coop announced.

Owen sat up straighter. Maybe he'd drifted off too, but Mackenzie had purposefully avoided looking at him. She couldn't bear to see his anguish, which had to be growing with each passing mile, and not be able to do anything to help him other than sit with him and pray.

She even regretted asking to come along. She'd been far too pushy. She shouldn't have butted in at a time when Owen had to deliver such hard news to his parents. But she'd already come to care for him, and she wanted to be available—not halfway across the state—if he decided she could help.

"You'll see the helipad below." Coop's deep voice came over the headset. "But don't freak out over how small it is. I've never missed yet." He laughed.

This was Mackenzie's first trip in a helicopter, but she liked adventure and hadn't been concerned.

Until his comment.

She looked out the window. Tall evergreens circled what looked like a postage stamp-sized clearing.

"Oh, I don't like this," she said.

"Relax." Sierra waved a hand. "The helipad is bigger than it looks from up here."

Mackenzie wanted to believe Sierra, but she had to start tapping her leg to release her jitters. She'd once been such an adventure girl and had turned into a wuss over the years. She really needed to get out and do things before she found a guy and settled down to have a family.

Family. Wow, was she really thinking about that?

What would Owen be like as a husband and father? He didn't talk a lot, maybe saying ten words on the flight. Imagine if they'd had to travel by car for six hours together. *Would've been the longest road trip ever.* But maybe that wasn't his true personality. Maybe he'd been silent due to his faulty memory and the stress of telling his parents their child, his sister, had been murdered.

Either way, she knew one thing for sure. She wanted the chance to discover the answer. But where could that lead if she didn't want a commitment before experiencing more of life's adventures? Nowhere. Better to keep her feelings in check and start keeping things between them strictly professional.

The helicopter slowed and started the descent toward the circle. She gripped the closest thing and held tight.

Owen looked at her. "Tense much?"

She looked at him. *No. Oh no.* She'd clamped her hand on his knee. She noticed Sierra watching her. Mortified, Mackenzie jerked her hand free.

The chopper descended. Greenery soon engulfed them as the helicopter slowly lowered, the rotors thumping overhead. The chopper hit the ground with a soft bounce and settled into place.

"Exactly like I promised," Coop said. "No miss."

"But you woke me up." Kelsey laughed.

The laughter took away the last of Mackenzie's anxiety, and she let out a long breath.

Everyone removed their headsets and hung them on hooks on the walls, then unbuckled seatbelts. The equipment, samples, and Cassie's remains were in the van and they had nothing to unload tonight.

Coop slid the door open, and the chilly night air swept in like an invader. Mackenzie still wore her jacket from hiking, but the lightweight fabric didn't do much to ward off the near freezing temps.

Coop held out his hand and helped Mackenzie down. "Thanks for flying AirCoop."

She wrinkled her nose at his comment. "Next time, if there is one, I'll trust you."

He gave a salute.

"Congratulations on the upcoming baby," she said.

"Thanks." He beamed a smile. "Grace is almost three, so

we figured it was time she had a sibling. She's a spitting image of Kiera and this time, I'm hoping for a Mini-Me."

She smiled at his incredible happiness.

Owen jumped down, and both Coop and Owen turned to offer their hands to Kelsey.

"I know I've gotten big, but I don't need two guys to help me. Still, chivalry is dead for most people, so I will accept." She made a big production of placing her hands in theirs.

Sierra hopped out on her own, clearly proving she'd done this many times. "Parking lot's across the road. Your sister should be waiting there."

Sierra set off along a path lit with landscape lights and leading through the nearly forest-thick trees. The rest of them traipsed behind her, and Mackenzie enjoyed seeing the ferns and underbrush glowing in the lights on the edges of the path. They reached and crossed a two-lane highway to a well-lit parking lot. Ryleigh had pulled her slate blue Volvo SUV in next to a white Veritas van.

"I'll drive." Sierra glanced over her shoulder. "We'll all be praying for your family, Owen. Let us know if we can help beyond the recovery and forensics processing."

He nodded his thanks, a gloomy look on his face.

"Night," Kelsey said, and the two of them headed for the van.

Ryleigh got out of the car and waved. She was the only woman in the family with short hair. Starting in middle school, she'd been the tomboy athlete of the family and had kept her hair short for years for easier competing. Now she claimed as an FBI agent she didn't have time to mess with long hair, and she also hoped the male agents would take her more seriously. A theory Mackenzie doubted because with her sister's big blue eyes and generous mouth, she was a real beauty. Short hair or not, how could guys miss seeing that?

Mackenzie reached the car and introduced Owen to her sister.

Ryleigh thrust her hand out. "Mac told me about your loss. I'm so sorry."

"Thanks," he mumbled and gripped her hand.

Or was it a grumble? Either way, Ryleigh cast a questioning look at Mackenzie.

"We should get going," Mackenzie said.

Owen might be grumpy, but he hadn't lost his manners and opened the passenger door for Mackenzie then climbed into the back.

No one spoke as Ryleigh got them on the road.

They'd traveled a good distance on the highway leading to the western Portland suburbs when Owen leaned forward between the seats. "Thanks for picking us up."

Mackenzie looked at Ryleigh for her reaction. She gave a sharp nod, but the tightness around her mouth hadn't relaxed.

"Do you want my parents' address now?" Owen asked.

"No need," Mackenzie said. "Ryleigh will be stopping at home, and I'll drive you wherever you want to go."

"Oh, right. Good idea." Owen settled back as if he planned to clam up again.

"Ryleigh's an FBI agent." Mackenzie knew Ryleigh would likely ask questions about the investigation and this way Owen knew she would understand any technical details.

He leaned forward again. "What's your specialty?"

Great. He actually seemed interested.

"Information technology with a focus on cybercrimes," Ryleigh said.

"I have a lot of respect for you guys." Owen smiled at the mirror. "I have like zero interest in that stuff, but our IT guys have saved my bacon more times than I can count. Both when I mess up my laptop and on investigations."

"We are pretty special. Just ask us." Ryleigh glanced in the mirror and laughed.

Owen cracked a smile. "How long have you been an agent?"

"Recently passed my five-year anniversary."

He tilted his head. "Like the job?"

"I do." Ryleigh paused and was quiet for a long moment. "You see a whole lot of awful in five years though."

Owen's eyes narrowed. "That's the truth."

"See." Mackenzie looked at her sister. "That's why it's time to join us at the company. We desperately need your IT skills."

Ryleigh sighed. "They've been pressuring me since I hit five years."

"You had to fulfill the requirement to join the family business," Owen said.

Mackenzie looked back and locked gazes with him. "I didn't think you would remember that."

"I remember every word you've said."

Their gazes held, and they connected on a deeper level. Maybe because she knew who he was now and his struggles. His pain.

She should look away before Ryleigh caught onto her attraction, but Mackenzie was frozen in time.

Ryleigh cleared her throat.

They both snapped free like they'd been caught making out in public.

"How long have you been a detective?" Ryleigh asked.

"I joined the force right out of college and was a patrol officer for eleven years. Been a detective for four."

"You still like it?"

He planted his hands on his knees. "I wouldn't want to do anything else."

Mackenzie admired his conviction and desire to continue to do the job that she'd left behind. She was grateful for men and women who kept at it even after seeing the terrible things Ryleigh mentioned.

"That's where we differ," Mackenzie said. "I wanted to move on."

"I'll bet you were good at it, though," he said. "At least from what I've seen."

"I was pretty good." She patted herself on the back and laughed.

Ryleigh looked in the mirror. "Are you married? A family?"

"Very much single," Owen said emphatically. "No time for relationships. You done interrogating me now?"

"What?" Ryleigh glanced up at the mirror.

"Don't worry." He cracked a half smile. "It's a law enforcement habit that we don't even know we're doing."

Ryleigh shared a sheepish look with Mackenzie.

"Don't look at me," Mackenzie said to her sister. "I'm not the one grilling him."

"Okay, fine, I was, but I wanted to find out a little bit about the guy who caused my sister to nearly break down in tears when she told me about him. And the looks between you..."

"I didn't—"

Ryleigh flashed up a hand. "Save it. You were completely emotional, and you know it. You might be a philosophizer and free thinker in your own world a lot of the time, but you don't usually wear your heart on your sleeve."

Mackenzie's first impulse was to argue, but why? Owen's situation tugged at her heartstrings, and she couldn't deny that. But she also wouldn't discuss her connection to Owen with her sister in front of him. Wouldn't discuss it at all. So she leaned back on the headrest and closed her eyes for the drive.

"Nice place," Owen said.

Mackenzie opened her eyes to see their big Victorian house in a sought-after Portland neighborhood come into view. "My sisters, cousins, and I bought the house a few years back. We all live here."

Ryleigh pulled to the curb and shifted into park. "Anything else you need?"

Mackenzie shook her head. "Thanks. I owe you one."

They all got out, and Owen looked at Ryleigh. "Mind if I drive your car?"

"Not at all. Just no high-speed chases." She laughed and headed up their walkway toward the house recently painted white with black shutters. Mackenzie always thought the house looked warm and inviting at night with the perfectly maintained landscaping highlighted with low voltage lighting.

Owen looked at her. "Do you mind if I drive? Figure since I know the destination and a few shortcuts it will be quicker. I know I don't have my license on me, but I promise to obey all the laws and not get pulled over."

A stickler for rules, she wanted to say no, but she didn't have the heart to disappoint him.

"Have at it." She slid back into the passenger seat and closed the door.

The Volvo had seemed roomy with Ryleigh behind the wheel, but Owen took up far more room. Both physically and with his commanding presence.

He set off, still seeming pensive. At this time of night, the drive to Vancouver should take twenty to thirty minutes. Depending on where his parents lived. So what should she do? Try to engage him in conversation or remain quiet? He had to be thinking ahead to his visit. She'd done many death notification calls, and they'd been the hardest part of the job. Even harder than autopsies. In the death call, with one quick knock on a door, she irreparably changed lives. That was hard, and she'd never had to tell a loved one.

But she'd witnessed the deep grief in her aunt and uncle after Thomas died. It was still in their eyes. They tried to hide it and put on a good face, but she often caught the lingering sadness at family gatherings. Not just in them. Everyone had a moment of remembering Thomas and mourning his absence.

Decision made. She wouldn't bother Owen with meaningless chatter. She sat back until he drove into a suburban neighborhood of newer homes. He pulled into the driveway of a two-story gray house with black shutters.

He shifted into park but left the car running and looked at her. "Thanks for the ride. What time do you want to meet in the morning?"

"You don't want me to come in with you?" she asked.

He flared his nostrils. "I could honestly use your support, but my parents would think they had to hold it together because you were there."

"That makes sense." She gave him what she hoped was a sincere yet sympathetic smile.

"I'll borrow my mom's car to go tell Cassie's husband and likely come back here for the night. Then pick up my files in the morning."

"How about we meet at eight at my place? I'll make breakfast for you."

"Sounds good."

"Do you need the address?"

"I remember it."

Of course he did. She was coming to see he had an excellent memory, which must have made forgetting his identity even worse.

He unclipped his seatbelt but stared ahead instead of getting out.

She reached for his hand. His skin was icy cold.

"Let me pray for you before you go in," she offered.

"I'd like that." His desolate tone cut into her heart.

She took a breath and bowed her head, first silently asking God for the right words. She wanted God's help, yes, but she also wanted Owen to be comforted by her words for his difficult task ahead.

Owen found his mom and dad in their family room, all the furnishings the same for as long as Owen could remember. His dad was lightly snoring in his worn leather recliner, his mom reading a book in front of a blazing fire in the gas fireplace. Owen had to force one foot in front of the other to join them. He was about to change their lives in so many horrible ways. He'd seen it often enough on the job. That he'd have to break such heartrending news to his parents had never crossed his mind until Cassie went missing.

His mom looked up and smiled, but it quickly evaporated. "What is it? What's wrong, son?"

He crossed over to her, stopping to gently shake his dad's shoulder on the way.

"I'm just resting my eyes," he muttered and blinked a few times. "Owen. Guess I dozed off."

"He has bad news," his mom said. "I can see it in his face."

Owen sat down next to her and took her hand.

"It's Cassie, isn't it?" she asked.

Owen nodded.

"She's been found, and it's not good."

Owen nodded again. "I'm sorry, Mom...Dad." He looked back at his dad. "But we recovered her body today."

"Oh. Oh. No. It can't. I..." His mom clutched his hand with iron strength. "How long? When did she die? How?"

"I don't have any answers other than to tell you I followed up on a lead on another investigation I was working and found her in the desert near John Day."

"Desert? John Day?" His mom blinked in rapid succession. "I don't understand. She said she was going hiking."

"Perhaps she went hiking there." Owen's dad came to sit and put an arm around Owen's mom.

"Could be." Owen kept his gaze trained on them. "We're basing her ID on the clothing she was last seen wearing and her necklace."

"The one we gave her on her eighteenth birthday," his mom said.

Owen nodded. "Since it was custom made, the odds of anyone else having one like it and wearing the exact same outfit is astronomically high. Still, the lab is running DNA and they'll use her dental records to confirm."

Pain creased his dad's face. "That means you can't ID her by looking at her."

"Correct." Owen would do his very best to never share the details with them. "I'm so sorry."

"How are you dealing with this?" his mom asked in her true selfless mom behavior.

"Don't worry about me." He tried to smile but failed. "It's you I'm worried about."

She blinked a few times, and he noticed how deep the lines had become around her eyes since Cassie's disappearance. "I guess I'm numb. I figured after all this time, that this day would come. I didn't expect you to be the one to find her, though."

"Me neither."

"That's got to make this even more difficult for you." His dad's voice broke.

Owen worked hard not to fall apart and be strong for his parents. "Not easier for sure."

"I hate that for you, but in a way, I'm glad you were the one to tell us." His mom took a shuddering breath and let it out slowly. Tears spilled from her eyes. She released Owen's hand to throw herself into his dad's arms.

She broke down. Deep, agonizing wails of pain. Almost animalistic. Owen's dad held her, but tears flowed down his face too.

"I'll make a pot of coffee." Owen fled to the kitchen and leaned his back against the door.

Why hadn't he let Mackenzie come in with him? He needed support. Something he'd always gotten from his parents. Two of the finest people and parents in the world, but he couldn't let them worry about him now. They needed to grieve and find their own peace.

Owen could call Mackenzie. No. Continuing to rely on her meant he cared about her more than he wanted, and that was unfamiliar territory for him. He'd put off getting involved in any relationships until he located Cassie.

Maybe it was an excuse not to face the real issue. That someone else he cared about might disappear. If he didn't add anyone beyond his parents to the list of loved ones, he didn't have to worry about them. Perhaps that would be different if he could trust God to protect others. But he couldn't, could he? Not after Cassie.

"Why did you let this happen to our family?" He forgot all about Mackenzie's suggestions and cast the words out in frustration. "Just why?"

Then his own tears came, and he swiped at them. He'd expected Cassie's death since the investigation went cold.

Sure, he'd held onto some hope. His job told him not to. And yet, he had. Had prayed to God for Cassie to be the exception to so many missing people. That she had somehow simply walked away. But why would she?

She was happy. Had a great life. Loved her husband. Owen didn't particularly like Keith. He was cocky and could be controlling at times. A problem some police officers faced when they couldn't turn the job off at home. Husbands were often the first and best suspect when a wife went missing, but Owen's cop radar said Keith was telling the truth about her disappearance, and he was sincere. No deceit at all.

No one searched harder and longer for Cassie than Keith.

A sob tore up Owen's throat, but he wouldn't let it escape, and he swiped at his eyes. He couldn't let go, or he would completely lose it, and that wouldn't help his parents.

Keep moving. Do something productive.

He crossed the room and gathered the items to brew the coffee. The piping hot liquid was soon dripping into its pot, the sound making him think of how Cassie's life had dripped away.

Was the bullet really her cause of death? When did it happen? And who killed her?

He had to know. Would move mountains to find out. And then, make her killer pay to the full extent of the law.

Only then would he rest.

12

Mackenzie should have left but she couldn't. Not after Owen's dejected posture as he strolled up to the house, then stood outside the door for a few minutes before lifting his shoulders and going inside. She wanted to be here in case he changed his mind. Or even if he wanted her company to tell Cassie's husband that they'd found her.

Her phone dinged, an email from Nick. He'd attached his background report on Cassie. Mackenzie sent a thank you reply, and then started reading the six-page report. Nick hadn't included any information that Owen hadn't already shared about his sister. Once they knew she was Owen's sister, they could've stopped Nick's background check, but he might have turned up surprises. It looked like she led her life just as Owen had described.

The garage door rose, and Owen walked toward a beige sedan, head down. At the vehicle, he looked out the garage door and paused. He started for her side of the car.

She lowered her window and peered up at him. "Hi."

"You stayed," he said.

"In case you needed me."

He took a shuddering breath. "Wouldn't mind the company to go see Keith."

"Of course."

"He moved to Salem this year to take a job at the Salem Police Department so it'll be a long drive."

"No worries. I'm glad to help."

He watched her then rested his hand on hers where she'd laid it on the open window. "You're a very special woman, Mackenzie Steele."

Heat crept up her neck. "Just doing what I would want someone to do for me."

"Don't play it down. You're special, and I want to be sure you know it."

She didn't. Not in so many words. As the middle child in the family, she'd often received less attention. But she'd learned to deal with it. Not that her parents didn't show their love for her—let her know that they were proud of her. But the spark Owen was offering had been missing from her life, and the wonder of it captured her like nothing else ever had. Like a cozy fireplace on a snowy day.

"Let me tell my parents that I'm not taking the car, and I'll be right back." He gave her hand a quick squeeze then went back through the garage and into the house.

She lifted her window, letting the warmth from his touch and kind words ease out the chill from the horrific day. Not that it could erase it for long, but for a moment she felt full. Complete.

Thank You for Owen. I hate the circumstances under which we met, but thank You for bringing him into my life.

She should also ask God to show her the *reason* he brought her together with Owen, but right now she didn't care. Didn't care that she didn't want to be tied down. She just wanted to bask in the heartfelt look he'd given her and help him cope.

He returned and punched a code into the keypad to close the garage door then climbed in the passenger seat. "I'll put the address in your GPS."

He tapped it in, and she reversed their earlier route to the interstate highway. Most importantly she clamped her mouth closed and resisted the burning urge to ask how it went with his parents.

He sat back and didn't speak. Her heart ached for him, and the silence felt like sitting on a bed of nails.

"FYI, I got the background report on Cassie from Nick," she said to break the silence. "Nothing we don't already know."

"Not surprising." Owen turned to look at her. "Thank you for staying. I have to admit after I told my parents, I wished you were waiting for me."

She didn't know what to say other than her heart ached for him, and she was glad to help. Things she'd already told him, so she kept quiet.

He faced forward and stared. "They took it hard. Not harder than I expected. I think they were in shock."

"I would imagine so."

"After so much time with Cassie missing, you prepare yourself for this kind of news, but can never be ready for the reality."

She wanted to say the right thing and took her time replying. "Coming from a law enforcement family, we all knew someone could lose their life. Still, it was a shock when we heard about Thomas. Even more, because he'd left the force to run Steele Guardians. So you think the danger is gone, but not in our world. It's everywhere and getting worse."

"Murders are climbing to an alarming rate I never thought I'd see." He fell silent.

"When I was on the force, I got lost and swept away by

135

the world's brokenness. It was heightened when Thomas died. That made everything personal."

He looked at her. "You seem to have recovered."

"Recovered? I don't know that I did. That a person can. But it helped to leave the force and not see every day how man could hurt their fellow man. Now I can wake up and see joy still comes every morning. I embrace that as much as I can."

"I think it's going to take me some time to get there."

"Of course it will. Maybe it will help to think of God grieving over the evil in this world and that He grieves over what happened to Cassie."

"He could've stopped it."

"He could stop it all, but then He would have to take away our free will."

"Right now, I would give that up to have Cassie live."

"Was Cassie a believer?"

"Yes."

"Then she's in a good place." She looked at him. "I know that sounds cliché but it's true."

"My mom said the same thing before I left." He looked down. "I'll have to try to remember that and other things you've shared with me."

"I don't mean to be patronizing by saying your grief is insignificant due to Cassie going to heaven. Your grief is very real, and I am here for you to talk about it all you want or need."

He nodded then leaned his head back on the seat.

She let him rest and would wait for him to speak again. She was honored he opened up to her at all. The guy she'd first come to know had been pretty quiet, but that Owen hadn't known who he was. This was Owen who knew very well who he was.

The miles rolled under the tires until they were out of

the metro area, the humming making her sleepy. She spotted a sign for a gas station. "Mind if we stop for coffee?"

"Not at all."

She pulled off at the exit and into the brightly lit station. "You want a cup?"

"I had some with my parents, but I'll be glad to stretch my legs." He climbed out.

She left him behind, poured a cup of black coffee that looked like sludge for herself, and dug into an icy freezer for two ice cream bars. Ice cream was her go-to when she felt down. She paid and found Owen leaning against the side of Ryleigh's car, his ankles and arms crossed. His whole body vibrated with tenseness like a taut guitar string. She was afraid he might snap.

Without a word, she handed him the ice cream. He arched a brow but took it. She set her cup on the roof of the car and leaned next to him. She opened her bar and bit into the coffee ice cream coated with chocolate, chopped almonds, and toffee pieces. He opened his too.

They stood there eating. Not speaking. But a bond was forming. One she could almost reach out and touch.

"Good," he said when he'd finished the last bite and licked the stick. "Thank you."

"You're welcome." She took the wrapper from his hand and disposed of them both in the trash.

Back at the car, she reached for her coffee, but he caught her hand and drew her into a hug and held her tightly. His desperate struggle for meaning and understanding emanated from him along with the warmth that chased away the damp evening chill.

Nothing romantic about his hold, but a desperate need to connect with another human being when a life had been lost too soon. When the world's evil had intervened in a vibrant life. When it was the closest thing to receiving a hug from God.

"Thank you for everything," he whispered against her hair. "You've made this bearable, and I thank God for putting you in my life."

Ah, yes. Maybe this was God's purpose in bringing them together. Nothing romantic, but Christian love.

She was glad to be God's hands on earth. Honored even.

So why was she disappointed it might be the only reason she connected with Owen?

Owen pounded hard on the door to wake his brother-in law and each second Owen waited, his dread grew in seeing Keith. Not as much as with his parents, but the added anguish was twisting his gut all the same. Once again, Mackenzie waited in the car. Owen regretted having to ask her to stay, but Keith deserved to hear the news without a stranger facing him too.

A sleepy Keith in a T-shirt and sweatpants answered the door. "Dude, do you know what time it is?"

"I do." Owen pushed his way past Keith and went directly to the leather couch. He didn't let any time pass before breaking the news.

"I knew it." Keith started pacing. "I knew she wouldn't just up and leave me."

Owen didn't know what to say to that as he didn't know the intimate details of Keith's relationship with Cassie, so he said nothing.

Keith marched back and forth. "I need to go to John Day. Talk to the sheriff. Demand action."

"You don't want to do that, Keith." Owen made sure to sound like he was asking when in fact he was demanding. A police officer like Keith would rebel at being told what to do, and Owen didn't need the added burden of babysitting Keith. "I'm working the investigation, and you can be sure I won't quit until her killer is behind bars."

"I gotta go. I just have to. I have to do something." He eyed Owen. "Besides your supervisor isn't going to let you work this investigation."

"I took leave, and he can't stop me."

"But you won't have access to any of the information we need."

"Sheriff Wheeler agreed to use the Veritas Center for all forensic testing, and their forensic anthropologist recovered the remains. Wheeler authorized me to get the reports from all of them."

"Anthropologist?" Keith shoved a hand into his thick blond hair. "She was that far gone?"

Owen nodded and regretted letting anything slip.

Keith let out an anguished cry and ran his hand over his face, sliding it up and down in frantic moves as if trying to erase the news. "What was she doing there?"

Owen's question too. "It's early days. We don't know."

"She was dressed for hiking, but we've never gone hiking out there. Too long of a drive, especially during the week. I figured she would've gone to a local park like we usually did." He let his hand fall. "Boy, was I way off. Maybe if I'd considered it at the beginning we would've found her before someone took her life."

"Don't beat yourself up," Owen said, though that was pretty much what he'd been doing since he'd discovered the body was his sister.

Could he have done more? Figured out where she'd gone? But how?

Keith planted his bare feet on the beige carpet. "I won't stand on the sidelines now."

"Give me a few days. That's all I ask. If I haven't made any progress, we'll revisit the idea of you joining in the investigation."

Keith rested his hands on his hips and fired his practiced cop glare at Owen. "Fine. But if you don't give me regular updates, I'll be in John Day so fast your head will spin."

"I can call you twice a day."

"See that you do."

Owen got up to leave.

Keith grabbed Owen by the shoulder. "You better not be jerking me around."

"I'm not. I'll update you like I said. More often if I discover something." Owen shrugged free and headed for the door.

Notifications over, Owen now needed to produce a miracle and find a strong lead to go on. Not something he could do on his own. Only God could accomplish that.

Problem was, Owen wasn't sure God was on his side right now.

13

_____

Nearing eight in the morning, Mackenzie placed the last piece of flatware on her long dining room table and stood back to assess it with bleary eyes. All told, she'd gotten two hours of sleep before she'd showered and made breakfast for Owen. She was baking a bacon, egg, pepper, and onion casserole that Teagan often made for their dad, and the savory scent filled the air. Mackenzie wanted the breakfast to be perfect and prayed it would help give a moment of relief from the grief she knew would plague Owen for some time to come.

Voices came from the kitchen. She spun, her hand going for her sidearm. The outside doors were locked. Or at least they should be. She was home alone except for Ryleigh, who was upstairs sleeping because she'd ended up going on a stakeout late last night. And even if Ryleigh had woken up, short of going outside and around back to get to the kitchen, she would have to pass through the dining room.

Mackenzie cautiously opened the swinging door far enough to see into the kitchen. Her gran and grandad stood in the room and turned to look at the door.

She entered the room and let out a breath. "You scared me."

"Sorry. Didn't expect anyone to be home." Her grandad wiggled a wicker basket with a handle. "Just delivering some goodies your gran made for you girls."

He took out a pan of gooey cinnamon rolls with thick white icing, then two banana bread loaves, and three perfectly browned wheat bread loaves.

Her gran, curly silver hair in a messy style as usual, crossed the room and hugged Mackenzie. Tears formed in Mackenzie's eyes, but she looked at the ceiling to will them away. She was too emotional after seeing Cassie's body, seeing Owen's pain, and no sleep to withstand her gran's ability to get information out of her granddaughters. Gran could finagle info from a stone if she chose.

She released Mackenzie and looked her in the eye. "You're supposed to be on vacation. Don't tell me you cut it short to go back to work."

"No."

"Then what?"

"I'm making breakfast for an associate," Mackenzie said, trying to be vague but knowing her gran would persist until she got all the details. Mackenzie had to fend off the inevitable questions and get them out of the house before Owen arrived.

Her gran's eyebrows rose under the deep red-framed glasses. "Must be someone special to not only end your vacation but for you to *cook*."

"Just an associate I'm helping with a murder investigation."

"Is he handsome?"

Ah, here we go. Mackenzie would answer to move them forward, and she would help unload the basket too, which also contained cookies and brownies. Her gran spoiled them something fierce.

"He's very handsome." Mackenzie took out the pan of frosted brownies, wishing she could face-plant into the pan instead of facing the grand inquisition.

"Single?"

"Yes."

"Interested in him?"

"Yes." There was no point in lying when her gran would flush the truth out of her. "But I won't do anything about it."

The doorbell rang. Mackenzie sighed. Relief or fear? She didn't know.

"Oh, good." Gran's beautiful broad smile could warm even the coldest day. "We can meet him."

Mackenzie wanted to groan but held back. "Don't say anything, Gran. Nothing. The murder victim we're investigating is his sister, and he just found her remains in the desert. He's hurting and doesn't need any prodding on what his intentions are for me."

"Oh, dear." She clutched her chest. "Of course not."

Mackenzie turned to her grandad. "That goes for you too. But also no prodding on the murder investigation as I know you're already itching to do."

His big brown eyes narrowed behind silver-framed glasses with thick lenses. "Got it."

She headed for the foyer, letting the kitchen door swing closed behind her, hopefully telling her grandparents it was time to leave. It was futile, but a girl had to try.

She straightened the basic navy and white striped knit shirt she'd paired with jeans. She'd gone through her closet multiple times to choose her outfit and finally stopped primping for Owen and put on something comfortable for the long drive back to John Day.

She opened the door. Owen stood looking down at his

booted feet. He wore black tactical pants, a tan T-shirt, and a water-repellant jacket. He looked ready to do battle. Under the jacket, she spotted an outline of a gun at his hip.

He looked up, his dark eyes tormented. She didn't think. Didn't speak. Simply stepped out into the brisk and very cold wind to give him a hug. He didn't back away but clutched her tightly. She could go on and on being held by him, but she heard footsteps from inside. Her grandparents were on the move.

She pushed back and caught the glimpse of an army-green pickup at the curb. "I see your truck wasn't stolen."

He shook his head. "But my Jeep is missing. So must've driven that."

"Hopefully, we'll find it." She backed inside. "Just a quick warning. My grandparents stopped by and want to meet you. I told them very little, but I did mention we're working an investigation together, and your sister is the victim."

He nodded and pressed his lips into a narrow line but didn't speak.

"This way." She led him to the dining room.

Her gran stood next to the table place settings, and she held a coffee pot. Her grandad stood behind her.

"Owen Greer, meet my grandparents," Mackenzie said. "Artie and Eloise Steele."

Her grandad stepped forward and held out his hand. "Pleased to meet you."

Owen shook and smiled. An earnest smile, which Mackenzie had no idea how he managed. "You too, sir."

Her grandad let go of Owen's hand and waved his. "Sir. Harumph. I might be old, but I'm just plain Artie."

Owen's smile widened, and he looked at her gran who waved at him. "And I'm Eloise. We don't stand on formality in our family. Life's too short for that."

"Go ahead and sit," Mackenzie said. "And I'll get the

food."

"I've got it covered," her gran said. "Starting with the coffee. Would you like a cup, Owen?"

"Please." He pulled out a chair for Mackenzie.

Her grandparents shared an approving look.

She sat, and Owen took the seat across from her.

Gran poured his coffee first. "Cream or sugar?"

"Black, please."

"Attaboy," her grandad said. "Enjoy all the goodness."

"Most people in our family like it black, except this one." Gran tapped Mackenzie's shoulder. "She likes it strong like we all do, but it barely looks like coffee when she gets done with it."

Mackenzie looked at her gran. "You make it sound like that's a bad thing."

"Bad?" Her gran poured the rich black coffee in the big stoneware mug. "Not at all. It makes you unique, and you are. Down to the color of your hair." She kissed the top of Mackenzie's head. "You have always marched to the beat of a different drummer. I find that absolutely fascinating, and I love waiting to see what you will do."

"Thanks, Gran." Mackenzie smiled at her grandmother. "I have to say, I think I'm a lot like you."

"Well, of course you are. And look how fabulous I am." Her gran chuckled.

"We'll get the food on the table and take off," her grandad said.

"You're not joining us for breakfast?" Owen asked. "If there's enough food it would be nice if you could."

"Thought you'd never ask. Been a long time since our breakfast at four." Her grandad pulled out the chair next to Owen.

"Artie, stop." Her gran raised a warning hand. "We're butting in."

Mackenzie wanted to agree with her, but for some reason Owen seemed to want them there. Maybe having such open and caring people helped him deal with his grief. Or at least distracted him and postponed it until he was alone with Mackenzie. Would he always associate his sister's death with Mackenzie? Man, that would be awful. Just awful.

"Not butting in at all." Her grandad stared her gran down. "We were invited, and it would be rude to say no."

"He has a point, Gran," Mackenzie said. "And with the goodies you brought, we have plenty of food."

"Okay then. But Artie, you're going to help set the extra place settings and bring in the food."

"I can do that," Mackenzie said.

Her gran shook her head. "We will earn our keep."

Mackenzie nodded as there was no arguing with her gran when she decided something like this, even if she earned her keep weekly and then some. She brought baked goods, meals, and even cleaned at times, spoiling all of them.

She set the pot on a hot pad and departed, her grandad tromping behind.

Mackenzie waited for the door to swing closed behind them. "That was nice of you to ask them to stay."

"I like them, and I don't get to see my grandparents enough. My mom's parents are the only ones still living, and they retired to Florida."

"I can't imagine not seeing mine every week. Sometimes I complain about it, but they really are special."

The door opened, and her grandad came in with a tray of plates and silverware. He started setting the place next to Owen and looked at him. "You fish, son?"

Mackenzie groaned, and Owen cast her a questioning look.

"I should've warned you about that. Grandad is obsessed with fishing and thinks everyone should do it." She smiled fondly up at him. "Actually, I'm surprised it took him so long to ask."

He waved her off. "When you fish, all the peace and quiet is good for the soul. Plenty of time to contemplate and talk to God without the world's pressures interfering."

"My dad's an avid fisherman," Owen said. "I went with him when I was a kid, but I couldn't handle all that downtime and was too wiggly for him. Sorry."

Her grandad brought the tray around to the other side. "Might be different as an adult."

"Maybe." Owen tilted his head.

"Would be worth a try, right?" Her grandad finished the second place setting and retrieved the tray. "I'd be glad to take you out anytime. Or maybe you want to go with your dad."

"Yeah, maybe. He could use a buddy right about now."

Her grandad nodded and left the room.

"How are your parents doing this morning?" She flashed up a hand. "Wait. Scratch that question. That's one that we all hated getting after Thomas died. How do you answer such a question? I know how they're doing. I've seen it in my aunt and uncle."

"Thanks for being concerned though," Owen said. "It's really set in overnight, and my mom is especially upset. But then my dad has always been kind of stoic, so he's likely hurting as badly but not showing it."

Stoic. A word that described Owen. Maybe he took after his father.

The door swung open again, and her grandad backed into the room with a tray and held the door with his foot. Carrying another tray, Mackenzie's gran entered. They held the casserole, cinnamon bread toasted a perfect brown, caramel rolls, and the bowl of fresh fruit Mackenzie had prepared earlier.

They placed the dishes on the table and sat.

"Let's pray," her grandad said.

They all joined hands, and he led them in a prayer of thanksgiving for the food and added one for comfort for the Greer family at the end.

At the Amen, Owen squeezed her hand hard, and she almost winced. Seemed as if he'd really embraced the heartfelt prayer. She had the best grandad in the world.

Her gran offered the casserole to Owen. "A family favorite."

He scooped out a large serving.

"I see you brought your cinnamon swirl bread and caramel rolls." Mackenzie took a piece of toast from the plate and then switched the dish with Owen for the casserole.

Her gran took a large serving of the fruit and smiled. "Nothing but the best for my girls."

Owen lifted a roll dripping in caramel sauce onto his plate. "If these rolls are as good as they look, there won't be any left for the girls."

"Now aren't you the sweetest boy." Gran gave Mackenzie and Owen pointed looks.

He glanced at Mackenzie and blushed a bright red.

"Mackenzie told us to stay away from matchmaking." Her grandad spread a thick slab of butter on his toast. "And now you've gone and embarrassed him. Suppose that means I can bring up the investigation."

Mackenzie shook her head. "What good does it do to talk to you two?"

"None." Her grandad grinned. "And I figured a smart woman like you would know that by now."

"I don't mind talking about the investigation." Owen

took a big bite of the roll and groaned. "Good." He swallowed. "What do you want to know?"

"I'd like to know if you got your case files and what your LT had to say," Mackenzie jumped in while her grandad finished chewing his bite of casserole.

Owen set down his roll and grabbed his mug to take a sip. "I got them, and he decided to let me proceed under his supervision. Means I have to check in with him a few times a day, and as he said, call him before I approach anyone that I might make mad."

"Which if you're doing your job right, could be most anyone," her grandad said.

"Right. Still, if I don't plan to *make* them mad, and they happen to *get* mad, I can beg forgiveness." Owen grinned.

"Attaboy." Her grandad smiled.

Her gran slapped her hand in his direction. "Now don't encourage him, Artie."

Mackenzie explained to her grandparents about Owen's memory loss. "Anything in the files that helped you remember why you were in John Day?"

"Plenty." He took a sip of coffee. "I'm investigating a murder in Camas. The guy, Jamar Bussey, was gunned down outside his house. Slugs recovered from the body are .308 Winchesters."

"A rifle then," Mackenzie said.

Owen swallowed his bite. "You know your guns."

"Know enough," she answered.

"Made sure all of my girls know their weapons," her granddad said. "This guy have a sheet?"

Owen shook his head. "Not even an arrest for shoplifting."

"A .308 is one of the most popular hunting calibers, especially for deer hunting," her grandad said. "And makes sense that out in John Day you could be looking for a hunter."

Owen nodded. "Which is why I initially went to John Day to visit OffGrid Outfitters where a Ned Leach works as a guide. He's Jamar Bussey's good friend and was visiting Bussey the week he was murdered. The two had a heated argument in a bar before Bussey was gunned down, and Leach had supposedly left town. I haven't been able to confirm that he actually did leave, and he's my number one suspect in Bussey's death."

Mackenzie set down her fork, and it clanked on her plate. "His job makes him a strong suspect then."

"Yes, though my detailed background check on him shows he's clean. But he wouldn't return my calls, so I planned a surprise visit. Problem was, when I got here, he was out scouting for the spring hunting season and wasn't due back for a week. His boss gave me coordinates of the location where I could find him, and I hiked out there. That's where I was attacked."

"It's odd that he'd be scouting on the land where my rental property sits," Mackenzie said.

"Apparently, OffGrid Outfitters has a hunting lease with the owner of the property for the outer reaches of their land. I didn't find him, but after I found the remains and came around the butte, that's when I was attacked and left for dead."

"You think it was this Leach fella?" her grandad asked.

Owen nodded. "Don't know who else it would be."

"But how would he know who you were?" her gran asked.

"I figure his boss called Leach after my visit to give the guy a heads-up that I was looking for him and that he'd given me his location." Owen planted his hands on the table. "But I'm just speculating, and that's the first question I plan to ask Leach's supervisor when I get back to John Day."

"And the second question?" her grandad asked.

Owen gripped the edge of the table. "Where in the world can I find Ned Leach?"

~

The car came to a stop, and Mackenzie jolted awake, her mind struggling to figure out her location. She blinked and looked around as Owen shifted into park in the OffGrid Outfitters' lot. A large sign with a logo that included a rifle, kayak, and fishing pole sat above an old log cabin with worn logs and green trim.

She stretched and looked at Owen. "I'm embarrassed I slept so long."

"I'm glad you did." He removed the key from his F-150 with all the bells and whistles and incredibly soft leather seats. "You needed it."

"I'm sure you need sleep too, and I could've driven some of the way."

He patted his dashboard. "I don't let just anybody drive my baby."

She rolled her eyes, and he chuckled.

"Ready?" he asked.

"For a pit stop, definitely."

"I'm sure they have a restroom you can use."

"Let's hope so."

They stepped into the nippy but dry desert air and climbed the rustic wooden steps to an old door with splotchy green paint. An aged copper bell chimed above the door. The dark and shadowy place held a hint of a musty smell. Two desks sat in the large front reception area, and a table held refreshments, including a pot of coffee, which Mackenzie eyed with longing. It would be her first stop after her restroom break.

They moved deeper into the space to the desks and

stopped next to one with boxes piled on top that were filled with personal items like picture frames. The other desk was empty and covered in a fine coating of dust.

Owen tapped the boxes. "Their receptionist used to sit at this desk. Wonder what happened to her."

"Their business could be slow during the off-season, and they lay her off."

"Could be."

A man came barreling out the doorway in the back wall. "Help you—" He caught sight of Owen. "Oh, it's you again."

Mackenzie wasn't surprised that the man remembered Owen from his earlier visit. Owen was very memorable, and a visit from a police detective would be as well.

"Hello, Mr. Hatch." Owen eyed the man. "Mind if we use your restrooms? Then I'd like to ask a few follow-up questions."

"Better make it quick. I'm run off my feet right now. My receptionist quit, and the new one doesn't start for a week."

"Won't take long." Owen turned toward the other wall where a faded restroom sign jutted out from the logs. Mackenzie didn't want to miss any questions, so she hurried into the ladies' restroom. She did take a moment to straighten her hair that had tangled into a frightful mess in her sleep.

How could she have slept for most of the drive? Embarrassing. But it helped. She was more alert and ready to grill a suspect. That had to count for something.

She stepped out, and neither Owen or Mr. Hatch were around. She fixed a cup of coffee with a liberal dose of creamer and sugar, then went through the back doorway to a small office. The door stood open, allowing her to see inside. Hatch sat behind a neat and tidy desk in the middle, his back to her with his phone to his ear. Two chairs were placed in front. Animal heads and fish filled the log walls.

The desk nameplate read, *Owner, Heath Hatch.*

"Chill out, Ned," he said into his phone. "I don't know what he wants this time, but I'll call you as soon as he leaves."

Was he warning Leach about Owen's visit? Likely.

She leaned against the doorjamb and sipped her coffee as she waited for him to finish his call.

"I don't know. I gotta go. They'll be out soon." Hatch lowered his phone and turned. "Oh, you. You're out. Thought it might take longer."

"Obviously," she said as Owen came up behind her. She looked over her shoulder. "Mr. Hatch was just on the phone telling Ned about your visit."

Owen glared at Hatch. "You called Leach?"

Hatch shoved his phone in his pocket. "Who I called is none of your business."

"It is if you're impeding a murder investigation."

"Murder?" Hatch came to his feet. "You never said anything about murder."

"Didn't I?" Owen sounded innocent. "So you were talking to Leach. Did you call him the other day when I was here too?"

Hatch's eyes flashed like a hunted wild animal. "I...well... yeah. I did."

Owen's whole body stiffened. "Sit."

Hatch didn't say a word but dropped onto his desk chair and crossed his arms. This was the first interview since Owen was approved to work Cassie's investigation. First guy he made mad. First time Owen would have to ask his boss for forgiveness. But Owen was a strong man, and she believed he could handle his boss's wrath.

Owen gestured for her to take a seat too. She did, and he sat on the edge of the desk.

Hatch scooted back. "I didn't know it was that serious. I

wouldn't have called him if I did."

"I was assaulted at the location where you provided the coordinates. Hit over the head. Left for dead and my Jeep stolen."

"Man, oh, man." Hatch ran a hand over his face. "Ned wouldn't do that."

Right. This guy seemed out of touch with reality.

"How well do you know him?" Owen asked.

"Real well. Been working for me for ten years. Not a lick of trouble."

"None?" Mackenzie asked. "In ten years. Hard to believe."

"Okay, maybe he got mad at some of the more entitled jerks he took out hunting. Not a one of us hasn't. We're just better at hiding it."

"You guide a lot of those types of people?" Mackenzie asked.

"Unfortunately, yeah. They have money to burn and our expeditions don't come cheap." Hatch frowned. "Not only do I have to pay the guide, which if you want one with experience you have to offer a good salary to keep them from leaving for the outfit down the road. Then I gotta feed the guests for the duration of the hunt. Not baked beans or MREs. No, they want gourmet all the way. And I have to own and maintain enough equipment to outfit them. And then there's the horses we use. Vet bills. Feed. That all costs a pretty penny these days."

"Why do it, then?" She took a sip of her coffee, now the perfect drinking temperature.

"I make enough so my wife can stay home with the kids. I'll never get rich for sure, but point blank, I love it. Don't have to sit behind a desk like this all day. Except when the receptionist pitches a hissy fit. Just because I asked her to do her job right, and she bolts like a skittish colt out the door, never to be seen again. The new one was at her last job for a few years, so maybe I can get a few out of her too."

Not with an attitude like that, Mackenzie resisted saying.

"Where's Leach now?" Owen asked.

"Still out scouting bears."

"What kind of vehicle does he drive?" Mackenzie asked.

"Ford pickup. White. Late eighties Lariat. "

"What make of rifle does he usually use?" Owen asked.

"Hmm, well depends on what he's hunting, but his all-round favorite is a Sig Sauer Cross."

Mackenzie had heard of that. A pricey rifle for sure.

"Do you know what ammo it takes?" Owen asked.

"They have varying models, but his is chambered for .308 Winchesters."

The same caliber used to kill Bussey. Mackenzie resisted sharing a knowing look with Owen.

"Get on the phone and call Leach back in," Owen said. "Don't mention that I directed your call."

"Okay, but he might not answer. Reception even for SAT phones out there can be sketchy." He picked up his SAT phone and placed the call.

"Put him on speaker," Owen directed.

Hatch punched the button.

"The cop still there," Leach asked.

"Leach. Good. Glad I caught you. I need you to come back today."

Mackenzie liked the way he ignored Leach's question.

"You setting me up for the cop to question me?" Leach asked.

Hatch's gaze frantically searched the area, and he didn't answer right away. "Cindy quit. Walked off the job. Got a new receptionist hired, but she can't start until next week. I need help running the office."

"The other guides are hanging out waiting to be called

back to work. Ask one of them."

"You know the business better."

"They all know it better than Cindy did, so they can do the job."

"This is an order, Leach."

Mackenzie didn't like the demand. Could suggest to Leach that Owen was here waiting to talk to him.

"I'm staying put." Leach's tone brooked no argument. "Scouting is going well, and it's gonna pay off big time in happy customers when they bag their bear. That's far more valuable to you than me answering the stupid phone."

"But..."

"Look, I said no. Fire me if you don't like it." The call ended.

Hatch slammed the phone onto the desk. "Sorry, man. I tried. You heard me. Leach knows he's too valuable to me to fire him. He's one of the best guides in the area, and my repeat customers ask for him the most 'cause they almost always bag their game with him."

"Then we'll have to go to him," Owen said.

"You experienced hikers? Just asking because the terrain in the area he's doing recon in is pretty rugged."

"We have our own guide," Mackenzie said. "Far more capable than any of your guides."

Hatch scowled. "Not from this area, then."

"No," she said.

"You'll give me Leach's coordinates and directions?" Owen asked.

"Yes."

"And you won't warn him I'm coming after him."

"I won't."

"One last question." Owen locked gazes with Hatch. "Does Leach wear glasses?"

"Yeah. Yeah, he does."

14

In downtown John Day, Owen stood back and let an elderly woman pass, as Mackenzie chatted on her phone with Ryan. The old lady didn't recognize Cassie's picture. No one had. Not one! He and Mackenzie had shown the photo to hundreds of people on the street, and Owen couldn't take many more rejections. Time to stop. Especially with the sun dropping behind the horizon, leaving the place illuminated only by streetlights. The pedestrians were thinning to a trickle, leaving the number of people to canvass at nearly zero as dinnertime approached.

Mackenzie ended her call and shoved her phone into her purse. "Ryan's on his way. Said he'd bring all the gear we need again. He'll drive the company truck and bring a four-seat UTV so we can better access the more rugged area where Leach is scouting now."

Owen nodded. "I'm going to owe this guy big time."

"No worries," she said. "At least that's what he'll tell you. He and his brothers live their faith big time by providing services for others, and they're always willing to help."

"Is it only the three of them on their team?"

She shook her head. "Started out that way, but now

there are six guys. I think two of the other guys are brothers. I'm not sure if the third guy is too, but I think he was in the military with one of the Maddox brothers. I know they're all former law enforcement or military."

"If they're all as capable as Ryan, then they're a good team to have if you need to head out into Oregon's vast wilderness."

"Actually, people from all over the country come to them for survival training."

"Bigger operation than I expected." Owen's attention was grabbed by Ernie's Bar and Grill's flashing red neon sign coming to light and cutting into the darkness like a beacon.

Owen's stomach rumbled. "Let's get something to eat, and we can ask the staff about Cassie too."

"You don't have to ask me twice." She chuckled and hurried ahead of him down the street.

They entered the dim building with older furnishings and a worn wooden floor. The sign said to seat themselves. Owen led Mackenzie to a private booth in the back. She took a seat facing the door, and he scooted in next to her.

She raised her eyebrow at him.

"You know I can't sit on the other side any more than you can." He—like other law enforcement officers—developed habits on the job. One was never sitting with their back facing the door so they could see any trouble coming.

"You should see when my family goes out to eat together. We race to get the seats facing the entrance." She laughed.

They both grabbed a laminated menu from the holder.

Owen didn't have to read beyond the first section of the American cuisine. He settled on a prime rib sandwich and stowed his menu.

Mackenzie looked up from hers. "That was quick."

"I know what I like." He gave her a suggestive look, telling her he liked what he saw.

She blushed and returned her attention to the menu.

He'd been flirting. Something he was terrible at, and her reaction proved it. He should stay in his lane. Be blunt and tell it like it was. Starting now, he would stop trying to be subtle about his feelings.

But why be anything at all? He had to find Cassie's killer not encourage a relationship with this amazing woman. That meant not leading her on and ignoring this interest that kept him confused.

Simple, right? Not.

Their waitress appeared at the table. She was young. Real young, maybe eighteen, with long red hair and a freckled face. She wore a white shirt and black pants. She tapped a pen on her order pad and looked at Mackenzie. "What can I get you?"

Makenzie looked up. "I'll have the deluxe hamburger with fries and iced tea to drink."

The waitress jotted it on her pad and turned her attention to Owen.

"Prime rib sandwich and fries. Coke for me."

She noted it. "Be right back with your drinks."

Before leaving Vancouver, Owen had gotten his backup phone from home and restored all of his data, including the picture of Cassie that their mom had taken on Cassie's last visit. He held it out. "Before you go, do you recognize this woman?"

The waitress studied the screen. "Not really."

Owen swiped to a detailed shot of Cassie's necklace. "She would've been wearing this necklace."

"That's pretty unique, so I think I would've remembered if I saw it, but I don't." She tucked the pen behind her ear. "You should ask Ernie. He owns this place, and he's what they call a super-recognizer."

"What's that?" Mackenzie asked.

"A person who never forgets a face. Even if they only get a glimpse of them." The waitress shook her head. "It's kind of freaky."

"Can you have him come see us?" Owen asked.

"Can do." She spun, and her rubber soled shoes squeaked on the floor.

Mackenzie shoved her menu back into the holder. "I've never heard of a super-recognizer."

Owen unwrapped his silverware from the paper napkin. "I worked with a guy once who fits that criteria. The waitress is right. It was freaky. He could look at a crowd, and then pick out individual pictures of every single one of the people. Even a week or more later."

"I wonder how they do that."

"I checked into it after that investigation and found not a lot of study has been done. But they apparently pick up a lot of pieces quickly and put them together like a puzzle."

"Fascinating." She leaned back. "But I would hate to have it. Think of all the people this guy comes into contact with in his restaurant, and he remembers all of those faces. Must be overwhelming at times."

Owen nodded and sat back as the waitress dropped off their drinks. "Ernie will be out with your food."

"Thank you." Mackenzie's gaze trailed the waitress as she departed.

Owen waited until she was out of earshot. "I'd like to run out to my truck and get a map to plan our visit to Leach tomorrow."

"We could look at a map on our phone."

"Humor me." He stood. "I'm old school on this."

He hurried outside and hunched under his jacket to keep the bitter wind at bay. He'd parked his pickup at the end of the block and got out his map of the area and a pen. A white truck was idling across the street, catching Owen's attention. Too bad Owen couldn't see through the tinted windows and get a glimpse of the driver.

The vehicle was parallel parked, and what Owen could see of the license plate was plastered with dirt. Looked like a Ford to him, but could be a Ram too. The lighting just wasn't good enough to be sure and both had rounded wheel wells.

Was the driver watching them? Was it Leach? Had he come back from scouting?

Nah. The driver was likely just early for a take-out order, and Owen was likely letting his cop code speak to him again. He'd knock on the window and would embarrass himself and his department, maybe make a guy mad who would call Sage and report Owen. Wasn't worth it for nothing concrete.

He went back to the restaurant, glancing back every few feet, but the truck remained in place. He entered the dark establishment. A perfect venue for someone to lurk in the shadows.

Mackenzie was watching the door. Studying every step he took. Not in a clinical way, but in the way a woman watches a man she's attracted to.

Did she know she was doing it? Probably not. But he felt it clear to his toes. And he liked the feeling. A lot. Still, he ignored it. Or at least he did his best.

He dropped onto the firm bench seat and pressed the map out in front of him, careful not to touch her. "Let's see where we're headed in the morning."

He ran his finger along Highway 26 heading toward John Day from Portland until he located the exit Heath Hatch told him to take. The narrow road wound south for miles then forked off. He trailed the right fork then slid his finger east until he located the final road, nothing more than a wide driveway, and their destination.

He drew a dark circle around it. "I don't like this location at all."

Mackenzie frowned. "If you mean there's only one way in and out, then I agree wholeheartedly."

He nodded, thankful for her quick observation. She really did think like a law enforcement officer and that added to his attraction. A woman who understood his career. His mindset. His sacrifices. That was a rare woman indeed.

"Could be an ambush if Hatch ignored me and told Leach we're coming," Owen said. "We'll be on foot, leaving us totally exposed. Ryan's UTV will help but won't give much more protection. But if we come under fire, we could move to safety faster."

She met his gaze, a suggestion of fear in her eyes. "You really think this guy's going to open fire on us?"

"If he's the jerk who knocked me out and stole my Jeep, then yes." Owen laid his pen on the map. "Besides, after hearing he uses a Sig Cross, I gotta figure the guy is seriously into marksmanship. That rifle isn't cheap, and it was designed based on input not only from hunters, but military snipers and elite long-range shooters, so it has stellar accuracy."

"Not something the average hunter might need," she said. "But he *is* a guide and might simply own an expensive rifle to do his job well."

"True. I could be reaching on this because I want a solid suspect. I need you to keep me in line there."

"I'm glad to keep you in line." She chuckled.

He got out his phone. "Let's get a look at the topography. If it's mountainous and the only entrance is a pass leading to his coordinates that would make things even more problematic."

He chose a satellite view on a map program and held it

out, allowing Mackenzie to see it. "The final road rises in elevation, but the land is flat before that, and we should be fine at that location. But looks like we'll have to go on foot for a good bit of the trail."

She frowned. "Maybe we shouldn't bring Ryan in. I hate to put someone else in danger."

She had a point. "I don't want that either, but he impressed me as a guy who could handle himself. Besides, the terrain is more rugged than I expected, and I don't think it would be wise to go alone."

"You're right. We need him." She narrowed her gaze. "But I'll lay out the situation for him and leave it up to him."

"Of course."

A chunky man with reading glasses resting atop his full head of gray hair stepped out of the kitchen door carrying two plates. He marched straight for their table.

Owen circled the final destination and folded the map.

The man held up the first plate. "Burger?"

"That's me," Mackenzie said.

He put her plate in front of her and then settled the other one in front of Owen. "I'm Ernie Jamison. I heard you wanted me to look at a picture."

Owen displayed Cassie's photo.

"Yep. She was in here. Sat at the bar. But her hair color was different. Brown." He peered at Owen.

"She must've dyed her hair then." There hadn't been any evidence of hair dying at her home. So she had to change it after disappearing.

Did it mean no one abducted her, that she didn't get lost? Seems likely if she was in this place alone. Was she trying to hide her identity? But why?

"Even if I didn't have the whole super memory thing going on, I woulda remembered her," Ernie said.

"Why's that?"

Ernie let out a long breath. "One of the local truckers was hitting on her. She made it clear she wasn't interested. He persisted. I was about to intervene when she expertly put him in his place, and the guy slunk out with his tail between his legs. Not before giving her a menacing look and telling her that it wasn't over."

Had this guy murdered her? "What day was this?"

"Can't say off the top of my head. The guy ordered our Kodiak Challenge meal that night. Figured he was trying to impress her. It's an eat the entire meal in sixty minutes and the meal is free kinda thing. It's not ordered often, so give me some time to look back on my receipts and I can find the day."

"Did she pay for her meal by credit card?" Mackenzie asked.

Ernie shook his head. "Cash. I remember because she left me a very generous tip."

"Do you know the trucker who hassled her?" Owen asked.

"Seen him before, but don't know his name. Works for a local metal casting company. Outfit called East Oregon Pipe and Foundry. They have an office right outside of town."

"Anything special about his rig that can help ID him?" Owen asked.

"Yeah. Yeah." Ernie's eyes brightened. "I know his truck. He has a red cab with a sleeping compartment. The other ones are mostly white and not as fancy."

That would help narrow down their search but only if no other trucker drove this particular rig. Might not matter if Ernie could ID the guy from having seen him.

Owen leaned forward. "If I can get pictures of the company's truck drivers, will you look at them?"

Ernie squinted at them. "What's this regarding anyway?"

Owen got out his credentials and displayed them. "Murder."

"Well, shoot, yeah." Ernie's tone raised and bounced around the room. "Glad to help. It might help to know that this guy has flaming red hair. Can't miss him."

"We can go by the casting company first thing in the morning," Owen said.

"If you don't want to wait, they run twenty-four seven, and the night manager might be able to help. Guy's name is Frank Urban."

"Good to know," Owen said. "Will you be working tomorrow?"

"All day." Ernie rubbed the back of his neck. "Don't tell me this murder happened in our sleepy little town?"

"Not in town, no." Owen opened the contact app on his phone. "Can I get your phone number so I can text pictures to you?"

Ernie rattled off his number. "Just let me know what I can do to help. You can count on me." He marched away, a purpose in his step.

"What do you make of Cassie's hair color change?" Mackenzie asked. "Do you think she was running from someone and trying to hide out here?"

He set down his phone and grabbed his sandwich. "But from who? There was no one in her life who wanted to do her harm. At least no one who turned up in the investigation."

"What about her husband?" Mackenzie reached for the ketchup and dumped a liberal portion on her plate.

"Keith? Nah. They had a solid marriage, and he was thoroughly investigated. Besides, he's a cop."

"Doesn't mean he didn't hurt her." Mackenzie paused, hands above her burger. "Cops abuse women more often than I would like to admit."

"I never saw a hint of abuse. No signs of intimidation. Besides, Cassie would've told me."

"Most women are too embarrassed to report it."

"True." He dunked his sandwich into the small bowl of au jus sauce.

She cut her burger in half. "You plan to follow up on this trucker tonight?"

Owen nodded. "We have to, right? Sounds like a promising lead we can't pass up."

Owen stood in the casting company foyer waiting for the manager to come out of his office. Mackenzie had taken a seat, but Owen was too antsy to sit so he walked around the space. He examined a bulletin board in the corner where the company posted the driver of the month's photo and name. A redheaded man stood in front of a red extended cab linked to an eighteen-wheeler.

"Come look at this," he said to Mackenzie.

She joined him and stared at the board. Her gaze flashed to his. "Could be our driver."

"Yeah, unless they have two truckers with red hair and red cabs." Owen dug his phone from his pocket and snapped a couple of photos. Owen texted the picture to Ernie and tapped his foot while waiting for a reply, but the dinner rush was a busy time and Owen might not get a quick answer.

The lobby door opened, and a stout man with a thick black beard and head of coffee-brown hair poked his head out. "Frank Urban, manager. You people want to see me?"

Owen got out his identification and displayed it then introduced Mackenzie as an associate. "We'd like to ask you questions about one of your trucks." Owen purposely said the truck instead of the driver to make his request less threatening. "Mind if we have a talk?"

Frank creased his high forehead. "Was one of my trucks involved in something bad?"

"Nothing like that," Owen said. "We only want to talk to you. In private."

"This way." Urban disappeared into a dark hallway.

Owen waited for Mackenzie to enter first, and they both had to hurry not to fall behind the man's long strides. He turned into a room at the end of the hallway. It was a small dark office with a single desk and three chairs, two of them metal folding chairs. The desk looked handmade from rough timbers perhaps harvested from Oregon forests. A ceramic ashtray loaded with cigar butts sat near the computer, the monitor was yellowed from smoke and the room reeked of it.

Urban dropped onto the cracked blue chair behind the desk. Owen didn't bother sitting. He wouldn't be here long enough. "Mind describing your truck fleet? Especially the cab design."

"All of our company trucks have white cabs with our black logo painted on the side." Urban leaned back, and the chair groaned as if wanting to die. "We also use contract drivers, and they drive their own rigs."

"Any of them have a red one with a sleeper?" Mackenzie asked, still standing next to Owen.

"Yeah, one. Nice rig. Owned by Hobert Tovar."

"Did I see his picture as driver of the month in the lobby?" Mackenzie's tone was totally innocuous.

"Yep. Been driver of the month for as long as I can remember. Smart driver and hard worker."

"Is he on the road for you right now?" Owen asked.

Urban nodded. "Had to take a load of fittings to LA. Been gone for two days."

"And before that?"

"He was off for a week after a trip down to southern California."

"When will he be back?" Owen's heart rate spiked over learning that Tovar was likely in town during the attack.

"Last time we talked, he was making good time. He's scheduled back early tomorrow. Around ten in the morning."

"What can you tell us about him?" Mackenzie's tone remained soft and non-threatening.

"What's to tell? He's a regular guy. In his late forties. Never married. Lives alone out in the boonies somewhere with his three dogs. Likes to hunt. Fish. A real outdoorsman when he's not driving."

Mackenzie shifted on her feet. "Any reason he never married?"

"Why? You interested?" Urban gave a deep belly laugh. "Okay, don't look at me like that. It was a joke. He's pretty easy-going, and I don't think he'd be real difficult to live with, so don't think that's the issue. Maybe he just never found the right woman."

The white pickup idling outside Ernie's bar came to mind. "What kind of personal vehicle does he drive?"

"Pickup. Older model Ram."

"Color?"

"White."

"What about his build?"

"I don't know. Six feet. Two-twenty or so."

"He wear glasses?"

"For driving, yeah."

Owen wanted to shove a fist up as this fit the description of the man who attacked him, but he resisted the urge. "I'll need his home address."

Urban sat forward, his eyes tightened. "Sorry. I think I've

said enough. You need one of them whatchamacallits that makes me say more."

Owen shoved his hands in his pockets. "You mean a warrant?"

"Yeah. Yeah." Urban nodded. "That's what I mean. The owner's a real stickler for following personnel rules so he don't get sued."

"I can get a warrant." Owen planted his feet and eyed the guy. "But I don't think you want to make me do that. I'll be granted access to all of your personnel files, and your owner probably won't like what I turn up. Maybe some immigration issues and undocumented workers will come to light."

"Fine." Urban grabbed a pen and paper. He flipped through an old-fashioned rotating card file and wrote down the information for Owen. He held it out, a surly scowl on his face.

"Thank you for your cooperation." Owen took out a business card and dropped it on the desk. "I would appreciate you not telling him that we're looking for him, and when he returns, give me a call so I know he's back in town."

Urban jutted out his chin. "You'd appreciate it, or you're forbidding me from calling him?"

"Forbidding." Owen spun and motioned for Mackenzie to go in front of him.

In the truck, he got on the phone to his lieutenant. "I need you to run a Hobert Tovar through the database for me."

"Gotta give me a reason to run someone," Sage said. "Can't just do it because you ask."

Owen brought his supervisor up to speed, which he needed to do anyway. "The guy could've been the last person to see Cassie alive."

"Can't think of a much better reason than that," Sage said. "Hold on."

Owen tapped a thumb on the steering wheel and counted. He'd hit two minutes when Sage came back on the call. "Guy's clean as a whistle. Has a commercial license and hasn't got a single ticket. Don't think I've ever seen that."

"So he's extra careful."

"Sounds like it."

"But why?"

"That's a good question. I know you're going to get to the bottom of it."

"What about home address and vehicles registered to him?" Owen got a notepad out of the console to jot down the information.

Sage rattled off the address, confirming the information Urban had provided. "First vehicle's a white '98 Ram pickup. His commercial rigs are 2021 Kenworth T800 sleeper truck tractor in red and a 2016 Great Dane dry van trailer."

"I'll update you as soon as I have any news." Owen hung up and relayed the information to Mackenzie.

"Tovar could just be an exemplary driver, I guess," she said. "But I find it as odd as your lieutenant did."

"Red flag for me too. Especially for as many years as Tovar's been driving." Owen looked at her. "He's a strong lead for me now. Especially since he fits my attackers build and that he likes to hunt and lives out in the boonies by himself where he could've killed Cassie and no one would know, then dumped her body in the desert."

"My thoughts exactly." Her eyes narrowed. "We should get Nick to do a deep dive on the guy. Leach too."

"I doubt he'll turn anything up on Leach that I didn't find for the Bussey investigation, but I'm not infallible. Pretty close though." He laughed.

She wrinkled her nose and got out her phone. "I'll get Nick working on it. Hopefully his report will help us prove that one of these guys is Cassie's killer."

～

The drive in the black of night back to Mackenzie's rental raised her awareness of the danger in her surroundings. With Owen behind the wheel, she was free to watch the wide-open desert spread out before her, going on for miles and miles. What had she been thinking all these years? Why had she rented a place so far from everything? Sure she'd been a law enforcement officer and safe for years, but Owen landing on her doorstep might just change her future vacation plans.

He pulled his truck to a stop in the circular portion of the driveway that led to the walkway. The moon barely shone a beam of light from behind heavy clouds as she opened her door. She hadn't thought to leave the cabin's outside lights on. The lights were activated by a motion sensor, but required a switch to be turned on. She hadn't wanted an animal skulking past and setting it off the night she'd arrived, so she'd flipped it off to get a solid night's sleep.

He looked at her. "If you'll give me the cabin keys, I can get the lights turned on."

"Not necessary." She slid from the truck and gripped her jacket closed against the freezing night air.

Crack.

A rifle report fractured the quiet.

A sharp sting pierced her arm. Fierce, breath-stealing pain.

She'd been hit.

She dropped to the ground, dust rising up to her face. Pain radiated up her arm and panic consumed her.

She gasped for breath.

"Mackenzie?" Owen called out, his voice frantic. "Are you okay?"

She opened her mouth to reply but couldn't catch her breath.

A bullet! She'd been hit by a bullet! Really and truly hit.

She inhaled deeper. Let it out.

That's it. In. Out. In. Out. Now think. Think!

"I'm fine." She clutched her arm. Blood seeped from her sleeve and coated her fingers. Was she really fine? No vital organs hit of course, but what about arteries? She didn't know her anatomy. Could she bleed out?

No. Please. No.

Another shot rang out, the bullet piercing the other side of the truck with a solid ping. The side near Owen.

"Owen!" she screamed. "Are you hurt?"

"Fine." His voice came from low to the ground. "You still doing okay?"

"Took a bullet to my arm." She hated how terrified she sounded. "Not sure how bad it is."

"I've pinpointed where the shots came from," he yelled back. "We should be safe at the front of the truck. Can you get around there?"

"Yes," she answered, but had no idea if she could actually fight the wooziness threatening to take her under.

"We trained you," she heard her grandad and dad say. *"You can do this. Keep your head and act rationally."*

They were right. Her panic was what was threatening to take her out. Not the pain.

She breathed in. Out. In. Then rolled to her belly and used one arm to army crawl backwards to the safe zone. She inched back. Slow but sure, reaching the front of the tire.

Owen met her on her side. He was also on his stomach.

Another rifle report. The bullet hit the dirt by her head. She cried out.

"Hold tight." Owen grabbed her good hand, clutching with a death grip, dragging her the final distance to safety.

She rolled over and sat up. The area swam before her eyes.

"Is the bleeding under control?" Owen asked, his tone calmer now.

The blood's warmth continued to seep into her jacket, but she didn't think the wound was life-threatening. "It'll be fine. Where do you think the shooter is positioned?"

"To our south. Just moved though to get off that last shot. Probably behind the barn or in it."

"Plan?" she asked as she didn't have the presence of thought to come up with one.

"Only two options. Stand to try to draw and return fire. Or call 911 and hunker down here until a deputy arrives."

"Drawing fire's too risky." *Especially with me only having one arm to use.*

"My thoughts too. What's the address here?"

She shared it with him, and he called 911. His phone must be set to dark mode as it emitted very little light.

"This is Detective Owen Greer with Clark County Sheriff's Office." He shared his badge number. "I'm taking gunfire at a rental cabin." He rattled off the address. "Suspect is likely located at the barn. We're out of the line of fire at the moment, on the ground in front of my pickup truck, but that could change. One person injured."

He listened, tapping his foot on the ground.

"See that they do." He ended the call and lowered his phone. "A deputy's a few minutes out, and they've made our call a priority."

A vehicle's motor roaring to life came from the barn area. They would both have to stand to be able to see the barn, risking their lives. Without discussing it, neither of them moved, but she cocked her head to listen.

The engine rumbled. Lights cut into the night. Tires raced over the gravel drive, heading away from the house.

"He's leaving," she said.

Owen shot to his feet to glance around the side of his truck then ducked back. "It's a full-sized pickup. Light color. Maybe white. Plates are caked with dirt. It could be the same vehicle I saw idling outside the restaurant when I got the map. It was gone when we left."

"Tovar and Leach both drive white trucks," she said.

"So could be one of them."

"Could be, but I'll bet a search of the DMV records would reveal plenty of white trucks in the area. I once read it's the number one color choice in pickups." Pain shot up her arm, and she clutched it tighter so she didn't cry out and raise Owen's concern even higher.

"It's possible."

"Makes me shiver to think he could have been following us from the restaurant, and we didn't know it."

"Yeah, it's unnerving."

"I hope the deputy intercepts him on the road on the way in."

"That could happen, but I suspect the shooter's smart enough to know that we called this in and is probably traveling off-road by now." He met her gaze. "I'll call an ambulance for your arm."

"Not necessary. It's only a scratch and the bleeding seems to have stopped."

"No need to be the hero here. I know what it's like to take a bullet."

She flashed her gaze up to him. "You do?"

"The cross tattoo." He tapped his shoulder. "Got it to cover the wound. Reminds me that God protected me that day."

"How did it happen?"

He took a long breath as if the story still troubled him. "Long story short, I served a warrant on a guy who had no priors for violence, and he didn't want to go to jail. Plugged me in the shoulder before my partner took him down."

"I'm sorry you had to go through that."

"I didn't think it was bad, but I ended up needing surgery." He looked at her but she couldn't make out his expression in the shadowy light. "Now I know we need to treat all gunshot wounds seriously. If you won't let me call an ambulance, then I'll drive you to the ER after the deputy arrives and releases us."

"I—"

He flashed up his hand. "Save your breath. I'm taking you and that's it. End of discussion."

She wanted to argue, but what was the point? He'd made up his mind. She didn't know a tremendous amount about him yet, but she knew when he decided to do something, he would follow through. Besides, he was right. She needed to have her arm looked at.

She'd been shot for goodness' sake. As much as she wanted to pretend she hadn't. To pretend she was shrewd enough to outsmart this evil villain and had strong skills to avoid danger. Sometimes danger came calling and there was nothing a person, even the most skilled in evasion tactics, could do about it and innocent people could die.

15

Owen wanted to punch the wall of the ER room. He should've been the one to take the bullet not Mackenzie. She had nothing to do with Cassie's murder, other than she'd rented a house in the wrong location. He was in her debt for all the care she'd provided for him, and this was the way he repaid her? By not keeping her safe?

Unacceptable.

Well, he could help make up for that now by ensuring she got the best medical attention, and supporting her in her pain. He would do whatever it took to help her out.

His phone rang. Talk about bad timing. He wanted to ignore the call, but it could be about the investigation. He had to answer. "Detective Greer."

"This is Ernie. You know, from the restaurant. I got your picture. Yeah, that's the guy who was hassling the woman you showed me all right. No question."

Tovar just shot to the top of Owen's suspect list even if the guy was supposedly out of town and couldn't have been shooting at him and Mackenzie at the house. But just because Urban said Tovar was out of town, didn't mean he was. He could have driven through the night, pretending to his boss that he was still on the road so he had an alibi for the shooting. Would be easy enough to do, though it would break the driving laws.

And even if he didn't shoot at them, didn't mean he didn't kill Cassie. Leach could be the shooter because he feared being arrested for Bussey's murder.

"I also located the day she was in here," Ernie said.

"And?" Owen held his breath and willed Ernie to say the day Cassie disappeared. When he mentioned a date a few weeks later, Owen blinked as he tried to process the news. His sister had been alive for *weeks* after going missing. "Say that again."

Ernie repeated the date. She hadn't been abducted right away as Owen had always believed. Was Ernie the last person other than Cassie's killer, to see her alive? Could be.

"Is that helpful?" Ernie asked.

"Very." Thoughts bounced like ping-pong balls through Owen's brain. "Do you know where she was staying?"

"No, and as far as I know, she didn't talk to anyone other than to shoot this guy down and order her dinner."

"What did she order?"

"I remember because it was a kid's meal. She had mac and cheese, chicken nuggets, and applesauce. Adults don't often order those."

Owen wasn't surprised. Cassie loved macaroni and cheese.

"Thanks, Ernie. Text me a picture of that receipt, please." Owen ended the call and shared the news with Mackenzie.

"Wow. Where was she staying all that time?"

Owen shrugged. "Now more than ever I want to talk to Tovar as soon as possible."

"Hopefully, he'll be back when Urban said he would be."

"What if he's already back and was the guy who shot at us?"

Mackenzie blinked her long lashes. "It's possible, right?"

Owen nodded.

The door opened, and an older nurse with glasses on a chain around her neck hurried into the room and handed a gown to Mackenzie. "Get undressed from the waist up and put this on. Opening in the back."

Mackenzie smiled at the woman. "Will do."

"I'll return with supplies, and the doctor will be in shortly." The nurse spun and exited the small room as fast as she'd entered.

Mackenzie stared at the gown.

Owen really wanted to stay and make sure she was okay, but she wouldn't want to get undressed in front of him. "I guess this is when I need to leave the room."

"Actually, I need some help getting my jacket off."

"Of course." He gently removed the sleeve on her non-wounded arm first and then moved to the injured side. He cringed at the blood saturating the fabric and prayed once the wound was revealed that the bullet hadn't done serious damage to a muscle or tendon.

"I'm not sure I can do my shirt either, but I'm not getting undressed in front of you." She blushed a crimson red. "Maybe you could go get the nurse."

"I can do it and still make sure you're covered."

She clutched the gown like a shield. "How's that possible?"

"Once when my parents were out of town, Cassie got appendicitis, and I had to help her get into a gown too. She didn't want to undress in front of me, but she was in too much pain to do it on her own, so I figured out a way."

He gently removed the gown from her hands. "You can slide this under the front of your shirt, and I'll tie it behind your neck. Then I can release your uninjured arm and you can slide it into the gown under your shirt. After I pull it closed in the back, you can do the injured arm too. Then I pull your shirt over your head, and you're fully covered the whole time."

"Sounds sort of like the way the shy girls changed out for PE." She gave him a soft smile. "Let's do it so we can get out of here faster."

He pulled the hem of her shirt forward, and she slipped the gown under. "Reach inside from the neck of your shirt with your good arm and pull it up for me."

She followed his directions, and he soon had the gown tied behind her neck and her uninjured arm inside.

He moved around the bed to her wounded side. "Hopefully the sleeve hasn't dried to your skin but this might hurt.
"

"Go ahead and treat it like a Band-Aid. Rip it off and get the pain over with."

"You're taking this quite well."

"There's not much I can do about it, so why not make the best of it?"

Her positive attitude told him a lot about her. "Most people would milk it for all it's worth. I respect your attitude."

She smiled at him again, and it warmed him clear through. She was quite a woman. She possessed many qualities he admired. How could such a fantastic woman possibly still be single? Obviously, it was her choice because there had to be any number of men who would want to marry her. Maybe had even proposed in the past. He didn't like that thought, but what was he going to do about it?

Nothing, that's what.

He pulled the soft fabric free from her arm. She gasped.

"Sorry." His word sounded trite even to his ears. Why couldn't he think of something better to say?

"Couldn't be helped." She sounded positive, but gritted her teeth together.

"Can you slide your arm out?" he asked.

"I'll try."

She slowly pulled her arm toward her body, and he helped by tugging the sleeve free. She held the gown in place with her other arm as he helped direct her injured arm into the sleeve. He got his first look at the long gaping open wound slicing across her arm in an angry red stripe. He didn't know how deep the injury went, but at least a half inch of flesh was exposed. He had to swallow hard to keep from uttering something he didn't want to say. Instead, he lifted her shirt over her head and fastened the last tie on her gown and stepped back.

"Thank you. I couldn't have done that without help." She smiled again, but it wobbled this time.

Likely the pain.

He reached for her hand, but the door opened before he could connect. The same nurse bustled into the space carrying an IV fluid bag. "Let's get this going so we can get some pain meds onboard."

"I don't need pain meds," Mackenzie said.

"You're in pain," Owen said. "Please don't say no."

She shook her head. "I don't want my judgment to be cloudy for when we go back to the cabin."

As much as he wanted her to be more comfortable, he understood her motive. He would do the same. He doubted anyone was lying in wait for them again, especially if there was still a police presence, but stranger things had happened. Holding his tongue was a struggle.

"Your choice," the nurse said. "But it's standard proce-dure to start an IV."

"Go ahead." Mackenzie looked like she wanted to roll her eyes, but restrained herself.

The nurse set to work inserting the needle in the crook of Mackenzie's arm and connected the IV bag.

The same young doctor that Owen had seen earlier in the week stepped in. He glanced at Owen. "You again. How's the memory?"

"Nearly all restored," Owen said.

"Glad to hear it."

"I guess he's the doctor who treated you," Mackenzie said.

Owen nodded.

The doctor approached the bed. "Ms. Steele? I'm Doctor Patterson. Tell me what brings you to the ER tonight."

Mackenzie pointed at her wound and explained the shooting, leaving out how she felt about it or if she'd been terrified, just shared matter-of-fact details.

Patterson looked between them. "The pair of you live dangerous lives."

"Turns out I'm a detective, and Ms. Steele is a former detective."

"Ah, these injuries make more sense then." Patterson moved to Mackenzie's side and examined the wound while the nurse finished adjusting the IV settings on the pump.

Mackenzie grimaced, and her whole body stiffened as she gripped the edge of the gurney with her good hand. She didn't cry out as the doctor poked and prodded around the wound, but she clamped her lips together.

The nurse finished and gave a satisfactory smile before stepping back.

Patterson stopped poking Mackenzie's arm and looked her square in the face. "You know I'm required to report a gunshot wound to the authorities."

"I know," Mackenzie said. "A deputy came out and took my statement so it won't be a surprise to them."

"Good. Good." The young doctor's shoulders relaxed. "Looks like you escaped with a minor injury when it could've been far worse."

Thank God for that.

"I don't want to downplay the injury, though," Patterson said. "This wound is still serious and deserves to be treated carefully. Your greatest risk is infection. We'll clean the wound with water, and then pack it with gauze and apply a bandage that you'll need to change twice a day."

Mackenzie gaped at him. "You aren't going to stitch it up?"

Owen got her unease. That was a huge wound to be left open.

Patterson scrubbed a hand over his face. "We don't like to close surface gunshot wounds. The bullet isn't clean and it can leave bacteria in the wound. Suturing it traps the bacteria in place. If we leave the wound open, you can irrigate it twice a day with clean water to wash out any bacteria that might form. I'll also prescribe a preventative antibiotic."

Mackenzie frowned. "Sounds gross, but okay."

Owen agreed. Sounded gross. But he wouldn't comment and make things worse for her. She would need help changing that bandage, and gross or not, he would be right at her side taking care of it each time it needed changing.

The doctor performed a similar neurological exam to the one he'd done on Owen. Then he looked at her. "The nurse will clean and pack the wound for you, but I see nothing else to be concerned about. I'll give you a prescription for pain medication, but please take it only if you need it."

"I probably won't even fill it, but we'll see how it goes."

The doctor gave a tight smile. "Any questions?"

Mackenzie shook her head. "I think it's pretty straight-forward, right?"

"Yes. Exactly." His smile broadened. "It was nice to meet you, Ms. Steele."

He offered his hand for a fist bump. She obliged him. He nodded at Owen and departed.

The nurse patted Mackenzie's knee. "Let me grab the supplies I need, and I'll be right back."

She marched out of the room.

"She reminds me of the Energizer Bunny." Owen worked hard to smile when he still wanted to punch that wall.

Mackenzie smiled. "That wasn't so bad. Thank you for all your help."

"Shoulda been me."

"Shouldn't have been either of us." She didn't look away. "You think this was Leach or Tovar?"

"Either one, I guess. Both are hunters. Looked like a large caliber slug in my truck door."

"Rifle."

"Exactly." He shoved his hands into his pockets as the wall tempted him again. "I'm glad the sheriff agreed to bring Sierra back to process the scene in the morning and the ballistic guy too. What's his name again?"

"Grady Houston. He has the slug Sierra located in the desert and will be able to compare them."

Owen had considered this but figured he had to be reaching. "You think whoever killed Cassie is still using the same rifle?"

She shrugged then winced in pain and stopped. "I've seen criminals do dumber things than that."

"Me too."

The nurse rushed back in, carrying cleaning and bandaging supplies. "Let's get that cleaned out, so you can be on your way. Pay attention to my procedure as you'll need to follow it twice a day."

"Thank you," Mackenzie said cheerfully but reached out for Owen's hand and clenched it tightly.

He would do just about anything at the moment to take her pain away. To be the one lying in that bed.

Please, let her pain diminish and don't let the wound become infected.

The nurse irrigated the wound, and Mackenzie's whole body tensed as if in a complete body muscle spasm. She tightened her grip with an iron force and looked up at him.

He couldn't stand by and not comfort her. He stroked her head, loving her silky hair. "It'll be over soon."

Her mouth trembled and tears came to her eyes. He bent closer. "Breathe. In. Out. Deep. Repeat."

He started breathing in a deep pattern, and she soon copied him. Her body relaxed.

"All clean," the nurse announced. "Let's get that bandage in place."

She pressed the remote, and the bed motor whirred to life, the head of the bed rising. Mackenzie continued to hold his hand, but he took a step back.

The nurse efficiently packed the gauze and wrapped the wound. "We'll send you home with a few days' supplies, but then you'll need to get some at the pharmacy."

The doctor poked his head into the room. "All finished in here?"

"She's good to go except for removing the IV," the nurse said.

"Be sure you keep the wound dry for three days," Patterson said. "Come back if there's any sign of infection such as redness, swelling, increased pain, or fever."

"Will do."

He backed from the room.

The nurse removed the IV. What a waste, but Owen knew it was protocol. Mackenzie had to be frustrated that the IV was coming out less than thirty minutes since the nurse put it in, but on the bright side, the ER staff were working fast to get her released.

"Go ahead and get dressed, and I'll get your discharge paperwork going." She stepped outside.

"Want to reverse dress with my help?"

"Yes, please."

He stepped to her and hated putting on the blood-soaked shirt, but they had no option. They worked together, and when the nurse returned with discharge instructions, Mackenzie only needed to put on her jacket.

The nurse explained everything in detail then put the paperwork and bandages in a plastic bag. "Any questions?"

Mackenzie shook her head.

"Then you're free to go." The nurse smiled and exited the room.

He grabbed Mackenzie's jacket.

"I was a deputy for years and was never shot." She shook her head. "I leave the force—and that's when I'm hit. Crazy."

All his fault. He would like to persuade her to stay home tomorrow. Sit by the fire and relax. She wouldn't of course. Meant he would have to do better. Step up his game. Make sure Ryan stepped his up too, because when they headed into the desert in search of Leach...

They would be exposed.

Mackenzie didn't know what to make of the sight ahead of her as she and Owen pulled off the road into her rental property driveway. His body rigid, Ryan stood facing Deputy

Dahl at the end of the drive, their posture rigid and angry as if they might come to blows.

"What do you think's going on there?" Owen asked from the driver's seat of her car.

"Park and let's find out." Mackenzie hated to see Ryan so upset. As soon as Owen stopped, she got out and approached the pair.

"Ms. Steele is expecting me." Ryan crossed his arms.

"It's okay, Deputy Dahl," Mackenzie said. "He's right. I am expecting him."

Dahl nodded. "We aren't letting anyone into the cordoned off area until after your forensic team gets here and processes the scene. Means you'll have to leave your vehicles here and walk in."

"Cordoned off area?" Ryan asked.

"I'll explain later," Mackenzie said.

"Are you expecting anyone else?" Dahl asked.

"No." Mackenzie put her good arm through Ryan's and led him back to her car.

Owen got out to join them, and she told Ryan about the shooting.

He ran his gaze over her. "You okay?"

"Fine."

"She's in a lot of pain but won't admit it," Owen said.

Ryan looked at Owen. "You probably figured out by now that she's pretty stubborn."

"Oh, I have. Trust me."

"Um. I'm right here." She chuckled. "Let's go inside and plan our trip tomorrow."

"You're not still going," Ryan said.

"Of course I am." She led the way around the crime scene tape, ignoring the bullet hole in Owen's truck. Her arm seemed to ache more as she skirted the scene. Probably a mental reaction to the location where the bullet had pierced her arm. She picked up her pace and got the cabin door open.

A sigh for making it home okay slipped out before she could stop it. She looked at the guys. "I'm going to make a cup of tea. Anyone want one or anything to drink?"

"I'll grab a glass of water." Owen joined her in the kitchen. "And if you go sit down and tell me how to make your tea, I'll do that too."

"I'm not helpless."

"I know. I just want to help."

"Let him do it if he wants to," Ryan said, coming in for his own water. "Besides, it might be fun to watch him fumble around in the kitchen."

Mackenzie rolled her eyes and looked at Owen. "Start by boiling water in the kettle on the stove."

She reached for the canister of teabags that she'd brought from home. "Then dump one of these in the cup and pour the boiling water over it. That's it. Simple."

"Yeah, I can do that." He gave her a flirtatious smile.

Did he know how he was looking at her? It was the same look he'd given her a few times since the injury. Was he interested in something with her? At some point, she'd have to figure that all out and how she felt about it, but not tonight when her arm ached so badly. It was all she could do to pretend she wasn't in serious agony.

She took a moment to go to her bedroom and change her shirt then came back to sit on the sofa by Ryan.

She faced him. "Have you had a chance to look at where we're going tomorrow?"

Ryan nodded. "And in the light of your attack, I think I better get my brothers to go with us. We would benefit from some overwatch."

"You're that worried?" Mackenzie asked.

"He has a reason to be." Owen stepped into the space

but didn't sit. "I would rest easier if we had additional support too."

"Then it's settled." Ryan got out his phone. "I'm sure they can drop whatever they're doing and get here by morning."

Ryan stepped to the far side of the room to make his call, and Owen dropped onto the sofa, his gaze alert and watchful. He was more worried for their safety than she'd been, but her concern was growing by leaps and bounds now.

"I'm gonna look up Tovar's address. See if it tells me anything about him." He got out the piece of paper from Urban and typed the address into his phone.

She doubted just looking at Tovar's property would tell them anything, but she appreciated that he was distracted from fully focusing on her. She felt helpless sitting there, and she didn't want free time to think about the pain either. When the kettle whistled she went to tend to it.

Owen lurched to his feet. "Hey, I got that."

She waved her hand. "Go ahead and keep looking at Tovar's place. I want to pick out my tea anyway."

In the kitchen, she opened the canister and located a bag of chamomile. She didn't need caffeine, and chamomile was soothing, plus she really liked it. She turned off the stove, poured the water over the teabag, and the calming aroma filled the air. After the water turned a rich color, she discarded the bag, went to sit with Owen, and set her mug on the table to cool.

She heard Ryan say goodbye to his brothers, and he returned to the living room. He dropped into a leather easy chair. "They'll be here by nine."

Owen shook his head. "Just like that? No questions asked and they come running?"

Ryan nodded. "That's what brothers are for."

"I always wanted a brother," Owen said. "Cassie is my

only sibling. Correction *was* my only sibling." His voice broke.

Mackenzie had to fight not to take his hand. But she wouldn't do anything in front of Ryan to make him think she and Owen were more than associates working an investigation. There was no way she wanted to point the focus on them when the emphasis needed be on their trip to the wilderness tomorrow and on praying that Leach wasn't planning an ambush.

16

Mackenzie approached Ryan and his older brothers Russ and Reid, making sure not to show any pain from her gunshot wound even though it throbbed like the drumbeat of a marching band. The men stood near the house in the morning sunshine, organizing packs when Mackenzie and Owen stepped outside. Ryan and the middle brother, Russ, both had dishwater blond hair, but Reid's hair was dark as the desert nights. Russ was the biggest of the three men, really built. Reid and Ryan were of similar muscular yet more wiry builds.

She introduced Owen and watched as the men sized each other up. Having grown up with mostly girls, she'd had a lot to learn about men. Her eyes had been opened in law enforcement where sizing up of the other guy was commonplace.

Reid was the first to break free and look at Mackenzie. "Good to see you again, Mac. How long has it been since you and your family were regular campers?"

"I refuse to answer on the grounds that it would make me sound really old." She laughed.

Reid and Ryan laughed with her, but Russ barely

cracked a smile. He'd always been the serious one. Ryan was the joker. Reid had a good balance of both. Seemed as if that hadn't changed.

"Are you ready to get going?" Russ asked.

Ryan rolled his eyes. "To the point as always."

Russ eyed his brother. "Something wrong with that?"

"Nope. Just saying."

"Let me grab my bag and then I'm ready," Mackenzie said.

"Ditto," Owen said.

She started to turn, but Ryan gently clasped her wrist. "There's no shame in sitting this out."

"Would you if you were me?"

"No, but..."

"But you're a big tough guy, and I'm just a girl." She jutted her chin at him.

He grinned. "And suddenly we're back to when we first met and you had to prove you could do anything I could do."

"And did I?" She challenged him with a look to tell the truth.

"Yeah, and sometimes better." He laughed and released her wrist.

She headed for the cabin, and Owen continued on to the guest house. Inside the cabin, she stepped past the duffel bags Ryan had dropped inside while she and Owen had been changing her bandage. She made quick work of using the restroom then grabbed her backpack, but on the way out, stopped to pack crispy chocolate chip cookies her gran had sent back with her. The guys had brought MREs, but they would appreciate the treats.

Owen was waiting for her with the other guys. The moment they saw her, they silently hefted their packs loaded with overnight gear. Owen had grabbed a Kevlar vest and rifle from his truck and was clipping handcuffs on his belt.

Ryan looked back at her. "We'll take both vehicles so we have two UTV's on the end. You and Owen can ride with me, and we'll let these two bozos drive by themselves."

"Bozos?" Reid put Ryan in a chokehold and knuckled his head. "I can still take you if needed, so watch who you're calling names."

Russ glanced between them. "And I can take the pair of you, so do what he said."

She laughed at the brothers. She'd loved summers spent watching them interact. They might be more than fifteen years older now but still boys at heart. Quite an accomplishment since they'd experienced tragedies and hardships. All of them seeing tough things in their law enforcement careers, but Reid especially, losing his wife to cancer and now raising a daughter by himself.

Mackenzie gave credit for their ability to remain young at heart to their wonderful parents and the slower lifestyle of Shadow Lake that had to help restore them all when they'd moved back home to start Shadow Lake Survival.

Owen opened the passenger door for Mackenzie. "You take the front. More leg room."

"You have longer legs." She slid into the back seat instead.

Owen mumbled something that included the word stubborn and climbed in front.

It wasn't that she liked riding in the back. She couldn't see any potential danger as well, but her smaller size made her better able to fit. Not to mention she was with four very capable guys. If danger lurked, they would spot it. And since she was in back, they were less likely to see her grimaces of pain that she was sure the rutted roads would bring.

Ryan got behind the wheel. "I'll get flak from my

brothers for wasting time if I get lost, so I already put the coordinates in my map program."

She leaned forward. "It's fun to see the three of you together again."

"Yeah, we're a real laugh riot." He grinned in the mirror and cranked the powerful engine.

She sat back while he got the vehicle on the main road and watched out the window as the miles flew by. "We really need a plan for when we get there."

"Way ahead of you," Ryan said. "My brothers scout the area while we wait in the vehicle."

"If Leach has an ambush planned," Owen said. "I should be the one to take fire. Not them."

"Besides," Mackenzie said. "Leach might be lying in wait, not fire on Russ and Reid, and wait for us to appear."

"Could be. But unless you both have wilderness survival skills that you didn't demonstrate yesterday, my brothers know how to work this kind of terrain better than you do. If they take fire, they can also take cover much faster."

"True," Mackenzie admitted, though she didn't want to sit back and wait.

"Let us do this for you," Ryan said, his tone conciliatory. "If at any time they determine it's better for you to be on the trail, then they'll let us know, and we can join them."

"Okay," Mackenzie said. "I don't like it, but I'll agree."

"I'll reluctantly agree as well." Owen looked at his phone. "No cell service. Can I use your SAT phone to update my lieutenant?"

Ryan handed it over to Owen.

They fell silent, and Mackenzie listened in as Owen brought Lieutenant Sage up to speed on the investigation. Ryan seemed to be listening too as he maneuvered the truck down winding roads. Owen gave a concise update, and his call ended in a matter of minutes. She waited for him to speak, but he shifted to watch out the windows.

She didn't bother him or Ryan for the remainder of the drive but checked her email on Ryan's SAT phone and found a report from Nick on Leach and Tovar in her inbox. Hoping to see a strong lead, she carefully read each report then slid forward between the seats. "I got Nick's report on Leach and Tovar. Nothing we didn't already know, but he said he's still running algorithms and could have added information later."

"I don't get it," Owen said. "Potential murder suspects aren't usually this squeaky clean. They both have to be hiding something, and we're missing it."

"I get that feeling from Tovar for sure," she said.

"We have to work harder to prove it."

She didn't see how much harder they could work, but they reached their destination so she dropped the subject.

Ryan parked in an area overlooking the rugged trailhead. His brothers pulled in closer to the opening leading into the secluded hunting grounds. Russ and Reid got out and added earbuds for their communication devices to their ears.

Ryan put in an earbud too and clipped a mic to his shirt. He bent his head foreword. "Yeah, I read you loud and clear, bro. Check in every five minutes. No exceptions."

The men put on Kevlar vests and strapped on sidearms. Russ withdrew a rifle from a padded case. He gave Ryan a salute, and the pair set off down the trail. Ryan got binoculars out from the center console and rested his hands on the steering wheel to peer out the front window.

Time ticked by slowly. The air in the truck seemed to evaporate.

"I don't like this waiting," Mackenzie said. "How far will they go before determining it's safe?"

"Based on our review of the satellite footage, they'll keep hiking until they get a visual on Leach's campsite. If they spot him, and he's not on the offensive, they'll give us the all clear."

"Means we could be sitting here for some time," Owen said.

"Yeah, but they'll report in regularly, and that will help."

Owen looked at Ryan. "You and your brothers seem to know what you're doing."

Ryan snorted. "You sound surprised."

"I didn't mean it that way. It was a compliment. Maybe I'll take some survival classes with you when this is all over."

"Be glad to have you. Not that you need many survival skills in the metro area. But the big one is coming, and we can help with that."

Though Mackenzie didn't want to think about it, he meant that Oregon residents should be preparing for a big earthquake that statistics said was overdue.

Mackenzie thought about how the last few days had played out. "I'll come too. I was looking for peace and quiet on this trip and got adventure. If I'm hoping to do more adventurous things in the future, does that mean I'll only get the peace and quiet?" She laughed.

Ryan joined in. "You always were the risk taker of the family."

"I've lost that and want to get some of it back."

Owen looked over the seat. "Nothing wrong with being risk averse. Means whoever's in a relationship with you doesn't have to worry."

"No relationship planned."

"Oh, come on." Ryan rolled his eyes in the mirror. "The chemistry between you two is like mixing a beaker of the wrong items in a chemistry lab. Ready to explode at any time."

Mackenzie didn't know how to respond. Owen obviously didn't either as he clamped his lips closed and turned back to the front.

"Fine," Ryan said. "Keep ignoring it. Why, I don't know. You're two single consenting adults who could find happiness together." Ryan touched his microphone and tilted his head. "Roger that."

"Your brothers?" Owen asked.

Ryan nodded. "They're moving out of sight. No sign of Leach." He lifted his binoculars. "You really think he's your guy, or are you liking the truck driver more?"

"Tovar might be a better suspect right now. He was seen with Cassie and threatened her. Leach wasn't, but I'm liking him for the murder of my Vancouver victim and the attack two nights ago."

"Still, it could just be about that for him." Ryan looked at Owen. "Nothing to do with your sister, right?"

"Right," Owen mumbled.

"We won't know until we get face time with him," Mackenzie said. "Which should hopefully be soon."

"And I hope we recover evidence that concretely points to Leach as our killer in both investigations." Owen patted his backpack sitting on the floor. "I brought along evidence bags and disposable gloves in case we need them."

"Good planning." Ryan suddenly came alert and listened. "My brothers have the campsite in view. No one's there. Which means they can't confirm it's Leach's site. What do you want to do?"

Owen jerked open the door and shouldered his backpack. "We're going in."

∽

Ryan handed Mackenzie a Kevlar vest, something she wished she didn't have need of. But they could be heading into danger, so she quickly put it on and fastened the Velcro. It was big but would still protect her. She double-checked the clip in her sidearm, and after Owen grabbed a rifle, the three of them set off.

Scrub dried from the nearly rainless fall and winter dotted the flat ground. Every step they took kicked up dust that faded into the clear blue sky. The temperatures hovered around fifty degrees with a cool breeze blowing across the landscape.

Ryan led the way, following numbered flags on steel posts his brothers had inserted into the ground. He carried a heavy pack, and Owen had another pack Ryan provided strapped to his back. Owen seemed to have recovered from his attack and was moving along at a great clip.

She carried her belongings in her own backpack. It jostled her arm, radiating pain and leaving her struggling to keep up. The terrain turned more rugged, and they had to scale boulders. Her arm complained, but she bit her tongue to keep from crying out and slowing them down.

Ryan set a fast pace, but all three of them continued to survey the landscape, looking for danger. They reached a narrow pass in the large boulders, and Ryan raised his hand. He pointed at an outcropping nearby where the glint of metal flashed in the sun.

"Take cover. Now!" He scrambled behind a butte.

Owen helped Mackenzie move into the space and followed behind. A gunshot broke the quiet. The bullet hit the wall behind him and splintered the rock formation. Birds flapped into the air.

Her heart leapt into gear.

Ryan pressed his mic. "We're under fire." He glanced out. "Flag sixteen."

Ryan listened intently. "We'll hold. Let us know when to move."

He turned to Owen and Mackenzie. "My brothers will approach from the west and take a few potshots at the shooter to draw his attention. That'll allow us to circle back and move in behind him. Be ready to go. We'll have to move fast."

"The shooter wants me," Owen said. "I'll give you both a head start and bring up the rear."

"No!" Mackenzie shook her head. "I won't let you make yourself a target. We all go together, or we don't go at all."

"Agreed," Ryan said. "No need to be a hero. My brothers will keep him busy, giving us plenty of time to move. Let's get into position. Owen first. Mac in the middle. I'll have the back."

Owen frowned at Ryan, but he slipped past Mackenzie, squeezing her good arm and giving her a warm look as he eased by.

She smiled at Owen. "It'll be okay. We'll *all* be okay."

He nodded but his expression remained uncertain. "Stay near me, but leave a bit of room in case he does fire on me."

She nodded, not wanting to think about that happening, but knowing she had to be prepared for it.

Gunshots rang out. Peppering the rocks above.

"Move!" Ryan shouted.

Owen took off. Mackenzie and Ryan charged after him.

He kept glancing back at her. He needed to stop doing that or he might fall.

Rifle reports exploded in the air, but they didn't take any fire.

"Cut across now," Ryan called out.

Owen veered to the right, and they swiftly moved over rugged terrain to the tall outcropping where Leach had taken a stand. Owen eased along the face of the rock wall until they'd passed Leach's location. Owen pressed his back against the wall. She and Ryan joined him. They stood there, one with the rocks, and panted for breath.

Ryan pressed his mic. "We're in position to climb the butte and take the guy. Keep distracting him."

The firing stopped then resumed in earnest. One bullet after another.

Boom. Ping. Boom. Ping.

Rock peppered the air in every direction.

Breathing normal now, Owen looked at them. "Ready to move?"

"I am," she replied, eager to get cuffs on Leach.

"Me too," Ryan said. "When we get near, I'll take a stand to cover you, and you can make the arrest."

"Roger that," Owen said.

"I'll have your back too," she said. "But won't interfere in the arrest, so it can't be called into question."

Owen gave a sharp nod. "We go on three."

He lifted his fingers to count. His third finger rose. He took off. They climbed over larger boulders, scrambling on all fours at times, while taking turns on overwatch to protect the others.

They crested the top of the butte.

The roar of a UTV sounded, and Leach piloted the vehicle over the ridge, fast heading away from them.

"No!" Mackenzie raced ahead until she had a good view of the UTV. She drew her handgun, but he wasn't brandishing a weapon, and she couldn't fire on a man who wasn't threatening her life.

He turned and drew his handgun.

"No!" Owen yelled.

She searched for cover.

Leach popped off a shot. The bullet whizzed by her head.

Another pop of the handgun.

Owen tackled her, holding her tightly in his arms. They rolled and rolled, her arm screaming in pain. The cliff edge loomed ahead.

"The edge!" she screamed and tried to change course but failed. "We're going to go over."

Owen's muscles tensed. His feet gained purchase. He jerked his body hard but held her tight. He reversed their course. Whipping them away from the cliff. They rolled to a stop in the other direction.

His body was crushing hers. Painful, but she'd never felt safer, even with the precipice three feet away.

"Got you covered," Ryan shouted. "Vehicle disappearing to the west."

Owen brushed the hair from her face. "Please tell me you're not hit."

"I'm not hit."

"You're sure you're okay?" He scanned her face.

"Yes, other than I can't breathe." Her voice sounded like a strangled cry.

He raised up on his forearms, but remained covering her.

She gulped in a breath and heard the rumble of the UTV's engine fade into the distance.

"Sorry." He scooted off and helped her to sit.

Ryan joined them. "Stay here. I'll head up the butte to take a better look and report back."

"Be careful." Owen looked like he wanted to go with Ryan but was hanging back because of her. "Ready to try standing?"

"Yeah, I'm good." Just embarrassed. "I'm sorry we didn't get him, but maybe Ryan and his brothers can track him down."

Owen gave a sharp nod, but his lips pressed together

confirmed his disappointment. "We need to get a forensic team out here to collect shells and slugs. We also need to request a warrant to search Leach's property."

Ryan jogged back to them. "My brothers are on their way, and we'll go after Leach. Now that he knows we're after him, we don't have to take a quiet approach. We'll get the drone in the air."

"Can I use your SAT phone to call the sheriff?" Owen asked. "I want to get a forensic team out here and a warrant going for Leach's property."

"Sure thing." Ryan got it out.

Owen stepped away to make his call.

Ryan looked at Mackenzie. "You doing okay?"

She nodded and watched Owen as he talked and grabbed the back of his neck.

"You're worried about him," Ryan said.

She kept her focus on Owen. "Is it that obvious?"

"Very," Ryan said.

She watched Owen shove a hand into his hair, looking like he wanted to pull it out. "He's desperate to find out who killed his sister, and it's eating away at him."

"And after losing Thomas, you know how that feels."

She shifted her attention to Ryan. "Not to the same extent. Seems like Owen thinks he's responsible for not protecting Cassie. Something I never felt for Thomas. So it's doubly hard on Owen."

Ryan tilted his head. "Can I make a suggestion?"

"Sure."

"Let me and my brothers go after the guy. We'll move faster and be more likely to find him." Ryan locked gazes. "You and Owen can go search Leach's place. That'll take Owen out of the danger in case he forgets to be careful."

"Like I just did, you mean."

"Didn't say that."

"But you were thinking it."

"Well, yeah." Ryan moved closer. "This offer is as much for you as Owen. You may not want to admit it, but you're personally invested in this too."

He was right. Of course he was, but as he'd said, she didn't really want to admit it because that meant admitting Owen had become important to her. "I don't know if Owen will go for that."

"Here's the thing," Ryan said. "Leach has worked this desert as a guide for years and knows every inch of the area. The odds that we're going to find him out here are pretty slim. Could take all night if we do. You could be better off searching his property and maybe finding something that could help pin the murders on him."

"Okay," she said, her gaze moving back to Owen as he paced over the dusty ground, his steps frantic and that hand still locked in his hair.

All she had to do was convince him to leave the area where they'd come under fire by the man they believed had killed his sister. Performing a miracle was likely easier.

17

Thankful Sierra had finished processing his truck, Owen pulled the vehicle into Leach's driveway. He searched the area and didn't like the look of it. Not at all. If Mackenzie's frown as she stared out the windshield told him anything, she was equally unsettled. Leach's house scored an eight on the scale of one to ten—ten being the worst—for the most difficult property to get to. They'd barely made it over rutted and washed-out dirt roads that were hardly passable to find this secluded property.

Ditto for Sheriff Wheeler and Deputy Dahl. Dirt and mud coated their cars parked by the front gate. The pair stood at the mouth of the driveway where overgrown weeds ran down the middle with abandon, and tire marks were worn into the dirt. Wheeler used a large pair of bolt cutters to clip the padlock securing the gate.

Owen idled his truck to wait for the men to gain access and drive onto the property. He looked at the no trespassing and beware of the dog signs posted in multiple locations on the fence and gate. They'd also been mounted on the fence leading to the property. "Leach seriously doesn't want company."

"He's an antisocial guy for sure." Mackenzie peered out the window. "How in the world does he manage to be civil to the hunting parties he takes out?"

"Probably bites his tongue a lot because he makes good money as a guide, and that supports his lifestyle of living out here in nowhere." Owen narrowed his gaze. "At least we have cell service out here in case we run into trouble."

"Agreed." She turned her attention back to the gate where Wheeler dragged the heavy chain free of the metal web.

Dahl pushed the gate in, the angry groan and high-pitched squeal audible inside the truck. The two men got back into their vehicles and drove onto the property. Owen shifted into gear and followed them. He went slow to take in the area. The brush he rolled over whispered against the bottom of his vehicle. Their vehicles startled birds that winged their way skyward. Dogs barked from somewhere on the property. Definitely outdoors. Hopefully, they were restrained or in a kennel.

About a half mile in, Wheeler and Dahl stopped by a small house. Owen expected the end of the driveway to open into a clearing, but weeds seized the land all the way to a single-story log cabin with a green metal roof and large stone fireplace crawling up the side.

Despite the overgrown condition of the property, the log cabin looked to be in good repair. A large barn-like garage with oversized doors sat further down the way and also looked to be in good shape.

"Odd," Owen said. "The guy takes care of his buildings, but he doesn't mow his lawn or cut the weeds."

Owen parked behind the police vehicles, the dogs' barking growing more frantic. The two officers walked up the three wooden stairs to the porch. Dogs didn't race out and attack so Owen assumed they were somehow restrained. Mackenzie slid out before Owen could turn off the engine. She hurried through the weeds mowed down by the officers. Owen caught up to her. Up close, Owen saw that the black door and trim paint was peeling. So maybe the place wasn't in such good condition after all.

Wheeler pounded on the door. Leach couldn't be home but someone else might be, and it wouldn't do to bust in and frighten them. The occupant could think they were intruders and draw down on them.

Owen tapped his foot until Wheeler gave Dahl the clearance to move. The deputy slammed his battering ram into the worn wood. The door splintered open and snapped back at him. The barking grew hoarse and desperate.

Dahl set the ram down, raised his weapon and stepped inside, pausing just inside the door. "Police. If anyone is here, show yourself now!"

They waited. The time ticked by slowly. Owen continued to check outside for any threat. No one pulled onto the lot or came running, and no one exited the rooms inside.

"Let's get in there." Wheeler pushed on Dahl's back, and the pair of them moved ahead.

Owen waited for Mackenzie to go first, then he brought up the rear.

The house was dark and dank smelling. Thick logs made up the living room walls, and the kitchen held a simple line of worn wood cabinets on one wall with ancient brown appliances on the other.

The hallway led to the right, and the four of them started down it. Pink and black tile covered most of the narrow bathroom walls and floors, and the sink and bathtub were dotted with mold. Two bedrooms were located on the right side. One was stacked full of boxes and discarded household items. The next one held an iron-framed double bed with a worn quilt rumpled at the foot. An old dresser painted white with handles made from antler pieces stood in the corner.

They didn't encounter anyone, the ongoing barking the only sound.

Wheeler turned to them. "Place is clear. Let's get it searched. If we each take a room, we can be done right quick and get out to that garage."

"I've got the living room." Before anyone could argue, Owen headed for the hallway.

"I call dibs on the main bedroom," Mackenzie said.

"Dahl, you take that spare bedroom. See if you can make any sense of all the garbage in there. I got the bathroom and kitchen. Let's move."

Owen crossed the tan carpet—more brown and black with dirt than the original color—to the desk in the corner. The top drawer held past-due bills for utilities, cell phone, and taxes. A few of them were two months behind, and the property taxes were a year in arrears.

So Leach had money issues. Maybe why he fought with Jamar Bussey in Vancouver and why he killed him. Owen would follow that as a line of inquiry.

The huge flat-screen TV looked fairly new. Sitting in front of it was a nice leather recliner. The guy couldn't pay his bills, but he'd bought a big TV and pricey chair, and Owen had seen a satellite dish outside too. Owen guessed the man had set his priorities, or he could've stolen the items.

Owen opened the cabinet doors in the corner to find another set of doors locked with a strong hasp. He broke the lock and revealed several rifles hanging neatly in a row. Owen had learned a lot about weapons over his career and recognized one as a Mossberg's Patriot rifle. He knew it fired .308 Winchesters.

Could be the firearm used to kill Cassie, or maybe Leach

had that rifle with him. If he did, hopefully he hadn't ditched it. They would have to get these weapons to the expert at Veritas.

The rumble of an engine drifted through the open front door. Owen spun and charged for the door.

"Incoming vehicle," he called out to the others. "I'll check it out, but be on alert."

Hand on sidearm, he remained in the shadows until an older blue Ford Explorer stopped next to Owen's pickup truck. The Explorer's door opened, and a tall skinny woman with stringy gray hair got out.

He stepped back into the house. "Stand down. It's a woman. Not Leach."

He went back to the door to find her looking around. She stared at the police cars, appearing jittery and a little spooked. She started for the porch but stopped by the patrol vehicles and looked in the windows. She stood there for a moment, running a hand over her face as if deciding what to do, but then turned and marched toward the steps.

Hand on his sidearm, Owen stepped out. He introduced himself and planted his feet on the wooden floorboards that squeaked under his weight. "And you are?"

She stopped at the base of the steps, a wary look on her face. "Della King."

"And what business do you have here?" Owen asked.

She jerked her head toward the side of the house where the barking originated. "Came to feed the dogs for Ned. He's out scouting for his job. He pays me to take care of the dogs when he's gone." She challenged Owen with a lifted chin. "And what are you doing here?"

"We believe that Mr. Leach was involved in a crime that we're investigating." He watched her carefully for her reaction. She blinked a few times, but no look of disbelief or even a question in her eyes.

"You don't seem surprised that he was involved in a crime," Owen said.

She shook her head. "I don't think he's ever really gotten into trouble with the law, but he's skated a fine line over the years."

Curious. "Are you friends?"

She shook her head. "I do odd jobs around the area for extra spending money. He got my name from one of the neighbors, called me and asked if I would feed his dogs when he was gone. That was about ten years ago, I think. We came to an agreement on a fair amount, and I've been taking care of them off and on ever since."

"He always pay you?"

"If he didn't, you wouldn't see me standing here now." A sharp smile tightened her long narrow face. "I love dogs, but I don't do this for free."

"Do you know Mr. Leach well?"

She tapped her chin. "Strange. I thought I did, but now that you ask, can't say as I really do. My only conversation with him is when he calls to tell me he's going out and for how long. Then I make sure I'm here to collect the money when he gets back. We shoot the breeze a little bit. Mostly about his work, but that's about all."

"Do you know if he has a girlfriend or friends in his life?"

"Not a girlfriend that I know of. But then like I say, I don't talk to him much. On friends, I've never seen anyone here, but I know he hangs at the local bars with that creepy trucker who drives for the casting company."

Could she be talking about their other suspect, Hobert Tovar? Did these guys know each other and conspired to murder Cassie?

"Creepy trucker?" Owen played dumb. "Could you be more specific?"

"A very unfortunate-looking guy who likes to hit on every woman in sight." She rolled her eyes. "He's always bragging about his big fancy rig. As if anyone cares."

"Do you know this guy's name?"

"Yeah, but I forget. It's as odd as he is, though."

"Hobert?"

"Yeah. Yeah." Her expression brightened. "That's it. Hobert Toner or something like that."

"Tovar."

"Right. That's him. Weird as they come. No matter how hard he tries, I've never seen a woman go home with him. And believe me, he tries hard with pretty much any woman who comes close."

Owen handed her his business card. "Give me a call if you think of anything else about Leach that could help."

She took the card and nodded.

She marched through the grass toward the side of the house, and Owen went back inside. He told the sheriff and Mackenzie about Della King and shared the information she provided.

Owen faced the sheriff. "Do you know this woman?"

Wheeler shook his head. "I'll run her name. See if we get any priors." He stepped out of the room.

Owen faced Mackenzie, glad to note the dogs had quieted. "I also found a cabinet full of weapons. I'm certain one of them uses .308 Win cartridges. We don't need to call the Veritas staff out here to collect evidence. See no sign of a crime here, but we should ship Leach's weapons to Veritas along with the slugs and casings from when Leach fired at us. And spring for the cost of a morning delivery so we get results sooner."

"Agreed." Mackenzie's phone rang. She looked at the screen, and her eyes lit up. "It's Emory Jenkins. Veritas DNA expert."

"Has to be our DNA results from the remains." Owen wanted the report to confirm Cassie's death, but he should've already faced facts and accepted them.

Cassie was dead.

"I'm putting you on speaker, Emory," Mackenzie said. "So Owen can hear the news."

"No problem," Emory said. "I'm sorry I'm later than we promised, but I've finished processing the DNA results from Cassie's crime scene."

"And you're going to confirm that Cassie is the victim." Owen's shirt collar threatened to strangle him, and he had to breathe deep for air.

"Actually, no," Emory said. "It's not that straightforward."

"How's that?" Owen asked.

"Processing of the DNA from the recovered remains was pretty straightforward, but I got hung up when I went to compare my results to the report on file from when she went missing. I noticed some oddities in the original report that makes me question if it was processed correctly."

"And?"

"And I think before we discuss any results, it would be good if you could bring me Cassie's toothbrush or hair sample if you still have them so I can run the DNA again."

How could this be? More waiting. "I'm guessing my parents still have those items."

"Could you confirm that and have them deliver it to my lab as soon as possible?"

"Of course, but what do the preliminary results tell you?"

"I'd rather not speculate. Not when discrepancies are skewing any results. I'm sure once I process the items from your parents, the results will be clear-cut."

Owen couldn't be more frustrated with what he thought

would be a concrete answer to the DNA question. "So they must not match if you have a question, right?"

"I didn't say that." Emory was talking in riddles. Hinting at the fact that she believed the remains to be Cassie's but not coming right out and saying it. Owen wanted to keep pressing her for details, but she was doing this as a favor, and he didn't want to make her mad.

Besides, he didn't think she would tell him anything more, and he was just wasting time. "I'll ask my parents about the items you need, and Mackenzie can text you their response."

"Sounds perfect." A smile was back in Emory's tone now. "We also recovered DNA from the slug extracted from the rock outcropping. We ran it through CODIS. No match."

"Makes sense as neither of our prime suspects have a criminal record and won't be in the database," Owen said. "We're hoping to have a suspect in custody soon, and we'll overnight his DNA swab to you, if that's okay."

"Of course. I can compare the results to the bullet sample, and by the time we have that processed, the DNA recovered from bullets fired at Mackenzie's rental property will be ready."

"We have another crime scene too." Mackenzie told Emory about Leach shooting at them in the desert and the guns in this house. "Those slugs and casings will be overnighted along with the weapons we found here."

"You can count on us to process it all as quickly as possible while maintaining our accuracy," Emory said.

"Perfect." Owen let go of some of his frustration.

They would know within forty-eight hours if Leach shot Cassie and then fired at Owen and Mackenzie. That was assuming, of course, that the overnight service delivered the items in the morning, and he located and arrested Ned Leach for shooting at them in the desert.

18

Mackenzie eyed Hobert Tovar outside the casting company as he tossed the sponge into his bucket from washing his truck, suds and water flying everywhere. He swiped wet hands on his jeans and strode toward the building, which was nothing more than a one-level concrete structure with a set of concrete steps under a canopy. A small sign on the wall said Office. Tovar didn't go willingly, but Owen had threatened to haul Tovar into the sheriff's office for questioning if he didn't sit down and talk with them. That got him moving.

She and Owen followed their suspect across the lot, passing tall cement towers with white smoke billowing into the air. She remembered the things Owen said Della King had mentioned about him hitting on women. Mackenzie shuddered at the memory of his leering gaze when she'd introduced herself. Even as Owen threatened the guy, Tovar had tried to charm her. The creepy guy coming on to her was more painful than the ache in her arm.

Tovar entered the building and led them to a small room with a table and four chairs, a Coke machine, microwave, and refrigerator humming loudly in the corner. He sat at the head of the wooden table caked with food residue and jutted out a pointy chin.

Owen sat across from him, and she took the chair next to Owen.

She studied the guy in the bright light from the fluorescent fixtures above. She could only come up with one word to describe him. Homely. He exceeded two hundred twenty pounds, and he was at least six feet tall. His out-of-control frizzy head of red hair topped a face put together all wrong. His nose was crooked. Not as if it'd been broken, but as if it were placed askew on his face in the womb. His lips were too full, forehead too high, and his ears reminded her of car doors left open.

Owen held out his phone. "I'll be recording this interview."

"No," Tovar said. "Don't want you to."

"Fine," Owen said, sounding not at all putout. "We can run down to the sheriff's office instead and record it there. Or we can do it here. Your choice."

Tovar slunk down in his chair and crossed his arms. "Just get to it."

Owen tapped his phone and announced the date and time and who was in attendance for the interview. Then he took a deep breath. "You like to hunt with a rifle?"

Tovar didn't respond, just cast a come-on look at Mackenzie.

She glared at the guy. "Answer the detective, or he'll be slapping cuffs on you and hauling you in."

Tovar lifted his chin higher. "So what if I hunt? You one of those Bambi lovers or something?"

"Nothing wrong with hunting as long as it's not for humans," Owen said.

Tovar's mouth dropped open. "Who do you think I am anyway?"

"We have an eyewitness who places you hitting on a woman named Cassie Collins in Ernie's Bar and Grill."

"Hah, shows what you know." Tovar sneered. "Ain't been in there in weeks."

"This didn't happen in the last few weeks." Owen shared the date Ernie had provided.

"I've never known any woman named Cassie. And I talk to a lot of women and don't consider it hitting on them as you say." He leaned his chair back on two legs and rocked. "I'm single and always looking for the right woman."

"She clearly wasn't the right woman as she asked you to leave her alone and you didn't."

Tovar stopped rocking midair. "That doesn't sound like me at all. Women really enjoy talking to me. Your eyewitness must be mistaken."

"No mistake." Owen opened a picture of Cassie on his phone and held it out to Tovar. "Her hair was brown when you harassed her."

He looked at the picture. "Don't recognize her."

"You also threatened her after she put you in your place." Owen's tone held a healthy dose of irritation now. "Telling her this wasn't over."

"Nah, doesn't sound like me at all."

Owen's nostrils flared. "How about being a man and fessing up to it?"

Tovar lifted his shoulders. "Not gonna say I did something I didn't do just to make you feel better. Now if that's all, I have work to do, and I need some shuteye after my long haul."

Mackenzie didn't want to walk away. She wanted to keep pressing Tovar, but he clearly wasn't going to confess to harassing Cassie, much less killing her.

"Where were you last night?" Owen asked.

"On Highway 395, pedal to the metal to get back here this morning."

"Stop anywhere along the way where someone can confirm you weren't in town?"

"Nope." Tovar tilted his head. "Why? What do you think I did?"

"What about Monday night?" Owen asked. "Where were you then?"

"Hmm, Monday. Probably on the road. Don't remember. But we can check with the boss. He'll know if I was hauling for him."

"You work exclusively for this company?" Mackenzie asked.

Tovar shifted to look her in the eye. "They pretty much keep me busy, but I do take the odd loads when there's enough downtime so as not to violate trucking laws."

"Any odd jobs this week?" she asked.

"Nope." He narrowed his eyes. "Seriously, what do you think I did?"

"That's all of my questions for now." Owen stood. "But in the words you used in parting with Cassie. This isn't over. Not by a long shot."

Tovar smirked as he dropped his chair legs to the floor and raced from the room. She and Owen followed at a slower pace. By the time they got outside, he was hosing down his truck, a fine mist spraying back at him.

What Mackenzie wouldn't give to be able to have Sierra process the inside of his cab to see if Cassie had ever been inside. Though, with the way he kept the truck's exterior clean, he probably cleaned his interior as meticulously and frequently, likely leaving little if any evidence behind.

Mackenzie trailed Owen to his truck and climbed in. He ran around the front and got behind the wheel. She kept her attention pinned to Tovar, who whistled an uplifting song as if the visit meant nothing to him.

She slammed her door harder than needed, the pain reverberating up her injured arm. "Either he's really bothered by our questions and trying to make us think he isn't or he couldn't care less."

"Not sure which." Owen cranked the truck and headed toward the exit. A quarter of a mile down the road, he turned into a dirt drive and made a three-point turn to point the truck at the road. He pulled forward and stopped behind an outcropping of rocks.

"You're planning to follow him," she said.

Owen nodded and got out his binoculars. "If we *did* spook him, let's see what he does and where he goes."

"Seemed like he was hiding something even if it isn't what we're looking for. There was certainly a thread of unease running through the conversation."

"Yeah, I caught that too and hope to unravel it to see where it leads. But it could be something simple like the guy grows more pot than Oregon laws allow, and he's afraid we'll find out."

She swiveled to face him. "If you're game, I have an idea of something we might try."

"I'm game for anything that's legal and can help."

"There's this technology I heard Nick Thorn talking about on another investigation."

"The Veritas IT guy." Owen lowered his binoculars and glanced at her. "What technology?"

"I don't remember the exact name of the computer program, but it can analyze a recording to determine if the person is lying."

"I've heard of that." Owen glassed the road again. "If I remember right, the accuracy of the findings is controversial."

"Right, but Tovar doesn't have to know that. If Nick analyzes the recording and finds Tovar is lying, we can use that as leverage to get Tovar to confess."

"Then I say we go for it, as long as this Nick guy doesn't charge us an arm and a leg to do it."

"He won't." She eagerly dug out her phone and placed the call.

"Nick Thorn," he answered.

She identified herself. "I'm still working that investigation with Detective Owen Greer from Clark County."

"If you're calling for results on the algorithms on Leach and Tovar, they're still running."

"Actually, I'm calling because we could use your help again. Owen's here with me, so I'm going to put you on speaker if that's okay."

"Go ahead."

She tapped the speaker button and then updated Nick on the investigation. "I don't remember the name of the program, but it's where you analyze a suspect's recording to see if he's lying."

"Voice Stress Analyzer or VSA," Nick said.

"Yeah, that's it. We'd like to have you review a recent interview to determine if our suspect is lying."

Silence lingered on the phone for a moment. "I can do it, but the accuracy isn't something that would hold up in court."

"How does it work?" Owen asked.

"The human voice has micro tremors—tiny frequency modulations—in it. When the suspect lies, the involuntary nervous system causes an inaudible increase in micro tremor frequency. A VSA program can detect and quantify changes in the voice frequency."

"But it's not accurate?" Owen asked.

"Studies have called the accuracy into question. The real

value of the program is to be able to tell a suspect that a computer will analyze their voice in the answers they give. This causes them to be more truthful. It's called the bogus pipeline effect, which basically says people might give truer responses when they fear getting caught in the act of lying."

"And that works?" Mackenzie asked.

"Not all the time, but yes. It works."

"Since we've already done the interview can you review it, and then we can tell him it was done and that we know he was lying?"

"Of course. It can work that way too. But again, not always."

"Do you think it's worth the time to do it?"

"Yes."

"I hate to ask, but is this something you could do quickly and not charge us the going rate?" Mackenzie asked.

"I can have one of my techs run it, and that will minimize the cost."

"Thanks, Nick. I'll email the audio file as soon as we end the call."

"I'll be waiting for it."

Mackenzie disconnected the call and looked at Owen. "AirDrop me Tovar's interview file, and I'll email it to Nick."

Owen got out his phone and transferred the file. She quickly sent the message and waited for him to confirm receipt. Before he could, Tovar's red rig drove past.

"Show time," Owen said and pulled onto the road behind their suspect.

Mackenzie stowed her phone, forgetting all about the recording and pointing her full attention on their suspect. Maybe tailing him would bring the lead they needed.

～

Owen hung back, especially slowing on the winding curves. "Looks like he's heading for home."

Owen had looked up Tovar's address after the shooting. The two-acre property was located about ten miles from the casting company. Mackenzie hadn't seen the images, and he wanted her to be familiar with the layout.

He glanced at her. "You should take a look at Tovar's property in a map program in case we go in."

"Will do." She got out her phone, the light glowing on her face in the dimness of his pickup.

"Wide open area," she said, but Owen already knew that. "No place to take cover like we did while we waited for him. But there's a stand of trees we can take cover behind about a half mile before we get there and then hike in closer to his place."

"Sun will be down in a few minutes. We'll wait there until dark to go in."

"Sounds like a plan." She bent down to her backpack and pulled out two protein bars. She handed one to Owen. "Tovar has a long driveway. Wouldn't hurt to fuel up for the hike."

"Thanks." He smiled at her thoughtfulness. "Mind opening it for me?"

She tore off the end of the package and handed the bar to him.

He chomped a bite of the chocolate bar, a gooey caramel layer melting in his mouth. "Good."

"I eat them at work a lot when I stay late and don't want to order in dinner."

He swallowed his bite. "Do you work late often?"

"I did, but this trip was meant to be a start toward living life outside of work again."

"You can change just like that?" He gave her a long look before focusing back on the road.

"If I restructure some things, I hope to. I've also been trying to get Ryleigh to join the company. If she agrees, she'll lessen the work load for all of us. But she's holding out."

"What's her hold up?"

"She likes her position at the FBI too much."

"You don't want to pressure her into the change because she wouldn't be happy."

"Exactly. She'll have to come to the decision on her own. But it doesn't stop me from pointing out the benefits on a regular basis." She laughed.

He laughed with her.

She glanced at her phone. "That stand of trees is about a mile on the left."

He slowed to scan the edge of the road for a safe place to pull over. Tovar continued ahead, and Owen lost sight of the man's vehicle. What if Tovar kept driving instead of going home? Odds were in their favor he wouldn't, but Owen couldn't guarantee that.

He located a wide spot shielded with trees, slowed to a crawl, and waited for a car coming toward them to clear. He backed into place, putting his vehicle in position for a fast getaway if needed.

He shifted into park. "We'll go in to get a better look. We'll wear vests and take a rifle."

She shot him a look, her eyes wide. "You think we'll need the firepower?"

"I was thinking more about using the scope for clear distance views, but the rifle might be needed too." He turned the key and got out to open the back door, making sure his door latched with quiet precision.

Mackenzie joined him, and he retrieved the same vests they wore when they went after Leach. Ryan had insisted Mackenzie keep the one he provided with her at all times. Owen wanted to be her protector—not let Ryan do the job.

Too bad. Ryan had the right supplies. Mackenzie was blessed to have a friend who cared so much about her. As long as they only had a friendship, Owen could deal.

She slid into the vest and gasped.

"Your arm?" he asked.

She nodded, but didn't speak.

"If you're not able to handle your firearm, I'll need you to stay here."

"I'm good," she said. "It might hurt, but I can manage it."

He looked past the tree line to a sky littered with a million stars and full moon, the diffused light helping illuminate the area. Perfect for finding their way in the dark. Not perfect for camouflage as they moved.

"We should stay close together. Make our footprint less obvious." He slung his rifle strap over his shoulder and soundlessly closed the back door.

He started off, silently letting his boots hit the packed earth. Mackenzie fell into step close by.

"Would be a beautiful night to stargaze." Her low, husky tone rolled over him like a warm breeze.

Ah, yes. Easy to imagine. Sitting in the desert with her at his side. Sharing a quilt for warmth and being at peace under God's amazing creation. But would Owen be at peace? Or would thoughts of Cassie losing her life in the desert intrude? He'd have to work hard to control them. The same way he'd had to work hard to deal with her disappearance. The pain had become more manageable over time, but the anguish lived as an unquenchable ache in his gut. He should've been able to protect her. That was his job—serve and protect—and he couldn't even do it with his own family.

He let out a breath.

Mackenzie eyed him. "What's wrong?"

"Thinking about Cassie. Was it day or night when she

was murdered? Was she alone? Terrified? Or did the killer shoot her from a distance, and she didn't know what was coming? The not knowing is eating at me."

Her hand slid into his. He didn't pull away but gripped her soft skin. They walked like that. Side-by-side. Hand-in-hand. The night surrounding them. And something akin to peace settled into his heart. Not complete peace. Not when the fresh ache of loss was still there. But a tight knot inside loosened.

Until the lights from Tovar's complex radiated into the sky like a halo around the compound. And it was indeed a compound. A ten-foot-tall stockade fence surrounded the area that held the trucker's house.

"That fence says he's trying to hide something," Mackenzie said.

He squeezed her hand and released it to retrieve his rifle. He paused to peer through the scope. "He has cameras and security lights mounted on the two front corners of the fence. We'll have to keep our distance and hike around to see if there's an area not covered by cameras where we can get close enough for a look inside."

Mackenzie nodded. "Question is, what's the reach of his cameras?"

"Most home security cameras have a seventy-foot range. Doubt these are basic home cameras though. Professional cameras can see up to seven hundred feet." He adjusted his scope. "We'll use the scope to locate additional cameras and lights, but to estimate yardage as we walk too, so we don't activate either one."

"So we have to stay around two football fields away then," she said.

"That's right." He resumed walking, making sure to pause and check their distance and correct their course when needed. They strode parallel to the property and arrived in the back without triggering any lights, and hopefully, not activating cameras either.

He ran the scope over the back. "No cameras or lights. We can get closer."

"What if he has guard dogs?" she asked.

He looked her in the eye. "He's on the road a lot so odds could be in our favor. But if we hear barking, we double-time it back to the truck."

She nodded.

"Stay behind me." Owen set off toward the compound, making doubly sure of his footing to keep from triggering any sound.

Please don't let there be dogs.

Silence. Every step. No barking. No alarm. No bright lights calling them out.

Owen reached the fence and slung his rifle over his shoulder. He located a small gap between the boards and peeked inside. A single-story rectangle of a house painted prison gray with a flat roof sat in the middle of the compound. A large metal pole barn stood close to the rear fence, old and dilapidated and held together with rust. Tovar had parked his red cab near the house where lights glowed from a large window on the side.

Owen stood back. Mackenzie took his place and leaned in. He was aware of her as a woman, not a fellow law enforcement officer. Not just now, but most every time he laid eyes on her. He'd come to see her as a woman he would like to get to know better.

What if he did pursue her when this was all over, and he couldn't shake her involvement in the investigation, and he let that fester? Would he always associate Cassie's death with Mackenzie?

"Tovar's coming out of the house," she said, her voice rising with excitement. "Headed toward the barn."

Owen wanted to shove her out of the way and look, but moved down the fence until he found another open slot. He leaned close and spotted Tovar coming straight for them, a gun at his hip, flashlight swinging in one hand and a covered wicker basket in the other.

Had he made them? Should they take off?

He didn't have his weapon out, and he was whistling. And he was carrying a basket, which seemed odd if he knew Owen and Mackenzie were watching him.

Owen would hold tight, but be prepared to run. He crooked his finger at Mackenzie to join him at his vantage point that provided a look inside the barn too. She crept toward Owen, and he resumed peering through the fence.

Tovar slid the door open, the metal groaning on rusty hinges and revealing the inside of the barn. He turned on a light and the beam shone down on an old-fashioned cellar door built into the earth.

Was it a root cellar, and he was simply getting food he'd stored inside? Could be why he carried a basket.

Mackenzie arrived beside him and rested a hand on Owen's shoulder. He reluctantly gave up his spot. She stared for a long moment, then gave Owen a quizzical look.

Owen took another look through the fence. Tovar lifted the cellar door and started down.

"Back away from the door or no food for you tonight," Tovar called out. "I mean it, ladies. If you want to eat, be quiet and do as I say."

What in the world?

Owen shared a questioning look with Mackenzie whose shocked expression said it all.

Tovar was holding women in the cellar.

A door hinge groaned and cries of distress rose up. Female, high voices begging in Spanish.

Owen knew rudimentary Spanish. At least enough to

224

understand their pleas. Tovar was holding these women captive, and they begged for him to let them go.

And it didn't take any language skills, foreign or otherwise, to understand the crying.

"I said be quiet!" Tovar's raised voice carried up the stairs. "This is all the food until breakfast, so share it."

How much food could that basket hold? Probably not enough for all the voices. He turned back to Mackenzie. Her face was tight with anger, her fists clenched.

Owen looked back at the fence in time to see Tovar drag a woman out of the cellar. He had a shackle on her wrist and a rope tied to it. He tied the other end of the rope to his belt loop and bent to close the cellar.

The woman struggled to get free.

"Now don't do that, sweetheart." Tovar's soft and soothing tone made Owen want to hurl. "We're going to have a lavish meal. Nothing like the others have. I've planned six courses and a scrumptious dessert. Don't you like that word? Scrumptious. It means *delicioso*."

She said something Owen couldn't make out.

"Don't be afraid. After our meal, you can take a long soak in the tub to wash off the grime from the trip." He stroked her hair from her face and she cringed. "And I have the most wonderful outfit for you to wear. You will be spoiled beyond what you have ever known, and then we will have a good time together. Yes, a very good time."

He removed his hand and started toward his house. The woman dug in her heels. Tovar jerked on the rope and looked back at her. "Fight me and we go straight to the good time. Cooperate and you will have the meal, bath, and fine clothing."

She let out a long sigh and started walking. He led her across the lot and into the house then closed the door with a solid thump.

Owen swallowed his anger along with his need to go after the guy and pummel him. Owen pointed at his truck for Mackenzie. He stormed away from the property and turned to check the distance with his scope. He'd gone the required seven hundred feet, but added even more distance to keep from slowing them down by having to stop and check the spacing often.

At his truck, he turned to Mackenzie. "Are you thinking what I'm thinking?"

She grimaced. "Tovar is into human trafficking, and he's abusing the women before he sells them."

Owen clenched his hands. "I hate thinking about how many women are in that cellar, but makes sense that as a truck driver he could move people and imprison them out here without being detected."

Mackenzie frowned. "The question right now is, what do we do about it?"

"Exactly." He clenched his hands around the steering wheel. "Because we sure aren't going to leave those poor women in there."

19

Owen had fixed his binoculars on the house for going on thirty minutes, making sure Tovar didn't leave as they waited for Sheriff Wheeler and his SWAT team to arrive with a warrant to raid Tovar's compound. It took every bit of Owen's self-control not to bust through the fence, cuff the man, and free the woman Tovar had ruthlessly hauled to the house. But they had to handle this raid by the book. No way Owen would let Tovar escape prosecution. Hopefully, the six-course dinner and bath took a long time.

"I wonder how many women he's trafficked here." Mackenzie stared out the window.

Owen lowered his binoculars. "A part of me wants to know, the other part doesn't. It could've been going on for years, and I can't get the image of Cassie having been in that cellar out of my head."

Mackenzie met his gaze. "Do you really think he kidnapped her and brought her here?"

"I think it's highly likely, but maybe he never put her in the cellar with the others." Owen clenched his teeth. "She would be a real prize to a guy like him, and he likely dragged her straight to his house like he did with the woman we saw."

"But if he had Cassie here, why take her out to the desert to kill her? Why not do it here and bury her on his property where no one was likely to find her?"

"Maybe he was worried someone would investigate her disappearance, find out he talked to her, and come looking for her like we did."

Vehicles humming closer caught his attention. He shifted his binoculars to the other side of the truck. Four patrol cars rolled down the road, the occupants turning off their headlights before they reached Owen. Thankfully, the bright moon gave them plenty of light to safely pull to the side of the road.

The sheriff led the team and parked nearest to Owen. Owen dropped the binoculars and bolted from his truck to join Wheeler, who scrambled out of his car. Mackenzie hurried over to them.

Wheeler waved a folded piece of paper. "Warrant. Signed, sealed, and let's deliver it with a bang."

Three deputies wearing black tactical clothing got out of the other cars and came forward. They wore armor-plated tactical vests and carried black helmets. All of them slung assault rifles over their shoulders. The first deputy brought a heavy battering ram and the second man a big metal pry bar. Only three men on the SWAT team. Not a surprise for the size of the county. But it would be enough with the sheriff, Owen, and Mackenzie to invade Tovar's compound and arrest the creep.

Wheeler looked at Mackenzie. "Since you're no longer a sworn officer, I can't give you an official role in this arrest. "

"But I—"

Wheeler held up his hand. "I get that you don't like it,

but we can't give Tovar any reason to call his arrest into question and escape prosecution."

She raised her chin. "So you're going to make me stay here."

"I should, but I'll let you bring up the rear and remain at the fence until we've detained Tovar."

"Thank you." Her words declared her gratitude, but disappointment deepened her tone.

Wheeler moved his attention to Owen. "My men will take the lead. We'll stay out of camera range and follow the same path you did to the rear of the compound where we'll remove a section of the back fence and go in that way to catch the guy by surprise."

"Sounds like a solid plan."

"I have ambulances and support workers on standby. After we've detained Tovar, we'll call them in and move on to the cellar to free the women."

Owen nodded. Wheeler might have seemed all bluster so far, but he was handling this situation like a well-trained officer.

Owen held out his hand. "Lead the way."

The men marched off, and Owen followed, steeling himself for what they might find in the cellar. Better to focus on the positive. They were going to save these women. A good thing. A very good thing.

His body flooded with adrenaline, and he had to work hard to move slowly and stay behind the men. Mackenzie strode with purpose alongside him, her face pale and tight in the moonlight. Seeing women abused this way had to be doubly hard on another woman.

Cassie. His sister. Her sweet innocent face came to mind.

Had Tovar indeed brought her here before he hauled her out to the desert to kill her? If he'd kidnapped her, he couldn't let her live. Not after she'd seen him and could identify him. What about these women? They could identify him by sight too, but if they were illegals smuggled from a border town, he probably didn't fear reprisal from them.

They'd soon know. Maybe not about Cassie, but about the women in the cellar.

The SWAT team moved steadily over the hard ground to the back of the property, checking distance through rifle scopes as Owen had done. The team might be small, but they seemed capable.

At the rear fence, the deputy shoved his pry bar behind pickets to loosen them. Another worked them free and quietly laid them on the ground. Owen's body vibrated with the need to get in there, and he wanted to hurry them along. He didn't of course. Remaining quiet was of utmost importance if they wanted to surprise Tovar before he ran or destroyed any evidence. Or took the woman he held hostage.

The men repeated the process until they'd cleared a wide opening. The deputy holding the battering ram went through the opening first. The others followed, then Wheeler and Owen.

He turned back to smile at Mackenzie, who was frowning. He knew she understood the situation, but he didn't want to leave her behind. She gave him a smile and thumbs-up. He nodded his thanks at her good wishes, appreciating that she could take her situation in stride and go with the flow.

He took off after the other men and caught them midway to the house. Their footfalls were silent over the packed desert soil, inching slowly toward the building with one light still burning from the front room. The first team member took a stealthy look in the window.

He turned and raised two fingers. Owen let out a long breath of relief. Tovar and the woman were still in the front room. Owen wanted to get a look inside too, but the deputy signaled they were going in. The guy with the battering ram slammed it into the older wooden door. It swung in and bounced back, but he'd stepped out of the way.

The second and third deputy burst in, yelling, "Police! Stay where you are."

Sheriff Wheeler followed, then Owen. Finally going in. Finally going after Tovar. Finally arresting the creep.

They turned to the room where the couple had been sighted. Tovar was sitting at the end of a dining table, the woman on the far side. He jumped to his feet and started to come around the table. The first deputy pulled Tovar's arm behind his back and pressed him against the wall.

Tovar glared over his shoulder. "What's the meaning of this?"

The deputy slapped cuffs on Tovar and read him his rights.

"I've done nothing wrong," Tovar protested.

Owen went to the woman who was dressed in a black shirt with a colorful pattern at the neck. Her plump face was smudged with dirt, and her eyes terrified. She was crying and trembling.

The wrist shackle Tovar had hauled her around by was attached to a hasp mounted on the table covered in takeout dishes of specialty foods. The custom table hasp said Tovar had likely done this before.

Owen squatted next to her. "I'm Owen, and I'm a detective. What's your name?"

Her terrified gaze cut around the room. *"No hablo mucho ingles."*

Just as Owen suspected. She didn't speak much English. Owen repeated the question in Spanish.

"Juanita."

231

"Are you being held here against your will?" he asked in Spanish.

"*Sí.*"

He asked about the other women in the cellar, and if Tovar had brought them all here in his truck.

"*Sí. Veinte mujeres.*"

Owen looked at Wheeler. "Twenty other women in the cellar."

Wheeler got in Tovar's face. "How long you been doing this, scumbag?"

"Doing what?"

"Locking up defenseless women in a cellar in your barn."

Tovar's expression held no guilt. "Haven't been in that cellar in ages. If someone put women in there, I don't know nothing about it."

Owen scoffed. "I saw you go in there less than an hour ago to bring Juanita out and heard you talk to the women."

Tovar snorted. "Not possible. My cameras would've alerted me. Got the best of the best."

"But you didn't put them at the back of your property, and it was easy to skirt around the fence to avoid them and surprise you." Owen smiled.

Tovar snarled. "You don't have any proof other than claiming you saw me go to the cellar. Your word against mine."

Owen glared at the slippery suspect. "I wasn't the only one who saw you. There's another witness."

The man clamped his mouth closed and glared at Owen.

The deputy searched Tovar, frisking him roughly. His hand came out of Tovar's pocket holding a ring of keys. "Could be one for the woman's shackle on here."

Wheeler grabbed the ring and stepped over to Juanita.

He smiled at her, but she continued to tremble. "I won't hurt you."

Owen translated.

Wheeler kept smiling, likely to ease her worry. He flipped through the keys to a small one and inserted it in the lock on her wrist. The shackle came free.

"*Gracias.*" She rubbed her wrist and peered at him, terror still firmly lodged on her face.

Wheeler looked at Owen. "Tell her to stay here with the officers while we release the others and someone will be here soon to help all of them."

Owen explained the best he could, making sure she knew she was safe and no one would hurt her.

She nodded, but her gaze remained wary as she ran a hand through her long black hair that was tangled and frizzy. She was likely afraid of the police and especially afraid of the men in their intimidating black helmets and dark clothing with vests, but Owen couldn't change that right now. If only Mackenzie had been allowed to join them, she could provide comfort, but she couldn't be in the same room as Tovar. Couldn't enter the house until it was processed for evidence.

Wheeler faced Owen. "You speak Spanish. Come with me to the cellar."

Owen nodded, but his gut twisted with visions of what he would see and hear. He'd always had a vivid imagination. Helped him think outside the box on the job, but right now he wished his brain would shut down the visions.

Wheeler looked at the first deputy still standing near the door. "Take the keys and get the gate open. Bring them back here then double-time it to your vehicle to take this bozo to lockup. Get him processed right away. Prints and DNA. Then we'll get it to Veritas to run and compare to our evidence."

"Roger that." The deputy marched out the door.

"What evidence?" Tovar asked.

"Evidence you murdered Cassie Collins."

"Hah. Just like I figured." Tovar shook his head and rolled his eyes. "You bozos are going to strike out. I didn't murder anyone."

Tovar sounded convincing, Owen would give the guy that, but it didn't matter. The evidence would confirm or deny his guilt.

Wheeler pointed a sharp look at his other deputies. "The pair of you babysit this guy while we free the women. Make sure Juanita is comfortable, but doesn't go anywhere."

Hearing her name, Juanita jerked her gaze to Wheeler.

"He's only telling his men to be sure you're okay, and that you should stay here," Owen told her in Spanish and made sure to end with a smile. "We'll be back with the others soon."

Wheeler charged out of the room, and Owen hurried to catch up to him. Outside, Wheeler paused facing the gate where the deputy was checking keys. Wheeler got out his phone. "Dahl, good. We've breached the house, and Tovar's in custody. Call the list of resources I left with you and get them out here ASAP."

He tilted his head as if listening. "Don't know if there are injuries or not. We're going to the cellar now. Send the ambulances just in case. Pronto."

He ended the call and shoved his cell into his pocket as his deputy ran over and gave Tovar's key ring to Wheeler.

"Keep moving at that speed," Wheeler said to his man.

"Roger that." The guy ran toward the gate and disappeared in the dark.

Wheeler dangled the keys and looked at Owen. "You ready for this?"

Was he? He highly doubted it.

Mackenzie craned her neck as Sheriff Wheeler and Owen talked to the deputy who'd gotten the gate open. Owen and Wheeler spun in unison and marched her way, determination in every step.

Finally! The women would be freed. At least she hoped that was their goal.

Owen looked at her. "Tovar's in custody. The woman he dragged to the house is free. Looks like we got here in time."

Mackenzie let out a long breath. She'd worried they'd be too late, but thankfully, they'd spared the poor woman from more turmoil. Mackenzie wanted to go to the house, give her a hug, and tell her everything would be okay.

But would it? Would she ever get over the trauma of being kidnapped and held against her will? Being dragged like a slave to the door and closed in with a creep like Tovar? Mackenzie doubted she would recover from such a thing.

Please don't let Cassie have shared the same fate.

If they learned that she had, how would Owen handle it? He loved his sister very much. That was clear in his every step in this investigation. Would he recover enough to lead a normal life? Could he get over Mackenzie being a part of the investigation—or would he think of Cassie every time he looked at her?

No. Stop. Don't think about yourself now. How incredibly selfish. If God wanted her to have a future with this man, she would.

The most important thing to consider and do right at the moment was pray for him, Wheeler and his men, and especially for the women. They all would need God's amazing restorative power to overcome such a traumatic experience.

"Hang tight in case we need your help with the women," Wheeler said, in an unusually uplifting tone.

She nodded, hating the situation, but if she could help, she was glad to stay. And for her own sanity glad to remain put. She would witness the joy of the terrified women freed from their captivity without the memory burned in her brain forever of seeing them in the cramped cellar.

20

Owen followed Wheeler into the barn, where he flung open the cellar door. The women began crying.

Owen's gut tied in a tight knot, and he offered a prayer for God's guidance in their actions.

"Go first," Wheeler said. "Say something to calm them, so they know it's not Tovar and that we're not going to hurt them."

Owen cautiously stepped down the dark cellar stairs. He located the light switch and flipped it on, flooding the small landing with a warm yellow glow that belied the task at hand. A thick wooden door with solid hasp and padlock awaited him at the bottom.

He knocked on the door and did his best to introduce himself and Wheeler in Spanish. "We've arrested Tovar and are going to let you out. Please don't rush the door. I don't want anyone to get hurt. There will be people out here to help you."

Sobbing noises sounded behind the thick wood, but a shout of *Alabanza Jesús* rose above it. Owen agreed. Praise Jesus. He hoped none of the women were hurt and in need of medical attention.

Wheeler stepped in front of Owen and tried a few keys in the lock before he landed on the right one, and the lock fell open. He stowed the keys in his pocket and dropped the lock in the dark corner of the earthen floor, then pulled open the hasp.

He looked at Owen. "Brace yourself for what we'll see and smell. We're going in."

Owen gave a sharp nod and faced forward when his whole being wanted to run away. But running was in direct opposition to what a law-enforcement officer did. They were trained and had the desire to protect the innocent at all costs. Even if it meant seeing women who were terrified, stressed beyond the breaking point, and likely filthy from their time in captivity.

The sheriff pulled the door open, and the odor of human waste and unwashed bodies stormed out. Owen fought his gag reflex. Wheeler coughed a few times, but recovered. Owen sure didn't want the women to see his disgust and add to their distress.

The small room was dark, smothering like a dungeon. He located a light switch outside of the room and flipped it on. The barest of light from a single bulb bloomed inside. The women gasped and closed their eyes.

Owen hadn't expected this response. Not at all. They'd been kept in squalid conditions—that he expected—but the creep Tovar hadn't allowed them any light.

Oh Lord, how could You let this happen?

Owen didn't believe he'd get an answer, but he had to cry out or he couldn't bear what he was seeing. While the women remained standing as if frozen in place, blocking their eyes until they could handle the barest of light, Owen counted the number. Got to seventeen and added one for Juanita then had to scan the room for the final three. Two women squatted in a corner, and one sprawled motionless on the dirt floor among dirty food containers.

"Perdona." Owen slipped between the women. "The one on the floor. What's her name, and what's wrong with her?"

"She needs water," a nearby woman said in solid English. "Her name is Valeria, and I'm Elaina. No one has enough water, but she suffers more."

Owen knelt next to her and cringed at her sunken eyes and loose skin—just a shell of a woman pretending to be alive. Sirens sounded outside the barn.

Owen looked at Elaina. "That will be the ambulances. Tell everyone I'm going to carry Valeria out first to get her immediate medical attention."

"Sí. Sí. We thank you for your kindness. And will bring the other weak sisters out too. The rest of us can wait." She turned to the women and fired off rapid, urgent words.

They moved like a wave toward the wall to make room for Owen. He scooped Valeria into his arms, the odor so intense he had to hold his breath until he got outside or hurl all over her.

He gulped a breath and glanced at Mackenzie. "Tovar didn't give them enough water. She's severely dehydrated."

He rushed to the first ambulance as another one backed in next to it. The EMT slid down from the driver's seat and came around the back.

"This is Valeria."

The medic took a good look at her. "Let's get her on a gurney. She's badly dehydrated. Needs an IV immediately."

"There are nineteen others inside." Owen moved closer to the back of the vehicle. "Two more who are weak but not this bad. The others seem stronger."

"I'll get fluids started on her and then call in a third rig." He climbed into the ambulance. "Let's not waste time taking the stretcher out. Figure we can get her in here okay."

Owen agreed, and with the EMT's help, he eased Valeria onto the stretcher. She moaned and shifted, but didn't wake.

Owen left her in good hands and returned to help Wheeler. On the way back to the cellar, he paused to look at Mackenzie. She could help Valeria, and he didn't care what Wheeler thought. "Can you sit with Valeria in the ambulance? I don't want to leave her alone, and the EMT will have his hands full."

She nodded and jogged toward Owen. As she came even with him, she paused to give his arm a squeeze, then hurried to the ambulance and climbed in.

Amazing. A quick touch by Mackenzie and his steps were lighter as he made his way back to the women. Elaina climbed out of the cellar, her arm around one of the sickest women, another woman on the other side.

Owen connected gazes with the sheriff who stood at the cellar entrance. "While the medics tend to the sicker women, I'll head to the house for water and whatever food I can find for the others."

Wheeler gave a sharp nod, his face pale and jaw tight.

"This way to the ambulance," Owen said to Elaina and led them and the pair of the stronger women who helped the other weaker woman toward the second rig.

The sicker women sat on the bumper and held hands, their eyes cutting around in fear. The taller medic spoke Spanish and offered them comfort as he treated one of the women, his partner treating the other.

Owen instructed the helpers to take a seat near the fence. Heads and shoulders down, they complied without a word. Their unconditional obedience broke Owen's heart as much as the horrid conditions.

Owen looked at Elaina. "I'm going to the house for food and water."

"I will help you." She glanced at the women by the fence. "Let me tell them where we are going, and that they should have the others sit with them."

She didn't wait for permission but crossed to the fence and gave the instructions. Owen waited, thinking of all the questions he would ask Elaina on their walk to the house.

She quickly joined him, her eyes narrowed. "Will Tovar be at the house?"

Owen glanced ahead. One patrol car sat out front. Hopefully, it didn't belong to the deputy Wheeler told to transport Tovar. "He should've been transported already."

"Part of me wishes he is still here. I would like to tell him off." She lifted her shoulders. "To talk to him while I wasn't his prisoner."

A perfect opening for Owen's questions. "How did you come to be his prisoner?"

"The cartels, of course." She spit the words with venom. "In my country, they are known for engaging in sexual trafficking. They target poor communities. The women often lack basic education. The cartels promise a better life. More money and romantic relationships. Exactly what most of these women dream of. Or the cartels even resort to blackmailing."

Owen nodded. "I'd heard it was a big problem in Mexico."

"Of course, the women don't get what they want. They are placed in terrible conditions while guarded or locked up. They're drugged, raped, mentally abused, tortured, and even murdered." Elaina shuddered.

"And this is what happened to you?" Owen asked, though he hated to do so.

"Sort of. We were all taken, but I would not give in and encouraged the others with me to band together and rebel."

She lifted her shoulders. "I am educated and could outsmart their men. For our rebellion, we received frequent beatings, which on the one hand was good because we were too incapacitated to be of use to them. They hoped their beatings would deter us, but we persevered and became so difficult that they did not want us."

Owen could just imagine their horrid lives. "And is that when Tovar came in?"

She nodded. "He is known in the border towns for human trafficking. Even has the nickname, Don Juan, because he believes he is seducing the women he forces to have sex with him. He buys women the cartels don't want. Either difficult ones like us, or women who are all used up or too strung out to be of value to them. Tovar then transports them here, and sells them to men who aren't as particular."

Owen shook his head. "That's really revolting, and I'm so sorry that it happened to you."

"I appreciate your kindness." She smiled at him, temporarily eliminating the pain in her eyes. "But you have rescued me from it, and now I hope I can go back to my real life."

He even detected a note of optimism in her tone, which totally blew him away. "Do you want to go back to Mexico? Aren't you afraid it will happen again?"

"My work is important to me. I come from a wealthier family than most of these women, and am fortunate to have an education. I have devoted my life to teaching in the slums. I suppose I could continue my work in the United States if they would allow me to seek asylum here."

"If that's what you want, I'll do my best to make it happen." And he would. Not only for her, but for the other women too, if they so desired.

They reached the house and climbed the steps to the

porch. The deputies stood right inside the room where Juanita remained sitting in the same chair.

She caught sight of Elaina and raced across the room to hug her. *"Eres libre?"*

"Sí. Alabado sea el Señor por enviar a estos hombres."

She'd asked if Elaina was free, and she'd replied praise the Lord for sending the men. The words made Owen feel good. For a moment only.

He looked at the deputy. "We're here to get food and water for the women. I'll check out the kitchen."

Elaina excused herself to follow Owen to the run-down and dirty kitchen. An old white stove top was caked with food, the refrigerator door and handle held greasy prints, and smelly garbage overflowed the trash.

"Looks like we could catch something in this room." He put on gloves and gave a pair to Elaina.

She slid her fingers into the gloves. "It is a palace compared to the places the cartel had us living."

If only he'd taken a moment to think before speaking, he could've been more sensitive to her plight. He opened cupboard doors and found a stash of protein bars. "These will be perfect."

He located a paper bag and stuffed it full.

"There is water under here." Elaina pulled out a rusty metal chair from a table pushed against the wall covered in stained and worn floral wallpaper.

Tovar had stacked pallets of bottled water below the Formica table. Owen tugged the bottles out and placed them on the discolored tabletop. "Plenty of water. If you can carry the protein bars, I've got the water."

She reached into the bag and freed a chocolate chip bar and took one of the water bottles from the heavy plastic "For Juanita."

243

He nodded and let her lead. They stopped to deliver the items to Juanita, who pleaded to come with them.

"Sorry," the deputy said. "My instructions are to keep you here."

"We'll ask the sheriff when we get back if you can join us," Owen said in Spanish and quickly headed for the door. The muscles in his arms strained under the weight of water, and he couldn't stand around and still carry the heavy load back to the barn.

Elaina caught up to him.

Owen stepped past Tovar's red cab. "Tell me how Tovar hid you from customs agents."

"He has false walls that he builds into a room in the back of his truck. They fold flat against the back wall when not in use." She shuddered. "The walls are soundproofed, and he also gagged us. He has tie-downs on the floor where he bolted us in place."

Owen hated hearing the details but he needed them to question and prosecute this man. "How was he able to handle such a large group of women at one time without any of you escaping?"

"The cartel workers helped herd us onto the truck in Mexico. Here, he took us off the truck one at a time. We were cuffed, and he attached a rope that he tied to his belt." She shifted the bag higher. "And, of course, he was armed. He said he would shoot us if we tried to run."

"Are you willing to testify in court as to what happened?"

"With Tovar, yes. Specifics on the cartel, no. They have long arms that reach into your country. They would find and kill me."

"They should pay."

"Nothing you can do is going to stop them. Why risk my life for nothing? But I can help stop Tovar at least." She peered at him. "I am more than happy to testify against him, and I know the others will be too."

They reached the women who were now seated in a neat row by the fence. Owen set down the water and ripped open the plastic. He handed out the bottles, and Elaina followed him with the bars. The women attacked them both.

When he'd finished distributing the items, he faced Elaina. "You need to eat and drink too."

"I can now that I know everyone is taken care of." She took out a bar and collapsed onto the dirt. He opened a water bottle for her and helped other women who were struggling to get theirs open.

Wheeler tipped his head at Owen and stepped back. Owen joined the sheriff.

Wheeler planted his hands on his hips. "Social services is five minutes out. We'll wait to question the women until we get them settled and provide medical checkups."

Owen relayed the information on Tovar that Elaina had shared. "She said she would testify against Tovar but not share any details on the cartel."

"Not surprising." The sheriff looked at the women.

"Are you okay with Juanita joining the other women?"

"Not before I do a thorough interview with her."

Owen didn't like the answer, but Wheeler was in charge. "This will likely be the biggest investigation your county has faced, and we need the best in forensic sciences to process this truck and property."

Wheeler fisted his hands. "Wouldn't doubt if the feds will want to get in on it."

"Likely," Owen said. "And it would be good if we had those forensics in hand before they do so you can retain control."

Wheeler arched an eyebrow. "Who says I want it?"

"You do. You're guaranteed a reelection landslide if it's handled properly."

"If not, it's career suicide." He lifted his shoulders into a hard line "But I can handle it. Call your forensics dream team in."

Owen eyed Wheeler. "Same deal. I get information from them once you have it?"

"Same deal."

Owen resisted shooting a hand up in victory and headed for Mackenzie to make the call to Veritas. He wasn't going to waste a moment before finding proof that Cassie might have been here before she was murdered.

Anticipating interviewing Tovar, Mackenzie looked ahead from the passenger seat of Owen's truck and gritted her teeth. He parked between a pair of fading lines in the deserted lot of the Grant County Jail located in Canyon City. The front sign stated the jail had been built in the late nineties, and the county had painted the box of a single-story building a drab beige. Mackenzie had looked up the jail details on the way over to learn the place held forty-one beds. Not a large detention facility by any means.

Owen tapped a code into his gun safe located in the console of his truck. He stowed his sidearm inside the small box and gave her a pointed look. "I'd have to surrender my weapon once I get inside anyway. You can't carry inside a government building."

She got the not-so-veiled hint and unclipped her holster to set it in the box. He secured the safe and double-checked the lock.

He studied her face. "Ready?"

"As one ever is to go inside a correctional facility."

"At least this one isn't terribly old and falling apart." He pulled his key from the ignition.

They got out. The chirp of his alarm activated by his fob was the only sound breaking the quiet.

Faces of the broken women hounded her on the walk across the lot. The medic said Valeria would be fine after she received enough fluids, as would the other women. At least physically fine. Regaining mental health would be a struggle Mackenzie couldn't begin to comprehend.

How did they come back from being treated so horribly? Sure, they were happy to be free, but that would soon pass, and the grim reality of how cruel man could be would settle in. Something they already knew from the conditions they'd been held in before Tovar bought them.

As Owen opened the door, she prayed for the women and kept praying until they reached the desk.

Owen flashed his badge at the deputy sitting behind bulletproof glass, and they signed in. The deputy asked Mackenzie for ID. She wouldn't be allowed in the interview, but the sheriff approved her to watch a live feed in a nearby room. She wanted to be able to personally grill Tovar, but they had to follow strong legal practices to make sure this guy didn't skate on these charges, and she would do whatever it took to put him away for life.

Sheriff Wheeler opened the door leading to the jail. "Right this way."

He led them down a narrow but well-lit hallway to an interview room and unlocked the door.

"You can watch in here." He stared at Mackenzie as if he thought she planned to argue with him. "Please don't try to leave and make me regret my decision to allow you in here."

"I won't. And thank you." She pushed open the door and crossed the room to the computer sitting on the table. She

247

pulled back her shoulders, steeling herself for seeing the man who'd taken twenty-one women against their will.

In a word, he was a monster. A brutal, unfeeling monster. She hoped she could contain her anger when his face appeared on her screen, and she prayed that Wheeler and Owen could do that same thing when they came face-to-face with a living, breathing monster.

21

Owen paused before reaching Tovar's interview room and faced Wheeler. "Are you willing to turn over Tovar's DNA sample and prints taken in booking to the Veritas center?"

Wheeler narrowed his eyes. "Why would I want to do that?"

"They can turn around the DNA much faster than the state, who I assume you will send it to."

"I have to follow procedure. Don't want Tovar's attorney to find a loophole that calls the results into question. Same goes with fingerprints. Have to respect his privacy."

"Not that he deserves privacy, but I get it." Owen shoved his hands into his pockets. "Then can we at least give Tovar a cup of water that I can get DNA and prints from?"

"*That* I can do. Hang tight, and I'll get the water." Wheeler strode down the hallway.

Owen glanced through the interview room window. Tovar sat at a small table, his back to Owen. A woman with short curly red hair and wearing a crumpled gray suit sat next to him. His attorney. Court-appointed, according to Wheeler's earlier phone call.

Footsteps took Owen's attention to the sheriff coming back balancing four plastic glasses of water. "Didn't want to single him out and make him think we were up to something with the water. Hopefully he's thirsty and will drink it."

Owen held the door for the sheriff. He stepped in and placed the water on the table. Owen entered but waited for the door to close with a definitive click before sitting on a metal chair next to the sheriff and across from Tovar.

Tovar fired off a combative stare. The woman looked bored. Not a good look for an attorney representing a man faced with a high number of serious counts against him.

"I'm Olive Pritchard," she said in a monotone. "Court-appointed attorney."

Tovar leaned back in his chair. "Don't think you're gonna get much out of me even with this chick here representing me. So far, I'm not impressed with her skills."

Pritchard looked like she wanted to say something back to him, but compressed her lips.

Wheeler reached out to punch the record button for the audio and video recording. He listed the names of the people in the room and looked at Owen to start.

Owen shifted on the cool metal chair and took a long drink of his water and hoped it would cause Tovar to subconsciously do the same thing. "Let's start with you telling us why there was a woman shackled in your dining room."

Tovar looked at his fingernails as if bored. "Don't know. Got home from my trip, and there she was at my table."

"Come on, Tovar," Owen said. "You expect us to believe that?"

He smirked.

"Tell us about the women in the cellar," Wheeler said.

"Like I told you at my place. Don't know nothing about them. Check my security video feed. You won't see me bringing any woman onto my property."

"But we will see you driving your truck and trailer through the gate," Owen said. "The trailer we've had towed to your place from the foundry and confirmed the false walls inside. Top forensics experts will be going over it and will undoubtedly produce evidence of the women having been in the truck."

Tovar's face held zero emotion. He took a long drink of the water. "Like I said. I didn't do it. Had to be someone else."

Owen worked hard not to show his excitement over the possibility of a DNA sample on the glass. "Then why do all of the women identify you as their jailer?"

Tovar shrugged, his expression disinterested.

He was a cold and calculating man, but then he would have to be to deal with Mexican drug cartels and to treat human beings the way he'd treated those women.

"You know." Tovar suddenly shot forward. "Now that I think about it, I have a friend who looks a lot like me. He's used my truck before too. Maybe he brought the women and planned to move them before I got back from my recent haul to LA, but I got back early."

Owen had to grip his knees to keep from calling out the lie. "Then tell me who this friend is."

"Guy's name is Ned Leach. We go way back. He has a key to my gate."

"Then he'll be on the video feed arriving with the women."

"Should be, but maybe he went to the back and took my fence apart like you did." He ended with a snide smile.

Owen clamped harder on his knees to keep from

punching the guy. Tovar had an answer for everything so far, but Owen wouldn't let it go. "Tell me about the night you hassled Cassie Collins."

"You still going on about that chick you showed me the picture of? I told you. I don't know her."

"If she was in your truck that night," Owen said, not giving up, "our forensic team will find evidence of that."

"Nah," he said. "Nah. No way they can do that. If she was in my truck, which I'm not saying she was, I've cleaned my truck hundreds of times since the date you said it happened."

He had a point, but one Owen wouldn't concede. "All it takes is a single hair."

Tovar's face paled. Just for a moment before he recovered and scoffed at Owen. Still, he proved he wasn't quite as cocky as he was trying to make out.

Time for Owen to go in for the kill. "You'll be brought up on an untold number of charges for those women, but here's the thing you need to remember, Tovar. A single murder charge trumps all of them."

Tovar pressed his palms flat on the table but didn't speak.

"Maybe it helps to know we have a program that reviews your answers," Owen said. "Tells us when your voice modulation changes for a lie. Your earlier interview proved you were lying about knowing Cassie. I'm sure this one will too. When a jury hears you lied to us about knowing Cassie and tried to hide your involvement, they'll be even more inclined to give you the death penalty."

"Fine," Tovar said between his teeth. "I talked to her in the bar, but that's it. I didn't see her again, and I sure didn't kill her."

"But you threatened her," Owen clarified.

"Maybe. I don't remember. Sometimes I just spout things off when a chick blows me off like she did."

"Do yourself a favor, Tovar," Wheeler said. "Tell us what you did with Cassie, and we'll make sure this goes easier on you."

"The only thing you can do to make *this* easier is to release me." Tovar crossed his arms and leaned back, cocky smirk back on his face. "Since I know you won't, you might as well quit wasting your time. I have no intention of answering your questions."

Owen sat forward. "Maybe it will help if I refresh your memory. You shot Cassie out in the desert about two years ago. In a location where Monday night you decided I shouldn't live either. You hit me over the head and left me to die." Owen cast his own snide smile at Tovar. "As you can see, I'm not dead."

"Yeah, I can see you're not dead," he finally said, his tone and manner calm. "But again. I don't know what it has to do with me." Tovar looked at his attorney. "I'm tired. I need to rest. Can we stop now?"

Prichard closed her binder. "As my client said. He's tired. We'll take a break."

Owen pushed to his feet. "No worries. We'll be back after the forensic evidence is in and the DA is ready to charge you. You're going down not only for the abduction and unlawful imprisonment of twenty-one women, but Cassie Collins's murder as well."

Mackenzie used the hand on her uninjured arm to protect her eyes from the dust swirling like a tornado under the chopper's rotors as the big machine landed outside Tovar's fence. Owen stood next to her, his whole body tight and rigid as it had been since Tovar's unproductive interview a few hours ago.

The helicopter touched down, and the rotors slowed, now more of a *thump-thump-thump* than a smooth whirring hum. The pilot's door opened, and Riley Glenn hopped down. Mackenzie would recognize the blond hair of Blackwell Tactical's other pilot anywhere. He slid open the back door, and weapon's expert, Grady Houston, was the first one out, followed by computer expert, Nick Thorn, and team criminal investigator, Blake Jenkins.

"Who are these guys?" Owen asked.

Mackenzie told him as she watched Grady help down Ainslie, his wife and team photographer. Blake held out his hand to Emory, his wife and DNA expert. A pang of jealousy bit into Mackenzie when she saw the sweet smiles the couples shared. Maybe she wanted to be in a serious relationship more than she'd realized. Or maybe she just wanted it now that she'd found an incredible man.

Last, Riley and Blake helped Sierra and a very pregnant Kelsey down. Mackenzie was extremely thankful Kelsey would travel this far again, but didn't know why she'd come along.

Mackenzie updated Owen on the women's identities. "Looks like they sent most of the team."

Owen stared at them. "Impressive."

Riley unloaded equipment from the back of the helicopter and each team member grabbed a bag or two, leaving the larger bins behind. They started toward the gate. Mackenzie was reminded of slow-motion action in a movie when heroes arrived on scene. These men and women might not face down danger in their jobs, but they were still heroes in Mackenzie's book. They worked long hours to help put criminals behind bars. Often for little or no pay.

They stopped in front of her and Owen, and she did the introductions.

"Thank you for coming." Owen smiled. "I didn't expect so many of you."

Blake widened his stance. "We don't do things halfway, and an investigation of this magnitude requires our full effort. I'll be coordinating the collection of evidence and compiling the findings as they come in."

"He's our taskmaster, and he's very good at what he does." Emory grinned at her husband.

He chuckled, but turned his attention back to Owen and Mackenzie. "I'd like to tour the property with you to set priorities, but if you know your number one priority for each of our team members, they can get started right away."

Owen looked at Mackenzie. "I say we have Sierra and Emory start with the truck used to transport the women and maybe Cassie. Grady can look for weapons and ammo, and Nick can check the truck for GPS recordings and then search for a phone. Tovar didn't have one on him at booking."

"I concur," Mackenzie said.

"I'll also look for a computer." Nick gave a tight smile. "And by the way, I finished reviewing Tovar's interview recording. He lied to you like you suspected. Seems as if he remembers Cassie and that he was at the bar that night. But like I said, this process won't hold up in court."

"I just told him about your review of his answers, and he confirmed knowing her," Owen said. "Can you review the interview I just did too?"

"Sure." He jerked a thumb at his teammates. "These guys are bound to take much longer to finish than me, and I can do it while I wait."

"Thanks, man," Owen said. "We'll email the interview to you."

"Your shipment of weapons arrived first thing this morning," Grady said. "Two of the rifles were chambered for the .308 Winchesters, but neither were a match for the bullet that killed Cassie. Or any of the ones fired at you at the rental."

Owen's hands clenched. "What about the slugs from the most recent scene we sent along with the weapons? You have anything on those?"

Grady shook his head. "I wasn't able to process them before I hopped onto the chopper."

Owen's shoulders tightened. "I was hoping for some good news for once."

"I get that." Grady offered a tight smile. "Not sure if this is good news or not, but I *can* confirm the slugs Sierra recovered from Cassie's murder scene were fired from the same gun used to fire at the two of you outside the rental house."

Owen's mouth fell open. "Whoever shot at us, likely killed Cassie."

"We can't be sure who fired the gun. Someone else could have gotten ahold of it between the murder and now, but it was the same weapon for sure."

Owen frowned. "I guess I just want it to be Tovar."

Mackenzie laid a hand on his arm. "We'll find out who killed her. How can we not with all these experts on our side?"

Owen gave a firm nod. "You're right."

"I wish I had more DNA results for you," Emory said. "DNA from the bullets Grady just mentioned should finish in about twenty hours, and I imagine your parents told you they brought Cassie's old hairbrush in. That sample is also running and should complete tonight."

"We also have a glass from Tovar in the truck," Owen said. "We were hoping you could run it for DNA and prints then compare to the ones you've collected."

"Sure." Emory smiled.

Mackenzie looked at Kelsey. "Are you here to help the others?"

She shook her head. "Since we found the remains in the desert, and Tovar is a suspect in the murder, Blake thought we might find clandestine graves on his property. I'll scan the area with my drone to see if he's right."

Mackenzie couldn't believe she and Owen hadn't thought of that.

"This scene could take a few days to complete," Blake said. "We don't want to delay evidence processing so Riley will be staying on, and we'll be sending evidence back to the lab with him tonight and then twice a day until we finish here. The glass can go with him tonight. Any of our team members who are finished or aren't needed will return too."

"Sounds like you thought of everything," Mackenzie said.

"A couple of my techs are on the way in our van with added supplies and will provide additional manpower," Sierra said.

"You're like the cavalry." Mackenzie laughed.

The others joined in except Blake, who looked at his team. "We'll get you set up, and then I'll take that tour with Owen and Mackenzie."

He clapped his hands, and everyone started into motion, appearing very eager to get to their work. He clearly still thought of himself in his former role as sheriff, except he was now sheriff of this posse of talented forensic team members.

Mackenzie turned to lead him on his tour, but when the sight of the abused women came to mind, she dreaded seeing the scene again. How many other women had fallen victim to Tovar's sex trafficking—and what had become of them?

She glanced at Owen. His whole body had become tight with stress. He could be wondering the same thing as Mackenzie. Or worse, he was wondering with each step if Cassie had faced the same fate before she was brutally murdered.

22

Owen and Mackenzie moved from expert to expert. Owen had high hopes for this team and wanted early forensic leads that could be used to persuade Tovar to confess. So far though, Sierra and Emory had struck out on locating clear-cut evidence to point to Cassie having been in the truck.

He looked at Mackenzie and made sure his disappointment didn't show in his expression and kept it from his tone. "How long has it been since we've heard from Ryan?"

She looked at her phone. "An hour. I'm guessing he'll check in again soon."

"It would be good if we could get Leach into custody too. Maybe he'll break in an interview. Or now that we know Tovar is blaming Leach, we can pit him and Tovar against each other to get one of them to talk."

She rubbed the back of her neck. "You think Leach will crack? He seemed pretty strong when Hatch called to order him to come in."

Owen wouldn't be discouraged. "That doesn't mean he'll remain that way when under arrest."

"You could be right," Mackenzie said, but her tone didn't convey belief in her statement.

"Got something here." Kelsey's voice carried on the wind from behind the barn.

"Let's go." Owen bolted for the near side of the rusty barn that hadn't been cordoned off.

Mackenzie's footfalls behind him confirmed that she followed, and Blake jogged from the direction of the truck to meet them. They rounded the corner to find Kelsey pounding stakes into the soil about ten feet behind the barn. She faced them, shielding her eyes from the sun.

Blake stopped in front of her and took a wide stance. "What do you have?"

"Three clandestine graves."

"Human?" Owen asked.

She nodded. "My GPR scan confirms human remains."

Owen shoved a hand into his hair and resisted pulling it out. "I sure didn't expect that."

"Me either," Mackenzie said. "But if Tovar's been doing this for a while, and he hasn't taken better care of the women than the ones we rescued today, stands to reason that some of them didn't survive."

Blake nodded. "The very reason I had Kelsey come along. I'm actually surprised she only found three."

Kelsey rubbed her lower back. "I'm not done scanning the area yet."

Mackenzie shook her head and kept shaking it. "When we followed Tovar, I had no idea we'd find all this."

"I wish I was more surprised than I am." Kelsey's solemn tone got to Owen. This woman had to have seen so many horrible things. How and why did she keep going in her job? "I'll get these graves marked out and then finish scanning the property."

"With two acres to scan," Mackenzie said, "won't that take a lot of time?"

"Not as long as you think." Kelsey drew another stake

out of her backpack. "It would be unusual to find remains on the outer edge of the property, so I expect that to go faster than near the house and barn."

"Because murderers don't like to move bodies far for burial?" Owen asked.

"Yes. Killers are often lazy and dig shallow graves close to where the victim has died. This isn't always true, however. Serial killers often don't fit this pattern."

"If Tovar killed Cassie, and these women died in his care, he would technically fit the FBI's serial killer criteria. But honestly, if these women died due to neglect, the charges could fall under manslaughter."

"No matter how you look at it," Blake said, "we have at least three bodies to recover. Are you the one who can authorize Kelsey to do the work or do we need to contact someone else?"

"The local sheriff is taking lead on this investigation," Owen said. "I'll give him a call and ask him how he wants to proceed."

Owen stepped away. He knew his role right now. Persuade Wheeler to let Kelsey excavate until she could determine the condition of the bodies. If they were skeletonized, she would continue. If not, they would need to call in the local medical examiner.

Owen didn't want these victims to have been buried long enough to be skeletonized, but he knew Kelsey's capability and had no idea of the local ME's skill in recovering buried remains and determining cause of death.

If that was the case, the best Owen could do was to request Wheeler call in the Oregon State Police medical examiners to recover the remains and do so quickly. Because at this point, they were only speculating that the victims were women who Tovar had bought for sex trafficking. The team could be wrong. Totally wrong.

He could be a true serial killer, having murdered other women like Cassie and buried them on his property.

~

Nearing eight o'clock, Owen pulled onto Tovar's property with a stack of pizzas on the passenger seat of his truck, a late dinner for the Veritas team. He wished he could say it had been a satisfying day with copious evidence to point to Tovar's part in killing Cassie. Not so. Some evidence had been recovered, but would need processing to determine the evidentiary value, leaving Owen feeling helpless much of the time. There wasn't a lot for him or Mackenzie to do on-site other than answer questions and bring food for the workers.

He'd been working hard to keep Wheeler on the right track as regards to the three victims Kelsey had found. She hadn't located any additional graves and had unearthed enough of the remains to determine the recovery did not fall within her domain and asked the sheriff to call in the medical examiner. She'd confirmed the victims were women who she believed to have been in the ground for less than a year. That was all she would speculate on. She protected the graves with tarps, and thankfully, Wheeler called OSP, who would send someone out first thing in the morning.

Owen parked near the house and jogged around his truck to retrieve the pizzas and drinks. He crossed the lot to a large canopy where he'd earlier helped Blake erect a table and filled coolers with refreshments. The Veritas team and Mackenzie were taking a break in lawn chairs that Blake had added to the area.

Mackenzie hurried up to him to remove the pizza boxes

from on top the drinks and place them on the table. "Thank you for picking these up."

"I'm glad to do something to help." He set the boxes on the table next to snacks that he and Mackenzie had purchased earlier in the day and turned to the team. "Get the pizza while it's at least a little bit hot."

He flipped open the top three boxes revealing a pepperoni, a sausage, and a cheese only pizza. The pizza place was miles away, likely leaving the pizzas lukewarm. Not Owen's appetite. He'd endured the smell for the drive but wouldn't take a slice before the real workers had gotten their food.

The men hung back and let the women go first.

"Go ahead, Mackenzie," Blake said.

She shook her head. "I appreciate your manners, but I'll wait until everyone on the team has theirs."

Owen looked around for the rest of the team but didn't see everyone. "Should I go get Riley and Kelsey?"

"He took off with evidence while you were gone, and Kelsey went back with him," Blake said as he plopped three large slices of pepperoni pizza on his plate.

"He took Tovar's glass, then?" Owen asked.

Blake chomped a bite of pizza and nodded. "Along with copious hairs and prints located in Tovar's truck."

"Anything more you can share on that?" Owen asked, eager for that lead he so desperately wanted.

"Nothing much, really." Blake grabbed a bottle of water. "We found untold red and black hairs, but we also found a few strands of long brown hair."

Owen's interest piqued. "Can you tell if it was dyed?"

Carrying her plate and water, Sierra dropped into a chair. "Yes, but not in the field. I need to use Surface-Enhanced Raman Spectroscopy to look at the hair in the lab. I'll be able to not only tell you if it was dyed, but can likely identify the brand of dye used."

"Can one of your techs perform this test?" Owen asked.

"Probably, but with something this important, I'd like to handle it myself." Sierra picked up her water bottle.

"But most importantly." Emory approached, her plate holding sausage pizza. "The hairs we recovered contained follicles and will give us nucleic acid DNA which is the best DNA for comparison to the sample your parents provided for Cassie."

Owen's hopes of proving Tovar had kidnapped Cassie skyrocketed, but he tamped them down as it was way too early to think these hairs came from Cassie. "How long will it be before we have DNA?"

Emory looked at him. "The glass should be pretty straightforward and processing time will be less than the hairs. The flight back to Portland is about an hour and a half. Then it'll take a few hours for my team to get the samples, and if all goes well, you can figure about twenty-four hours from then."

Owen did the math. Tomorrow night at around midnight. "That'll be late. Will someone still call then with the results if he matches any of the other samples?"

"We will," Emory said.

Sierra set her slice of cheese pizza on the plate she balanced on her knees and dabbed her mouth with a napkin. "We'll also be lifting his fingerprints and comparing them, and that'll go faster."

"And you'll update me right away?" Owen asked.

"You can count on it." Sierra smiled.

The men finished loading plates with thick slices, and Owen waited for Mackenzie to approach the table. She chose the last sausage pieces and opened the new box below before sitting. Sausage was his favorite, so he took three large pieces and a seat next to her.

Owen looked at Grady and chewed the tangy pizza. "Any

luck in locating a rifle that could've been used to kill Cassie?"

He nodded and set down his slice. "Found a Sig Sauer Cross. It's chambered for a .308 Winchester."

"Seriously?" Mackenzie sat forward. "That's the same rifle that our other suspect usually uses."

"These guys know each other?" Grady asked.

"Friends."

"Makes sense," Grady said. "Buddies are known for having gun envy and trying to one-up the other guy. But in this case, there's really nothing else out there better than the Cross right now. At least in my opinion. So maybe Tovar bought the same one just to be equal with the other suspect."

"But now that you have the weapon, you can fire test shots and compare ballistics," Owen said. "And that'll tell us if this's the gun used to shoot Cassie."

"Actually, no." Grady reached for his drink.

"I thought that's the way ballistic testing worked," Owen said.

"Usually does, but there's something you need to know about this model of Sig. The barrel can be removed and replaced by another barrel—even one chambered for another caliber. Means the slugs might not match this gun, but it doesn't mean the gun didn't fire the bullet."

Owen's bubble burst. "Did you find any other barrels?"

Grady shook his head.

"Doesn't mean one doesn't exist," Blake said. "If I killed someone with this rifle, I'd ditch the barrel."

"Yeah, me too," Owen reluctantly admitted. "What about finding a unique mark on the casing from the firing pin? Is that possible?"

Grady emptied his water bottle. "It's possible, yes. The firing pin indent is actually more reliable as an identifying focus than extractor or ejector markings, except for a few weapons not in play here. But...and this is a big but...if the weapon was fired frequently between finding the casing and recovering the weapon—say a thousand rounds or so—it may be more difficult. That would potentially change the indent marks a significant amount. Besides, we didn't locate any casings at Cassie's scene for comparison."

What a turn of events. And not a good one. They could have the murder weapon in their possession, and yet not be able to prove it was the gun that killed Cassie. Unbelievable!

23

The anguished howl of a wild animal startled Owen awake. He glanced at the clock. Four a.m. He should go back to sleep, but his heart was thumping too hard. He slid out of the warm covers and looked out the guest house window toward the main cabin. Lights burned in the living room and kitchen windows.

Mackenzie had turned out the lights hours ago. He was positive of that. He'd waited until she'd done so before going to bed. He'd asked to sleep on her couch to make sure she remained safe, but when he'd suggested it, she rolled her eyes and shooed him toward the guest house, assuring him she'd be fine.

Did the lights mean there was something wrong?

He hurried to get dressed, ignoring the residual pain from his attack, then raced for the house. Through the sheer curtains on the front window, he caught a look at her sitting on the sofa.

He let out a long breath and knocked softly on the door to keep from startling her. "It's Owen."

The soft sound of her footfalls padded across the floor, and she opened the door. She wore black yoga pants and an oversized Oregon State sweatshirt, but her feet were bare. "What's wrong?"

"Nothing." He smiled. "Couldn't sleep. You too?"

"My arm is aching." She stepped back. "I just made coffee and will share if you ask nicely."

She giggled like a schoolgirl, and he loved that she could let go of the pain in her arm to find humor.

He hated that she was in pain, but her humor made him release his anguish in a way that only she could bring out. What was it about this woman? He sure wanted to figure it out. "May I please have a cup of that delicious smelling coffee?"

"Sit and I'll get you some." She strode toward the kitchen. "My gran sent back a loaf of banana bread. Want a slice of that too?"

"Oh yeah." He smiled at her but she'd turned to face the coffeepot and couldn't see him. Probably good as he was likely sending all kinds of mixed signals her way.

He went to stand in front of the roaring fire she'd built, but faced the kitchen. He enjoyed the warmth to his back and the scent of woodsmoke, but he couldn't take his eyes off her fluid movements. Interesting, but her sparkly blue toenails fascinated him more. Extremely feminine for a woman who'd proved she could toss on a vest, strap on a firearm, and hold her own in a gunfight. He loved the contrast.

Not the only thing he loved about her either. So many more things, like her personality, her strength, her faith, and how she lived it. Once he had Cassie's killer behind bars, could he let go of everything in his past and start something serious with Mackenzie? Would she be receptive? After all, he hadn't been the most pleasant guy to be around since he'd met her.

She padded toward him, those toenails catching the overhead light and sparkling.

"Something fascinating down there?" she asked.

"Your polish," he said, choosing to be open with her.

"Ah, that." She paused and wiggled the toes on her right foot. "I splurged for vacation. I checked the average temps for the area and packed accordingly but foolishly hoped it might be warm enough to wear sandals."

He sat down. "Nothing foolish about hoping. Sometimes hope is the only thing that keeps us going."

She set the mug and plate on the table near Owen before sitting and crossing her leg to dangle her foot. "You're talking about Cassie."

He nodded. "My hope for finding her alive might be gone, but I can hope to find her killer and make him pay."

"So which guy are you liking after today's events?" She reached for her mug. "Leach or Tovar?"

He picked up the banana bread and broke off a large bite then chewed it while he gave her question some consideration.

"Good bread," he said. "Do you think your gran will adopt me?"

"I'm sure she would. Especially if we were dating."

His mouth fell open.

"What?" she asked. "You know a real connection and attraction has been simmering under the surface since we met. We've denied it, but as Ryan said, why?"

"I just..." Owen shook his head. "Maybe after I find Cassie's killer."

He couldn't miss the disappointment in her eyes. So maybe she did want to get together with him. Scary and yet fantastic.

She took a sip of her coffee. "Back to my question, then. Which suspect do you like for it?"

He would answer this time to keep them out of the personal realm. "I think Tovar is higher on the list for me right now, but only because he had contact with Cassie. That could change after we have Leach in custody and can question him. I still like Leach for Bussey's death, and after someone has killed once, they are more apt to kill again." Owen grabbed the steaming coffee mug and blew on it. "Did you hear from Ryan after I went to the guest house?"

She nodded. "He texted at ten. Said they were hitting the hay but would update me in the morning."

"Then that's on hold, so after the sun rises, we go back to Tovar's house to see if the Veritas team located anything overnight."

She gave a heavy sigh. "I didn't like leaving them there. Not at all. If they can't sleep then I shouldn't be able to either. Maybe that's what kept me tossing and turning, not the physical pain."

"I agree. Maybe we can do something to help them."

"Like what? We don't have any expertise in the forensic world, which is why they didn't need us there."

She was right, but... "Do you have enough supplies in the kitchen to make breakfast and take it to them?"

"Yeah, sure. I stocked up when we were in town." She smiled. "Why didn't I think of that?"

"Tiredness?"

"Could be." She peered at him. "How good are you in the kitchen?"

"Well, um..." He probably shouldn't have suggested something that he wouldn't be much help with. "I can make toast without burning it."

"A necessary skill. Can you scramble eggs too?"

"Honestly?"

She nodded.

"I've never done it."

She tugged him to his feet. "Then you're about to learn."

She took him by the hand and led him into the kitchen. She tossed him a black apron that said, World's Best Barbecuer. "Put that on."

He groaned.

She arched an eyebrow. "You want to work in my kitchen —you follow my rules."

"Yes, ma'am." He saluted her.

She laughed and slipped a plain blue apron over her neck. "Don't tell my gran that I'm channeling her. She'd love it, but I'd never live it down."

"My lips are sealed," he said. "Except maybe to finish that coffee and banana bread."

"Go ahead and grab it while I get out the ingredients we'll need." She shooed him away.

He bolted for the family room, tying the apron on the way. He'd never put an apron on in his life. At least this one was black and made for a guy. He wouldn't be caught dead in something frilly. Unless of course Mackenzie asked him. Then he would probably put it on in her presence only.

He'd never acted this way before. Smitten was the word that came to mind. He was starting to see why guys who really fell for a woman did things they normally wouldn't be caught dead doing.

He grabbed the plate and mug and hightailed it back to the island and sat. He shoved a large piece of the bread into his mouth then chased it down with coffee. The banana flavor and crunchy walnuts were heaven in a loaf. "If your gran ever did adopt me, I would seriously have to up my workout game to make up for the calories consumed."

"She's responsible for half my workouts." Mackenzie laughed and faced him. "Time to crack eggs. Tell me you've done that."

"Um. Well...no. My mom is kind of like your gran, and

she's always spoiled me. And after Cassie went missing, she threw herself into feeding me all the time, and I couldn't say no because it helped her attitude so much. I kinda go by their place for breakfast three or four times a week." It was likely more often than that, but he didn't want to admit it to Mackenzie.

She smiled at him. Maybe she appreciated his devotion to his mom.

She crooked her finger. "Come here, and I'll show you how."

He polished off the bread and took another sip of coffee before joining her at the sink.

"I'll do a few while you watch. The important thing is not to get shells in the bowl. But if you do, we can fish them out."

She expertly, or at least it seemed expertly to him, cracked four eggs then slid the carton to him. He hit the first one on the bowl and it crumbled in his fingers, leaving them dripping and gooey.

"Not that forceful." She took his hand and put a fresh egg in it then gently tapped it against the bowl. He should be paying attention to the technique, but all he noticed was the touch of her fingers and warmth from her body.

He discarded the shells and turned to look at her. Her face was inches from his. Gooey hands or not, he bent down and kissed her. He didn't know how she would react, but he didn't expect her to twine her hands around his neck and draw him closer.

The kiss deepened, and he wanted to hold her, but egg goop kept his hands away. She didn't seem to notice he wasn't holding her but wormed even closer. His whole being exploded with emotions he'd never experienced before.

He almost said forget the mess he would make of her clothing with his eggy fingers and pulled her tighter, but his phone rang, bringing him back to reality. He drew back. "I should get that. Must be important at this time of the morning."

He quickly rinsed his hands and dried them then dug out his phone. Lieutenant Sage.

Owen answered his supervisor's call. "LT, what's up?"

"Hope I didn't wake you." The guy never engaged in small talk. He was a straight to the point guy. So this couldn't be good news.

"I was up," Owen said. "What's going on?"

"There was a fifty-car pileup in dense morning fog on I-5 heading north out of Salem."

"That's rough." Owen was sorry for everyone involved but this was not the first massive pileup on I-5 in fog so not a surprise. "Is there a reason you're calling to tell me?"

"Five people died, and when I saw the list of fatalities, I thought you would want to know. Keith Collins was there and got out of his vehicle to try to stop oncoming traffic. He was sandwiched between an eighteen-wheeler and van. He didn't make it."

"Oh, man. No." Cassie's husband had died. Blood rushed from Owen's brain. He dropped onto the stool. "Have my parents been told?"

"Figured you'd want to do it."

Want to? No way. Have to? Yeah.

He listened to Sage's platitudes offered in true sympathy, but not hitting the mark. Mackenzie came over to him, a question in her eyes as she rested a hand on his arm.

Oh, man. Here he was considering a relationship with her, but why? Life was fragile. Could be fleeting. He knew that. Had known that. Experienced it with Cassie. Now Keith.

How could Owen think he could even consider getting hurt like that again? Even for someone as amazing as

Mackenzie? He'd only been deluding himself. He needed to forget that kiss. Forget a future and stay in the single lane where he belonged.

~

Mackenzie rode in silence as they headed back to town to interview Tovar again. Breakfast had been a hit with the Veritas team, and Mackenzie was glad she was able to provide it. Some of the team members were wrapping up their work and getting ready to head back to Portland. Sierra was taking off to start processing recovered evidence, but she was leaving Chad behind to finish areas she hadn't gotten to yet. They hadn't located anything else of interest but had a lot of items to process that could provide valuable leads.

The forensics discoveries were important to Mackenzie but of equal importance was the change in Owen's mood since they kissed. She'd suspected he had feelings for her, and it was obvious in the kiss. But his phone call from his lieutenant put a real damper on things.

He even seemed to regret having kissed her.

She got it. He'd lost his brother-in-law. Of course he was down. But it was more than that, as if he'd internalized it deep at his core. Maybe he feared losing her like he'd lost his sister and brother-in-law, so he'd pulled back from getting involved. It all made sense, and she would talk to him about it. Not now. Now it was time to get Tovar to crack.

Her phone rang, and she spotted Ryan's name.

She answered the call. "You're on speaker, Ryan. I'm in the truck with Owen."

"Leach is long gone. We reached the end of the wilderness area. He ditched his UTV. Figure he drove off in a vehicle he'd parked here."

"You didn't see where he went?" Owen asked.

"He was gone by the time we got here," Ryan said. "No sign of a campsite or fire. He probably had enough of a head start and took off last night."

"Then we're going to talk to Leach's boss to see if he knows where Leach is." Owen cranked the wheel and did a U-turn, the tires squealing.

"We'll need to hike back to our trucks," Ryan said. "But we can take the road, and it'll be a shorter hike. Still, it'll take a few hours."

"Can we pick them up?" she asked Owen.

"Maybe, but if we find out where Leach is, we'll need to head straight to that location."

"Don't worry about us," Ryan said. "Focus on Leach and keep in touch. If you can come get us, fine. If not, it's not the first time we've had a long hike."

"Thanks, man," Owen said.

"Yes, thanks," Mackenzie added. "I'll let you know what Leach's boss has to say." She ended the call.

Owen gunned the engine, and the truck sped over the bumpy road to the outfitters company. Owen whipped into a spot by the rustic building and slammed on his brakes. The truck was still rocking when he was out the door and waiting for her by the steps to the office.

He opened the door for her, and they stepped into the large room.

"Be right out." Heath Hatch's booming voice came from his office. He continued talking but had lowered his voice. He was either on the phone or with someone.

She looked around, surprised to see that the receptionist's desk had been cleared off and a nameplate sat on the metal top. Polly Plummer.

Owen paused by the desk and stared at it then moved on.

Hatch stepped into the room. "Oh, it's you two."

"Do you know where Ned Leach is?" Owen asked.

"He called in this morning. Said he finished scouting the area he was in and was headed to the Troy Unit."

"Can you give us coordinates for his camp?"

"Sure, but you might not find him there."

"Why not?" Owen asked.

"He's kind of obsessed with kayaking, and if I know him, he's out on the Grande Ronde River instead of doing his job. He doesn't think I know he spends plenty of my time on his hobby, but like I said before, he's the best guide out there, so I cut him some slack."

"Where can we rent a boat or kayak if we need to go after him?"

"Good luck with that. He's super skilled in a kayak. The store in Minam has rentals. Can't miss the place. About all that's around there. He rents a kayak there instead of hauling one with him. I think he does it to hide that he's wasting my money in paying him."

"Thanks for your cooperation." Owen headed for the door.

Mackenzie caught up to him outside.

He opened her truck door for her and met her gaze. "Time to go after Leach. The guy's our number one priority right now. No way he's getting away this time. No way."

24

The sun was directly overhead as Owen and Mackenzie neared the boat rental store. With each passing mile, Owen was jonesing to make those miles speed by faster. Much faster than the many that had passed under his truck with Mackenzie at his side. They'd called Ryan and his brothers to join in Leach's apprehension, and the guys were on their way. A recent update put them an hour behind Owen and Mackenzie. Still, they might arrive in time to assist in taking the guy down.

Mackenzie's phone rang, and she grabbed it. "Putting you on speaker, Sierra. Owen's with me. Please tell me you have something for us."

"I do actually. Two things."

"Go ahead." Mackenzie held the phone out so Owen could better hear.

"First, I heard back from the forensic optometrist. The optical glass we found in the location where you were attacked, Owen, fits Ned Leach's prescription."

Owen shot a fist up. "Leach has got to be our killer."

"Not necessarily the killer," Sierra clarified. "But he broke his glasses at some point in that area."

"And the second thing?" Mackenzie asked.

"The fingerprints on the bullets that were fired at you at the cabin are a match to the prints found on the bullets Ned Leach fired at you when you tracked him to his camp yesterday."

"So it was Leach who shot at us both times?" Mackenzie asked.

"Looks like it, but he could've just loaded the bullets into the magazines that were used and gave them to someone else."

"Someone like his friend Hobert Tovar," Owen said.

"Which means neither of the findings are conclusive," Mackenzie added.

"Exactly," Sierra said. "But they do point strongly in Leach's direction and would be very damning in court. Grady is working on comparing the bullets recovered from yesterday's shooting to see if they match the others we recovered, and test firing the guns he took into evidence. He said he would call you when he knew more."

"Thanks, that's great," Mackenzie said. "We're in a sketchy area for cell service. Have him leave a message if I don't answer, okay? And thanks, Sierra. We owe you big time."

"Yeah, you do." She laughed and disconnected.

Mackenzie pocketed her phone. "You liking Leach more for Cassie's murder now?"

"Yeah, and it's even more of a reason to find him." Owen pushed the speed limit until he reached the single-story log store with a green roof. He parked and rushed inside with Mackenzie.

An older man was helping a young guy who seemed lost, and Owen didn't want to interrupt. He got in line to wait to ask his own questions. He glanced around the basic convenience store that also carried fly fishing gear, survival gear, and inflatable boats for sale.

Mackenzie stared at the wall of bins that held hundreds of fly-fishing baits. "My granddad would be in heaven in this store."

"Has he ever been here?" Owen asked.

She shrugged and took a picture of the wall. "If he hasn't, when I show him this picture, he'll be making a trip out here."

"It seems like a great place to camp when you're not hunting down a potential killer."

"Can I help you?" The man behind the counter with a silvery head of hair smiled at Owen.

Owen displayed his badge. "And you are?"

"Bob Grainger. Store owner."

Owen stowed his credentials. "We're looking for Ned Leach. We think he might have rented a kayak or boat from you this morning."

"Ned, yeah. He was in. Rented a kayak. His favorite one. Says yellow brings him good luck and the hull of this composite one is yellow."

"I'd like to rent a boat or kayak for two," Owen said.

Grainger's forehead creased. "If you're hoping to catch up to Ned, that's not possible before dark by paddling a boat."

"You have any motorized boats?" Owen asked.

"I have a few, but we don't rent them."

"Leach is a suspect in a murder investigation. I—"

"Murder?" Grainger slapped his hands onto the worn wooden counter. "Leach? No way."

Owen pinned his gaze to Grainger's skeptical face. "Leach is indeed a suspect. I need you to provide me with a motorized boat so I can reach him today."

"Well." Grainger ran a hand over his head, leaving

silvery tufts of hair sticking out. "You'll need an Oregon permit. Won't let you go without it no matter who you are. You can go online to ODFW's site to apply and pay."

"I can use my phone to do that."

"While you do, I'll get the boat ready." Grainger frowned. "You been around boats much?"

"Enough."

"The river has several rapids that you should know about. The most difficult is only a class III. I can include a map so you can be prepared before they surprise you."

"That will be most helpful. Go get that boat ready ASAP." Owen leaned against the counter and got out his phone.

Grainger took off through the back door, leaving them alone in his store. Not a good move on his part. Sure, Owen was a police officer, but that didn't mean he was a good one. Still, Owen was thankful for the owner's cooperation.

Owen got the ODFW website open on his phone. He located the correct application and started filling it in.

Mackenzie faced him. "Have you really been in a boat often enough to safely handle this one?"

"I know the basics. Besides, I'm sure the guy will provide us with life jackets, and you're familiar with boats, right?"

"Yes," she said. "Maybe I should take control."

"I'll let you know if I need your help." He sounded a bit testy as Mackenzie turned away. He would have to apologize once they got on the river. He completed the form, used a credit card he'd retrieved from his safe at home, and received a receipt with his license information to display for Grainger. "We're all set. I'll just grab the rifle and some ammo from my truck."

He bolted out the door to retrieve the gun he'd also brought along from his place and a few boxes of ammo that he shoved into his cargo pockets. Back inside, he found Mackenzie setting water bottles on the counter.

"We need to stock up on basic supplies," she said. "Just in case we don't find Leach right away and have to spend the night on the river."

"Sounds like a good idea." Owen started down the nearest aisle, and she took the adjoining one.

He retrieved protein drinks, two heavy blankets, and a couple of headlamps. He added the items to the water on the counter. "What about waders or a rainsuit? It's not supposed to rain, but we would be warmer if we had them."

Grainger returned. "I'd go with the rainsuit. Waders could fill with water and slow you down."

Owen grabbed two rainsuits, guessing at Mackenzie's size, and added them to the pile at the counter along with a pair of binoculars he snatched along the way. He'd used his credit card to pay and couldn't wait to see his LT's face when he explained the charges.

The owner bagged their purchases. "I can't charge you for the boat because I'm not licensed to rent it. Just lending it to a friend. But I want to see that water license."

Owen displayed it on his phone.

"All's in order." Grainger handed Owen the bags. "Let's head outside, and I'll get you launched with instructions."

Owen and Mackenzie followed the man over a rocky hillside down to the river where a boat was tied to the shore and bobbed in the water. A cold wind whipped along the river, and he dug out the smaller rainsuit from the bags and handed it to Mackenzie.

"I'm glad you thought to buy these." She ripped open the package and slid her feet into the pant legs.

Grainger gave concise and detailed instructions on the motor and boat, along with basic safety items for both of them to follow. Owen dressed in his rainsuit as he listened.

The fabric cut the wind down, and he was thankful for the extra protection.

Grainger got a bag out of the boat and handed it to Owen. "You'll want to stow all your supplies in the dry bags I provided. Especially your cell phones. You'll find the river map in this one. Let me grab some ice for your water and a few sandwiches too. You might need them."

Grainger took off up the bank before Owen could tell him they'd had lunch on the drive and didn't need the sandwiches. Nor did Owen care if his water was cold, but they might indeed want the food later in the day.

Grainger came barreling down the hill with a bag of ice and another bag holding food. He put it all in the cooler and then Owen added the bottles of water and protein drinks.

Grainger shared the best location where Owen could get off the river and call Grainger to come get them.

"Your phone won't likely work out here. Take my SAT phone." He dug the phone from his pocket and held it out for Owen.

Owen waived a hand. "We can't take your phone."

"Humor me. I'd feel better if you had a way to communicate."

Owen would take it so the guy didn't worry, and it might come in handy too.

"Thank you for all your help." Owen put the phone in a small dry bag then pocketed it in his rain jacket.

"Take care, Detective Greer," Grainger said. "It's not a hard river to navigate, but the current is swift, and you don't want to become a victim of carelessness."

Owen shook hands with Grainger and put on his life jacket as he waited for Mackenzie to do the same thing. "Let's listen to Grainger and use the small dry bags for our cell phones too. Just in case."

They both inserted their phones into small bags and

secured them in zipped pockets. He considered putting his sidearm in a bag, but wanted to have it available if needed.

Mackenzie made her way to the boat's front seat, and he took the back, placing the rifle within reach. He used an oar to push off the murky bottom. Once the motor cleared the bottom, he lowered it into the water and started it up. He wanted to let it rip and go racing down the river. Not that the motor was big enough to race anywhere. But even if it were, he had to be mindful of Mackenzie in the boat with him and be more cautious.

He might be willing to risk his own life to catch Leach, but he wasn't willing to risk hers, even if the guy could be Cassie's killer.

Mackenzie wedged the river map between her knees and pulled up the hood on the rain jacket, then tied it against the wind whipping up the river. The cold set her arm to aching something fierce, and she had to fight not to cry out when they hit hard bumps that jostled her.

The wind howled, and the boat speed didn't help keep her warm. But surely, they would gain on Leach soon, arrest him, motor to the first exit location downriver and haul him off to jail. The warmth would return, and the arm would hurt less. At least she hoped.

If only it were all as simple as it sounded.

She lifted the binoculars and scanned the rapidly flowing river. She couldn't determine how far they'd come, but the water started to move faster, and she heard a roaring noise ahead.

She scanned the area ahead, but didn't see a change in the current. She looked back at Owen. "Map says the first rapids are coming up."

"Sounds like it too."

Her stomach knotted at the thought of an inexperienced person at the helm. "You good to pilot the boat through them?"

"Should be, but why don't you take the SAT phone in case we need to make a quick call." He leaned forward to give her the phone.

She grabbed it then lifted her jacket to clip the bag to her belt and slide it into her jeans pocket. Safe and secure should they have to call for help.

Please don't let us need it.

She tucked the map into her pocket and slung the binocular strap over her neck so she could hold onto the seat straps. Owen hit the rapids called the Minam Roller head on. Water splashed over the boat's bow. They bumped and rocked down the faster water. Nothing more than waves like you might find in the ocean surf.

No biggie. Hopefully the others would be as easy.

She consulted the map and her watch. Red Rock next, where a giant boulder rose up from the water and sat midstream, leaving the clear route to the left. She turned to warn Owen and describe it to him. "We should be approaching it in fifteen minutes or so."

"So steer left?"

"Yes. I think it will be obvious once we see it." She lifted her binoculars again to get a good look and be able to give him ample warning.

The canyon walls rose along the river banks dotted with basalt ledges and soaring ponderosa pines. She knew the river flowed from The Wallowas, the second highest peaks in Oregon, and that volcanic activity with lava flows formed the steep canyon solidifying into layers of basalt ledges.

Near a large ledge, she spotted a bright yellow and gray kayak dragged onto the rocky shore.

Leach! Was the kayak real or her imagination? She blinked a few times. Glassed the shoreline again. *Yes!*

"Leach's boat is pulled up on the right bank just ahead." She handed the binoculars back to Owen so he could take a look.

He scanned the area. "No sign of Leach though. I'll land this thing just shy of his kayak, and we can get out to look for him." Owen returned the binoculars to her. "Be ready to draw your weapon."

He changed course from the left side of the river to the right and aimed for the bank where they would land. She kept watch. Only a short window of opportunity to land on the bank and the zone was perched between two areas of the basalt.

The boat puttered closer.

She lowered her binoculars and prepared to leap onto the rocky bank.

Leach appeared from behind a stand of trees. He cupped his hand over his eyes. Took off running for his kayak.

"It's Leach," she shouted. "Looks like he's going to try to make a run for it. Could be armed, but I don't see a gun."

She rested her hand on her sidearm and wished Owen could lift his rifle, but he had to keep his hands on the motor to stop them from crashing into the massive boulder.

"I'll try to cut him off." Owen corrected course again.

The large boulder in the water loomed ahead of them like a barrier playing chicken with them, daring Owen to keep moving closer. He did, continuing on their course.

Leach jumped into his kayak. Pushed off the rocky landing with his paddle. Turned his kayak to head out to the open water.

His smaller boat was more maneuverable than theirs but Owen kept up with Leach, facing their bow straight for his boat. Leach didn't go for a gun, so she couldn't very well fire hers.

So what then?

A grab line ran along the bow of his kayak. If she could snag it, Leach couldn't get away. She got on her knees. Slid on her belly over the rigid side of their boat. Reached out and prepared to seize the line.

"No, Mackenzie!" Owen shouted. "Back in the boat. You can't hold him in this fast water."

Adrenaline fueled her, and she believed she could do it. She leaned out further and snagged the grab line with her good arm, the other holding to the boat. Her wound screamed at the exertion. She let the pain work for her. Give her motivation to hold on to the man who likely shot her.

He gave a mighty roar and slammed his paddle down on her hand.

She yelped in pain but took a deep breath and held fast.

He hit her again, harder this time, whipping her body out of the boat.

The water swallowed her. Her face. Head. She gasped at the icy cold liquid. Her lungs filled with frigid water, and she went down into a black void.

25

"No!" Owen shouted

Leach cackled like a madman and paddled away. Owen's brain screamed to chase Cassie's killer. His heart screamed to save Mackenzie.

Mackenzie. She had to come first.

The large rock loomed ahead. Owen threw the motor in reverse and kept his eyes on the water, watching for Mackenzie to surface. He knew she would. The life jacket would ensure that. For now.

She popped up, coughing and gagging. Sputtering.

He held out an oar and slowed the engine to a crawl.

She reached up. Missed it. The oar passed her by. He dropped it into the boat. Bent over the side. Grabbed hold of her hand and lifted with every ounce of his strength. The current threatened to rip her free. He held fast, and with his free hand revved the throttle to reverse against the demanding current.

The large boulder loomed ahead. The boat inched back, but the current wanted to drag them forward.

Mackenzie clutched his wrist with her other hand, looking at him. Pleading for help.

His arm strained under her dead weight. "I won't let you go."

"The water is freezing," she got out between chattering teeth.

His heart broke. Shattered. He had to do better for her. Just had to.

He pushed the motor harder. Got the boat into a position to angle into shore. Lifted his arm to bring Mackenzie higher out of the water. She was like an anchor. Ripping his muscles. Burning, straining.

He changed the motor to move the boat forward and pointed the bow toward the shore. He rammed into the rocky soil. Mackenzie's body grew lighter. She must be touching bottom.

She released him. "Go ahead and let me go. I can get to shore now."

He let go, the remaining pieces of his heart shattering. She clambered onto the rocky beach. Had the remaining strength to grab the boat bow and direct it into a dry spot, then she collapsed.

Killing the motor, he catapulted over the seats and out of the boat to tug it further up land so the current couldn't sweep it away.

He bolted over to Mackenzie and looked her over. "Are you hurt anywhere?"

"Just my pride." She shivered like a frightened animal.

"Your hand is okay where he hit it?"

She looked at it. "It's sure to bruise but nothing's broken."

"You have to get out of those wet clothes." His anger at Leach tripled. "I'll get the blankets and give you my rainsuit. You can go behind the trees and change into it."

She nodded.

He grabbed the dry bag containing the blankets, thankful for the supplies they'd bought and for the bags Grainger had provided. He raced back to Mackenzie and shed his rainsuit.

She had the SAT phone in one hand and her cell in the other. "I'll call Ryan. They can intercept Leach downstream."

She looked at Ryan's number on her cell, then stowed it, and with a shaking finger she dialed the SAT.

Owen held out his hand. "Give me the phone and get changed."

She handed it over without comment and gathered up his suit and took it and the bag with blankets toward the trees.

He faced the water.

"Hello," Ryan said.

"Owen Greer here." He explained what was going on and asked for Ryan's location.

"We're approaching the store."

"Head downstream to the Wallowa River Bridge in Wallowa. Leach will probably get out there and try to hitch a ride."

"Roger that."

"We'll continue downstream as fast as we can and see you in Wallowa. Keep me updated at this number if anything changes, and I'll do the same." Owen stowed the phone back in the dry bag then shoved it into a pocket of his tactical pants and zipped it closed.

He counted in his head, each second like an hour, as he waited for Mackenzie to return. He finally heard footsteps crunching on the stones behind him and glanced over his shoulder.

Mackenzie headed his way, dwarfed by his rainsuit. She'd draped a blanket over her head and one over her shoulders, was carrying the dry bag with one hand, and was holding up the oversized pants with the other.

She seemed to be shivering less, but that could be wishful thinking.

She smiled at him. "I'm ready to go after Leach."

"The Maddox brothers will try to intercept Leach in Wallowa. We have a few hours ride till then. Will you be okay?"

"Might have cold feet but otherwise the blankets and your suit will keep me warm."

He tried to remain where he was, focusing on anchoring his feet on the soil, but he couldn't stand there and do nothing. He could've lost her. Like he'd lost Cassie. He was seeing how fleeting life was and God was telling Owen to grasp every good thing he could before it was gone.

Mackenzie was a good thing. A very good thing.

He swept her into a hug. He was likely smothering her with his tight hold, but he had to do it. To reassure himself that she was alive and okay.

"Don't take a risk like that again, okay?" he whispered against the blanket on her head. "I can't lose you. You're already too important to me."

She leaned back and looked at him, a smile on her face. "I'm glad you finally told me that. You're important to me too, and I don't want to lose you either."

He returned her smile. "I don't know where that leaves us. But right now, we have to get on the river, go after Leach, and put him behind bars. Then we'll be free to figure this" —he wagged a finger between the two of them—"out."

~

Mackenzie tied the oversized waist of her pants with a rope from the supplies Grainger provided and shivered under the

290

pair of blankets. She worked hard to stop her body from shaking so Owen wouldn't see her discomfort. He would feel bad about her being dunked in the water when it wasn't his fault. She'd reached too far. Sure, she believed she could do it, but it was still her fault.

That was a problem she faced in her life. A big one. Always trying to reach beyond what was safe or comfortable. Except when she'd been a deputy. Then caution reigned, and she'd suffocated under that. Until she not only left the force to help in the family business, but also to regain that freedom she'd had to put aside to make sure she stayed alive and that she protected innocent lives at all costs. If she planned to be in a relationship with Owen, she might need to quench her thirst for adventure. But wouldn't that be suffocating again? Wouldn't she have to let go of who she was to be with him?

They approached another set of rapids and water sprayed over the bow as the boat plunged through the uneven water. She might want to dwell on Owen's declaration of how important she was to him. Maybe meaning love? Like? Whatever she called it, she needed her complete concentration as navigator to keep them safe on the water.

She directed Owen through the rapids to calmer water. She lifted her binoculars and scanned ahead. She didn't expect to see Leach's beached kayak. He was likely planning to make a run for it. Maybe gaining access at the Wallowa as Owen thought. Or even going further down to where the Grande Ronde ran into the Snake River and Class IV rapids would challenge them in their chase.

This river was accessible by road in only a few spots, restricting the places he could get off the river. And it was their job to have Ryan and his brothers concealed at each stop in advance of Leach's arrival.

But soon it would be dark, and if Leach didn't get off the

river in Wallowa, they would be forced to camp for the night.

Please let him ditch his kayak at Wallowa. Please!

The wind kicked up, and she huddled deeper into her blanket, feeling guilty for taking Owen's rainsuit which could be cutting the wind for him. He had to be cold, but she suspected his single-minded determination to catch Leach was keeping his mind occupied, and he might not even notice the cold.

She rested her elbows on her knees and lifted the binoculars, scanning the area ahead.

The SAT phone rang from behind her. She spun on the seat to look at Owen.

He was digging it from his pocket. He handed the bag to her, and her cold fingers fumbled to answer. Thankfully, it continued to ring.

She tapped the button. "Ryan?"

"Got Leach in sight in my binoculars. We're hidden in the trees. I don't see you yet. How far out are you?"

"It's hard to tell without any real landmarks until the bridge, but based on time, I'd say about five minutes away."

"Do you want us to apprehend Leach or tail him?"

She knew what she wanted Ryan to do, but that didn't mean Owen didn't want to be the one to stop Leach. She turned to ask Owen that same question.

He waffled for a moment, looking up and then down. "Apprehend."

She relayed the answer to Ryan.

"Roger that. Will call back when we have him in custody."

Liking the certainty in his tone, she stowed the phone and pocketed it in her jacket then resumed watching in the binoculars. The bridge soon came into view.

"Landing area just ahead on the left." She scanned the

bank. "I see Leach's kayak, but I don't see Leach or the Maddox brothers."

Owen opened the throttle, and they churned faster toward the rocky landing.

She scanned further up the bank to the hillside covered in fir trees. Nothing. No one.

"Maybe they've apprehended Leach and took him to their truck," she said, though that made no sense. Ryan would've called to tell her.

Owen angled their boat toward the shore, fighting the current that tossed the boat in mighty jolts. The rough ride made it difficult to keep the binoculars to her eyes. She ignored the bouncing and focused higher up the incline.

Movement caught her eye. A person was charging down the bank toward the water but she couldn't make out his ID.

"Someone running toward the water," she reported to Owen.

He gunned the boat, and they glided toward the shoreline. He lifted the motor. Began rowing. Frantically. Furiously. Slapping the oars into the water and jerking them out in even strokes, until they hit the rocks.

A man wearing camo like Leach had on cleared the trees. He backed toward them. He held a rifle in his hands. At the edge of the outcropping and surrounded by brush, he skidded to a halt and took a wide stance for support.

She scanned the horizon to locate the Maddox brothers. They'd broken cover, and she spotted them at a distance. They were no longer hidden from Leach's viewpoint, and he faced them, so had to see them too. Seemed by Leach's lack of checking to his rear that he hadn't seen her and Owen arrive. He could be blind to their movements. A perfect scenario for them.

"It's Leach," she said to Owen. "On his own."

Owen didn't wait for her to get out of the boat but bailed

from the back. Sloshed into the water. Grabbed the tow line and tugged the boat deeper onto the shore.

The SAT phone rang. She grabbed it and answered.

"I see you," Ryan said, sounding out of breath. "We're closing in on Leach. We'll cut him off and herd him in your direction."

"Got it." She ended the call and relayed the message to Owen, who had drawn his sidearm.

He signaled that he planned to move ahead, which he did. Taking slow, silent steps.

Deadly steps.

She wanted to shout at him to stop. All Leach had to do was spin, raise that rifle, fire one shot, and Owen could be dead. She had no doubt that Leach was a fine marksman and would hit his target if he tried.

Thankfully, Ryan eased closer, keeping Leach's attention. Ryan dropped down behind a large boulder and pointed his rifle at Leach. "We have you cut off, Leach. Put down your gun."

She followed behind Owen, her sidearm raised. Inching toward the unmoving suspect, as if he were frozen and didn't know what to do.

The Maddox brothers, rifles raised, slowly closed in from the top of the hill.

Fifty feet from Leach, she stopped and took a stand behind a boulder. Owen continued on. One foot in front of the other, surprisingly graceful for his size. He inched closer. Foot by silent foot. Moment by moment.

His foot hit a patch of gravel. The rocks grated, the crunch sounding like an explosion.

Leach spun, his rifle rising as he moved.

"Don't move!" Owen shouted, gun trained on Leach.

The man didn't listen. He kept his rifle raised. Owen had every right to shoot him.

Instead, with a mighty roar, Owen launched himself at Leach. Shoved the suspect's arm to the side. Leach's rifle flew free and down the hillside.

Owen dropped his own weapon, and Leach grabbed for it. Owen knocked it out of reach and wrestled the man. They scrapped, rolling side-over-side. Arms flailing, growing closer to a sharp ledge on the hill that would plummet them down to serious harm.

Hands grabbed. Legs kicked. Inching closer. Closer to the precipice. The fall precariously close now.

"Owen, the edge!" she shouted as she moved toward them. "You're too close."

Owen roared and flipped Leach onto his stomach. Owen emerged like a mighty predator and whipped Leach's arms behind his back, shoving them up. Leach cried out.

Mackenzie reached the pair and trained her gun on them, praying her wounded arm or beaten hand wouldn't give out on her from the strain of her swim, and she couldn't correctly brace her weapon.

"Don't move, Leach." She filled her tone with a confidence she didn't feel right now. "I won't hesitate to pull the trigger."

He ceased struggling and lay like a statue. Breathing hard, Owen retrieved the handcuffs from his belt and fastened them to Leach's wrists.

"That hurts," Leach complained.

"Not as much as it's gonna hurt to spend the rest of your life in prison for killing my sister and leaving me to die in the desert."

"Sister?" Leach asked.

"Cassie Collins. I plan to see you get the maximum penalty allowed for her death." Owen jerked Leach to his feet. He searched him and removed a cell phone, wallet, keys, and knife from his cargo pockets and shoved them into his own pockets.

He then forced Leach to march away from the sharp ledge. He settled Leach on the ground near a boulder. Owen read the man his rights.

Mackenzie took the moment to retrieve Owen's gun and a SAT phone that had fallen from Leach's pocket. They could check the call log to see who Leach had been talking to. She clipped it on the rope holding up her pants and handed the gun to Owen.

The Maddox brothers joined them.

Owen faced Ryan. "Your truck nearby?"

"Just up the hill."

Owen looked at Mackenzie. "Let's get this murderer secured in the truck."

"I...didn't...kill...your...sister." Leach ended with a snarl. "I don't even know a woman named Cassie Collins."

Ignoring his statement—as did the guys—Mackenzie followed them up the incline, her boots squishing from the dunk in the river.

"You look like a drowned rat." Ryan took her arm and helped her navigate a large boulder.

"I feel like one."

"We'll get the heat on in the truck and see if we can't put an end to your shivering."

Owen glanced back, a thundercloud in his eyes. It was as if having the cuffs on Leach allowed him to let go of that focus and see everything else around him, and he wasn't happy that she was cold.

They climbed in silence the rest of the way, darting in and out of tall and baby evergreen trees. At seeing Ryan's truck, she let out a long sigh. It was a sight for sore eyes, but it would be a tight fit for all of them. She sure didn't want to sit next to Leach, but she suspected Owen did—to make sure his sister's killer didn't escape.

He got out his cell phone, brought Wheeler up to speed in a quick conversation then faced Mackenzie. "We'll pick up my truck, get you some dry clothes, and then haul this guy to the jail in Canyon City."

She nodded, and didn't know which she looked forward to most. Dry clothes or interrogating the man who likely killed Owen's sister.

～

Owen pulled into Canyon City about thirty minutes later than he planned due to his pitstop at the store in Minam. He hadn't wanted to take the time to pick up his truck, but getting dry clothes for Mackenzie and telling Grainger where he could find his boat and kayak was important too. Owen hoped he hadn't damaged the boat. He would pay for any needed repairs or for a new one. How could he not when Grainger's generosity saved them and allowed them to take Leach into custody?

Owen parked in front of the jail and glanced in the rearview at Russ and Leach. Owen had wanted one of the brothers to watch Leach while Owen drove and Mackenzie warmed up under the heater. Of all the brothers, Owen chose Russ. As a sworn officer, he wouldn't allow Leach to call his arrest and handling into question.

Wheeler stepped out the front door to meet them. Owen had called him and asked him to be present for the questioning, and the sheriff had readily agreed.

Russ jumped down then hauled Leach out by the cuffs. Mackenzie and Owen both climbed out.

"And you are?" Wheeler asked Russ.

"Sheriff Russ Maddox. Emerson County."

Wheeler narrowed his eyes. "Long way from home, aren't you?"

Owen joined them. "We called him and his brothers in as trackers and guides, but then I put him on official duty as Leach's escort." Owen didn't add, he'd done that rather than let Russ drive, as Owen wanted to keep an eye on Mackenzie to make sure she was recovered from her river drenching.

Wheeler gave a sharp nod.

"He's all yours." Russ shoved Leach in Wheeler's direction.

"Watch it," Leach snapped. "I'm not a piece of meat."

"Just a man who'd kill a defenseless woman." Wheeler took hold of Leach's arm and started him toward the door.

Ryan pulled into the lot and parked next to Owen's truck. He and Reid made their way over to the others.

"Always a good feeling when you get your man," Ryan said.

Owen nodded. "Be a better feeling after we get him to confess."

"Good luck with that," Russ said. "The guy seems pretty determined to deny his involvement in the murder."

Owen shoved his hands into his pockets. "We'll see how long he lasts."

"We'll go ahead and take off unless you need anything else from us," Ryan said.

"Thanks. You've been a big help." Owen shook hands with Ryan and then his brothers.

Mackenzie gave each of them a hug, and Owen wished he was on the end of one of those hugs. But right now, he wished more than anything to face Leach and get him to admit to killing Cassie.

He looked at Mackenzie. "I'm sure Wheeler will let you watch the interview again."

"Sounds like a plan." She waved to the brothers as they departed, then walked alongside Owen to the entrance.

He looked her over. "You sure you're okay after the drenching?"

She tucked her arm into his and pulled him close. "Stop worrying. I'm fine."

They walked arm-in-arm to the front steps where she separated from him and her professional demeanor locked into place.

After clearing security, Mackenzie settled in the other room to watch. Owen approached the interview room door, and his body fairly vibrated with the need to punch the guy who smugly looked at him with his lips clamped closed. Leach's expression said he had no intention of admitting to Cassie's murder.

Meant Owen had to do a better job than ever in questioning a suspect.

Mackenzie didn't like the outcome of the interview with Leach. Owen had come up empty and anger glazed his eyes as they got into his truck. She didn't know what to say to him for fear of discouraging him even more. He deserved to experience his anger. His sister had been murdered, and even with forensic evidence that linked Leach to her death, they really needed more to convict the man.

She could help with that. "How about I call Sierra to see if they've located any additional evidence on Leach or Tovar?"

"Fine," he said. "I'll get us back to the cabin where we can evaluate the evidence we *do* have. Then I can present a better front the next time I question this guy."

She loved to hear that no matter Owen's anger, he

continued to think clearly. She got out the waterproof bag still holding her phone. Three missed calls displayed. She also had three voicemail messages.

She should probably have looked at her phone sooner, but she'd been intent on getting into warm clothes first. Then for the duration of their drive, not saying anything that could help Leach, so she'd shoved the phone into her pocket and forgot about it. Then the interview took over.

"Three missed calls from Sierra," she told Owen as she navigated to voicemail. "All within the last hour."

"Must be important." The anger in Owen's eyes morphed into interest.

She played the first voicemail on speaker.

"Call me the minute you get this message?" Sierra said. "I've got something very important to tell you."

"Sounds urgent for sure," Owen said.

Mackenzie played the second voicemail, basically a repeat of message one. She started the third one running.

"Where is everyone?" Sierra's exasperation sounded through the speaker. "You're not answering, and I can't get ahold of Wheeler either. Call me!"

"You heard the woman." Owen gave a tight smile. "Call her."

Mackenzie tapped Sierra's number and hit the speaker button.

"Finally," Sierra said. "You're not going to believe this."

"What?" Mackenzie and Owen asked at the same time.

"The DNA from the remains found in the desert came back," Sierra said. "It's not a match for Cassie. The dead woman isn't Cassie."

26

"What?" The word erupted from Owen. He could hardly think, much less drive. He whipped his truck to the side of the road and skidded to a stop on the shoulder, gravel flying everywhere. "What do you mean, not Cassie?"

"Are you positive?" Mackenzie asked, sounding way too calm for Owen's liking.

"Of course, I'm positive," Sierra said. "Emory never makes a mistake. And she says not only does the DNA *not* match the sample brought in by Owen's parents, but it came back as a match in CODIS for a Grace Gale from Salem. She has priors for soliciting."

Owen had to trust the FBI's Combined DNA Index System, didn't he? But really, his sister might not be dead? Couldn't be. Just couldn't be, could it?

Is this some sick joke, God?

"She wore Cassie's clothes and necklace." Owen shifted into park.

"I can't explain that," Sierra said. "But trust me when I say these are not Cassie's remains that we recovered."

"What about dental records?" Mackenzie asked. "Did Kelsey have a chance to review them?"

"Not yet. Cassie's dentist is old school and doesn't utilize the electronic program we use to download dental and medical records. He procrastinated on sending the hard copies despite repeated requests, so Kelsey sent her assistant over to pick them up this morning."

"Can she compare them to be sure?" Owen asked.

"Sure, but, Owen," Sierra said. "There's no doubt. These remains aren't Cassie's. I thought that would make you happy."

And he should be, but... "I'm having a hard time believing there might still be hope that she's alive."

"Then let me get Kelsey moving on those x-rays to put any question you might have to rest," Sierra said. "I'll get back to you as soon as possible."

"Thanks, Sierra." Mackenzie ended the call.

Owen looked at Mackenzie. "I don't know what to believe."

Mackenzie held his gaze. "I think you have to go with Emory. She's an expert and wouldn't be wrong."

"Then why did Leach knock me over the head out in the desert and shoot at me at your place?"

"He might not have killed Cassie, but he could've killed this other woman, and he was afraid you were going to investigate. Or he was afraid you were coming after him for Bussey's murder."

"Yeah, I guess." Thoughts bounced through Owen's head, and he tried to focus them. "And makes sense when he keeps saying he didn't know Cassie because the victim is Grace Gale."

"Exactly." Mackenzie smiled at him. "Maybe we'll find she's somehow connected to Cassie."

"I'll get the slugs from Bussey's body to Veritas for Grady to compare. Maybe we can link Leach to both deaths *and* the shots fired at us."

"And I can help with getting info on Grace Gale." Mackenzie held up her phone. "The fastest way is to have Nick at Veritas do a background check."

"Yes. Right. Good thinking."

Mackenzie made the call, and Owen let the investigation play through his brain, trying to find any item that this news would change or that they hadn't dug into deeply enough. He ran through the leads. Through the forensics. He landed on the outfitter's office and seeing the nametag on the receptionist's desk.

Polly Plummer was his sister's best friend's name. She was named after a character in the Chronicles of Narnia, and she died a year or so ago. He doubted the name Polly was very common these days. More specifically, he doubted there would be many Polly Plummers in the state. Though there could be one for sure. Still, the name nagged at his brain.

Did this woman have something to do with Cassie's disappearance? Time to find out.

He got out his phone, dialed his lieutenant and updated him. "Can you run the name Polly Plummer for me? Living in Grant County I think and could have something to do with Cassie's disappearance."

"Hold on." The click of Sage's fingers striking the keys on his keyboard came through the phone.

Owen could easily visualize the guy hunched over, pecking out the name in his one finger typing pattern.

"No Polly Plummer in the area," Sage said.

Odd. "What about the state? I think she'd be around thirty."

"Hold on again."

As Owen waited, he tapped his thumb against the steering wheel and listened to Mackenzie finalize her call with Nick.

"Got three entries," Sage said. "The only woman under fifty is the one with a Portland address. Want me to email the driver's license to you?"

"Now, please."

"On its way." He fell silent for a moment. "Anything else I need to know on this investigation?"

"Let me chase down this lead, and I'll get back to you." Owen hung up before Sage pressed him for additional information. He glanced at Mackenzie and shared his thoughts about Polly and his conversation with Sage.

She pursed her lips. "Interesting. Nick will get us something on Grace Gale within the hour."

Owen's phone dinged, and he opened the email with the driver's license. He held it out to Mackenzie. "Just as I suspected. This is my sister's friend."

"This's odd." Mackenzie tapped the photo. "Look at the license expiration date. It was renewed a few months ago."

Owen shifted into gear. "Let's question Leach about Grace Gale and Polly. Maybe he'll know what's going on. As a bonus, maybe we'll get a confession to murder before the day is out."

Leach's attitude grated on Owen from the moment he stepped in the door to the small room with cinderblock walls. Leach hadn't lost any of his cockiness, sitting at the table, his arms crossed, slumping in his chair with his chin pointed toward the ceiling.

Owen gritted his teeth to keep from wiping the smirk off the guy's face and sat across the table from him. Wheeler took the seat next to Owen, his posture rigid and unyielding as he turned on the recorder and stated the names of the people present. For some reason, Leach had decided he didn't need an attorney and would represent himself. Foolishness, but it could work in Owen's favor.

Leach lowered his chin to eye Wheeler then shift his gaze to Owen. "You might as well turn around and leave. You're wasting your time if you think I'm going to tell you anything."

"Hmm." Owen leaned back in his chair, stretching his legs out under the table. "That's exactly what Tovar said before he turned on you. Told us you shot and killed Grace Gale in the desert. Shot her point blank then tried to burn her body to cover it up, but thought it would take too long and the members of the party you were leading would come looking for you. So you dumped her body in the creek."

Tovar hadn't said a word, of course, but Owen worked hard to hide the lie in his expression and tone.

Leach looked from Owen to Wheeler then back. "Tovar doesn't know what he's talking about."

"That's odd," Owen said, planning to take a big risk. "He said he was present when you killed her, and he would testify to what he witnessed. The judge will look more favorably on you if you admit your role instead of Tovar testifying."

Leach tightened his arms. "Tovar wasn't even there."

Ah, yes. Now they were getting somewhere. "Wasn't where?"

"In the desert that night she died."

"So you *did* kill her?" Owen asked.

Leach leaned forward. "Before I say anything more, I want a deal. I tell you what Tovar is doing, which is far worse than killing a woman."

"We can make sure the judge knows you cooperated in bringing a terrible criminal to justice," Wheeler said. "That should shorten your sentence. But this offer is good today and today only."

Owen knew Wheeler couldn't make any promises to shorten Leach's sentence. If he'd had an attorney present they would've pointed that out to him. Now Owen didn't know what the creep might do.

"Then fine," Leach said. "Yeah, I killed her."

Owen resisted shooting up a hand in victory or letting his expression reveal his satisfaction.

Leach cocked his head. "But like I said, it's not nearly as bad as what Tovar does."

"And what might that be?" Wheeler acted uninterested in Leach's answer, but Owen knew the sheriff was very interested.

"He smuggles women into Oregon and sells them for sex. After he starves them and rapes them. Some of them have even died. Three, I think. They're buried behind his barn."

"And I assume you're willing to testify to that," Wheeler said.

Leach crossed his arms again. "The jerk rats me out, he gets the same thing in return."

"Why did you kill Grace Gale?" Owen asked, bringing them back to the issue Owen most wanted explained.

Leach frowned. "She was camping out there and caught me poaching."

"Poaching?" Wheeler gaped at Leach. "That's worth killing someone over?"

"I had to do it. If I was charged with poaching, I couldn't be a guide anymore. I don't know nothing else." Leach sat up in his chair and gripped the table edge. "Would have to go work at the foundry or something and being inside all day would kill me. Might as well put a bullet to my head now."

"That's why you attacked me when I discovered the

body," Owen stated. "You were afraid I'd figure out you killed her and arrest you."

Leach shook his head. "Didn't even know the creek had dried up until after I coldcocked you."

Owen blinked for a few seconds to process. "Then why attack me?"

"You figured out I killed my friend Jamar and were going to arrest me." He sat back. "Wasn't going to jail."

The guy didn't sound the least bit sorry for this murder either. Owen hated dealing with creeps like this.

But since he brought up Bussey, it would be a banner day if Owen got a second confession out of this guy. "I would've only arrested you because you *did* kill him."

Leach stared at Owen. "It was an accident."

"You don't accidentally shoot someone long distance with a rifle."

"Yeah, well...well..." He sputtered as if he couldn't come up with an explanation. "He deserved it."

"No one deserves to be gunned down," Wheeler said. "No one."

"I had no choice. None. He was going to ruin my life too."

"How?" Owen asked.

"I got drunk the night before he died and told him about the chick I killed. That Grace Gale lady. He said if I didn't turn myself in, he would. Like I said, I wasn't going to prison so he had to go."

Owen shook his head in disgust. "So you compounded that mistake by trying to kill me too. Instead, you left me to die a slow death if I didn't find my way back."

Leach scoffed. "I actually thought you were dead. Couldn't find a pulse. So I drove your Jeep to an abandoned property, hiked back, and got my UTV."

"And it was you who fired on me near Ms. Steele's rental cabin too."

"You wouldn't let it go." Leach eyed Owen. "Another time I didn't have a choice."

"You always have a choice. You just make bad ones." Owen could hardly look at the guy anymore. He'd gotten every confession he needed and had only one last question. "Where can I find my Jeep?"

Leach described a location near his property. "I tossed the keys somewhere around there."

Owen made note of the address. "It better be in good condition."

Leach sneered at Owen. "I didn't hurt your precious Jeep."

"No, you just killed your friend and a young woman who did nothing to harm you." Owen locked gazes, letting his revulsion flow through his expression. "Makes you the lowest of the low."

27

Owen approached Polly Plummer's apartment in a sketchy area of John Day. Junky cars, weeds, and peeling paint blowing in the cold wind did not make a good first impression. Mackenzie strode next to him. He should never have brought her into such a neighborhood, but he had no idea what to expect. Maybe he would be more comfortable if the sun wasn't setting, casting shadows around the building where unsavory characters could hide.

He lifted his hand to knock but couldn't bring himself to do it. Couldn't be disappointed one more time by a lead that turned out to be nothing. Nick's report said the woman behind this door had been using the identification of Cassie's friend Polly. Owen could simply be looking at a matter of identity theft. That was the most logical explanation. Criminals often took on the identity of deceased individuals.

Then why did his gut tell him it was more than that?

"It's okay if you can't do it." Mackenzie slipped her hand into his. "We can come back when you're ready."

"I want to find out if this woman knows something, and

yet I don't." He clutched Mackenzie's hand tightly. "It's been such a rollercoaster. Cassie's missing. Then we think she's dead. Now we don't know again. I don't know which one is worse—not knowing what's happened to her or knowing she was dead? I just don't know."

Mackenzie laid a hand against his cheek. "You're strong enough to handle whatever you discover."

"I'm not so sure of that anymore." He sucked in a long breath of the crisp night air. "When you fell into the river, I was reminded of how fleeting life can be. One second you were fine, the next you could've died. I'm still reeling from that. If this woman tells me Cassie died. I don't...I just...I don't know what I might do."

"But God brought me through, and I'm fine," she said with conviction. "Which means not everyone dies, goes missing, or suffers a great tragedy."

"God did take care of you, but will He always?" Owen searched her face for answers he knew she couldn't give. "We can't count on that. Not when it might be in His plan to allow someone to die. Was it His plan for Cassie to die?"

"I can't say it wasn't, but what we have to do is cling to His promise. If we love Him and are called according to His purpose, He works all things for our good. Not some things. Not the things we want. But *all* things."

"Yeah," Owen admitted but didn't want to. Because God's idea of what was good for Owen wasn't necessarily Owen's idea of what was good for him. But still, God made that promise in the Bible, and Owen believed it. And if he embraced his beliefs, he could move forward now. Accept whatever he learned from this woman.

He gave Mackenzie a gentle kiss on her cheek, released her hand, and knocked as hard as he could on the door. For all he knew, Polly might not be home or she wouldn't answer the door.

He waited. Let out a long breath and knocked again. Sucked in more air. Held his breath.

He put his ear against the door. Footsteps sounded on the other side. A light in the portico above came on. He took a step back and held his breath.

The door opened. A woman peered at him from the opening. He blinked. Hard. Trying to clear his eyes. To see reality, not what he hoped to see.

Was he seeing the truth? Was the woman standing in front of him his sister? His sister!

"Owen?" she said. "How did you find me?"

Owen's heart soared. *His sister was alive! Truly alive!*

Owen crushed her to him. "You're alive! I can't believe it."

Thank you, Father! Thank you!

Cassie didn't let him hold her long, but pushed free and looked over his shoulder. "Did you tell anyone you found me? Is anyone with you? Not Keith. Please say you didn't tell Keith."

Owen studied her and didn't like her nervous demeanor. Was she hiding something? Maybe something illegal?

In any event, he wasn't going to tell her Keith was dead while standing out here on her doorstep. "Can we come in and talk?"

"Not until you answer my question. Did you tell Keith where I am?"

"I didn't tell him," Owen replied, being vague.

Cassie fixed her frightened, almost terrified gaze on Mackenzie. "Who are you?"

Mackenzie cocked her head. "Mackenzie Steele. I've been helping Owen look for you."

Cassie continued to peer at Mackenzie, her gaze sharpening even more. "Why? Why do you want to find me?"

"It's okay, Cass," Owen said. "She's helping me because I

lost my memory and landed on her doorstep. It's a long story, but she won't hurt you if that's what you think."

Cassie's dyed eyebrows raised. "Do you know my husband, Keith?"

Mackenzie remained steadfast under Cassie's stare. "No."

Owen rested a hand on Cassie's shoulder. "What's going on? Why are you so jumpy?"

"Come inside, and I'll tell you." Cassie stepped back and rested a shaking hand on the doorknob.

Owen stepped over the threshold, but stopped next to his sister. No way he would let her out of his sight for even a second.

Mackenzie entered and passed them. Cassie double-bolted the door, tugging on it and checking the lock. She was clearly afraid of someone. She started down the short hall, and he trailed her to a small living room holding only a worn plaid couch and small older model TV.

"Go ahead and take a seat." Cassie gestured at the sofa. "Sorry about the lack of furniture and the thrift store things. I haven't been able to save enough money for much more than a deposit and first month's rent to get out of my tent and into this place."

Mackenzie sat on the couch, and Owen sat next to her to leave room for Cassie, but she plopped down on the carpet. Owen shifted to get comfortable on the lumpy cushion that released a musty smell.

"Why did you disappear?" he asked, still barely able to believe she sat in front of him.

"Keith. He's been abusive since our first year of marriage. Started out with occasional beatings." She clutched the edge of her T-shirt and fidgeted with it. "I could handle that, but he escalated. Then I found out I was pregnant. I couldn't bring up a child in that environment."

Pain tightened Owen's gut. "You have a child?"

She shook her head. "I miscarried shortly after I left."

"You went through that alone?" Owen gently took her hand. "I'm so sorry."

"It was probably for the best."

"Why didn't you tell me? Why run away instead?" Owen heard the anguish in his tone. What might she be hearing? "I would've put Keith in his place and protected you."

She withdrew her hands and sat on them. "But what could you actually do to make things better? Keith's a cop. Cops stick together, and they wouldn't believe any accusation I lodged."

Fair point. "Did you report any of the times he hit you?"

"No. He threatened me each time with a worse beating if I did. When I had visible bruises, I made sure not to go anywhere anyone would recognize me outside of work. I got to be a makeup master, covering everything with concealer."

Owen held onto his knees to keep from punching something. The pain Cassie had caused him and his parents by running away could have been prevented. The pain she endured could've been prevented. "You know I wouldn't have been on Keith's side. Never. No matter the brotherhood."

"I know. But you couldn't have stopped him either. Admit it." She fired a challenging gaze at him. "No one would believe me except my family and that sure wouldn't stop the guy."

Owen sat back, his mind racing with questions, his body tense with emotions. How had he not known she'd suffered abuse for years? "You could've come to stay with us instead of taking off."

"And put you all in danger? No. I wouldn't do that to Mom and Dad for sure. And you? You could handle yourself with Keith. No doubt. But you might've snapped and killed him. I couldn't risk any of it. And I couldn't risk any of you knowing where I was. Keith had to believe I'd been abducted or murdered. That would make taking on Polly's name a whole lot easier."

"I should have known the minute I saw the nameplate that you could pull that off." He explained about seeing Polly's name at OffGrid Outfitters. "As Polly's executor, you had access to all of her files and paperwork. And with the dyed hair, you look enough like her that you could get away with using her photo IDs."

Cassie nodded.

And now here she was. Alive and well. "We found a woman's remains in the desert this week. We thought it was you."

"Oh, Owen, I'm so sorry. I heard about it, of course. Everybody in the area is talking about it, but they didn't share any details." Cassie tilted her head, giving him the quizzical look she'd used since she was a toddler. "What about her made you think it was me?"

"The victim wore the clothes and necklace you were had on when you disappeared. The necklace with the infinity heart that Mom and Dad gave you on your eighteenth birthday. Her name was Grace Gale. Did you give them to her?"

Cassie shook her head. "I changed clothes at a rest area and threw them in the trash. I had to get rid of the necklace too. I hated to do it, but I knew it could identify me, and I couldn't risk anyone seeing it. And if Keith did hunt me down, I would take off again, but I couldn't risk him finding it if I had to leave it behind. So best to get rid of it right up front."

"Grace must've gotten your things from the trash then," Mackenzie said.

"Sounds like it." Cassie nibbled on her bottom lip, then

suddenly sat up straight. "If you found me, so can Keith. He said he owns me, and he'll never quit searching for me."

Owen sat forward. "He's not looking anymore."

Cassie's eyes lit with hope. "How do you know?"

"He was killed in a foggy pileup on I-5 early this morning."

"Really?" Her posture lifted. "You're sure?"

"I haven't seen his body if that's what you're asking, but yes. My lieutenant called to report Keith's death."

"Then I'm free. Really free. I can come home." Cassie smiled and clapped a hand over her mouth. "I shouldn't be so happy. Especially that Keith died, but I have to admit to wanting to be with you all again, and his death makes that possible."

"Yeah." Owen leaned down to Cassie and took her hands again. "You can come home. Should we call Mom and Dad now or head to Vancouver to surprise them?"

"Surprise them." Cassie jumped to her feet. "Let me change and pack a few things, then we can leave right now. That is if you want to take me."

"Want to take you? Are you kidding? Just try to stop me." Owen laughed, feeling lighter and more optimistic about life than he had in years.

"Be right back." Grinning, Cassie bolted from the room.

The weight that had been bearing down on Owen for so long disappeared. Lifted. Released. He was free from the bonds he'd imposed on himself. His sister had a new start, and so did he. He wouldn't waste a minute of his new life.

He looked at Mackenzie. "Will you come with us?"

She arched an eyebrow. "It's such a personal family moment. Are you sure you want me there?"

He took her hands in his. "I've never been more sure of anything in my life. Without your help, I would never have found Cassie, and my parents will want to meet you. But not as much as I want them to meet the woman I hope will soon become a very big part of my life."

Near ten o'clock, Mackenzie hung back as they walked up to the Greer house and Owen rang the doorbell. The moon hung bright in the clear skies and a frosty wind whipped in from the west. She tightened her coat and hunched into the collar. Cassie stood behind Owen to hide from her parents when they opened the door and make the surprise even greater. Both siblings were practically vibrating with excitement, and the contagious emotion saturated the air.

The door opened, and a shorter woman with silvery hair answered the door. She blinked hard. "Owen? Forget your key?"

"No. Can you get Dad?"

"Sure, but why?"

"I have some good news for once."

Her face paled. "Is this about Cassie? Did you find the person who murdered her?"

"Yes and no." Owen shifted. "Just get Dad, okay?"

"Okay, but I don't know why you're acting so odd." She went back into the house, but left the door open, and the yeasty scent of recently baked bread drifted out.

Cassie squeezed Owen's waist and danced. "I can't wait to see their faces."

Owen looked over his shoulder. "I hope the shock isn't too much for them."

"They'll be fine." Cassie sounded sure.

Mackenzie didn't know. This surprise was a big one, but a phone call would carry an equally big shock, and she agreed this wonderful news should be delivered in person. It'd been important for Owen to tell them in person that Cassie had died. How could it not be equally as important to be face-to-face to share the good news?

His mom returned with a tall gentleman who resembled Owen in so many ways Mackenzie couldn't list them all. But the man's facial structure, thick head of hair, and the same height and broad shoulders as Owen stood out for her.

"Son." His forehead furrowed, and he took his wife's hand. "What's going on? You've got your mother in a state."

"Cassie's alive," Owen said.

Mackenzie had hoped he would come right out with it like this.

"What?" His mother's eyelids fluttered, and she clutched her chest. "But you told us you found her remains."

"I did, but the DNA didn't match the sample you brought in."

His father's eyes narrowed. "Why should we believe that these latest DNA tests are accurate?"

"Believe them or not, she's alive." Owen reached behind and drew Cassie forward.

"Oh, my goodness!" His mother fanned her face. "Sweetheart. It's you. It's really you!"

Cassie threw herself at her mother, whose arms came around Cassie. "I don't know what to say. Oh my! Oh my! Praise God for this miracle! Praise Him! Praise Him!"

"Amen to that and let me get in on some of that hugging." Their father swiped tears from his eyes. "I never thought I would be able to hug you again, honey. Oh my goodness. I can't find the right words, so get over here for that hug."

Cassie let go of her mom and flew into her father's open arms.

Tears flooded Mackenzie's eyes, and she didn't even try to stop them. Why should she? As Mrs. Greer said, Mackenzie was witnessing a miraculous day for this family. God's blessings after a terrible time in the desert. Reminded Mackenzie of God's welcoming open arms waiting for her for when she'd strayed in the past. He never gave up on her. Never failed her. Just like this father's love she was witnessing. Mr. Greer had never given up on Cassie until science told him his daughter was dead. But now, now he was overwhelmed with the same joy Mackenzie had when her Heavenly Father welcomed her back into the fold. The joy that came each morning when she woke up and remembered she was a child of God.

Owen looked back at her and held out his hand. She took it, and he drew her forward to cradle her under his arm, his warmth chasing away a bit of her chill. "Mom. Dad. I would like you to meet someone special to me. This is Mackenzie Steele. She took care of me when I lost my memory and helped me find Cassie."

His mother cocked an eyebrow. "But I can see that's not all."

Owen shook his head. "If she agrees, we're going to be seeing a whole lot more of each other."

"She agrees." Mackenzie chuckled.

"Then we've had two miracles this day," Owen's mother said. "Our beautiful daughter returned to us, and our son found a woman he wants in his life."

Owen rolled his eyes. "Now come on, Mom. That's not quite a miracle."

She glanced at her husband.

He tucked Cassie closer at his side, his arm tight around her shoulder. "Well, son, you've given us no reason to believe you might ever find someone and settle down. We'd kind of given up on that."

"We all figured you'd turn into a spinster." Cassie laughed.

Owen let out a breath. "I guess I can see your point."

Mackenzie looked at him. "Don't worry. I don't mind being your miracle. I can't think of a much better thing to be."

28

Three weeks later.

The Steele family's pastor gave the Easter sermon, and Owen held tight to Mackenzie's hand, thankful for her presence and for his sister on his other side. His parents sat next to her, and the rest of the Steele family and their extended family members filled the rows behind them.

The group totaled twenty-four people, all dressed in their Sunday finest. Mackenzie too, who wore a soft yellow dress and sky-high black heels that made her seem ultra-feminine. Nothing like the woman who hiked the dusty desert with him a few weeks ago. He loved that about her. One of the guys one minute—feminine and captivating the next.

"Easter is a story of hope," the pastor said. "When everything seems lost, there's still a future."

That's exactly what Owen had experienced. He'd lost hope and then found Cassie alive. But it could've gone the other way. And the pastor stated that no matter their circumstances, no matter their losses, no matter their pain, hope always remained. Owen had been hoping for a thing

—for Cassie to be alive—and he'd lost sight of his hope in someone else, God the Father.

He had to keep his focus on God. God always had plans for His people no matter what they saw before them. He knew the next move and the next and the next. That included the women they had found at Tovar's farm. Despite the horror they faced, they hadn't lost hope and now they'd all been relocated to good living situations and had a bright future ahead of them. Owen could take comfort in that.

The sermon ended, and they stood to sing the final song. Owen had failed to worship God the past few years. Shame mixed with the joy of forgiveness. He clutched Mackenzie's hand and when the song ended, hugged her tightly. "Thank you for inviting us today. The service was amazing."

"Of course." She slipped her hand into his. "I told you we have a fabulous church and pastor."

"Agreed." He turned to his family members who were talking to Mackenzie's parents. Her dad was sharing directions to their farm where Owen and his family would have an Easter meal with them. He couldn't imagine hosting a gathering for all these family members crowding around them, but Mackenzie said her grandad held a bigger meal on Christmas and today was a walk in the park for him.

The family departed, and they all greeted the pastor on their way out before getting into their respective cars to travel to the farm.

Owen started his Jeep that he had thankfully recovered and looked at Mackenzie. "I still can't believe you were raised on a farm."

"I could change into my overalls and boots and do some chores when we get there if you would like to see proof." She laughed.

"You look amazing in that dress, so I'll take your word for it."

"You don't look so bad yourself." She winked at him.

Owen loved flirting with her. Loved the lighthearted banter between them since finding Cassie, and realizing that life—no matter the twists or turns that he faced—was worth celebrating and rejoicing over all the time. Sure, he knew as time passed he would lose some of the appreciation for finding Cassie alive, but he hoped not to lose it totally and live each day with the excitement of new life. Especially today as they celebrated Easter.

At the farm, Owen found a secluded parking spot by a big red barn and looked at Mackenzie.

"You know the house is back that way." She jerked a thumb over her shoulder.

"I was hoping for a minute alone with you. Maybe we could take a quick walk."

"I won't argue with that." Her soft gaze held his, and a promise of something great permeated her eyes before she opened her door and let in a cool wind.

She slipped on a long sweater coat and joined him. "We'll want to head this way or risk encountering odors from my grandad's new cow."

He laughed, and they strolled around the back of a shed painted to match the barn where he discovered an empty field that seemed to stretch forever.

He didn't actually want to walk and the shed protected them from prying eyes, so he took her hand, the chill of her skin cold against his. "It seems like we've lost what's happening with *us* in the joy of my sister returning."

"That's okay." She smiled at him. "It's been a pleasure to see your family's happiness."

He tightened his grip on her hands. "That's great, but I

wanted to be sure you knew that I don't have any reservations about the two of us going forward."

"Ditto for me." She frowned.

He turned her to face him. "What is it?"

"Well...I might have one reservation."

His gut twisted. "What's that?"

"I want to be sure you're not still freaked out about losing someone you care about. You know I'm a risk-taker at heart. I'll try to change. I don't know if I can do it, but I'll try."

Was that all? Piece of cake. "Do I want to wrap you in bubble wrap and not let you face anything dangerous? Of course, I do. But your adventurous spirit is what makes you who you are. I would never ask you to change that. I like who you are. Very much." He slid his arms around her waist and drew her closer.

"I know I keep saying this, but ditto for me." She chuckled, then her expression sobered. "I think you should kiss me to fortify me for the coming meal."

"Your family's great. A meal with them can't be all that bad, can it?"

"There will be a lot of matchmaking going on. I mean *a lot*." Her eyes widened. "By the time we finish eating, you'll want to escape for sure. Another walk can be arranged."

"Then I guess I need that kiss as much as you do." He lowered his head and touched his lips to hers. They were soft, but cold like her hands. They quickly warmed as she snaked her arms around his neck and eased closer to him. Thankfully, her arm had healed well, and she seldom cried out in pain now.

Wow. Oh wow. He could spend hours kissing her. Had spent a lot of time thinking about it over the weeks, but the reality was so much better.

He drew her closer. Deepened the kiss. Ignored the soft mist that started spitting from the sky.

"I thought I saw you two sneak back here," Ryleigh's voice sounded from behind them. "I don't want to come between you when it's about time Mac found someone to kiss behind the shed, but Gran is calling us to the table. You can resume this mushiness after the meal."

Mackenzie pulled back, but didn't release her hold. "See. It's starting already. So buckle your seatbelt and hang on for the ride. It's going to be a bumpy one."

Thick slices of Gran's coconut cake resting on her best china made their way around the table, and Mackenzie almost let out her breath of relief. Almost. She'd made it through the ham, cheesy potatoes, green beans, and rolls without a single comment or question about her and Owen. Not one family member said a word. No one even hinted at their relationship.

How could that possibly be?

Her family. Her grandparents. Mom and dad. Aunt and uncle. Siblings. Cousins. All were usually opinionated and vocal about the latest family gossip. Were they seeing something in Owen that she'd missed and thought their relationship wouldn't last?

They sure weren't seeing any doubt or questions on her part. She was all in with this guy. And he reciprocated. Or at least she thought he did.

She glanced at him sitting next to his mother on one side, Mackenzie's gran on the other. Her gran said something, and Owen threw back his head to laugh with gusto.

He'd been laughing and animated the whole meal. Not giving off let-me-out-of-this-place vibes. So what?

"Okay, fine," Mackenzie said loud enough to draw the attention of everyone at the main table and the temporary table set up in the adjoining living room. "I give up. Why is no one saying anything?"

"About what?" Her gran batted her eyelashes behind the purple glasses she wore on special occasions.

"Oh, come on, now." Mackenzie ran her gaze over her relatives and other family guests. "Me and Owen. You comment all the time about me not finding someone. I finally do, and you go radio silent."

Her grandad looked at his watch. "One hour and seventeen minutes. Whose time was closest?"

Londyn shot to her feet at the other table. "Me! I win. No dishes for the rest of the year for me. Woohoo!"

Everyone laughed and chatter broke out.

Mackenzie stood. "What's going on?"

"We all decided when you two took a trip behind the shed," her dad said, sounding a bit uneasy, "to keep quiet and guess how long it would take for you to ask about it. Whoever had the closest time doesn't have to help with dishes for the rest of the year."

"Of all the dirty..." She sat but quickly got into the spirit of family pranks and laughed. "Good one."

"We thought so." Her grandad raised his sparkling cider glass. "To Mackenzie and Owen. May they find the happiness that my sweetheart and I've had for untold years."

"Untold?" Mackenzie's mom asked. "Does that mean you don't remember?"

"No, it means I'm not going to give the exact number to keep my sweetheart from clocking me for revealing how old she might be."

Her gran swatted his arm. "You should've stopped while you were ahead."

The family erupted in laughter and clanked their glasses together as they offered their heartfelt congratulations.

Mackenzie locked gazes with Owen and mouthed, "Sorry."

He gave a shake of his head and smiled, a broad, warm smile that curled her toes. She had to get this guy alone. Stat!

"Our cake is getting stale so eat up everyone." Her redirection worked. Her family members dug into fluffy yellow cake with coconut frosting dyed green to resemble grass. Gran had topped the pair of cakes with chocolate eggs and each plate held a few of those as an extra treat.

"Looks like a break in the rain too," her grandad said. "So we can get to that egg hunt."

Here they were, her, her sisters, and their cousins, all in their thirties except for Ryleigh, and their grandparents still held an Easter egg hunt for them. When they'd reached their teen years, their grandparents stopped putting candy and treats in plastic eggs, but included a charitable task that they each had to do before the next Easter.

An outsider might think that they wouldn't try to find as many eggs, but they remained competitive in their hunt and enjoyed the tasks throughout the year. Now they would do the hunt as a team with their significant others. Ryleigh was the only lone hunter this year, and there had been a lot of talk about that during lunch.

Peyton's fiancé Grant Logan had a five-year-old daughter, Sadie, and the family held an indoor hunt for her before they'd sat down to a late lunch. Her grandma, Judy, and Sadie would form a team for the outdoor hunt, after the sweet little girl's face had been cleaned of sticky frosting.

Mackenzie's grandad stood. "Let's get the leftovers put away, but we'll leave the dishes until after the hunt."

Chaos ensued as everyone got up, grabbed platters and

bowls, and hauled it all to the kitchen. Gran shooed all but Mackenzie's mother and aunt out of the room.

Mackenzie grabbed Owen's arm and drew him to the entryway where a table held Easter baskets from her childhood. Thomas's basket sat with the others, and the loss hit her like a fist to the gut.

"What is it? What's wrong?" Owen turned her to face him.

She pointed at the basket. "It belonged to Thomas. It's hard to be happy knowing he isn't here with us."

"I'm sorry, honey." He drew her into a hug. "After my scare of losing Cassie, I can imagine that only too well."

She leaned into him and let him cradle her head on his shoulder.

Ryleigh burst in. "Figured you two might be trying to find time alone again."

Tears in her eyes, Mackenzie looked at her little sister.

Ryleigh's eyes narrowed. "You're not upset over our prank, are you?"

Mackenzie shook her head and pointed at Thomas's basket.

Ryleigh's smile fell. "Ah, yeah. We're all missing him today. I don't know how Aunt Iris and Uncle Gene are coping."

"Because we know we'll see him again someday." Their uncle stepped into the room and picked up Thomas's basket. "Iris and I'll hunt for him and do his tasks throughout the year. It'll bring him closer still."

Mackenzie grabbed her uncle into a hug and then released him. "We can also pray."

He nodded, and tears fell from the strong man's eyes.

Mackenzie led the family in prayer, then they solemnly put on their coats.

"Now." Her Uncle Gene lifted Thomas's multi-colored

woven basket. "Thomas would want us to move on and do our very best in this hunt. I for one am going to skunk all of you."

He raced out the front door, lifting the mood again. Mackenzie knew hearts remained heavy, but they would all put on brave faces for her aunt and uncle.

Mackenzie hung back, waiting for Owen's mom and dad and Cassie to join them. "We have a basket for the three of you to hunt as a team if you'd like to join us."

"Are you kidding?" Cassie grinned and took a basket. "Any time I can win a challenge against my brother is a good day."

Owen gave her a playful punch to the arm. "Bring it on, girl. Bring it on."

She linked arms with her parents, the trio smiling jubilantly.

Thank you, Father, for bringing this family back together.

Owen took Mackenzie's hand and held her back as his family exited the house. He faced her. "I liked your family before today, but now I know why you're such a special person. I'm honored to be part of it. Unofficially now, but who knows, we could make it official in the future."

She rested her hands on his shoulders. "We really need to get to the hunt. Not because I want to skunk anyone, but because I want to claim my share of the charitable tasks."

"Like I said, a special woman. You have all of this in front of you." He released her and gestured at his body. "And you choose helping others."

"Yeah, but all of that will be there when the hunt is over. And then? Well then, I'll be glad to kiss you and make it better for letting you down now."

He laughed. "Woman, you are going to bring me a lifetime of surprises, and I can't wait to get started on that journey."

She grabbed his hand. "Then let's go. I know all of the best egg-hiding spots."

"Are some of them good for stealing a kiss too?"

"Absolutely." She grinned.

"My parents raised me not to steal, but in this case, I'm sure they'll understand and grant me immunity."

"No stealing required." She smiled up at him. "I plan to give you as many kisses as you want for the rest of our lives."

*

SHADOW LAKE SURVIVAL SERIES

Coming 2023 - When survival takes a dangerous turn and lives are on the line.

The men of Shadow Lake Survival impart survival skills and keep those in danger safe from harm. Even if it means risking their lives.

Book 1 – Shadow of Deceit - August 2, 2023
Book 2 – Shadow of Night - October 2, 2023
Book 3 – Shadow of Truth - December 2, 2023
Book 4 – Shadow of Hope March 2, 2024
Book 5 – Shadow of Doubt – June 2, 2024
Book 6 – Shadow of Fear – October 2, 2024

For More Details Visit -
www.susansleeman.com/books/shadow-lake-survival

STEELE GUARDIAN SERIES
Intrigue. Suspense. Family.

A kidnapped baby. A jewelry heist. Amnesia. Abduction. Smuggled antiquities. And in every book, God's amazing power and love.

Book 1 – Tough as Steele
Book 2 – Nerves of Steele
Book 3 – Forged in Steele
Book 4 – Made of Steele
Book 5 – Solid as Steele
Book 6 – Edge of Steele – May 1, 2023

For More Details Visit -
www.susansleeman.com/books/steele-guardians

NIGHTHAWK SECURITY SERIES

Protecting others when unspeakable danger lurks.

A woman being stalked. A mother and child being hunted. And more. All in danger. Needing protection from the men of Nighthawk Security.

Book 1 – Night Fall
Book 2 – Night Vision
Book 3 – Night Hawk
Book 4 – Night Moves
Book 5 – Night Watch
Book 6 – Night Prey

For More Details Visit -
www.susansleeman.com/books/nighthawk-security/

THE TRUTH SEEKERS
People are rarely who they seem

A twin who didn't know she had a sister. A mother whose child isn't her own. A woman whose parents lied to her. All needing help from The Truth Seekers forensic team.

Book 1 - Dead Ringer
Book 2 - Dead Silence
Book 3 - Dead End
Book 4 - Dead Heat
Book 5 - Dead Center
Book 6 - Dead Even

For More Details Visit -
www.susansleeman.com/books/truth-seekers/

The COLD HARBOR SERIES

Meet Blackwell Tactical- former military and law enforcement heroes who will give everything to protect innocents... even their own lives.

Book 1 - Cold Terror
Book 2 - Cold Truth
Book 3 - Cold Fury
Book 4 - Cold Case
Book 5 - Cold Fear
Book 6 - Cold Pursuit
Book 7 - Cold Dawn

For More Details Visit -
www.susansleeman.com/books/cold-harbor/

ABOUT SUSAN

SUSAN SLEEMAN is a bestselling and award-winning author of more than 45 inspirational/Christian and clean read romantic suspense books. In addition to writing, Susan also hosts the website, TheSuspenseZone.com.

Susan currently lives in Oregon, but has had the pleasure of living in nine states. Her husband is a retired church music director and they have two beautiful daughters, two very special son-in-laws, and two amazing grandsons.

For more information visit:
www.susansleeman.com

Made in United States
Orlando, FL
21 June 2023

34389859R00203